MW00813418

VINTAGE WORLDS 3
MORE TALES OF THE OLD SOLAR SYSTEM

VINTAGE WORLDS3

MORE TALES OF THE OLD SOLAR SYSTEM

EDITED BY

ZENDEXOR

AND

JOHN MICHAEL GREER

Vintage Worlds 3: More Tales of the Old Solar System
Copyright © 2020 John Michael Greer & Zendexor

All stories are copyrighted to their
respective authors, and used here with their permission.

Published by Founders House Publishing, LLC
Cover art by Court Jones
Cover and interior design © 2020 Founders House Publishing, LLC

Paperback Edition: November 2020

ISBN-13: 978-1-945810-52-7

This book is licensed for your personal enjoyment only. All rights
reserved. This is a work of fiction. All characters and events portrayed
in this book are fictional, and any semblance to real people or
incidents is purely coincidental. This book, or parts thereof, may not
be reproduced in any form without permission.

For more information please visit
www.foundershousepublishing.com

Published in the United States of America

CONTENTS

VINTAGE WORLDS 3

MORE TALES OF THE OLD SOLAR SYSTEM

INTRODUCTION
Along the Grand Canal

John Michael Greer

IT'S REALLY AN odd thing, this talent for imagining places that don't exist. As far as we know, all human beings share it, and use it in a bewildering diversity of ways. When religious people try to talk about that incomprehensible mode of being in which the divine is present, they turn to it—that's where we get the vivid imagery of Homer's Olympus, the Plain of High Heaven in the *Kojiki*, the vast celestial Rose of Dante's *Paradiso*, and countless others. When people concerned about the political life of their times try to imagine a different way for human beings to govern themselves, they turn to it as well—that's where we get Plato's *Republic*, Sir Thomas More's *Utopia*, Ernest Callenbach's *Ecotopia*, and many more.

Then there are those, no less brilliant though perhaps a little less serious, that have no purpose other than the simple goal of entertaining their listeners or readers. Those go back at least as far as the others, and perhaps further still. The island setting of an ancient Egyptian story of a shipwrecked sailor appears nowhere on the map; the countries crossed by Sir John Mandeville on his travels east to the Terrestrial Paradise were just as splendidly imaginary as Sir John himself. What makes this even more fascinating to me is that the Egyptian tale was originally read by people who saw nothing improbable in the mighty human-headed serpent who shows up in time to save the shipwrecked sailor, and a good many of Sir John Mandeville's readers saw nothing in the least improbable in the "men whose heads do grow below their shoulders" that Mandeville's inventor said he encountered.

The same complex relationship between fiction and belief runs all through one of my favorite examples of the genre, Vasco de Lobeira's *Amadis of Gaul*, the fourteenth century's epic fantasy bestseller. Readers nowadays are so used to the thought of imaginative fiction as a way to escape from prosaic realities that it may come as a shock to learn that fantastic tales of swords and sorcery were just as popular in the days when swords were standard military weapons and nearly everyone believed in the reality of sorcery. It's nonetheless quite true; Amadis, his love Oriana, his great opponent the evil sorcerer Archelaus, and his great protectress, the deliciously named sorceress Urganda the Unknown, were just as popular when knighthood was in flower as J.R.R. Tolkien was in a much later age.

The transition from one of these conditions to the other—from a period in which people write fantastic stories about things in which they believe or half-believe, to a period in which people write fantastic stories about things in which their ancestors believed but they don't—can be abrupt or it can be gradual, depending on the speed at which old beliefs unravel. Knighthood took a long time to go out of fashion. The theme at the center of this anthology falls on the other end of the spectrum.

Until space probes began to send back images of the airless and lethal wastelands to be found on other planets in our solar system, even the most sober scientists considered it quite reasonable to think that there could be intelligent life on Mars and Venus, and perhaps on other worlds that circle the same sun we do. It was thinking along those lines that inspired the creation of the greatest of all shared fictional worlds, the solar system of Golden Age science fiction, in which hundreds of authors penned tales of derring-do set in the jungles of Venus or along the Grand Canal of Mars—and all the while, many of them believed that it was just possible that something like their tales might actually be reality.

We know otherwise now. (It would be wrong to say "we know better"—the universe became a much poorer place on that bleak summer day in 1976 when the first Viking lander touched down on Mars and failed to send back pictures of Barsoom.) There is no Grand Canal on Mars, no lush jungles on Venus, no Twilight Belt on Mercury, and so on through the litany of places the protagonists of classic science fiction visited in their peregrinations around a solar system that never was.

Yet none of this makes the places enshrined in that litany any less suitable for stories written with no other reason than to entertain. For several years now, in print and on websites, stories about the Old Solar System have begun to find a niche in the literary ecosystem of modern imaginative fiction, and the two earlier anthologies in the Vintage Worlds series have helped to stock that niche with its proper inhabitants. This third volume has more of the same—lively, quirky, and highly readable tales of adventure in places that Sir John Mandeville and the shipwrecked sailor of the Egyptian story might not have found completely unfamiliar.

The Old Solar System, the solar system of classic science fiction, remains just as vivid a setting for tales as it was in its heyday. Right now, along the Grand Canal, adventure is waiting—and all you have to do is turn the page.

Coverage, world by world:

Mercury: *The Resurrection of Merrick Hardcastle*

Venus: *Home, Lady Penelope and the Drug Lords of Venus; Love in the Mountains of Venus*

Earth: *A Martian Iliad* (main setting), *Europa Dive* (first part); *On the Shoreline of Darkness* (first part); *Lady Penelope and the Drug Lords of Venus* (historical background); *Ghosts of Saturn*

Mars: *A Martian Iliad* (historical background); *Ghosts of Saturn*

The Jovian system: *Europa Dive; The Colorless Colossus of the Cold* (second part)

The Saturn system: *The Arc of Iapetus; Ghosts of Saturn*

Uranus: *Europa Dive* (historical background)

Neptune: *Cutter Pristine*

Pluto: *On the Shoreline of Darkness* (second part)

Levi Seeley grew up in the boundary between the Rocky Mountains and the Great Plains before heading to central Massachusetts to forage for wild edibles and earn a Master's Degree in biology. He has recently returned to Colorado, where he works in a genetics laboratory and writes fiction that explores how the mechanics of ecological systems can influence characters as they make their lives in environments that are more than passive backdrops.

One of the advantages that science fiction shares with historical fiction is the chance to take the long view and place events in the context of centuries and millenia. Levi Seeley's Home *is a fine example, a tale that weaves together the destinies of two human expeditions to Venus a thousand years apart...*

HOME

by Levi Seeley

TODAY IS THE one thousand year anniversary of the first Venus expedition. As a result of careful planning, I am pleased to say that it is also the beginning of the second Venus expedition.

Landing proceeded smoothly, and we established camp on a beach of mauve sand, fine and soft enough that none of us could resist walking barefoot. We are splitting into two teams. One team will be staying here to process samples from the ocean, while the other will begin making excursions into the dense forest ahead. I will be participating in the latter group, and I am particularly excited by the prospect of exploring this truly unknown territory, where the terrain was too rough for our pre-landing rover.

We will need to use climbing gear to get above the accumulated deadwood at the edge of the forest, but after that we are planning to move through the trees from branch to branch. The growth is far more dense than anything on Earth: Each great bough feathers out into a complex network of fine twigs, whorled with delicate leaves and overlapping each other from every direction. The leaves, obovate and just under a centimeter at their widest point, seem to be nothing but translucent flickers of green until you get close enough to touch them.

Photosynthesis on this planet must be unbelievably efficient, as the leaves allow so much light to pass through that visibility inside the forest, despite the foliage continuing upward for more than a kilometer, is almost as good as on the beach, albeit with an emerald tint. I suspect that this economy is the results of an evolutionary history spent under the clouds.

The most intriguing question is whether or not we will find macroscopic life in the forest. It would be quite strange if the gigantic trees were the only multicellular organisms on the entire planet, but so far we have seen no evidence to the contrary.

Captain's Log, Monday, August 16th, 2961

WITH GRIEF, I must report that the second Venus expedition has fallen to tragedy. We were attacked by something from the ocean, and I am the only survivor. We had intended to be cautious in approaching the forest, but our aquatic probe had plunged to such depths without encountering anything as complex as a colonial alga that we thought we could set up our equipment on the water's edge without concern.

The thing that came out of the water was larger than our ship, at least fifty meters tall and somewhat wider. It was crab-like, with a shell and large pincers, but displayed a seven-part radial symmetry and had no visible head or legs. It appeared to be covered in purple glass, the same hue as the sand, but slightly lighter in tone. I have to assume it had some kind of ventral mouth because I watched several of my crew members disappear as it dragged them under its body.

I alone was standing at the edge of the forest, double checking the condition of our equipment, when it happened.

The creature tore through the people by the water's edge within moments of emerging from the deep. I wanted to run for the ship—we had brought guns, although we hadn't bothered to keep them with us—but the creature made it there, and to the people standing by the ship, before I had a chance, so I started to climb.

I didn't abandon my crew. I only started to climb when there was no crew left to abandon.

Given the creature's size and speed, my only chance depended on getting away before it noticed me. I probably wouldn't have made it if it hadn't been for the Venusians.

There has always been speculation about what happened to the first Venus expedition. Their reports stopped coming suddenly, but the technology to receive transmissions from space was lost that same year, so most historians have assumed the problem was on our side. There was a lot of excitement two hundred years ago when communication technology was first restored to pre-war levels, but when our transmissions into space met with silence, the simplest answer was that none of the interplanetary expeditions had managed to leave eight hundred years of descendants. It would have been more surprising if they had, really: the expedition back then was larger than the small crew that came with me, but they would still have had to be extremely fecund to have created a self-sustaining population.

Apparently they were. I can't be sure it's them, but as I climbed for my life, I heard a distinctly human voice above me.

"Homianü thitta teknao! Yeh uitta hueh gonao!"

The words weren't in English, but perhaps the careful preservation of the ancient language wasn't as important to them as to us, or perhaps some other pre-war county had a Venus mission we didn't know about. Either way, the people who appeared in the trees above me, who threw down a rope and swiftly pulled me to safety, were human.

We traveled through the branches to their tree-dwellings, a trip that was short but utterly exhausting, and here they've been quite courteous, providing me with food and lodging in spite of the language barrier.

Captain's Log, Tuesday, August 18th, 2961

I AM STILL certain that the Venusians are human, although I think they may have some slight physiological differences— their facility in climbing through branches makes me think they tend toward having longer arms than humans from Earth. I'm sure much of their ability is acquired through practice and the development of muscular strength, but even so, something about their general appearance makes me think that there may have been selection in favor of climbing ability over the last thousand years. I haven't had a chance to see a Venusian's body that wasn't obscured by the complicated garments they wear, though, so I can't be sure.

The Venusian dress is quite surprising. They wear graceful robes comprised of many layers of flowing material that has the feel of silk, tied at the waist by a loose sash. I'm wearing one now, given to me by my hosts, and it seems like the most utterly impractical vestment possible for people that spend most of their time climbing through trees. I certainly get mine stuck on a branch, or several branches, every time I go beyond the thinned area immediately outside of a door, much to the Venusians' amusement. They don't seem to have any trouble, however, and I hope to learn their secret in time. Actually, I think I may have figured it out already: The Venusian tree-branching is extremely complex, but also extremely regular. I suspect the Venusians are simply so familiar with the pattern that they know precisely which areas they can slip through without having to think about it.

Aesthetically, the Venusians prefer fluid and naturalistic ornamentation in colors of rose, amber, and olive flecked with gold. The way they dye their clothing is quite fascinating, as each design has two faces—one which comes out in the dim emerald light outside, and one which is revealed only in the brighter, yellow chartreuse glow of their candle-lit interiors. Men's and women's garments differ only slightly, with the men's tending to hide animal motifs among abundant foliage and the women's being inclined to show vegetation interspersed with flowers and fruits. The overall effect is that of an alien art nouveau, where the straighter lines and sharper corners of Venusian vegetation are somehow reconciled with a gentle, curving conception of beauty.

As it happens, the illustrations on their clothing have been quite useful for my scientific work, because they show far more species than I've had the chance to encounter. The variety of the Venusian diet confirms that much of this assortment must be based on real organisms.

Their principal staple is a large fruit that combines the texture of an apple with the flavor of a pomegranate. This is eaten raw, in slices, and paired with sides of smaller fruits, roasted vegetables, and grilled meats. Most of the flavors and textures are quite unusual, but I have quickly grown to enjoy them.

I have manged to learn the names of at least a few of my hosts. The man who first called out to help me escape is Jonü, and he seems to be the primary one responsible for my well-being, assisted by a woman named Mara, who I believe to be his sister. These two have done the most to make me comfortable, although the Venusians have all been quite gracious and are understandably curious about their alien guest.

Captain's Log, Thursday, August 20th, 2961

I AM ONLY guessing at the date, assuming the Venusian sleeping schedule is a reasonable approximation of Earth days. Every electronic device I carry has run dead, and the only means

I have of charging them is the ship itself. I have been unable to communicate my desire to return there to the Venusians, although I have made some promising realizations about the Venusian language.

"Yeh ta Venüttü havuelkem," appears to consist of "to Venus" and "welcome" with some divergent pronunciation and grammar. The sound changes obscured some things which now appear to be clear derivations from English: The staple fruit is in fact called an "apülü" and they tell me, "Yeh dona falnao!" if I seem unsteady moving through the trees.

Once I realized this, I assumed I'd immediately be able to decode the Venusian language if they spoke slowly enough, but it has proven somewhat more difficult. For every word that clearly comes from English, there's another I can't place, and two more that seem obvious but have different meanings, and that's before trying to put the words together in a way that makes sense.

This is frustrating because, although my hosts have been generous, I can't shake the feeling that they're deliberately uncooperative when I talk about my ship. The big metal thing I came from that doesn't look like anything else on this planet shouldn't be such a hard concept to convey, especially when they recount the story of how they found me with abundant hand gestures to every new Venusian we meet.

Lest I sound overly suspicious, I'll end by mentioning that I have gotten closer to Jonü and Mara, and that I feel I can count two of Jonü's friends—Evanü and Güttü, both of whom were part of my rescuing party—as genuine friends among the Venusians. They have made no attempts at restricting my movement, and I have gotten better at navigating the branches, so I will simply have to go back to the ship myself.

Captain's log, Sunday, August 23rd, 2961

TAKEN BY THEIR hospitality, I have trusted the Venusians too much.

I woke this morning, somewhat later than usual as no one came to get me for breakfast, to find that all of my Venusian "friends" were missing. One of the Venusians still at camp brought me a meal, so I ate, assuming Jonü and the rest were simply occupied elsewhere. Mara made an appearance after some time, returning to camp from the direction of the beach. She seemed intent on keeping me occupied, as if to make up for her absence earlier, but her manner had an uneasiness I hadn't seen before.

In particular, she seemed to dismiss my questions about the others and try to divert my attention elsewhere. We might not speak the same language, but we've communicated enough for me to know that they're capable of figuring out the obvious question in response to a familiar name and miming an appropriate answer.

I decided it was time to return to my ship, so I tried to hide my suspicion as I told her the Venusian parting words, "Meh uelgoin," and made to leave the camp. She said something in protest, but that only increased my determination to go.

I've gotten better at climbing, and it didn't take long to make it to the beach. Mara followed, but she stayed back and didn't try to stop me.

When I got to the edge of the forest, I could see several Venusians, Jonü and the others among them, standing by my ship engaged in a bizarre task. They carried large bags and were spreading something red with grizzled lumps across as much of my ship as they could reach. I couldn't guess what purpose that served, but I wanted to stop it whether it was vandalism or something more sinister.

They had left ropes, tied high in the trees and hanging down to the base of the deadwood, so I grabbed one and was about to jump down when I heard Jonü shout.

"Pinshaü havkemin! Hueh gonao!"

The Venusians dropped their bags and ran toward the forest. They saw me, as they got to the ropes, but my presence seemed to concern them less than climbing up as fast as they could. I soon understood why.

The monster that had attacked my crew erupted out of the water and made straight for the ship. I believe the Venusians had been spreading animal entrails. The creature had ignored the metal spaceship the first time, but was now intent on attacking it, each pincher tearing chucks out of the ship and dragging them underneath its body, only to pull the wreckage of metal and plastic back after a moment and toss it aside.

The demolition was astounding, and the monster's raw power was more terrifying at that moment than it had been even as I watched it devour my crew.

The Venusians made it back into the trees as I gaped and, after a few glances and unreadable expressions directed at me, proceeded back toward camp.

I had expected some sort of fighting or altercation, but after that, there really wasn't anything to do. I might have been able to demand an explanation if I had been able to speak their language, but as things were, I could only watch as the creature rent my ship like it was determined to taste every piece just in case it proved to be edible.

I watched until the monster returned to the ocean, and then went back to camp. I'm not sure how to approach the Venusians now. However much I want to regard them as enemies after what they did, I am still lamentably dependent upon their hospitality to survive on this planet.

Thankfully, they seem content to allow me to remain in my sleeping quarters for the time being.

Captain's log, Tuesday, August 25th, 2961

NOT LONG AFTER finishing my last entry, Mara came to my

room. She brought dinner, for which I was grateful as I had missed the midday meal, and sat down for a time. I was torn between the desire to express my anger at what they'd done and the knowledge of my dependence on them—I still hadn't discovered where the food came from, much less how to obtain it myself.

She said a single word. "Sari."

The merciful similarity to English made it the best explanation I could have asked for, under the circumstances. I felt a little better about trying to deal with the Venusians by the time she left.

Even so, I wasn't exactly excited about the prospect of trying to spend the next day acting as though they hadn't stranded me here and destroyed everything I owned. Thankfully, Mara came to my room again the next morning and kept me occupied so I didn't have to face the others for a while.

We talked as much as we could manage, and I gather that, from the bits of English I've used, she has caught on to the relationship between our languages.

We compared vocabulary for some time, while she patiently allowed me to take notes, and I think I've learned more about their language from a morning with an understanding collaborator than I had in all the time I've spent previously. She tried to speak a bit of English too, and she seems as interested in my language as I am in hers.

For now, I am intending to continue this way. Hopefully a greater ability to communicate will prevent further difficulties until I can signal back to Earth.

Nothing I have with me can send a message that far, regardless of battery life, but I think I can manage something. I have been thinking about the communication devices on the ship. Even if they were damaged and torn apart in the wreckage, the creature didn't actually eat any of the metal, so the parts should still be there, and I think I know enough about the technology to rig a system that can get at least a simple message back home.

I still don't know the motivation for the Venusians' attack, so I plan to stay quite for the time being and only attempt to salvage material from the ship when I can do so unseen. Perhaps a greater ability to communicate will allow me to question their motives, or at least make excuses for why I want to go off alone.

Captain's log, Friday, September 4th, 2961

WITH MARA'S HELP, my progress in the Venusian language has been marvelous. Although I avoid potentially problematic subjects, I can generally understand most of what is said and express most of what I need to say. This has enabled me to integrate somewhat into Venusian life.

I have finally been able to see where our food comes from. In dramatic contrast to the simplicity of the ocean and the canopy, the forest floor is a dense maze of fallen wood, collected around and within the broad domes that form the roots of the trees, spreading out several meters before they meet the ground. Each root is blanketed by leafless flowers and fruits of stunning variety—symbionts, most likely—and animals seem to make their home everyplace that there's a fallen branch large enough to conceal them.

Apülü grow within the root domes, and it turns out that they are the fruit of the humongous trees. Fresh apülü has tough amber skin, the source of one of the principal fabric dyes, and grows in bunches that are nearly a meter across. I believe that they're something like aggregate drupes, although that's only an analogous term, as the native Venusian organisms have a clearly alien biology.

Gathering food on the forest floor is a matter of speed, and is closely tied to hunting. Spending too much time on the ground attracts kattü, pale white quadrupedal predators that don't hesitate to attack humans, so Venusians gathering fruit always travel with hunters that remain above them with spears ready—the kattü are actually a major source of meat in the Venusian diet.

I have become a regular member of Venusian hunting parties—hunting on Venus requires less agility than gathering, as the gatherers essentially act as bait—and I have developed quite a bit of camaraderie with my fellow hunters. Whatever ill will the Venusians had for my ship, they don't seem to extend it to me.

I have been able to get a closer look at a Venusian's body, and there are indeed slight proportional differences between them and humans from Earth, mostly relating to arm length. However, the sheer muscular development in the bodies of people whose primary mode of transportation is to pull themselves upwards creates the greatest difference in appearance, particularly for a woman, although I will say the the visual effect of the differences is not at all unpleasant.

I am still intending to return to my ship and cobble together a communication device, but it's easy to put that off as I'm getting more comfortable here. By the time I get to it, I'll probably be able to talk to the Venusians openly about what happened and get their aid in building the device.

Final Captain's Log, Friday, January 1st, 2962

OR AS THE Venusians would date it, Early Afternoon of the 1503 Day

I had almost forgotten about this journal, but I figured it would be better to give it a proper ending in case it becomes part of the Venusian lore or is someday read by another Homian explorer.

I have come to enjoy life on Venus. I don't know whether Earth will take the risk of another exploration mission after we, too, suddenly disappeared, but I'll be staying here either way.

The reason for the attack on my ship turned out to be quite

understandable: Apparently we managed to send a few messages to the first Venus expedition after the last one we received, and we naturally informed them of the war. When our messages stopped coming, they assumed that destruction had been total, and the story of Homian weapons leveling a whole planet survived in Venusian folklore. They were afraid I might have such weapons on my ship once they were sure I was, in fact, a Homian, but took it for granted that I'd be staying on Venus as their ancestors had.

That word, "Homianü" in its original pronunciation, is one of my favorite bits of the Venusian language. It seems the first people here were so insistent on referring to their settlement as "camp" and Earth as "home" that subsequent generations considered "kampü" to be the word for the place where one lives and "Homü" to be the name of a distant planet.

I've gotten a fascinating look at those early generations of Venusians in the lore books, which I'm now translating from English into Venusian. The first few generations kept journals, rather like this one, and those have been preserved. The Venusians were hesitant to show them to me until they were sure they could trust me, as they haven't been making copies. No one has been able to read them for a few hundred years and making the paper is a difficult process.

I may keep such a journal in the future, but it won't be a "Captain's log" anymore. My priorities have changed: I'm expecting a child, a son if the Venusian method of prediction is accurate, in just under five months. I'm planning on marrying Mara before that, and marriage is apparently a rather complicated affair here, so I'll be a bit busy for a while.

HERE ENDS THE record of the second Homian expedition to Venus.

Ariel Cohen was born in Israel, in a town call Bat-Yam, which means "mermaid". With a beginning like this, it was perhaps inevitable that he would be drawn to fantasy and science fiction all his life. He tried hard to be a "serious" person, majored in Computer Science, did his PhD in Computational Linguistics, and is now a professor of linguistics at Ben-Gurion University, Israel. And while this is his only second published fiction, he has published extensively on the science side of the equation, specifically on linguistics. Yes, linguistics is a science, even if it is sometimes indistinguishable from magic. For how is it possible for mere air vibrations, or squiggles on a piece of paper, to express ideas, thoughts, desires, feelings? Ariel Cohen lives with his wife Silvina and daughter Keren in Meitar, Israel.

As the label suggests, science fiction can draw on any branch of science, but the "hard sciences" such as physics and astronomy tend to get the lion's share of the attention. There have been some classic examples of linguistic science fiction—Jack Vance's delightful The Languages of Pao *comes instantly to mind—but few tales have embraced the fantastic dimensions of language with as much verve as Ariel Cohen's* A Martian Iliad—*or used classic SF as a resource for a new tale with as much panache...*

A Martian Iliad

by Ariel Cohen

Mars, Mars, bane of men, bloodstained stormer of cities!
-- Homer, The Iliad

MAULANA ISHAQ OBSERVED the faces of his men. Only their eyes sparkled in the dark, like diamonds on a velvet cushion, but that was sufficient for him to see their determination. "Enough is enough!" he cried. "For many years, the Iranians and Pakistanis have persecuted and terrorized the Baloch. And this accursed barrier they are building, right on their border, is just another link in the chain of oppression. They want to divide the Baloch, to separate us from our families on the other side. But they will not succeed! Tonight, we strike back! Tonight, we blow up the barrier!"

Ishaq went on, feeling his men's excitement rising, as they thirstily drank his every word, their attention fully on him.

Ishaq also had the full attention of Amanullah Achakzai, of the Pakistani intelligence service, hiding behind a rock on the hilltop. He couldn't hear Ishaq, being too far away, but, using his night-vision binoculars, could see him quite clearly. This is how Achakzai was able to see the tall, feathered creatures, which appeared out of nowhere. He could see the

Balochi rebels fall, one by one, before terror overwhelmed him and he ran away from the place.

SUSAN PICKED UP her ebook reader and clicked once again on Larry Niven's *Rainbow Mars*. She immediately typed the page number of the description of the Tweelers—so tantalizingly brief. The big, flightless birds, wearing tool belts, are only mentioned in a few sentences. They chase the main characters, Svetz and Miya, for a few clicks, but never catch up. And that's it. But could these few words contain some clue after all?

Suddenly, Susan froze. The description was longer than she remembered, longer than she knew it to be. Much longer. Wide eyed, Susan started reading the words that had never been in this story before.

She read how the nearest bird hurls a rock at the heroes' sailcar. How Svetz picks it up, and notices that it is wrapped in a sheet of paper. How Miya unfolds the paper, sees that it is covered in writing, and starts reading aloud.

TENIENTE JERÓNIMO GRANADO let his eyes flow over his boat, the Durango. He thoroughly disliked his job in the Mexican coast guard. But this time he was happy: he was going home. The twelve men on his boat had finished another really daring and adventurous mission in the Gulf of California, he thought wryly. Yes, there is only so long you can stare at the foam on the waves, with nothing to do. It was time to go back.

When he fell unconscious, he literally didn't know what hit him. Marinero Carreon didn't know either, but at least he managed to see one of the three tall, feathered figures, though even that at a blur. He had just enough time to pick up the mike of the transceiver and yell "¡Pájaros grandes!

¡Pájaros grandes!" before he saw the figure point something at him—and then he, too, saw nothing further. The Durango continued to rock gently on the waves, with no crew left to stir its course.

Susan's eyes were glued to the screen, as she kept reading the story she had known so well, but that now had additional, completely new words. Miya was reading from the piece of paper. It turned out to be a letter. Incredibly, impossibly, the letter was addressed to Susan herself!

Dear Susan,

I managed to convince the Tweelers to wrap this letter in a rock and throw it at Miya and Svetz. With a bit of luck, this letter will be recorded in the story. And I know that, sooner or later, you will read the story again—and this is the only way I have of contacting you, of saying goodbye.

So, at long last, I have made a difference, in a way that my dear brother Mitch will never be able to. There will be some record of me, if only as the author of a fictitious letter in a fictitious story in a fictitious world.

But I have to tell you, Susan, from here it doesn't look fictitious. It looks real, very real...

Captain Ou Dingxiang looked through his binoculars at the Chinese-Indian border, and the state of Arunachal Pradesh beyond it. As expected, there was nobody to be seen.

"Border, ha!" he thought to himself, derisively. This land was Chinese, had always been Chinese, and would be Chinese again, soon. But not, unfortunately, today. Today was just a small incursion, to remind the Indians who was boss around here. The orders of his company were to move in, make camp, and withdraw the next day. That's it.

Dingxiang thoroughly disliked these little games. If we

believe this place is ours, we should go in and take it—with all necessary force, he thought. If not, just let it be. But the government thought differently—they even sent a professional photographer to video the entire heroic operation, the brilliant military maneuver against a few barren rocks.

Dingxiang sighed and checked his watch again. Oh, well, he decided. Time to give the order. But he never did. The tall, birdlike creatures, which appeared out of nowhere, acted with lightning speed. In a matter of seconds, the entire company was unconscious. The creatures picked up the soldiers and carried them one by one. They even picked up the photographer, but not his camera, which was left behind, still rolling.

IT'S NOT THAT I wanted to be a hero, Susan. I admit, having a brother who is a decorated general is not easy. Not when you are a frustrated Ph.D. who couldn't get an academic job.

Well, I shouldn't complain. I do (or did) have a decent job, even if it wasn't in academia. But what will be left of me when I am gone? Mitch will have his heroic secret operations in the military, the little I know of which I will not describe, not even in this fictitious letter; you will have your novels and stories, which generations of SF fans will continue to appreciate; but I will have nothing! Not even children to carry my name. Not even a widow to mourn for me.

But that dinner, when you started telling these wonderful, amazing stories, was the beginning of a way to make a difference, though I didn't see it at the time...

SUSAN DIDN'T REALLY like Larry, although, or perhaps because, he was Mitch's brother. It's not that she disliked him; but he always seemed to be in the way. Always around at the most inappropriate time. Of course, Mitch said that, for her, any time when Larry was around was an inappropriate time.

Susan sighed. Another one of those dinners with him! Another dreary and boring event, full of meaningless pauses at best, or whining about his unsuccessful life at worst.

As always, the TV was on—Susan stealing a glance at it every now and then, to relieve the awkwardness. It was she, therefore, who first noticed the newsflash.

Mitch and Larry followed her gaze. "What are these things?" Mitch cried out. The screen repeatedly displayed footage of tall, feathery creatures, with long beaks and little black bags hanging around their necks. They were carrying what appeared to be the lifeless bodies of soldiers, taking them somewhere off camera. The news anchor described the complete disappearance of a Chinese infantry company. The Chinese Prime Minister was on screen, accusing India of the attack and vowing revenge.

"This is serious," said Mitch. "This sort of thing could start a war."

"Looks like it's already started," said Larry.

"You don't want to know what this reminds me of," said Susan.

"Not another one of your science fiction stories!" grunted Mitch, not without affection.

"Well, yes, actually" said Susan. "It's a real classic—A Martian Odyssey, by Stanley G. Weinbaum. But of course neither of you have read it, right?"

Without waiting for an answer, she continued.

"Well, there is this explorer on Mars, called Dick Jarvis. And he sees a creature that looks just like this: tall, feathery, long beak. Even the little black bag! He calls it Tweel."

"What is it like?" asked Mitch.

"Well, apparently very intelligent. But its way of thinking is different from ours, which makes it appear crazy sometimes. For example, Jarvis draws a diagram of the Solar System in the sand and indicates Earth as his home world, and Tweel seems to understand this. But when Tweel itself is asked where it is from, it starts jumping up and down excitedly, points frantically at various parts of its body and at various stars, and then makes a tremendous leap straight into the drawing of the sun…"

"Is it dangerous?" asked Larry.

"Well, depends. It doesn't attack Jarvis, but it is capable of violence. It uses a gun made of glass, which fires poisoned glass splinters.

"In fact, in one scene Jarvis and Tweel fight side by side, the two of them against an attack by twenty barrel-shaped creatures—Tweel with its glass gun and Jarvis with a gun that fires exploding bullets. They cooperate pretty well together, and fend of the attack. But then more of the creatures come, and—"

"All this is fascinating, of course," said Larry. "But what are you actually saying? That we are being attacked by Martians from a science fiction story?"

"Come on, Larry!" Mitch cut him short. "Let the Chinese deal with it. It's not our problem, anyway."

I AM SORRY I made fun of you that evening, Susan. But you have to admit the whole story was funny, something out of the Weekly World News: Bigbird from Mars Attacks Chinese Soldiers! I wouldn't have given it a second thought. And when, a few days later, I came to visit you, while Mitch was at the army base, it wasn't to talk about the Martians. But the reason is not important—because we ended up with the Martians after all, didn't we?

"WHY ARE YOU here?" demanded Susan, for the third time. She hadn't gotten a clear answer the first two times. And she got no answer at all the third time, because Mitch stormed in.

"Susan, I need to talk to you," he said urgently. And then he noticed Larry—"What are you doing here?" he asked.

Larry said nothing. Susan almost said "I didn't expect you home so soon!" but caught herself in time. Instead she simply asked: "What is it?"

"I need you to tell me more about these Martians," said Mitch, his attention, again, fully on Susan.

"This is why you rushed in like this? What, are they chasing you?" asked Susan incredulously. And then she noticed the look in his eyes and understood—this was serious. And bad. Really bad.

"Well, I guess I'd better get going!" said Larry.

"No... No," Mitch stopped him. "You might as well stay—so long as nothing said here leaves this room, do you understand?"

"Mitch, what is it?" asked Susan, her anxiety mounting.

"We've been attacked!" responded Mitch grimly.

"Attacked? Who was attacked? And by whom?" asked Larry.

"We, the United States of America. A patrol boat, near Clearwater, Florida. All eight crewmembers are missing. A second boat, nearby, saw birdlike creatures appear, seemingly out of nowhere, and the crewmembers falling one by one. They didn't want to open fire, for fear of hurting our men, and moved towards the first boat at full speed. But when they arrived, everybody—both our forces and the enemy, were simply gone."

"But why are you telling us this?" asked Larry. "How can we help?"

"Well, I turned to Susan, in fact," snapped Mitch. After the briefest of pauses, he continued: "Because something was found at the scene. A gun. Made of glass. Firing small glass projectiles."

This time, the pause was much longer.

"I've made some phone calls. What happened at the China-India border had happened before. It's just the first time that this was made public. Similar attacks were reported at the Iran-Pakistan border, the Mexican Gulf of California, Tindouf in Algeria, the Spanish island of Tenerife, and the Japanese island of Ukejima. And now Florida. Curiously, all attacks were on the 28th parallel north—all these places are at approximately latitude 28 north.

"All the attacks were against military personnel. In all of them, no survivors and no bodies remained—they were all captured, presumably alive. And... all the attacks were carried out by large, birdlike creatures. Looks like someone is going to great lengths to impersonate these Martians of yours. Why would anyone do that? I need you to tell me all you know about them."

"Well, I am not sure what more I can add to what I've already told you about that story," said Susan, "except that there is some question whether Tweel really originated on Mars. There are some Martian life-forms that Tweel doesn't seem to recognize: for example, the barrel creatures that they end up fighting.

"But I can tell you that Tweel's species appears in two more stories," she added.

"Really?" asked Mitch. "This Weinbaum guy wrote two more stories about them?"

"Only one", responded Susan. "In Valley of Dreams we meet more of Tweel's people..."

"We can call them Tweelers" interrupted Larry.

"Yeah, whatever," said Mitch. "What do we know about them?"

"Well, a long time ago, they traveled to Earth, to ancient Egypt, where they were revered as manifestations of the god Thoth."

"That's interesting," said Larry. "I once wrote a paper on metaphors in ancient Egyptian, and I read the Book of Thoth..."

"Is that so?" interrupted Mitch, without interest. "How did these Tweelers get to Earth?"

"The characters in the story actually wonder about this," answered Susan. "The human spaceship runs on nuclear power, but the Tweelers haven't discovered nuclear energy. At the end of the story, Jarvis gives Tweel the nuclear engine of his spaceship as a gift."

"OK, you said there was one other story?" Mitch said.

"Yes, but it wasn't written by Weinbaum. Another author, Larry Niven, wrote a story called Rainbow Mars. In this story, there are a number of races on Mars, including Tweelers. The races are at war with each other. Some of them kidnap members of other races, enslave them, and force them to become soldiers."

"Do they, now?" asked Mitch. "Now we are getting somewhere. Maybe this is why the attackers target military people—they kidnap soldiers to make them fight for them. Are these Martians a threat to Earth—I mean, in the story?"

"Not really," said Susan. "You see, they don't have space travel."

"Well, somebody is carrying out these attacks," said Mitch. "But who are they? And why go to the trouble of impersonating those fictitious Martians? They even made the glass of the gun look like it came from Mars!"

"What did you say?" asked Susan, very quietly.

"Naturally, the gun was sent to analysis," said Mitch. "The little bubbles in the glass did not contain regular air; they contained the gases you find on Mars, in exactly the right proportions. This is how you discover that a meteorite came from Mars, you know: most meteorites contain shock glass veins or pockets, which can be chemically analyzed."

"Yes, I do know this," said Susan emphatically. "But this is something that you can't fake. If the glass looks like it came from Mars, then come from Mars it did!"

"What do you mean, it can't be faked?" asked Mitch.

"You can't just put together the right combination of gases and inject it into your glass, because the bubbles form as the glass is created," explained Susan. "Think about it: Martian meteorites are very rare and extremely expensive. If it were so easy to fake them so that a chemical analysis wouldn't find them out, don't you think the market would be flooded with fake Martian meteorites?"

"So what, exactly, are you telling us?" asked Larry.

"Only this: the glass really came from Mars. Which means that the gun came from Mars. Which means that the attackers came from Mars."

There was no immediate reply to Susan's words: the two men simply stared at her for a long moment. Finally, Mitch broke the silence.

"We aren't seriously considering this, are we?" he demanded. "I mean, we have sent numerous spaceships to Mars, and have active rovers on the surface as we speak, and they failed to find any sign of life—not even bacteria, let alone Martians running around! And even if Martians really did exist, why wouldn't they appear as they really are? Why would they attempt to impersonate the characters from a story written by a human?"

"They don't. They really did come from this story," Susan replied.

This time, the ensuing silence was considerably shorter.

"Susan, you know you ought to explain this," said Larry.

"Of course," said Susan. "But I am not sure myself—I will just speak while I think, you know? Look, in many science fiction stories, we have different parallel universes, and characters can travel among them. And they can also travel in time, OK?"

"Yes, but this is not science fiction," said Mitch. "It's real life."

"Exactly! What is told in the science fiction story is not true in the actual universe. It is true in a fictitious universe, not our universe. But what if it really is possible to travel among universes and times? What if the Tweelers from Larry Niven's Rainbow Mars can travel to Stanley Weinbaums's universe, or to our universe?

"Suppose the Tweelers from Niven's universe are looking for slaves to fight for them. And suppose one of them, Tweel, travels to Weinbaums's universe, and encounters the human Jarvis. As described in the story, they fight the barrel creatures together; presumably Tweel is impressed with Jarvis's fighting skills, and with how quickly he bonds with it and joins forces with it to fight a common enemy.

"When Tweel comes back to its own universe—Larry Niven's—it tells the others, and they decide that humans are exactly the sort of soldiers they are looking for. So they want to travel to our universe and capture human soldiers.

"However, although they have the ability to travel from one parallel universe to another, which allows them to infiltrate our universe, this would still leave them on Mars; our Mars, but still Mars. To get to Earth, in any universe, they need spaceships. So, they travel to Stanley Weinbaum's universe, where they meet the humans and, as described in Weinbaum's second story, get the spaceship engine from them. And then they can travel to Mars in our universe, get into the spaceship, travel to Earth and start kidnapping military personnel. This explains why Tweel didn't recognize the barrel creatures—it came from Niven's Mars, which doesn't have these creatures, not from Weinbaum's, which does."

"Susan, you can't be serious!" said Mitch. "I don't even know where to begin—but here is just one point: where can they hide on Earth so that they are undetected?"

"In the past," replied Susan. "In ancient Egypt, where they are revered as manifestations of the god Thoth.

"Tell me", she suddenly turned to Larry. "You said you had read about Thoth. Do you happen to know if there was a special place sacred to Thoth in ancient Egypt?"

"I do, actually," replied Larry. "Thoth's main temple was in the ancient Egyptian city of Khmun."

"Let's google it," said Susan. "I bet it will be at roughly 28 latitude north."

And so it was. Susan continued to explain.

"You see, the Tweelers have a base at Khmun, in the ancient past. When they want to kidnap some soldiers and enslave them, they travel to our present, that is to say, they move forward in time, many years. But apparently they don't have efficient means of moving substantial distances in space."

"Why not, if they now have spaceships?" asked Larry.

"Well, spaceships can take you from one planet to another, but if you want to go from here to London, you wouldn't take a spaceship, would you?" Susan asked. "In the stories, they move by running and jumping, and they are very fast, and can travel a hundred and fifty feet at a jump. Of course, in Earth's gravity and atmosphere, they will be slower, but still quite fast."

"But jumps won't take them to China, Pakistan, Florida, Mexico," said Mitch. "They would just be stuck in Egypt!"

"Not really," replied Susan. "Suppose you traveled twelve hours ahead in time, but not in space. Where would you be? You wouldn't move; but the Earth would. It would turn half a resolution. So you would find yourself on the other side of the Earth. But, crucially, still at the same latitude! This is why all the attacks occurred at the 28th parallel—the latitude of Khmun. When they move forward in time they can find themselves not only in our time, but anywhere they want, so long as it's on the 28th parallel."

"Hey, wait a minute!" said Mitch. "This is getting way too crazy. I mean, how is it even possible to travel between times and universes?"

"Maybe it's not so far-fetched," said Larry thoughtfully. "If you think about it, our language travels to other times and universes quite easily.

"For example, the word *president* usually refers to the current president—Donald Trump. But when we say a sentence about the past or future, it can refer to different people: for instance, when we talk about the Great Depression, the word refers to Roosevelt. The word can even refer to presidents that never existed in our universe, but only in an alternative universe, as when we say that Hillary Clinton wishes she were president."

"Thank you, Larry, for your invaluable contribution," said Mitch. "Exactly what we need to deal with this problem: a linguistics lecture!"

"It *is* interesting, actually," said Susan. "But this won't help us in the case of the Tweelers, because their language will not let them talk about other times or universes. The Tweelers' language is very different from human languages: their words keep changing as time goes by. They can't even use the word *rock* to refer to the same object twice at different times. Weinbaum describes how even Tweel's name keeps changing every time Jarvis tries to communicate with it; at last Jarvis gives up and simply sticks with *Tweel*.

"However, in the story, Jarvis manages to teach it a bit of English. Tweel seems to grasp the idea that Jarvis's first name, Dick, remains the same all the time, and that, for Jarvis, its own name is always Tweel. It also learns a few nouns, such as *rock*, and seems to understand that the same thing can be called *rock* twice in succession—in fact, it seems greatly amused by this!"

"This is fascinating," said Larry thoughtfully. "Tell me— did Tweel do his crazy jump into the diagram of the solar system before or after this language lesson?"

"After, as far as I can remember," said Susan. "Why?"

"Because the question is…" started Larry, but Mitch cut him off brusquely.

"The question *is*," he said, "how we can defend ourselves against these birds. Even if you're right, Susan, and they really are aliens from science fiction stories—which I don't believe for a moment—how can we fight an enemy that appears out of nowhere, without warning, and then disappears again? But this is not for the two of you to deal with. If you'll excuse me, I must get back to Headquarters, and you two can carry on with... with whatever it is you were doing."

And then, as abruptly as he came, he left. Susan tried to catch Larry's eye, but he excused himself and left too.

YOU SEE, SUSAN, you were right all along. These aliens really can travel among times and fictional universes, they really keep slaves to fight for them, and they really did come from Rainbow Mars, *the story you are reading now, the story that, now, contains my letter to you.*

I know, because now this universe contains me too. Yes, I am one of their slaves. Very soon I will go into battle. I fear that unlike the other humans, I will prove a disappointment to the Tweelers; I am not a good soldier, to put it mildly, and my chances of survival are not promising. I know I will not be missed, not by my dear brother, and not by you, either. And I will certainly not be missed by the Tweelers! They hadn't really meant to kidnap me—but they had no choice. You see, I wanted to be captured.

How did I manage that? Very simply. I figured that when they travel to our present, they first pick the date, and then fine-tune the hours and minutes, so as to allow the Earth to move beneath them until they are exactly where they want to be. Which means that, if they start in ancient Khmun, they will first arrive at the same place, but in the present, and then continue carefully to their final destination, looking for prey.

So I bought a one-way ticket to Egypt, and a cab took me directly from the airport to the site of the Khmun ruins, near the village of El Ashmunein. There isn't much remaining there today, but I was able to hide among the few pillars that are still standing.

I didn't have to wait long before the Tweelers appeared, and then I simply jumped them. Out came the glass gun, and when I awoke I was on their nuclear-powered spaceship, on the way to Mars—that is to say, Larry Niven's Rainbow Mars, which you are now reading, Susan.

You see, I figured out the answer to Mitch's question, how to mount a defense against the Tweelers. They will never come again, I can assure you. Earth is safe, and so are you. And I am the one who did it! Yes, the little old linguist carried the day!

You were right. The Tweelers can travel to other times and universes. But how are they able to do it?

The answer has to do with their language. We can't travel to other times and universes, but our language can; in contrast, the Tweelers' language can't travel to other times and universes, therefore they themselves must.

Let me explain. If I want to talk about something that Tweel did, or something that it will do, or something that it might do, I can; and I use the same name, Tweel, in all these cases. Because, for us, the name remains constant through time.

But suppose one of the Tweelers wanted to talk about one of these things. How could it? The name Tweel only refers to it at one particular moment; so how can the Tweelers refer to Tweel at some other time?

The answer is they can't. There is simply no way for them to do this. But they have to! It is impossible to have any sort of reasonable communication without being able, every now and then, to talk of something lying outside the here-and-now. The only way they have of talking about Tweel of yesterday, or tomorrow, or Tweel that might have been, is for them to actually go to that time or universe. Then, they can talk about Tweel using whatever name it has in that time or universe. So, they solve the problem posed by what we might consider the poverty of their language in a remarkable, dramatic way. For them, of course, it is perfectly natural.

When Tweel learned a few words of English, and the notion that words can remain constant in time, this provided it with the rudimentary components of a communication system that allowed it to speak of other times and universes without actually going there. This was enough to disable its linguistically compelled ability to travel among times and universes. Remember how, when Jarvis inquired as to where it came from, Tweel responded with frantic jumping and pointing in all directions, culminating with a giant leap? This strange behavior was caused by its frustration and fear when it discovered that it couldn't travel to another universe, couldn't get back home, and was stranded on Weinbaum's Mars.

I know that this must be the reason, because I watched the Tweelers perform the same strange, frantic, desperate dance. This was right after I taught them a bit of English, right after they caught on to the insidious idea that the same word can refer to the same thing at different times.

Yes, the Tweelers have now lost their ability to travel among times and universes. Their minds have undergone irreversible change, reached a simple yet profound understanding, and this now cannot be undone. They (and I) are all stranded here, on Larry Niven's Mars. This is why they will never threaten the actual Earth again—I can tell you for a fact that the war of the worlds is over.

So this is how I saved the world—with a brief language lesson. Had the Tweelers come from a poem by Pope, rather than a science fiction story, perhaps they would have known that a little learning is a dangerous thing.

Violet Bertelsen is an herbalist, farmhand and amateur historian currently living in the northeastern United States. While a child, the woods befriended and educated Violet, who proved to be an eager student. She spent her young adulthood in a haze, wandering the vast expanses of North America trying to find the lost fragments of her soul in deserts, hot springs and rail-yards. Now older and more sedate, she likes to spend her time talking with trees, reading history books, laughing uproariously with fellow farmhands, drinking black birch tea and, on occasion, writing science fiction stories.

One of the many pleasures of imaginative fiction is the way it opens up standard elements of fiction to an epicure's banquet of variations. Violet Bertelsen's On the Shoreline of Darkness *is a good example; it puts its own unexpected and extraterrestial spin on one of the classic tropes of the horror tale...*

On the Shoreline of Darkness

by Violet Bertelsen

T HE POLYHEDRON PLUTONIAN spaceship docked in the pad at the Louisville terminal. The Plutonian men in their g-suits unloaded the crates of dried fungoid mass which had grown so popular in recent years. Dr. Diego Kraken watched the crates come off, his head shaking, wondering to himself. How did it seem so easy to live without the fungoid mass just a few years ago? Now everyone with half a brain is imbibing it all the time...even me. And...it's delightful, a mild euphoric that increases acuity of the senses, and allows for deep understandings, hidden connections to come to the light...very useful.

He observed the Plutonians, under their silver g-suits which prevented the earth's gravity from crushing their fragile bones. They'd evolved on an almost sunless planet, and yet they do not merely survive, they thrive, thought Dr. Kraken to himself, shaking his head. He worked on and off at the University of Planetary Studies in Chicago, and was considered one of the best research anthropologists. Beings on every planet of the Solar System avidly read his accounts of the last remnants of the ancient civilizations of the Earth's

Moon, the deserts of Mars, the eerie twilight belt of Mercury, the seas of Neptune...all of it. He had visited every planet in the solar system and most of the major moons. That is, all but one: Pluto.

Prior to the advent of the fungoid trade four years ago, little had been known about the most distant planet, or the strange pale men that lived there, with their windowless cities, fungoid gardens and distinctive polyhedron space craft. There was brief mention of them in the legends of the Neptunian Cetaceans who told fearsome tales of the pale humanoid beings who craved blood. Likewise, the Jovians had some folk tales of the horrible polyhedron space ships of legend that would snatch their children for some sinister purpose.

Certainly, these myths link up in a terrifying way, thought Dr. Kraken as he watched the polyhedron, so unearthly with its translucent, green and purple sides, being loaded with its Earth cargo; human children, aged about ten to sixteen years, no one older than eighteen.

Generalissimo Johnson had been happy to have an off-world market for the rapidly swelling convict population. Since The Coup, times had been dark: secret police, concentration camps, torture rooms; the entire apparatus of a high-tech police state. So far, Dr. Kraken had been left mostly at peace. Not even Generalissimo Johnson, who hated public intellectuals with a passion, wished to harm the celebrated Planetary Anthropologist, at least not yet. Although the professor had been brought in for questioning a half dozen times, and every time the sinister men with their fedoras and cigarettes had spent the better part of an hour discussing their various torture instruments and asking Diego to sign copies of his books for their wives and children.

This is my final frontier, thought Dr. Diego Kraken, afterwards what am I going to do with myself? As soon as he thought these words he had an eerie premonition of horror, and involuntarily touched the ray gun that never left his side holster. Dr. Diego Kraken had been putting off going to Pluto for a while now.

Given the tremendous speeds of space travel, there was always the reality of Einsteinian time dilation to contend with. While Dr. Kraken would only experience the passage of about one earth day on the space ship, the rest of the universe would experience the passage of the better part of ten years. Travelling to Neptune had been horrific for this reason. Everyone hated experiencing the effects of time dilation. Now though was different for the professor. Now he had no one to return to. He did a breathing exercise to calm his heart; *my flight is already chartered, and it's wiser to get out of Earth while space travel is still allowed. If things go Venusian I have a lot of friends I can turn to, no matter how many years have passed.*

The human cargo was led on board, and Diego walked up to the open bay of the ship, "Hello sir, here is my passport; I've chartered a flight with you to Pluto," he said with his characteristic outward pluck and confidence.

The Plutonian in his shimmering g-suit took the passport. His little black eyes became round when he read the name. "Professor Diego Kraken!" he exclaimed, "When the captain told us you would be coming onboard I couldn't believe it. I love your work! The Cetacean Myths of Neptune is my favourite book ever! Please sir, come on board."

And with that Diego said to himself, "Farewell Terra!" and stepped inside.

AFTER THE TAKE-OFF, the Captain was eager to meet the great anthropologist. He invited Dr. Kraken to his private study for a glass of whisky. "Ah, so you are the great author; you know I've read all of your books Dr. Kraken, indeed, they are what inspired me to become a pilot."

"Thank you, Captain, I am surprised that you were able

to get them all the way in Pluto," said Diego as he took a long sip of his drink. Watch this one he thought; he is more dangerous than he looks. Diego had learned to trust his intuition long ago; it had saved his life more times than he wished to remember.

"Yes, well. Please, call me Draque," said the obsequious Captain; "there are a lot of rumors and misinformation about Plutonians that I trust you will be able to set straight. We are voracious readers, and writers I may add. We get most of our books via Uranus, which of course is a major hub of some of the best libraries and publishing houses. The weather of their steppes is good for preserving paper and their great forests are an excellent source of paper pulp."

"Hmm, that is fascinating, Draque," pondered Diego. "I've never heard mention of Plutonians in Uranus; they seemed to think it was a dead planet."

"Why yes, they would. Look Dr. Kraken, I'll be straight with you; you have your...political situation on earth, yes, and it would be...unethical for me to press you on it, given the potential consequences. Well, Pluto has certain...arrangements that we wish to maintain. Utter secrecy concerning our trade with Uranus is one of them. Not everyone needs to know who trades what for what," said Draque sinisterly, as if testing the professor.

"With all due respect, how do you expect to maintain secrecy with your fungoid mass trade? It is so enormously popular, and for good reason. The last four books I've written have been under its influence," remarked Dr. Kraken.

"Well, hmmm...you must have noticed that the shipments only came after your Generalissimo Johnson took over," said Draque, now speaking with barely concealable malevolence.

"Hmmm, yes you're right; I hadn't put it together," pondered Dr. Kraken, nursing his whiskey.

"Suffice to say word won't get out from Earth; prior to The Coup there were over five hundred thousand radio operators on your planet. Now there are less than one thousand alive, following the strict scripts of your dictator. We are not concerned; loose tongues are in no one's interests currently. Have you considered that many people less travelled than yourself do not know or even care where their fungoid mass comes from?" and before Dr. Kraken could answer, Draque finished his drink. "More whiskey Dr. Kraken?" he offered cordially.

"Yes, thank you," said Diego.

Captain Draque looked out the side of the spaceship. "We are passing through the asteroid belt right now; don't worry, our pilots are skilled, very skilled. We believe on Pluto that men can be molded to their machines, that men are the machines of machines. Would you like to see what I mean?"

"Yes, of course!" said Dr. Kraken, his ears pricking up.

"Very good; come this way," said Captain Draque.

They walked down a flight of stairs to the control room. In spite of himself Dr. Kraken gasped.

In the helm was a body totally merged with the machine, like melted cheese. A spinal cord was visible and here and there the ripple of muscle. Captain Draque guffawed at Dr. Diego Kraken's involuntary fright. "And you consider yourself cosmopolitan!" sneered the Captain; "our trade ships are all operated by a body that has, since earliest youth, been conditioned to be an integral part of the ship. It makes it very easy to navigate; you just set a course on this monitor, and the pilot effortlessly traverses through space."

"That is so...efficient," said the anthropologist, disgusted.

"Indeed, you may wonder why we need a captain at all; I simply control the crew, keep them from getting rowdy and of course I set the course, although a trained monkey could probably do so as well in my place," said Captain Draque drily.

"Fascinating," yawned Diego, suddenly exhausted.

"Shall I show you your quarters?" asked Captain Draque.

"Please; space travel always makes me sleepy."

Captain Draque led Diego to a small room with a cot. "If there is anything you need, my good man, let me know. If you need to relieve yourself there is a button here that will launch the suction toilet."

"Many thanks," sighed the professor, ready now to sleep.

"Sleep well," said Captain Draque, returning to his study; "may you have sweet dreams."

ADA LAY THERE in her hospital bed, the cancer spread through her vitals; she looked at Diego, tears in his eyes: "Dad?"

"Yeah Ada?"

"I'm going to die, aren't I?"

Diego felt his heart sink in his chest; he wished he could trade places with her; he had already lost his wife Ruth to a Mars attack, now he was about to lose his only child.

"Ada…" he said stupidly, like a coward, like a man who couldn't look his daughter in the face and tell her the truth.

"I'm going to die, Dad." She said, a statement not a question. "I'm going to die…Do you think that there is someplace we go after we die?"

"Well, the Neptunians believe…."

"I read your book, Dad; what do you believe…I'm scared…"

"I…I…don't know; I haven't thought about it much personally."

Ada began to cry, "I can't die - I've barely begun to live! I'm just sixteen…"

Diego watched her helplessly, the daughter he had barely known, regretting bitterly that he had spent so much of her youth travelling and writing and now not sure what to say.

"I need to be alone," she said, "I need to think about this stuff myself. I'll let you know the next time you can see me."

There was an edge to her voice. They both knew that he had failed her.

"Ada, I love you."

"I love you too, Dad...bye..."

He stood there for a moment looking at her light brown skin and bright eyes and curly dark hair, and she looked away from him and out the window and he didn't want her to get cross and make an ugly scene, but didn't want to acknowledge that this would be the last time he would see her. With all his strength Diego made himself leave.

The next time he saw her was her funeral...

Dr. Kraken gasped awake, covered in a cold sweat in the strange room. He was haunted by these memories. He felt like crying but couldn't, and felt her ghost with him in this spacecraft so far away from Earth. "Oh Ada," he said out loud, "I am so sorry..."

He took two tablets of fungoid mass, got up and opened the door. Outside he saw that they were landing on Pluto.

Captain Draque found him, and smiling his vampiric smile said, "Welcome to Pluto, to the end of the Solar System, or as we say here; the shoreline of darkness."

"It is...dark here during the day," said Diego surprised in spite of himself, "I would say that it is about as bright as early dawn on Earth." His body felt light; low g-planets were in some ways more disconcerting than the giants. On Jupiter you went around in a g-suit to keep the bones intact, which kept things feeling very similar to Earth. Here he felt he could easily jump four meters off the ground, and even with intensive exercises his bones would rapidly atrophy. Best to leave here soon as possible, he thought to himself.

"Yes, there is much less light here than on Earth" said Captain Draque; "we will provide you with some specially made light amplification goggles if you should like."

"Thank you, I doubt I'll need them," said the professor, watching the human children being led onto little trains under the faraway sun, little bigger than a star but so bright. A cold wind blew. "It is frigid here!" he said shivering.

"For an Earthling yes, I'd imagine so. For us zero degrees Celsius is rather balmy," Captain Draque explained as he and Professor Kraken sat themselves on the passenger car of the same train. There were no windows. "May I ask why there are no windows?" asked the professor.

"Ah yes, it is part of our…foundational myth you would say. Secrets are important and there are grave dangers in looking out into the world. Much better to look inwards." Diego's hair rose on end at the lurching way Captain Draque was speaking.

"We are passing now the fungoid plantations where the agricultural cyborgs are welded to their machines, similar to the pilot. It is a pity you can't see them now, but you can trust my word, and I'll happily show you some illustrations when we get to the Capital; we are proud here on Pluto of our mechanistic efficiency."

"I'm eager to see."

Diego dozed; time-dilation caused the worst sort of jet lag.He awoke as the doors opened, and he looked outside in the frigid air. Craggy mountains, red and white; the odd fungoid masses further out and what appeared to be the agricultural workers, on stilts and augmented bone structures, loading the seashell-shaped masses into the open gondolas of freight cars. The skyscrapers, the same colors as the mountains, blood red and snow white, but without a single window, reaching upwards into the sky.

"That's enough looking around, professor, you'll catch a cold with your warm, human blood," scolded Captain Draque. "Let's go to the library where you can learn all about Pluto."

"Hmm, okay; I always prefer to form my own impressions first and then do book research," mumbled Diego.

"That is ill-advised here," said Captain Draque sympathetically, "I understand you have your scientific method you so treasure, but we too here have our...political realities, and it is safer for you to read the material that we have prepared for you."

"Ah...of course," replied Diego, a chill running down his spine. They entered into a smaller windowless trolley, which was crowded with pale Plutonian bodies, all of them hairless and with beady wide-spaced small black eyes. Professor Kraken took a tablet of prepared fungoid mass and, his brain duly fortified, listened carefully to snippets of conversation between two loud, new money merchants. Professions and spending habits were easy enough to discern anywhere.

"Markets been good lately," said one, big and gaudy in black shimmering clothes

"Oh yes; great influx of human blood," said the other smaller, but with more cunning in his voice.

"Helps the mind, great aphrodisiac!" said the larger one vulgarly.

"Couldn't live without it anymore, better than anything..." said the little one, with a note of resignation.

Professor Kraken clearer his throat and turned to Captain Draque, "I'm particularly interested in the biology of Pluto; the divergence with the Homo sapiens line, etc."

"Why of course," said Captain Draque, "easy enough; you'll learn that we have a tad bit more fungal admixture in our chromosomes and some fascinating differences in the structure of mitochondria. The fungoid growths and mycelial networks too may be of interested. I'll make sure that the royal librarian is well prepared to help you in your scientific inquiries."

"Many thanks, Draque."

"My pleasure." The trolley arrived at the boxlike, windowless library, made of the same bright red and white stone that seemed to be the major building material out here. Make note to brush up on the geological history of this place, thought Professor Kraken to himself.

They entered the library, and walked over to the main librarian's desk where a chubby Plutonian was deep in a book.

Captain Draque cleared his throat. "Excuse me, librarian!"

The librarian jumped up comically. "Oh, well; oh my!" he stammered, "I thought you would all be quite a bit longer getting here. Well then, there are books prepared, I've seen to that, indeed..." He was moving his big body around, clumsily, knocking down books here and there, before finding a big stack for Professor Kraken. "Yes here we go; if you have any questions, any at all, Professor, ask me. The scholar's room in the library has been arranged for your stay. We love your writing here and can't wait to read what you have to write about us!" said the Librarian, now tarrying to pick up the spilled books before returning to his reading.

"May I ask you a favor before we depart?" asked Captain Draque.

"Yes of course, you've been so helpful to me!" said the professor, almost feeling affection towards the sinister Plutonian.

"Would you sign my copy of The Cetacean Myths of Neptune?" asked Captain Draque pulling the volume out of his briefcase.

"Of course," said Diego Kraken, picking up a pen and writing: To Captain Draque; thank you so much for all that you have taught me. With all my best, Professor Diego Kraken.

"Thank you so, so much!" exclaimed Captain Draque, genuinely excited.

"Take care," said Dr. Kraken as Captain Draque again boarded the windowless train.

"Best of luck!"

Professor Kraken sat down with a sigh, and began to go through the books, taking notes. Apparently, Pluto was the oldest plane of the entire solar system. It was held together by mycelia which Plutonians harnessed to convey their rails. The rocks were fungal-mineral hybrids, totally unlike anything on Earth. The entire planet is an organism, realized Diego, perhaps not too different from Earth in her own way... After many hours of study, he had the Librarian show him his sleeping quarters, where he immediately fell into a deep sleep.

In the morning he awoke in a cold sweat, the same dream of Ada's farewell, the same horrible feeling of impotence, the same horrible regret. I only spent 3 years with her he thought fighting back tears, I missed most of Ada's short life because of the time-dilations of my space travels.... Not wanting to be alone the professor decided to chat up the librarian, rather than hit the books.

"Good day, librarian," said Dr. Diego Kraken.

"Ah good day, good day—was breakfast adequate?" asked the excitable librarian.

"Very much so, thank you; I'm curious about some lines of questioning that aren't accounted for in the literature. Things of a particular human interest."

"Yes, go ahead," said the librarian leaning back.

"Well, why do you import so many human children? It is interesting to say the least," asked Diego frowning.

"Of course, yes, yes, my apologies for the lack of appropriate literature; it is such a new institution here we don't yet have much published on it. Human blood is compatible with Plutonians since we share a common ancestor. Young blood is highly valued, it has been scientifically proven to reverse aging, increase our ability to think clearly and improve our vitality and virility. Of course, we breed differently than humans; we are all physiologically male and combine the sexual fluids of eight males to form the base of a new one. We also, like you, have sex for pleasure. Human blood increases our ability to create reproductive fluid, another reason it is so much in demand."

"Could you take me to see a facility for milking the human blood?" asked Dr. Kraken, sweating.

"Well, uh, I shouldn't, you know, I could get in trouble; but...you're a great writer and scholar and, well, as personal hero of mine. Although it's probably foolish of me... yes, I can pull a few strings and we can visit a factory tomorrow. I can arrange it to avoid suspicions," decided the librarian resolutely, "but...you'll owe me a favor."

"I will grant you anything within my capacity," said Diego, curious to what the favor would be.

"Take me with you when you leave. Your tales have inspired me greatly and more than anything else I wish to see more of the solar system, adventure about for a few years. Also, if I am party to betraying Plutonian secrets I shouldn't want to stay once they figure out what's happened," said the librarian, poker faced.

"Well, sure, I've helped dozens of folks immigrate across the solar system before. I promise to take you with me. You should be safe with me. By the way, what's your name?"

"Mephist."

"Okay Mephist; tomorrow morning it is; we visit the factory."

PROFESSOR KRAKEN HAD never been so horrified in his life; there was the phlebotomist explaining the situation concerning the girl strapped to the wall; her hands and feet severed and stuck into the fungoid machine which now overrode her heart recirculating and siphoning her blood.

"So you see," the phlebotomist explained, "we have made her a part of the circulation machine. This circulates her blood, siphoning it off at a sustainable rate. They usually last about three weeks before they must be replaced."

"What ultimately kills them?" asked Professor Kraken trying to conceal his rage.

"We're not exactly sure," said the phlebotomist. "but we believe it is something akin to sorrow, we make sure to drain them fully before this though, of course"

The girl moaned and writhed, struggling against the wall.

"Can she hear us?" asked Professor Kraken, increasingly upset.

"Probably, but she is already as good as dead so not to worry," said the phlebotomist. The girl seemed to hear and whimpered as if trying to make words.

"We have millions upon millions of such blood apparatuses all over Pluto," explained the phlebotomist cheerfully ignoring the girl, "with fresh shipments of young humans daily to restore our stocks. Now even agricultural cyborgs can afford warm human blood!"

The girl cried and mumbled to herself as if dreaming, and Dr. Kraken shook his head, sickened. Mephist the librarian cleared his throat; "May we see the holding tanks, sir?" he asked.

"Ah yes, come see the Earthlings in their cages."

The humans were held in great cages with feeding troughs, some were dispirited, some looked sick and some were angry and sullen.

"We keep them here at approximately fifteen degrees Celsius," explained the phlebotomist, "they huddle together for warmth. Those that approach psychosis we make sure to drain first as they are murder/suicide risks."

"Ah," said Dr. Kraken, seething.

"There is a good latrine system. Full turnover is about three months," continued the phlebotomist, "but with the increasing number of shipments, we have ourselves limited by faculties, not humans to drain." Dr. Kraken was hardly listening; in the cage was a young girl with light brown skin, bright eyes, and curly black hair.

"Ada!" he cried out loud.

"Excuse me?" said Mephist the librarian.

"May I speak to that human?" asked Dr. Kraken agitated, pointing to the girl who looked exactly like his daughter.

"Sure, no reason why not; she's slated to be inserted into the machine three days from now. No harm in asking her some questions," said the phlebotomist opening a little door to the cage.

Dr. Kraken entered and approached the girl, "Hi," he said.

"They're going to kill me in three days," said the girl, distraught, "my parent's were enemies of the Johnson dictatorship. I got sold to the Plutonians in exchange for fungoid mass....my name is Sarah, I am 16 years old. Please, don't let them continue doing this with the solar system totally indifferent. Please."

"Listen Sarah, you remind me of my daughter...she died of cancer years ago... It broke my heart. I can't let them drain you. I won't," said Dr. Kraken quietly to the frightened girl, and leaning over he whispered quietly in the ear, "don't worry Sarah, I promise that I will rescue you from here."

ALL THAT NIGHT DR. Diego Kraken and Mephist plotted how to save the girl; "do you think I could just simply buy her?" asked the professor.

"Hmm, seems doubtful; you would probably have to trade your blood for hers, which is highly unlikely, only blood from Earthlings younger than twenty years old is the least bit desirable." Said Mephist.

"Well, how about this; we go back tomorrow, grab her, and scram; Captain Draque told me that operating the ships is very easy since you have the pilots welded in and apparently without any volition," reasoned Diego.

"It could work; about half a mile from the blood factory is a fungoid mass plant with a docked space craft. If we could get her onboard we could perhaps escape," said Mephist.

"Do you have a ray gun?" asked the professor.

"Yes, and you?"

"Never leave Earth without it! Alright then! We have a plan; tomorrow we rescue Sarah."

THE NEXT DAY they returned to the blood plant, but there was no Sarah in the pen. "Where did the one I spoke with yesterday go?!" demanded Professor Kraken.

"She is being prepared to be attached to the circulation machine, you actually just interrupted me from the preparations," explained the phlebotomist, "should you like to see?"

"Very much so," said Diego his hand on his ray gun.

She was unconscious on the operating table. The bone saw lay next to her, the phlebotomist seemed pleased with himself; "Soon I will apply the tourniquets and then remove the first hand and it insert it here into the wall. I have a little stool that helps me jab the stump into the wall and then untie the tourniquet. We save more blood that way, and the stool helps save my back! Then I do the same thing with the foot on the opposite side. This creates a sort of diagonal bracing. Afterwards, the rest goes fast. With her limbs in, the wall myceliates around the body helping to support it."

"Ah," said Professor Kraken, "Faaascinating," and then he grabbed the phlebotomist's head in his hands and brought it full force onto his knee. To Diego's great surprise the head shattered like a melon filled with black blood. The lowered g-force! He understood in a flash: my muscles and bones are stronger than his because Earth is five hundred times more massive.

He slung the body of Sarah over his shoulder, and leapt

for the door. "Now to the space ship!" Dr. Kraken ran in great bounding strides on the low gravity planet. Mephist struggled to keep up, falling further and further behind. As they ran through the odd dark fungoid landscape an alarm bell sounded from the blood factory. Mephist tripped head over heals and screamed "help!" Dr. Kraken, bounded back, grabbed his arm and slung him over his other shoulder, "I never forget a promise!" roared the professor as he bounded on like a gazelle carrying both Sarah and Mephist.

They approached the spaceship and saw the long-limbed cyborg workers about three hundred meters away. Soon ray guns began to fire at them; Mephis jumped to the ground. He and the professor made zigzag patterns and fired back, slowly advancing. Mephist was a surprisingly good shot, one of the best that Professor Kraken had seen in all of his travels. "How did you learn to shoot so well?" asked Diego breathlessly.

"Video games!" cried Mephist as he shot the last factory gunman. The agricultural cyborgs were without weapons and had disappeared in the mayhem.

They advanced to the ship, Mephist opened the bay and they entered. "Where shall I set the course?" asked Mephist.

"Ganymede, moon of Jupiter. I have some good friends there who will loan you a gravity suit to protect your bones."

Mephist nodded solemnly, entered the information into the screen and they took off.

"Well, that was easy!" exclaimed Dr. Diego Kraken, sighing as they passed Neptune, "I imagined everything would be better defended."

"Well, from reading your accounts, Pluto is one of the most conformist and regimented planets in the solar system. People can hardly think for themselves and so they very rarely misbehave at all. That is why it was so easy to gain access to the factory; I simply lied through my teeth and claimed more clearance than I had, and no one thought that I might lie. The authoritarian structures have atrophied our imaginations. I'm more surprised that we experienced as much trouble as we did," explained Mephist.

"Interesting, I'll make note of that in my book. Oh drats! I left all my notes at the library," remembered Diego.

"Well you're lucky to have a librarian with you right now to help fill in your gaps!" offered Mephist with the odd vampiric smile that all Plutonians seem to have.

"Point well taken; I do hope Sarah wakes soon, it's been quite a few hours," worried Professor Kraken.

"She should, but it might take a few days."

" Ah."

They arrived on Ganymede later that day. The better part of four years had passed in the Einsteinian time-dilation. It took the better part of a week before Sarah opened her eyes. "Where are we?" she asked groggily.

"Ganymede, moon of Jupiter," replied Dr. Kraken; "we're in a hotel. I got a good rate; it's the off season."

"What happened? Am I dead?" she asked.

"We saved you from getting inserted into the circulation machine," said the professor.

"What…what are we doing now?" she wondered, tears in her eyes.

"Well, I have a lot of interplanetary royalties, so money's not an issue right now. I plan on writing about Pluto. Mephist is going to help fill me in with details; we're co-writing it," said Dr. Diego Kraken, Mephist in his g-suit beaming vampirically. "I'll need all the help I can get. I'm about a week off the fungoid mass and my thinking's a bit…disorganized. After the Pluto book I'm going to write about what's happening on Earth; I have some friends in high places throughout the solar system and maybe they could fund some political movements hostile to the Johnson dictatorship. From what I've understood his leadership has been bad for business, except for Plutonian business that is. Things have only gotten worse since we left four years ago. Maybe there could be some sanctions against Pluto after this; they're breaking quite a few laws."

"We were travelling for four years?" asked Sarah, eyes wide.

"No, we travelled for about eight hours, but we went fast enough to experience Einsteinian time dilation, so four years have passed everywhere where people were not travelling at similar speeds."

"That is so...eerie...this has all happened so fast, but taken many years for everyone else," said Sarah quietly "I'm stranded outside of Jupiter without a friend or any skills, exiled from my home."

"Sarah, please, don't worry," said Diego in a soft voice. "Ganymede is a big hub for business and there's a lot of opportunities here and lot of interesting characters; Venusians, Martians, even some Uranians.Real interesting scene, which is part of the reason I decided to come here rather than Mars, which is more desolate, or Earth where Johnson still reigns.I would suggest that you stay away from the space drugs and attend some of the free lectures at the University here, but I'm old fashioned like that."

"This has all happened so quickly," said Sarah, dazed.

"I want you to know that you can stay with us as long as you need, eat on my tab. No worries...it's important to me. Also, here's a key to your own room, number 27. And last thing...if you're up for it I want you to help me with the books," said Dr. Diego Kraken, "tell me about your experiences, have you be a viewpoint character."

Sarah cautiously took the key, and smiled uncertainly. "Thank you Dr. Kraken, I don't know..."

"You could help a lot of people by sharing your experience...but I don't want to pressure you just after you've woken up and before you've been able to shower or have a bite to eat. You can let me know what you decide in the weeks ahead. Don't worry Sarah, you've got all the time you need. Down the hall to the left there's a cafeteria and next to it are the showers. If you have questions about the hotel the receptionists are helpful, and I'm here too if you want to talk. Now, though, I must leave and lie down for an hour or two. It's been a hectic week, and hard to rest without the fungoid mass. Take care Sarah, I need to go to bed."

Sarah smiled and looked like she was going to start crying. Dr. Kraken sighed, and left her to her process, walking down the blue hall to his room. The girl was not Ada, and would never be Ada. Saving one girl didn't stop the horrific blood trade, and writing some books was a shot in the dark, a dangerous one at that. It was easy enough to imagine him failing in his objectives, and becoming a fugitive scuttled from safe house to safe house or meeting his end in some asteroid belt torture-room... He felt so little and limited compared to the evils of the universe, and the political problems on Earth. Dr. Kraken unlocked the door, and sat down on his bed. He looked at himself in the mirror mounted on the wall, meeting his own eyes. He thought; well, at least it's something, at least I'm doing what's in my capacity and doing it in good faith. What more can I do? Unable to answer the question, he turned the lights off and fell into a deep, dreamless sleep.

Under the alias "Zendexor", Robert Gibson co-edits the Vintage Worlds series and is the webmaster of www.solarsystemheritage. com. Born in London in 1954, of mixed Scottish and Belgian extraction, Robert works from home as a private tutor in Lancashire, England. He is married to Mary, who helps him with any maths that he finds too hard, and proofreads his fiction. His published works include the Old Solar System adventures Valeddom and the collection of linked tales set on the Seventh Planet, Uranian Gleams. Another Uranian story appeared in Vintage Worlds Volume 1.

Some works of Old Solar System SF dispense their wonders with a light hand, while others pile them on in glorious profusion. Robert Gibson's The Arc of Iapetus *belongs to the latter category: a dazzling tale of adventure, intrigue, and high strangeness among the moons of Saturn..*

The Arc of Iapetus

by Robert Gibson

1: the bait

WELL, SQUELCH ME, Trader Hurst," piped Ghilidb through its translator tube, in what it fondly imagined to be Earth slang, "I deemed you more ambitious than that."

It then stared with its three eyes at the human who faced it across the small wooden table in a dim corner of the largest tavern in Traw City. The stare was amicable, but challenging. Such shades of meaning can be easily expressed on a Rhean face, and the man knew enough to read them - and the Rhean knew that he knew—so both beings realized that a calculated risk had been taken.

Conversation halted while a conical Tethyan twirled past the table to deposit two tall glasses which brimmed with fiery *wepyj*—the favourite poison of Rhea's northern hemisphere.

"Ambitious," echoed Hurst, unoffended. The moment of tension seemed over. He had no interest in a quarrel with Ghilidb, who in the intervals between bouts of haggling could be as much friend as customer. And he had found it safe to tease Rheans; safe to pretend to misunderstand them, when it suited him. He could tell that Ghilidb was trying to propose some sort of risky deal, but he chose instead to view the being's words as a dig at his restrained life-style. "I suppose," the Earthman sighed, "there are more romantic ways I could spend the evening, than sitting in this dive, face to face with a vertical three-armed dumb-bell... On the other hand, this scene is less heavy with emotion, than some of the alternatives."

"Before the evening is out," trilled Ghilidb, "you may change your mind on that point, Trader - or should I say," and it lowered its voice, "ex-TIA-agent Hurst?"

This unexpected turn to the conversation caused the Earthman to slump in his chair, while his face expressed a sudden wave of past regrets. His moment of depression and semi-collapse usefully concealed the tensing of his right arm and the approach of hand to holster. Habit, merely—irrational, this habit of caution—for if his past became known, then so what? There could be no danger for him here. Not in this system of moons policed by the formidably benevolent, godlike Saturnians. Nobody—not even the Terrestrial Intelligence Agency—ever dared mess with the Saturnians.

The Earth Government probably suspected—though they would never admit openly—that the beings of the Ringed Planet could dominate the System easily if they chose. Fortunately for the other worlds, Saturnians were not imperialistically-minded. They merely insisted on good behaviour in their own back yard. And countless small traders and outlanders such as Seth Hurst throve under the umbrella of that insistent protection. When he thought of it this way, he even felt a twinge of guilt at the one indiscretion which had caused him to be booted out of the TIA...

"All right," said Hurst. "Let's stop playing games. Get back to what you were hinting. You've got a new client for me, is that right, Ghilidb?"

The furry dumb-bell rotated its three eyes in a gesture that meant "yes".

"And he/she/it is here, in this building, and you want to introduce us?" (Another gesture of assent.) "Well - and may I ask, what are you, old friend, getting out of this?"

A wheeze through the translator tube, that might have been a deprecating laugh, was followed by a glib flow: "In accordance with common practice, I welcome an opportunity to fulfil an obligation to a third party while simultaneously doing a favour to a friend. It is, how do you say, like disintegrating two Jovians with one neutronium bomb. Everybody benefits."

"I see." Hurst leaned back in thought. Useless to pump Ghilidb further; the Rhean would not be baulked of its little surprise. So meanwhile he, Seth Hurst, peaceful Trader, must decide, on scant evidence, whether to accept what might turn into an adventure.

New clients often meant new types of commission, new contacts, new routes, new destinations... Hurst knew his way around the Saturnian moons as well as anyone, but that wasn't much compared with what there was to know. Risk today, profit tomorrow - but why rock his boat, his battered but serviceable space-boat, when business was chugging along nicely as things stood? On the other hand, his curiosity was now aroused.

Ghilidb obviously believed it had something eye-twitchingly important up its non-existent sleeve. Who could it be, this mysterious new client? Anyone seated in the common room right now, perhaps? Hurst's eyes roved, scanning the tables. What he saw was merely the typically stupendous ethnic complexity of a low-gravity satellite-system. You got used to the variations in shape eventually, though it sure took a while, what with the furry dumb-bell Rheans, the conical Tethyans, the Dionian hexapods, the Enceladan ice-clankers... and the occasional Titanic blow-pots whistling like kettles on the boil. No one in this menagerie looked especially rich, or on the look-out for recruits, or governmental...

But then, a deputation from some other worldlet could have lodged elsewhere in Traw City, or in Cleth City in the Southern hemisphere, or any one of a dozen other places. No, wait, Ghilidb had agreed that the being was somewhere in this building. But since how long? Hurst thought back to his own arrival on Rhea, six hours ago. Had he witnessed any important convoy? His space-boat had nosed in through the usual cloud of other midget ships and the occasional liner. And there had been one of the giant grey spheres of the Saturnians, floating on its mysterious way within a few miles of Traw, but that could be left out of account - the "gods" do not interfere with the little races... All these thoughts did not take long to run through his head.

Hurst gave up on speculation. "All right, I'll take your bait, Ghilidb," he decided. "But look here—just because I once confided in you some of my life-story, I don't want you to mention it again, not even to me, and certainly not to another. Understood?"

"Fear not," piped Ghilidb. "The being whom I have in mind, will never deign to ask you for your history."

Hurst took a swig, draining his glass, and said: "Then so long as that's understood... I'm ready."

Ghilidb got up immediately and, with a complex gliding waddle, meandered away among the tables, while Hurst was hard put to it to keep up. He was led into a corridor and round a corner, through a door into a soundproofed area. He had said he was ready, but when the Rhean approached a private suite, and turned a handle without knocking, a wail of primitive protest rose within the Earthman's mind. Things were happening too fast—

Ghilidb stood aside, rigidly careful not to look into the room with any of his eyes. Hurst, by contrast, was not able to avert his gaze. Permission was denied him. He advanced, under compulsion, while the door closed behind him and he was abandoned in the presence of hugeness. He halted after one further step, and stood, arms by his sides, facing the centre of the room which was filled with the bulk of a Saturnian.

2: the hook

HURST'S LIMBS AND his mind would have given way, granting him the mercy of collapse into oblivion, but for the muscle-lock which kept him rigidly upright and which must have been induced by some invisible stream of command from his "client".

Aware that he was probably the first human being to see a Saturnian in the flesh, the Earthman had no relish for the honour—he would gladly have exchanged places with any of the countless scientists who had lamented their lack of knowledge about the rulers of the sixth planet.

In outline, the creature was just about acceptable to one's belief. Saturn, unlike Jupiter, is not a high-gravity world; though it is immensely huge, its frozen-volatile crust is so comparatively light that its surface pull is hardly more than that of Earth; therefore it is reasonable for the dominant species to tower on legs that look spindly in comparison with the massive pendulant torso. The effect is vaguely comparable to a colossal, leathery, six-limbed mis-drawn spider, whose "elbows" reach to a height of three yards.

That was Hurst's first impression. He might have corrected it if he had been given time for a second.

The wiry arms, which he had not at first noticed, moved—swung out and swung in—did something to an area of membrane, which became a sphincter, which opened and squirted a gob of semi-visible force like chaotic diamond jelly straight through the air to splat onto Hurst's face and into his soul.

Power surged into him, power he did not want, a terrible gift of understanding which he could not immediately digest. But he also knew that it had to be this way. A "conversation" between human and Saturnian was necessarily one-sided. His own contribution, if any, was bound to be unconscious – it would consist of what the Being wrung out of him in those moments of contact.

Then it was over. He tottered back against the wall, gasping. He sensed another blast of force, this time not directed at him. The door re-opened and he was clasped and dragged out of the room.

Now that he was no longer forcibly kept conscious, his exhausted mind dived into blackness. But not for long. He was soon slapped awake to the accompaniment of a high-pitched scolding. "Come on, Earthman, don't sink into it! It's all right if one does not sink!"

"Ghurrrrr," said Hurst, rolling his eyes, and became aware that Ghilidb, who was holding him, was alternating between shaking him and shaking itself.

"Earthman, it couldn't have been that bad. You're not even dead!"

"And you," croaked Hurst as his pulse-rate slowed towards normal, "you're not even trying to be funny."

"Of course not. This is too important—"

"Ghi, listen, you know what, I don't want to hear that word from you, and you know what else, Ghi, I'd rather you didn't try to introduce me to anyone in future... in fact," he rambled, "this is the last time I'll trust you, full stop..."

"Ah, be fair, Earthman. If I do a thing like this, it is because I have to."

Oddly enough, within a minute or so, Hurst began to see the other's point of view as clear as daylight, and with even swifter daybreak of awareness he grasped that he himself had no grounds for complaint, neither against the Rhean nor—and this was the dazzler—*nor against the Saturnian.*

For whatever a Saturnian might do to a human, was done only when the human deserved it. That was the sort of godlike bastards they were...

"Got it now?" asked Ghilidb, watching the Earthman's stumped expression.

"This is payback time, I suppose," nodded Hurst, resigned to his fate. Like a grub hatching in his head, the command, the mission plan would grow, till the details became conscious, perhaps all at once but more likely one stage at a time, and he would do the Saturnian's bidding.

"Payback?" chirped Ghilidb.

The Earthman, propped on one elbow, knew he had to get up and go, and yet he felt an urge to have one last say. There are times when a man feels he must leave a message to the world in general. In which case, the need is for a worthy carrier of the message. He looked at the Rhean narrowly. "I told you once, didn't I, about why I got myself chucked out of the TIA? Yeah, full of indignation, that I was. The one man who had landed on Saturn and returned to tell the tale – all right, it was against the rules, but I got away with it, I got back safely, yet instead of being praised for the exploit, and rewarded, I was cashiered. Probably would have been locked up, had not the Saturnians themselves intervened. Heaven knows how they knew where I'd been. They don't use radar, my detectors made sure of that, and I'd landed in a thoroughly deserted area. South Temperate Zone, longitude 130, no sign of activity for ten thousand miles in any direction – yet they must have known I'd been there. And then they sent a message to the TIA, telling them not to punish me, that they would keep an eye on me themselves... and so they saved me from klink... and now it's payback time. I must go..."

The Rhean helped him to his feet. "Where, Earthman?"

Hurst bent forward in a fit of coughing. He managed to say, "The Arc..." and then some inner compulsion closed his mouth before he could add, *of Iapetus.*

A sense of free will returned to him almost immediately afterwards. He could open his mouth again, could try again to say the name of that world.

But on second thoughts, he decided it was best to keep quiet. He would keep his own counsel, keep his options open...

and perhaps he might, after all, manage to play a lone hand.

3: the line

HURST EMERGED FROM the shadow of the inn's porch, into the open sunshine of Traw City.

Rhea feasts the eye with colour, despite receiving only one-hundredth the sunlight available to Earth. The glow, dubbed the "neon nacre", which pervades the biota of the Saturn system, gets right into the paint which is used to coat the architectural exteriors on those worlds, so that although rooms may be dim, the street culture shines.

The resulting splendour of Traw City's curved avenues was, for Hurst, a welcome contrast to the gloom of the inn. And though he was accustomed to the public beauty he saw, the Earthman appreciated it anew; he lingered with slow steps as he threaded the streets towards the space-boat hangar, for it seemed possible that he might never again see the famous glowing blue domes of Rhea.

Not lived in, lived on - the Rhean domes were packed with power plants, to emit light and heat through their surfaces, around which the citizens lived and moved on their exposed, outdoor housing-platforms encircling the blue hemispheres.

So when you stroll through Traw City, you see just about everybody in plain view; and when you come across the bizarre sight of Rheans doing something oddly familiar like beating their carpets—then, the mix of alien shapes with humdrum action can sear you with nostalgia for Earth.

Hurst smiled sadly; he knew himself well enough. If some twist of Fate were to return him to Earth, he would inevitably feel bittersweet longing for the other worlds. Spacers were like that.

But why these reflections, right now?

He recalled a line from literature: "You see, Watson, but you do not observe."

He, by contrast with Dr Watson, was observing as well as seeing; more acutely than was his wont. And perhaps this was not surprising, in view of what had happened to him. Every step he took, he was now aware of the slight "electrostatic" stickiness which forced him to make that much extra effort to lift his boot from the pavement—an extra effort which almost compensated for the tiny gravity of Rhea.

His flitting thoughts had perhaps alighted upon a clue, a hint concerning his present mission.

He clutched at it—gotcha! But no—the idea had gone! He'd been overconfident just then! But the idea was not gone for good, surely? Be patient, Seth Hurst.

Naturally, he wanted to work it all out himself, before the sealed orders in his brain were opened according to the Saturnian's timetable. His human vanity impelled him to try. But even if he failed the first time, he might get another chance. For it would come in bite-size stages, or so he hoped. Not all in one go, please, Fate! He wasn't keen on another wholesale mental shakeup, not even if it solved the whole mystery of the mission in one fell swoop; the price, he reckoned, would be too high.

Start again, thought Hurst. Think back to that observation about the boot, the stickiness of the stride.

It was easiest to allow the reminder he needed to rise at him out of the very ground he was treading.

Like all Saturn's moons—except Titan which was large enough for more normal options—Rhea depended for its life upon retaining an atmosphere by means other than the gravity of mass. Right from its inception the bio-field must have depended upon complexity as an actual force: the "pull" of a life-system so varied that it brought hitherto unknown laws into play; laws which could never be discovered outside its unique zone... The complexity of the most colourful coral reef on Earth was as nothing compared to the variety found on Rhea, where almost every organism was its own subspe-

cies. Only the highest forms, the intelligent forms, were stabi-
lized to any marked extent; and even then, races varied out-
rageously—some had two sexes, some three, some a larger
number... and some (like Ghilidb's) were sexless and instead
had 'grall', which meant that individuals could only digest
their food with the help of someone of the opposite 'grall'...
The capabilities of individuals varied just as drastically, some
being as keen-sighted as eagles, others as keen-nosed as dogs,
and others telepathic. As for the lower forms, the "ordinary"
animals, they presented such apparent chaos as to drive a
Terran biologist insane. Yet it was this "chaos" that generat-
ed the force that kept Rhea alive. The complexity-force, the
gravitation of variety, somehow fenced the air-molecules into
the bio-field, and, closer to ground, pulled at Hurst's boot-
soles as if he were shod with magnets on a metal path.

This made all the difference to the way he moved; it allowed him a grounded stride instead of the extravagant
soaring hops he would otherwise have made; it gave him, in
short, a proper world to live on. Admittedly the visual effect,
especially when one looked at a crowd, was eerily reminis-
cent of the motion of seaweed wafting in a current, rather
than of "proper" gravity, for solid bodies were "weighted"
only within an inch or two of the satellite's surface... Hurst's
brow furrowed as he sought furiously to guess where all these
thoughts were leading.

If only he could guess it in good time, before the Saturnian agenda opened its Page One in his mind...

Failure! Here he was approaching his space-boat hangar,
and he had not yet deduced the substance of his mission.

Ah, but perhaps he had managed to target the area where
the mystery lay. It ought to be something to do with evolution, with the history of life on Iapetus.

Something the Saturnians were scared of.

The Saturnians scared??

And at that moment the page began to open...

Hurst scrambled up the ladder into his tiny space-boat, ironically named *Jumbo*, and sat himself at the controls, sweating. The first briefing or instruction sheet in his mind now told him what he was commissioned to look for at Iapetus – and it was so fantastic that he almost managed to class it as delirium.

He could not evade the truth: insistently, like a sheaf of photographic evidence presented in court, the Saturnian knowledge displayed itself, incontrovertibly, before his mind's eye.

Hurst could not, would not believe it at first. Part of him protested so strongly that there came an adjustment, whereupon the thought receded. Perish all such thoughts! His mission must not be aborted by panic. If he had been given too much information, some of it had better be taken back, for he simply wasn't ready, wouldn't be ready until he reached his destination... Oh brother, he was in for it. He pulled the lever that sent the command to open the hangar roof and then even before the "clear" signal came on he pressed the take-off switch. *Jumbo* soared into the Rhean sky.

Within a quarter of a minute his ship was surrounded by the black of space.

4: the reel

SETH HURST TAPPED the keys of his navigation system, which in theory gave him all he needed to set course for Iapetus.

At the same time, he kept a naked-eye watch through the windows. This was for his own peace of mind, as well as the beauty of the scene. The pilots who live longest in the Saturn system are those who actually look where they are going.

The bulking glory of Saturn and its rings, the tiny brilliance of the Sun, the black of Space – these alone ought to have comprised the view. Not the satellites: they ought to be just dots, most of the time, hardly noticeable, except for Titan. Yet such was not the case.

Every one of the worldlets was accompanied by a coloured zone, a pale, glowing stain in the fabric of its surrounding space. Mimas, Enceladus, Tethys, Dione, Rhea, Hyperion, Iapetus and Phoebe, as well as the much larger moon Titan, each sailed through space seemingly surrounded by a lenticular smudge twelve to twenty thousand miles in diameter. The tilts of these haloes varied seemingly at random. Their hues differed: red (Mimas), pale green (Enceladus), purple (Tethys), white (Dione), yellow (Rhea), orange (Titan), light blue (Hyperion), violet (Iapetus) and dark green (Phoebe).

None of this parade of glowing zones could possibly be due to ordinary electromagnetic radiation. Detectors outside the Saturn system could not pick any of it up. These rays, uniquely, were rays that went so far and then stopped.

Some natives might know the meaning of it all, but if so they were not telling. Let the scientists back on Earth tear their hair over it, shrugged Hurst; he had his destination to worry about. Anyhow, the awesome spectacle of the "haloes" was comforting, in a way—it encouraged the hope that "seat of the pants" navigation within this mini-system would be possible if the need arose.

If one had to make a quick getaway in an alien ship, for instance...

What was he thinking of now?

Grimly, he concentrated on what he had just had learned for sure.

The Saturnians were genuinely, no kidding, afraid of the Iapetans.

Hurst groaned at the thought. The Saturnians—afraid! And he was being sent where they feared to go!

The trouble was, he could not refuse. The Saturnian intelligence was overwhelmingly able to convince. It was pointless to complain of "compulsion". He himself had no choice but to *want* to undertake this mission—whether he wished to want it or not.

Though he had no free will; though he were as a fish being reeled in to his doom – yet he could not disagree!

And all because of the fact he had learned. The news about Iapetus.

The Saturnian whom he had met had studied the place from orbit with remote-sensors so powerful as to enable it to carry out a species-count of the Iapetan biosphere.

The result was bad news, apparently. Left to himself, the Earthman would have struggled to understand why. His reaction would have been, "So what?" So what if the species on Iapetus were numbered in their thousands rather than in the tens of millions which were the norm for the Saturn system?

He did try to form that thought, but a blast of awareness put him right. A kaleidoscope of information-fragments, from previous inconclusive or contradictory studies, coupled with an amazing, deep-rooted fear of change (yes, the Saturnians were really worried!)—impressed upon him that the dominant race on Iapetus had something no one else had.

Call it Gravity Three.

Iapetus is small, too small to keep its atmosphere by means of Newtonian "Gravity One". Nor has it the species complexity to live by biotic Gravity Two, in the manner of Rhea and the other worldlets.

Yet the Iapetans walk their world and breathe air… and (Hurst felt a stab of accusation from the alien force within his mind) the Iapetan troublemakers are humanoid.

Sort out the mystery, you Man, said the voice in his head. If they know more than we do, they must be Time-cheaters of some sort. Need I say more? A threat to us all.

Hurst slumped at the console for some minutes. Then, wearily, he sat up, stretched and blinked. Ignoring the various navigational indicators and screens, his gaze roved through the control cabin window and out into the halo-splotched firmament.

The violet smudge surrounding Iapetus, the eighth moon,

had already grown noticeably larger in his field of view.

He stared while that world revealed itself as a disk, its equator banded by its incredible range of mountains, twelve miles high—the Arc of Iapetus.

5: the hand

As THE EIGHTH moon of Saturn swelled in the viewport, Hurst divided his attention between that vista and the magnified images he could get on his scanner. He detected a few dark urban patches on the approaching grey surface. The Iapetans, he knew, had towns and small cities. So far as was known, they had no space-port; they had not yet shown any interest in space travel. Nor did they show any warm welcome to visitors from their neighbouring worldlets. Only a few such visits had been recorded: fruitless embassies, a handful of unprofitable trade missions. And no authorisation had yet been granted for any scientific expedition. Therefore, not much was known about the place. In fact, the closer he got, the more Hurst felt he had to revise that knowledge-estimate downwards: rather than "not much", it was really a case of knowing absolutely *nothing*.

Come now, he told himself, it can't be that bad. Just the inevitable sense of fresh wonder and mystery you get when flying towards any world. I get it when approaching Earth, in fact. The sense that you're seeing it for the first time…

This reminder, of the many privileged moments in his space-roving career, brought a brief smile to Hurst's face, only to give way, next moment, to a grimace.

He had just tried to tap the key to bring *Jumbo* into a high parking orbit, about five hundred miles from the satellite's surface. No go. His fingers would not co-operate. His body wasn't obeying his mind.

Testily he grumbled at the Saturnian thing inside his head, the personality-fragment or whatever it was, which he now dubbed Perce.

I did think, Perce, that you might have left me a choice of landing-place, at least.

The space-boat was headed straight down towards the equatorial mountains. Hurst sighed. Had "Perce" really spotted something significant there? There on the heights where the air was too thin to breathe?

Perce, you're just an artificial compulsion, with no independent ego, no motive for self-preservation; I bet it's all one to you, what happens to me, so long as you get what you're looking for. You know that if I fail your master will simply try again with another you inside another mug like me, and what do you care, if I leave my bones on Iapetus along with the expendable psychological mechanism that is you—?

No answer from "Perce".

The austere white-and-grey world now more than filled the viewport. The equatorial heights paraded past the field of view, their comparative brightness gleaming like bared teeth.

Hurst reviewed what he had learned.

Iapetus was an exception to the complex biota of the Saturn system. Its species were numbered in mere thousands, not tens of millions. That was why it lacked their special biotic gravitation; its surface pull ought to be low. So the Iapetans must have discovered a third kind of gravity—not Newtonian, not biotic, but something else, which enabled them to retain their atmosphere. Whatever it is, this Gravity Three, should surely be beyond the resources of a small world to master. Yet they had mastered it, without outside help. They could only have done this, by a control of Time itself. *Understand, Earthman? Time-cheaters!*

No, said Seth Hurst, uneasily.

I think you do, said the "Perce" in him. I think you get it very well, actually. A small world can match a large one in research and development if it magnifies its available time with the opportunity for endless replays. Manipulations of reality. You therefore know that my ruthlessness is justified. This is the greatest ever threat to the existence of all the peoples of all the worlds. Go we must, go to the Arc and get proof, then get back to the Great World with our report; that will persuade the Great Ones to destroy the devil moon.

But why the Arc? wailed the appalled mind of Seth Hurst. Why these mountains? What do you see there?

The burst of brain-clarity was over and he got no further answers.

He shivered and wiped his brow of cold sweat. Altimeter readings showed he was now a mere sixteen miles from the satellite's median surface—about four miles up from the high peaks. Out the window he glimpsed a stunning cosmic bauble setting behind a mountain: Saturn, the Great World, looking about the same apparent size as Earth seen from Luna. Emotionally, it suddenly seemed to him that the Great World was no longer unrivalled; that Iapetus, so immensely larger in his present field of view, was indeed preparing some frightful stroke of usurping power, and that even the Saturnians did well to be afraid.

Jumbo continued its unstoppable descent towards the immense, world-girdling, arc-like range that distinguished the eighth moon.

Hurst began to spot some small buildings, that looked little more than huts, sparsely dotted amid the icy mountains. There was no "neon nacre" on Iapetus; magnification by means of the scanner showed the structures were pebble-dash in appearance, splotchy grey-white like the world itself, though darker than the ice on which they stood. Nothing to get impressed about, surely?

More silence from "Perce". He/it had seen something, evidently, and had decided they must head for it, and that was that. Hurst was a mere passenger. He ground his teeth.

And then—he saw it too. Through the scanner, he saw a long thin upward flow of movement climbing one of the valleys towards the summit ridge.

Jumbo made one final course adjustment and then smoothly touched down, in a pass between two rounded icy summits, directly in the path of the ascending army. For that's what it was—the driblet of information was kindly allowed him—an army plodding up towards the pass, for reasons he could not guess at.

Glumly he donned his pressure-suit and checked its oxygen supply and radio; then he went to the airlock.

Awe and expectancy vied with a sense of being played for a sucker, as Seth Hurst set foot upon the icy surface of Iapetus. *One thing at a time, one driblet at a time,* he thought to himself cynically, *that's how I get drawn in, isn't it. Don't tell me too much at once, else my mind would blow; just feed it to me piece by piece, so that I retain my usefulness.*

But wasn't it a good idea anyway? To enable a limited human mind to absorb an alien situation, should not the data be fed in step by step?

And as for the forced landing, could he really complain? What seemed like compulsion might merely be for his own good, and anyhow, one's own hunches were a kind of compusion. All pressures were simply input, like that of the sensors on board ship.

Thus he salved his pride, as he walked towards a silent watcher, a humanoid figure, one of a half-dozen visible on the sides of the pass.

The figure looked not much different from a tall, strangely attired Earthman. He wore a black-green leathery suit, a dark shapeless hat, and what looked almost like boxing gloves. The air pressure up at this height was far too low for Seth Hurst to breathe, yet the Iapetan wore no helmet, his face open to the sky.

As he approached, Seth scrutinised the man's neck but saw no translator tube. But it hardly seemed worth the trouble to worry about communication—was not everything being taken care of?

The problem was indeed resolved when Seth halted two yards from the Iapetan who then spoke in Tsvairp, the harsh though splendid tongue of the Titanic blowpots, which – minus the whistles—had acquired currency as the lingua franca of the Saturnian moons.

High-pitched due to the thinness of the air, yet projected with sufficient force to be clear, the meaning of the greeting was unmistakable. Seth liked the first word—pity about the rest of the sentence...

"Welcome! Another Earthman-volunteer from the Great World, sent here to the summits of Khurrn, to participate in our experiments."

Seth wanted to say: no, I am not a volunteer—and my allegiance is not to the Great World—since I am an Earthman I am a free man—

Of course, he could not say these things. He could not talk at all. But he could still think, could infer from the Iapetan's words that the Saturnian who had sent him here had tried before, at least once, with other "volunteers".

And I wonder what became of them...

But let me remind myself that I am not just any old guinea-pig – I am Seth Hurst, late of the TIA, the first and so far the only human being to land on the Great World and return alive –

Smiling, as if he had guessed the defiance in the Earthman's heart, the Iapetan stretched out an arm and with a slight bow stepped aside to invite Seth forward.

Spellbound in more senses than one – *if I ever get out of this, the fantastic knowledge I'll have gained!* – Seth Hurst walked obediently past the Iapetan, towards where the pass began to descend. He continued for some yards down the steepening slope, and stopped at a point from which he could clearly see the ascending army, which had now advanced to about a furlong below where he was placed.

To his inexpert eye (he naturally knew no details of Iapetan culture or history) those men, toiling upward in lines of infantry, looked more or less similar to the half-dozen watchers around him—except that they were wearing swords!

Then he turned his head and saw others, elsewhere in his field of view, differently attired. Same humanoid shape, but wearing bulbous furs. Hidden from the ascending army, they waited on either side of the defile.

A sense of doom invaded Seth's mind. He could not understand, could not accept the direness of the situation. Iapetus was an advanced world, yet here was a medieval tragedy in the making. The contollers on the summit of the pass were doing nothing to prevent the ambush. Was it all an illusion, a fragment of the past brought to life by a kind of holovision? Was this to be a kind of lecture-demonstration?

"Ready, Earthman?" piped the sardonic voice of the Iapetan Controller, and Seth felt his mind hurled out of his body. The scene whizzed past his eyes and his mind buzzed and jolted into a different setting—uprooted, transplanted— Next thing he knew, he was no longer space-suited; he was a Iapetan soldier, plodding up the slope, with his doomed comrades around him.

6: the brain

ACCEPTANCE WAS PART of the scene; otherwise he might have gone mad.

Lift a boot, push it down, lift a boot, push it down, like the plodding figures around him, planting one step after the next, muscles straining against the rough ice-slope, as Gravity Three pulls his pack-straps against his shoulders.

Yes, he accepted all that, he had to, but -

Worst was the depression of spirit that came from a conviction that he, and all around him, were headed for annihilation.

Could he warn them? Start a mutiny?

Sidelong, he caught glimpses of the bowed expressions

of the other men in his unit. Close up, they seemed maybe eighty per cent human in appearance. Their faces lacked animation, as no doubt did his own, the stress of the climb resulting in grim, set features.

Seth's mind wandered, shying away from this crazy reality. He preferred to muse...

What would far-away Terran scientists say of his plight, if they knew? Trapped as he was, his mind thrown into the body of a Iapetan soldier—no, it must be a dream; it could not be! He imagined (in a kind of comfort-reflex) that he was back on Earth, talking about all this before a lecture-audience at a scientific meeting... "It's obvious," he rambled, "that the Iapetan haughtiness of feature is a mere tropism; one should not deduce cruelty or ruthlessness from their thin lips or hatchet jawline..."

Only, come to think of it, the Saturnian, yes the *Saturnian*, had been afraid.

Go on, guess it, he told himself: the Iapetans, who have exterminated their rivals to become one of the few remaining species on their world, derive and extend their power from re-takes, from historical re-plays, and you, Seth boy, are in the midst of one right now.

Re-takes—or wipe-outs?

A faint song in the air, composed not of sound but of huge currents of emotion, made him picture second-chancers waving flags, proclamations: "Let it happen differently this time!" Perhaps this army was not doomed after all. Or perhaps it was, and the *other* side was tired of being doomed, and it was their emotion he could sense. Either way, he could not grasp the specific content of the songs. But he got their essential message. It was accessible to him because the more advanced a system the easier and more effortless its compatibility with other systems. So, it adjusts from one mental field to another as it slides into universality. No mistaking the theme: doomed infantry headed under incompetent leadership towards disaster.

It self-arranged for Hurst's own background, his native land on Earth:

> *And why stands Scotland idly now,*
> *Dark Flodden! on thy airy brow,*
> *Since England gains the pass the while,*
> *And struggles through the deep defile?*
> *What checks the fiery soul of James?*
> *Why sits that champion of the dames*
> *Inactive on his steed,*
> *And sees, between him and his land,*
> *Between him and Tweed's southern strand,*
> *His host Lord Surrey lead?*
> *What 'vails the vain knight-errant's brand?*
> *—O, Douglas, for thy leading wand!*
> *Fierce Randolph, for thy speed!*
> *O for one hour of Wallace wight,*
> *Or well-skill'd Bruce, to rule the fight,*
> *And cry— "Saint Andrew and our right!"*
> *Another sight had seen that morn,*
> *From Fate's dark book a leaf been torn,*
> *And Flodden had been Bannockbourne!—*
> *The precious hour has pass'd in vain,*
> *And England's host has gain'd the plain;*
> *Wheeling their march, and circling still,*
> *Around the base of Flodden hill...*

But not this time. Surely that must be the idea: that this time his host wasn't going to "gain the plain". This time, struggling through the deep defile, the English, or rather his bunch of Iapetans, were going to get well and truly clobbered; only, on the other hand, he wasn't sure how strong the analogy was, the "deep defile" might be just a coincidence, and in fact the topography was most likely irrelevant, in which case he had better hope that the tables were about to be turned some other way, so that the doom remained for the other side -

Breathless, confused thoughts. One clear fact: he had seen the ambush plainly prepared. If only he could talk to someone. He tried but he could not open his jaw. He could move some muscles but not others; he'd probably be allowed to draw his sword, when the moment came to do so, but it was no use trying to break the spell in advance and utter a warning to the other actors in this drama, who must be as helpless as himself; no use even to think of expecting them to step outside the flow of their own headlong verses, to discuss the practicalities of escape; *for there is no escape from this resurrected corpse of dead time. Resurrected, to be vivisected, its tendons of cause and effect about to be drawn out and poked around by the Iapetan authorities...*

This can't be the first such meddling, thought Seth; the Iapetans must have carried out reality-dissections many times before, to learn to perform plastic surgery upon their world's history, and soon, perhaps, they'd be making it *more* special, re-writing the history of the whole Saturn system, and then of the Solar System...

At that moment, public anxieties faded before a more personal dread.

The most ominous of sounds—a sudden rumble above and ahead of him, intermingled with bleats of terror carried through the thin air—prompted Seth to halt and draw his sword, his useless sword. The ambushers must now be rolling their boulders down! He gazed up-slope. So did his companions, but whereas they were troubled and alarmed, he was hopelessly sure.

Yet as it turned out, he was no more prepared than they.

Disaster was interrupted as the wedge of deep violet sky at the top of the defile was almost blotted out by a vast grey shape. In a split second it flashed a paralysing light, which rayed the incipient ambush into immobility. The boulders rolling down upon the ascending army were halted in mid-plunge.

The soldiers, including Seth, could not move an eyelid.

Then came a gradual relaxation, and he could blink, and breathe, once more. Up ahead, the boulders rolled again but gently, as they were let down feather-light.

Next the giant ship itself descended to touch the top of the ridge.

So, after all, thought Seth, there are some Saturnians who are not afraid of the Iapetans.

The thought was hardly framed when, with a stomach-turning sensation, he was clutched by some force which lifted him off the ground and drew him with outrageous speed to stand before an extruded gangplank beside the Saturnian ship.

Things had happened so fast, his guts were a-churn with contradictory emotions. Not exactly keen on another one-sided bout of communication with a godlike denizen of the Ringed Planet, he yet did not flinch from the prospect as he would have done a few hours before. His recent experiences still echoed so strongly inside his skull, that rather than fret about any alien, no matter how powerful, he was more apt to ponder the defeat and death of Scots King James the Fourth and the destruction of his army, amid the wavering glimmers of all the lost might-have-beens of Earth history. So he stood his ground, while a bulky spider-shape moved into view at the top of the gangplank, and began to descend towards him, followed by another.

The first Saturnian came to a halt a couple of yards away and towered over Seth. Though not sure how, Seth thought to recognize the one who was responsible for his mission. Yes, this was the being who had afflicted him with Perce – who had "spoken" to him in the inn on Rhea.

Yet the being, now, was... subdued.

Behind it loomed an ever taller bulk, perhaps a yard taller, and heavier. A fully adult Saturnian, guessed Seth—which would make the other one a mere adolescent. Guesswork, admittedly; but an inner voice strongly hinted that the guess was true, and now he felt new fear.

The larger Saturnian moved forward, to stand beside the lesser one, and then began, from a point on its midriff, to twitch. Oh, no, thought Seth thought: oh no, that diaphragm is going to open, just as the other one did, to spit probably a yet worse gob of truth...

But what actually happened then filled the Terran with amazed relief: amazement instantly accepted, for who could set limits to the powers of a *boss* Saturnian?—who could question the ability of the great being to clang out words in perfect, idiomatic English—!

"Earthman—well met—none too soon. This rogue," and it delivered a sideways tap at the side of its smaller fellow—"put a soul-tracer on you. Do you know what that means?"

"No—I'm not sure—yes I suppose so," gabbled Seth.

"Never mind. Fortunately, *I* also had one on *him.*"

A pause. Seth saw a chance to draw a rasping breath. "Sir..."

"I am Xagelthad. You may address me as Commissioner."

"Commissioner, I thank you for saving my life. And the lives of all these people..." He did not dare look round but he guessed the frozen army was still frozen, and whether or not the fighting would resume after the Saturnians had gone, at least the boulders had been deposited where they would no longer roll...

"You can and shall repay me, Earthman," said Xagelthad.

Seth drooped at the words; but he caught himself and straightened, though nigh exhausted with foreboding. Another and even more formidable mission at the behest of this more powerful Saturnian—was that what lay in store? What must be, must be.

"The tracer," the Commissioner went on, "would have

stopped its signal if reality-change had occurred. It did not, because we arrived here in good time, but why such an urge to meddle in the Iapetan scene at all? Tgimvaru here needs a lesson, and this is the occasion for it."

Seth licked dry lips, sensing he was suppposed to say something. "And I...?"

"You, Earthman, are going to help me teach this impulsive rogue *why* it is stupid to fear the Iapetans and their experiments. Humble him, Earthman!"

"What—how—"

"Demonstrate to him that even you have more sense than he does. Speak!"

This was no dream; he, Seth Hurst of Earth, really was being required by one Saturnian to deliver a put-down to another.

The ploy at once became crystal clear, so that he had no difficulty in seeing how he was being used. But what to say? And what was the penalty for failure? Unthinkable—literally—and so Seth Hurst's puny Terrestrial brain must somehow produce the goods; must without delay come up with an answer to satisfy Xagelthad.

Why is it stupid to fear reality-change?

He could give the obvious reply – could say, "Reality change, when it occurs, is retrospective so that it has always been so, so in a sense it had never 'occurred'; a wipe-out leaves no trace, and that means, no trace of itself. It swallows itself, and so there is nothing left to fear."

But might this clever answer seem trite? Insufficient, moreover, to cure those fears which occur in advance of the wipe-out?

Seth guessed that the Commissioner did not want this kind of clever answer. Rather, what was required was a low-level, practical view. Something to prove the point that a lowly Earth brain really can score over a neurotic though vast Saturnian rogue intelligence.

Seth opened his mouth... hoping that his tongue would find inspiration for itself—but at the same moment he understood why he was beaten: either he would fail to think of something, or else he would succeed, and if he succeeded, he would have experienced a triumph which he surely would not be allowed to take home with him.

Either way, he would never see Earth again.

7: the will

WITH A SHRUG of the mind Seth let his personal hopes fall away. Now he could lean back relaxedly against his last prop – his pride. This calm resignation in the face of doom brought its reward: he could grasp, at last, what to say.

He could give Tgimvaru his lesson in how not to worry.

"Of all crimes," Seth declared, "that of reality-change is least likely to spread, because the perpetrator must 'draw the ladder up after him', as it were. The guilty ones know full well they must make sure that the deed is only done once."

Xagelthad shifted, the mighty Saturnian torso wobbling with some unguessable emotion as it turned a degree or two towards its smaller fellow.

"Hear the Earthman," the Commissioner's voice clanged. "The thing can only be done once."

And don't, please don't, mention the further point I didn't dare make, pleaded Seth in silence. If someone who changes history must do so in such a way that the result also wipes out the invention of the change-mechanism itself, so that it has never been, and no such alteration can recur or, indeed, has ever occurred—if, in other words, time-tampering results in itself being written out of existence as part of the deal - is that really much comfort, if another part of the deal is the rise of the Iapetans?

But the younger Saturnian, the rogue Tgimvaru, did not protest. Instead, when it spoke at last, it said one simple, satisfied English word:

"Once."

It agrees with me, realized Seth with awe. It is content to believe in what I said.

The thing it fears can only be done "once".

Sizzling Saturn—I've convinced it!

And now the super-beings of the Great World could depart – leaving him to the care of the Iapetans, from which there would be no return. My ship? wondered Seth – is it still intact, or have Iapetans or Saturnians destroyed it? Academic question; they'll never allow me back to *Jumbo*. For me the next stage is to be put away.

Here it starts...

The scene blurred in front of his eyes. Minutes stretched. He saw the grey ships lift, their fields of influence fade... and he found himself no longer wearing the Iapetan soldier gear or, indeed, the Iapetan soldier body. Physically he was himself again, and he once more wore his own spacesuit, a temporary concession to his frail Terran needs. The Iapetan Controllers, four of them now, tall in their robes and huge gloves, stood around and murmured to him, making him understand that he was Iapetan from henceforth. They began to shepherd him back up the spine of the great ridge, the Arc of their world, and along its undulations, towards the laboratory complex which awaited him—

He consoled himself with his pride. Whatever might happen to him now, he had had his moment. He had spoken up and answered the great Xagelthad. All the more important to remember this, because compared with Iapetans or Saturnians, an Earth-human was hardly more than a "babe in the wood". Had it been the Saturnians, or the Iapetans, who had flung him back into his own body again, displacing his consciousness for the second time? Either of them could have done it, he guessed.

Now he must brace himself, must keep hold of his dignity by budgeting in advance, emotionally preparing for what these savants of the Eighth Moon were going to do to an Earthling who knew too much.

They escorted him towards the collection of gunmetal cuboidal buildings, impressive though not beautiful, which loomed ahead on the ridge-path. It would have been easier, no doubt, to build such a colossus in the lowlands, but of course, thought Seth (as his fancy virtually whiffed the ominous metaphor which curled like mist through the near vacuum), of course they had to build their time-laboratory up here on the Arc, the bent bow aiming its arrows of greatness at the rest of the System...

So—face the worst. Stand tall as you can against despair, thought he, as they ushered him in through the heavy doors.

But the interior was surprisingly inviting. Despite his self-cautionings the entrance hall, carpeted in gentle orange, with walls in golden tints, soothed his soul. Same for the chamber in which they bade him sit: an attractive lounge, though its seats were trumpet-shaped, upended thorns stabbing the carpet. This, a lab?

Perhaps it was to be expected, in the hands of a people so super-scientific that the science begins to become invisible, like artless art in the work of a great poet.

They gave him food and drink; they let him rest; and Ghwepp, the Iapetan who spoke English, softened him up with truths in strange parables.

"Not only living tissue, but also events, are cellular in structure... The "DNA" of an event contains the germ of all its possible outcomes..."

"Stem-cells of probability," murmured Seth, moved again by his pride to show them that he could follow what was being said, albeit weakly, hazily.

Ghwepp murmured, "Quite. They just need growth."

It was then that Seth really understood.

Not a moment too soon, it burst upon him that "wipe-outs" and "reality-changes" were altogether the wrong ways to think about what was being done.

No wipe-outs, no, nothing like that; instead -
Purposive evolution!

Gravity Three came from the *will*...

They were all looking at him.

It was time for him to undergo the experiment.

"Tell us," said Ghwepp, "about the time you landed on Saturn."

They had slid a screen in front of him, and his thoughts began to be pictured on the screen.

He might as well obey willingly. Certainly he could not blank out the memories. And besides, he would not. For this was the final mercy. If he had to be wrung dry, let it be through telling his captors what he was most proud to tell but could never have risked telling except when he was being forced -

As the good little ship *Jumbo* dropped the last fifty miles below the cloud layer towards the tawny glow of the Ringed Planet's surface, Seth Hurst was heartened by the stupendousness of the vista. Sharpening gradually out of the haze of distance, the prairie seemed to go on for ever. No Terran ship had ever detected the use of radar by the Saturnians, and customarily it was assumed from this was that the Great World must use some effective substitute, but Seth's idea—that there was no substitute; the Great Ones simply did not care—seemed ever more convincing as he gazed out of the cockpit window. Beings who possessed a planet on this scale would have egos and self-confidence to match its size, and would not feel the need for any snoopy defence network. With a bit of luck he could drop down, have a look around, and shoot back up again, taking with him the glory of being the first Terran to have stood upon Saturn.

He had descended to an altitude of fifteen miles when the sharpness of the detail below allowed him to note a splotch, perhaps on average twenty miles wide, on the prairie. It was a stain of relative brightness, like a sheen of sparkling dew. There was no reason to suppose it was anything dangerous; doubtless no more than a variation in the flora; but to play safe, he levelled out the ship's course and made for the edge of the twenty-mile patch.

Finally all his cautious trains of thought chugged to a stop as his ship touched ground and he faced the full immensity of his achievement. He was here. And nobody was around to challenge him, or to stop him getting away again. He was going to do it – he was going to be the man who attained Planet Six, the most formidable world in the System.

The indicators assured him he'd be able to breathe the air outside, and stand the temperature, which was mild, doubtless due to thermal activity below ground... Earthlings might live on this world, if it were not for the fear of the Saturnians. Seth shrugged; that was an insurmountable "if", and besides, he was happy to leave this planet to those who owned it. It looked good, but...

He stepped out of the needless airlock and into the waist-high Saturnian grass.

In the far distance, a few hundred miles off, loomed the hazy outlines of trapezoidal mountains. Apart from them, the scene was one of grass, grass, grass, interspersed every few miles by a dense hunk of taller, darker vegetation. The ubiquitous grass gave off a bracing scent, so that Seth found the air a tonic to breathe, yet there was something intimidating about its freshness, as though it committed the Terran soul to one type of greatness too many, one hugeness too far.

Absurd though it was even to think about surveying such a place to any meaningful degree, Seth decided he might as well poke his nose into something before he fled back into space. He remembered he had landed deliberately at the border of the brighter patch of grass. Well, before he left, he could at least walk over and have a look at that slightly different area.

He trudged through the "normally" tawny grass until he reached the border of the also-tawny-but-brighter sort.

Here he stopped for a while and listened to the ringing silence around him. *It was extremely important for him, just then, to look back and reassure himself that Jumbo was where he had left it, and that no other additions to the landscape had appeared within his 360-degree field of view.*

For now he strongly suspected that he had come upon a secret.

The realm of brighter grass was inhabited.

Semi-transparent humanoids, multitudes of them, six inches high, swarmed almost weightlessly over the grass-blades, hardly depressing them as they leaped from one to another. Their bodies were a very light blue, but they looked quite human.

They were leaping all the more urgently because they had seen him. Suddenly the edge of the bright area bristled with what looked to him like little pop-guns, made of stuff that looked solider than the folk who had constructed them.

Seth backed away slowly. He raised a hand in placatory greeting and farewell. He had seen enough. He did not want to become a new Gulliver ensnared by these Lilliputian Saturnians.

And were they the *Saturnians? He realized that the question made no sense. This planet was so vast, it need not have just one intelligent race.*

The midgets saw him retreat; they were content to see him go, without firing across that boundary which he had not violated. He hoped they understood that he had not been hostile. The possibility of his friendliness, at any rate, ought to have occurred to them. He waved again, and—was it a trumpet he saw? Some instrument that looked like it. A celebratory thing, anyhow. He glimpsed some wave-gestures just as the small trumpety sound washed through him.

Quite confident, those gesticulations…

And now the tone of the whole scene changed, for Seth remembered where he really was, remembered that he and his captors were watching these memories displayed on the screen in the laboratory up on the Arc of Iapetus.

And yet he felt a pull, as though his past exploit would not let go – would not admit it was merely a memory. So he felt he was living simultaneously in two times and places.

He overheard the self-satisfied Iapetans commenting on what he'd shown them.

"Stem cell event… we can grow real *Saturnians from these… they will be the Saturnians… humans like us, under our tutelage. We will finally take our place as overlords of the Great World."*

Seth spoke. He no longer cared what he said.

"That's what you think, fools that you are, Idiots of the Arc. Sure, you'll do what you think you'll do. And when you've done it, which will be the tail and which the dog? The real Saturnians will be the grass-people who invited me down there, without me knowing."

As soon as Ghwepp had translated his remarks, all the Iapetans laughed.

"Oh, so they invited you, did they?" Ghwepp chortled.

No, smiled Seth, not yet. But eventually they will have done, for what grows from events' stem-cells is the poets' power of re-defining victory and defeat; of making true what is not yet true.

"And Flodden had been Bannockbourne…"

The End.

Jamie Ross was a Canadian/Irish systems and software engineer living in rural East County Clare, Ireland. Growing up in the US and Canada, he and his brother Graham devoured every science fiction and fantasy book in their local libraries, from Edgar Rice Burroughs and Jules Vern to Andre Norton and Robert Heinlein shaping their life direction. He went on to study Aeronautics and Astronautics at MIT and graduated on to work on a diverse range of R&D projects including advanced spacecraft navigation and control systems, a Life Science centrifuge for ISS, as well as robotic missions to Mars and Europa. His brother picked up a PhD in fluid dynamics at Stanford and was instrumental in the Hubble Space Telescope and Gravity B spacecraft programs. On a more practical side, Jamie worked on the Iridium communications network and giant undersea tidal turbines in France and Canada. He first tried coming up with a story about asteroid mining years ago, ending up making friends with the top expert in the subject at the US Geological Survey which resulted in a proposal for mining lunar regolith but couldn't find the story that needed to be told. The story that starts here finally introduced itself in the competition for the first Vintage Worlds *and has sucked him into its expanding universe.*

Readers of Vintage Worlds 2 *will recall* Beyond Despair, *Jamie Ross' vivid account of first contact on Uranus. In this sequel,* Europa Dive, *Ross launches a further exploration of his version of the Old Solar System, sending a team of investigators down below the frozen seas of Europa to face realities that challenge everything they think they know...*

Europa Dive

by Jamie Ross

D R GRAHAM BURD sat in a steel and leather office chair in the Office of Director of Space Research, trying very hard not to show his confusion while watching the Director studiously ignore him as he scanned his personnel file. Twenty-four hours ago, he had been lecturing undergraduates at the University of Victoria on the fundamentals of fluid dynamics when two very serious-looking men came into the lecture hall and insisted he follow them. A helicopter trip to Vancouver followed by a flight by private jet to Montreal and the Canadian Space Agency Headquarters. He sat twirling his pen trying not to show his annoyance until his patience finally ran out.

"Director Richotte, exactly why am I here? What is so important to drag me out of my lecture and half-way across the country?"

Unperturbed, Jean Baptiste Richotte looked up from the files. "Dr Graham Burd, University of British Columbia graduate and one of NASA's leading geophysical fluid dynamicists specialising in the moons in the outer Solar System. Now you are teaching undergraduates basic physics? This seems like a step down in your career perhaps?"

Graham shrugged, "I was at Marshall in 2023 when the nukes went off and things in the US fell apart. I lost a lot of friends in San Francisco and San Diego and suddenly the affairs of far-off planets didn't seem so important.

"Besides, NASA funding was really frustrating; they spent more on air conditioning in Iraq than on the space program. Most of our proposals for solar system exploration ended up in the trash. Then the Americans called a Constitutional Convention after the Korean Incident and broke up the country into the four Republics. At the same time, the MarsOne mission disappeared without a trace and funding for space disappeared next. I had family back in Victoria so I was lucky I was able to come back and find work."

Jean Baptiste looked directly at him and asked, "Dr Burd, you have been following the events with the Lúthians I assume?" Graham laughed; after all, who had not been following the news of an intelligent species on Uranus three years ago?

The crew of the exploration vessel, Shining Star, had gone to Uranus to collect Helium-3 for the Eurasian Economic Union's new fusion reactors and it almost ended in a disaster and war.

It was only the efforts of the crew negotiating a last-minute peace that allowed a trade agreement between the Eurasian Economic Union and the Lúthian Council. Now there were three giant ships traversing the deep space between Earth and Lúth, the original Shining Star, the Aleksandr Kaleri and the Max Plank, all carrying raw metals and water to Uranus in return for Helium-3.

"Only what I have seen on the Metanet broadcasts. The Lúthians won't travel to Earth because of deep space radiation but they have synthetic beings called symbiotes who can withstand it and so act as their agents here. We now have abundant electrical energy with the new fusion plants online and as a result, they are opening up the Yukon and Nunavut for expansion. That's about it I'm afraid. I never did hear what became of the crew of the Shining Star?"

Jean Baptiste leaned back and looked intently at Graham before he responded, ignoring his last question. "What you probably aren't aware of is that we have formed a joint program with the Lúthians to explore the outer planets. While their fusion and biomechanical technology is superb, they had only just developed interplanetary travel. They had trouble getting through the upper atmosphere to space for a long time due to extreme winds.

"So our governments have decided to work together and share our technologies. As a result, I am now Co-Director of the Centre for Earth Lúthian Exploration(CELE) with Leader Myker of the Lúth Council. We already have a mission in mind around Jupiter."

Graham leaned forward, "You are actually going to send people out to the outer planets? What is the mission?"

Jean Baptiste smiled, "You did several studies on the oceans of Europa, did you not? How would you like to participate in a mission to drill into the ice crust and explore the oceans underneath with remotely operated submersibles?"

Graham's jaw dropped for a second; that was his dream mission but it had never gotten past concept discussions and when the American space program fell apart, he had given up on the whole idea. "Yes, of course, we planned that mission for years.. but I never expected it to happen in my lifetime!"

"The mission team will be lead by Captain Alexey Leonov from the Russian Federation Arctic Command with Dr Anna Shirshov, Arctic marine biologist, Dr Roger Davis from the New American Republic, a specialist in deep-sea ROV operations and Dr Marceau Frappier, an Antarctic biologist from the French Polar Institute. The Lúthians are sending several specialists as well. The last position is yours if you want it."

- Space Operations Centre, Star City -

AFTER A SHORT ride from the airport in an electric taxi, Graham found himself at the Space Operations Centre. It was a large facility housing mission control, astronaut training, engineering, communications, and other support functions. As most of the countries had now joined the EEU, the population at the Operations Centre was very international, which was obvious from the number of languages Graham heard as he entered the building. After checking in with the receptionist and getting his badge, he was directed to the conference room on the first floor.

Entering the room, he navigated through the milling crowd to the buffet tables with coffee, samovars of tea and an assortment of pastries. He grabbed a cup of coffee and a croissant surrounded by enthusiastic conversations all around the room, feeling very out of place. How had he gotten into this state? He used to be an outgoing extroverted young scientist pushing the edges of human knowledge and then somehow he had retreated into a safe, predictable teaching position. Why did he think he could step back into the pace of a fast-moving exploration program?

As he tried not to fall into a bout of melancholy, his thoughts were interrupted by a voice behind him with a distinct Texas American accent. "Dr Burd? I thought that was you I saw coming in. Hi, I'm Roger Davis from OceanTech in Dallas. We met at NASA Houston back before the War. After NASA folded, our company went back to oil and gas projects but I guess they are using modified versions of our deep-sea ROVs for this mission. I was trying to figure out what to expect on Europa so I pulled out some of your old papers on ocean dynamics under the Europa icepack. I was impressed but I still can't say I have any good idea what's down there."

Graham nodded, glad for the distraction from his morose thoughts. He scratched his beard and pondered an answer. "I am not sure I have confidence in our estimates any more either. Everything we used to think we knew seems to be wrong. I'm not really sure why they want me along." He laughed a bit self-consciously, "I'm just a middle-aged college lecturer these days."

Roger laughed and shook his head, "I wouldn't worry about that. These Chinese and Russian types don't seem to make decisions like that without a reason. I suspect they want someone along who can analyse the oceans as we explore them. You are still the best authority on Europa."

They were interrupted by a booming Russian voice from the front of the room. "Ladies and gentlemen, thank you for coming. If you will please take your seats, we have a lot of information to cover on this mission".

As they walked to their chairs, Roger turned to Graham, "I suspect that is our new commander, Alexey Leonov. I understand that he led the development of the big Russian Arctic science base they used for the core drilling study last year. The EEU must be taking this mission seriously if we get someone assigned with his credentials."

As they sat down at the table, an attractive woman with auburn hair sat down next to him. Quickly reading her name badge, he introduced himself: "Hello, I am Dr Graham Burd; you must be Dr Shirshov?".

Dr Anna Shirshov turned to him and shook his hand and smiled, "It's a pleasure to meet you, Dr Burd. My colleagues have told me good things about you!"

Graham found himself suddenly a bit tongue-tied as he realised he was really attracted to her. He was confused as he hadn't felt that way in many years. Something about Anna's smile was electrifying and he was having a hard time maintaining his professional composure.

"Uh, yes.. well, thank you. I have studied your work as well.. I look forward to working together." The room darkened as the wall display turned on and Alexey started the briefing. Graham shook his head thinking, that's great, Graham, what are you, twelve years old? That couldn't have been more awkward.

Fortunately, the rest of the briefing and side meetings prevented any further embarrassment but he couldn't get her out of his mind.

The next month turned out to be non-stop training for the mission. As they were put through physical fitness training, Graham found himself regretting ever giving up hockey. He really used to be in pretty good shape but now he found himself out of breath and falling behind the others.

Anna seemed to take pity on him though and would hang back and give him encouragement which gave him enough motivation to make it through the day. He found himself finding excuses to work with her and she didn't seem to mind, which pleased him, though he was half convinced her interest in him was wishful thinking on his part.

On the trip out from Earth to Lúth, they were all packed into the protective interior of the Max Planck freighter for radiation protection as the AI pilot guided the ship out to Uranus. Several weeks later, they entered geosynchronous orbit above Uranus, which apparently everyone now called Lúth (much to the disappointment of several generations of schoolboys).

There they docked with the new orbiting platform which serviced the Max Planck and the other interplanetary vessels moving Helium 3 and raw materials from Earth to Lúth and back.

After disembarking from the freighter, they had been met in the main Station conference room by the head of the Lúthian Council, Leader Myker, and briefed on the final details of the mission as well as meeting the final three members of the team.

The team now included two symbiotes: Sylan, a mining technician for the drilling operation and Ansil, a scientific technician, who would support the bio-survey operations. The third member, Fadek, was short and stout with a beard and Graham couldn't help but compare him with a dwarf from Lord of the Rings. Apparently, they were a different species of Lúthians who lived deep underground that the news broadcasts hadn't mentioned. Alexey told them that he was one of the top deep mining experts on the planet.

Once they had collected the additional crew members, they were escorted to the docking bay where the Lúthian exploration ship was being prepared for the trip to Jupiter's moon. Graham couldn't be more shocked at the red maple leaf logo with a Northern Loon and the words "Crazy Loon" painted on the nose of the sleek ship. He was confused. The pilot of the Shining Star, Elisabeth Williams, had been a Canadian, but the official story was that she died on the first mission to Lúth. He remembered that Director Richotte had avoided answering him when he asked what happened to the crew of the Shining Star. He turned and Alexey, Anna, Roger and Marceau were all staring with equally surprised looks on their faces.

"So maybe Elisabeth Williams didn't die after all", shrugged Alexey. They all looked at each other, then headed through the entry hatch as the symbiotes loaded the equipment in the cargo bays. Graham found his way through the crew quarters to the flight deck. As he was putting his gear away into a small locker, he was interrupted by a familiar accent which he guessed belonged to the enigmatic Canadian pilot.

"Dr Burd, welcome to the Crazy Loon; I will be your Captain for this flight." Graham stood up and turned around and stopped in shock.

The woman before him had silver-blonde hair and an attractive face, but then nothing else was what he expected. From her bright blue cybernetic eyes to the mechanical arms, sleek silver mechanical legs and a torso much like the symbiotes - he had never seen anything like her.

Graham stammered, "Elisabeth Williams? What happened to you... I am so sorry." He paused and looked away for a minute. "They didn't tell us anything; I didn't even think you were alive."

The woman smiled, "Yes Dr Burd, I am or was Elisabeth Williams. They call me Lizbeth here on Lúth and I have gotten used to the name. When I crashed on the surface during the Shining Star expedition, many people thought I died there and I would have. Fortunately, the Lúthians are brilliant when it comes to bio-organics and robotics so they decided to resurrect me using symbiote technology with my remaining human parts grafted in. Now I am a hybrid of sorts, one of only two that I am aware of."

"Two? Where is the rest of your crew? Director Richotte evaded the question when I asked him."

Lizbeth smiled, "They aren't really comfortable with the hybrids, any more than the Lúthians are. My first officer, Marika, was critically injured down under the surface so to survive she ended up being transformed like me.

"Jimmy and Ivan managed without major injuries so Jimmy was called back to Earth and has been overseeing the upgraded fusion drives like what brought you here. " She paused for a second, a hint of sadness crossing her face. "Ivan is down on the planet on a special assignment. They won't tell me the details and I haven't seen him in over a year."

Graham sensed the grief behind the last statement. "I'm sorry." He paused. "If I can ask you one other question?"

Lizbeth looked up, her smile returning. "Yes, sure."

Graham thought for a moment. "You are part Symbiote? I am not sure what that means; are you a cyborg, a human brain in a robot body? I'm sorry that was rude of me."

Lizbeth laughed, "I asked the same question but the answer is no. There is a semi-sentient fungal web that exists beneath the surface of Lúth with extensive neuro-electrical capabilities. The Lúthian bio-engineers found a way to control it and use it to control the organic matrix in the symbiotes. It regulates our body functions and repairs damage as well as improving our performance. It's the reason Marika and I can handle the deep-space radiation. We are organic and mostly human, even if we have some biomechanical limbs."

They were interrupted by the comm system: "Commander, please come to the nav centre - the final flight path to Europa orbit needs to be checked."

Lizbeth looked at Graham. "I'm sorry but that's all the questions I have time for. We have a lot of preflight checks to complete before we depart. Marika and I connect into the ship for the flight so I won't see you until after we land on Europa. Good Luck!"

As Lizbeth turned away and walked down the corridor, Graham couldn't help but think how different this Lizbeth was from the person his colleagues in the EEU astronaut corp had described. Back in the program she was the top-ranked EEU pilot and was known for her cold almost brutal efficiency. This new version seemed very different in more ways than one which was something else he had yet to understand.

- Europa Surface -

GRAHAM BURD STOOD on the cold dark ice of Europa looking up at the stars. He couldn't really believe he was here on the surface of a moon of Jupiter. As the Crazy Loon crew completed the final preparations in the distance, he was trying to shake his perception of not being part of the team. He had been out of the space program since the war and things had changed so radically since then that he was having problems processing everything.

His reverie was interrupted by the comm system in his helmet and he was brought back to the ice cold dark landscape of Europa by the familiar voice of Anna Shirshov in his earpiece.

"Dr Burd, I was hoping to find you. Roger would like our assistance in setting up the drilling module." He turned and watched Anna coming towards him across the ice. Even in her pressure suit, she still took his breath away.

As he admired her form silhouetted against the sky, it reminded him once again of the changes in the space program. The skintight fit of the new Newman counter-pressure suits left little to the imagination and his imagination tended to run wild around Anna anyway. Fortunately, Anna had on external armour and gear otherwise the distraction would overwhelming.

In contrast, the suits didn't do as much for a middle aged university lecturer, as the mirror in the crew quarters had reminded him with visual clarity. He was in better shape since training but he would never look like the 25-year-old he remembered. He shook his head, getting his thoughts back to the mission.

After she made her way over and stood beside him, he turned and said, "Anna, please call me Graham, Dr Burd is way too formal. It's funny, I was just thinking that there was a time when I believed we really understood the Solar System. Then our world as we knew it came to an end in the Korean Incident. After we met the Lúthians, any remaining confidence in our knowledge was destroyed. Sometimes I am just afraid that I am too old for this."

"Graham, I have to disagree. We all regret that we didn't get the science right before but we did the best we could. Now we just have to pick ourselves up and start again. I'm not that much younger than you and I believe we have to relook at all the scientific assumptions we had and find out what needs to be changed. I think you are too hard on yourself! I am very glad you are here with us and I am really happy you are here with me. You have helped me get through the fears I have about this whole trip into deep space."

Graham smiled,"Thank you. You are right of course and

I am really happy you are here with me as well." She looked up at him, her smile visible through her helmet. With that, she took his hand and they both stood side by side as the exploration ship silently took off and disappeared into the dark sky.

As GRAHAM AND Anna returned to the base camp, they saw that the Lúthian team had already constructed two pressure domes under Fadek's direction. Graham was impressed that the domes were built so fast and couldn't help comparing them to ancient Inuit Igloos he had visited back home. As he walked closer he observed that they even had a thick layer of ice covering the hard substrate and were dug a metre or so into the surface. He walked over to Fadek to congratulate him.

"Fadek, I'm very impressed; they look very functional."

Fadek looked up from his instruments. "Thank you, Dr Burd. This is a technique we use on Lúth in the highlands. We use the outer ice layer for both thermal and radiation protection. The dome on the left is our quarters while the right dome will contain the drill hole, controls and workshop. Your engineer, Dr Davis, is setting up the drill assembly with Dr Frappier's help."

Fadek stopped as the symbiote Sylan came up to them. "Savant Fadek? I have the well-site information you were asking for. The ice is 18km deep at the drill hole and I have calibrated the fusion drill for Dr Davis. We estimate at full output temperature, the drill will travel about 500 metres an hour through the ice so it will take about 36 hours to clear the borehole. Dr Davis and Dr Frappier are preparing the two probes and estimate they will have a communication range of about a kilometre from the borehole transmitter." He then bowed and left as quietly as he came.

Graham turned to Fadek with a puzzled look on his face

as the symbiote walked away. "Fadek, what exactly are the symbiotes? Lizbeth told me a little, but while they seem very intelligent, they don't seem to act on their own."

"They are servants, Dr Burd. The Symbiotes are bio-mechanical constructs, made from mechanical parts combined with organic elements incorporating "meshi" as we call it, a type of semi-sentient fungus. They were developed to serve the needs of the Lúthians who live on the surface. The mother of the meshi fungus is the source of all life on Lúth. In ancient times, it existed deep in the inner core of the planet and converted methane, heat and what hydrocarbons it could find into oxygen and nitrogen and built-up nutrients as waste. This eventually supported the development of the advanced forms of life that exist now.

"The people you know as Lúthians and my people were once the same race who evolved in the caverns and tunnels deep under the surface. They were our best and brightest and as they studied the "meshi", they learned how strands spread through the planet and connected everything. They were able to use this to develop a tame version which allowed the creation of the synthetic beings we call Symbiotes.

"At the same time they developed the Symbiotes, the scientists became more skilled at bioengineering and modified themselves and their children to be superior in their eyes. They became tall and slender and craved the open spaces on the surface.

"Symbiotes were deliberately designed without free will and as they became more capable, they were used to replace the work my people originally performed. As you might expect, we Keltans have differing opinions on the nature of Symbiotes than our Lúthian brethren on the surface."

Anna interjected, "So are you a different species now? How do you get along?"

Fadek frowned, "Eventually, we became two species: Keltans like me remain in the depths and the Lúthians live in their domed cities on the surface with their Symbiote workforce. While we trade and work together, it is safe to say we don't really trust each other."

Fadek turned back to his instrument pod, signalling that the subject was closed. To avoid the awkward silence, Graham and Anna decided that they should check out the new crew quarters. As they covered the distance across the ice to the other dome, Anna whispered to Graham on their private channel, "Those symbiotes remind me of angels. They serve their gods with no free will. What does that make Elisabeth?"

Graham shrugged, "I really have no idea. It brings to mind the analogy with the Garden of Eden. What happens when you introduce free will into the symbiote race? I would really like to..."

"Dr Burd, you have to come here and see this!" Alexey's voice came booming through the headset. Graham paused and looked at Anna. "Let's go see what has Alexey so wound up."

As they came around the stacked supply palettes, they saw Alexey holding two hockey sticks. "Your friend, Lizbeth, left us some presents! We have hockey sticks, skate attachments for our boots and even a couple of nets. I think that it's only appropriate that Russians and Canadians are the first humans to play hockey on Europa!"

Anna looked at Graham and they both broke out in laughter. "Alexey, game on! She didn't include any hockey tape for the sticks by any chance?" said Graham with a grin.

FOUR HOURS LATER, the team sat around the dining table in the crew dome sipping vodka and whiskey after several hours of the strangest hockey game in history. The Symbiotes had retreated to their charging stations and Fadek was watching the ongoing drill operation, muttering under his beard.

"Dr Burd, I see you haven't forgotten how to skate," Alexey laughed.

Graham grinned, "I am surprised I didn't fall more. I haven't played in while and the low gravity certainly adds a whole new element. Anna was a demon on skates though, and Roger valiantly defended the honour of Texas and best of all, none of us broke anything, so that's positive."

"Cheers to that!" Roger raised his glass as they all savoured their first night on Europa.

It was later the next day when the team gathered in the science dome to watch the final breakthrough to the oceans of Europa. As Fadek monitored the fusion drill, Anna and Marceau were preparing the first submersible while Roger and Graham went over the release procedures for the second one. Fadek would implant a borehole transmitter at the end of the ice tunnel connected to the surface by fibre.

The transmitter would provide communications through the cold water to the two vehicles and relay it to the control station in the dome. Submersible 1 was nicknamed the Jacques Cousteau, and would search for lifeforms while Submersible 2, nicknamed the Fritjof Nansen, would survey the water content and any geophysical structures.

It was late in the day when Fadek announced that the borehole was complete and the borehole station stabilised. Everyone clustered around the monitors in the science dome as they deployed the Cousteau and Nansen probes. Graham and Marceau were using Lúthian designed immersive displays to "fly" the probes through the darkness, the bright lights of the probes lighting up the darkness.

"Graham, what are those columns rising from the interior?" Anna was leaning over his shoulder. As the probe moved closer, they could see a ripple of lights moving quickly up and down the column.

Marceau brought the Cousteau upwards following the organic columns to the underside of the ice. "It looks like they spread out along the underside of the ice pack. The light pulses seem to travel all the way out to the smallest tendrils. It's almost like a nervous system."

Anna looked closer, "Marceau, can we use the Cousteau to take a sample of whatever that is?"

"Don't do that!" growled Fadek. They all turned as Fadek looked over their shoulders at the displays. He seemed visibly agitated. "We don't know anything about the lifeforms here. It is dangerous to disturb anything. There is something oddly familiar about this and it has me concerned."

Anna looked at Graham and they turned to Alexey, "Commander, what do you think?"

Alexey frowned, "I agree with Fadek, I think we need to be cautious. Don't disturb anything until we have more data."

Marceau was steering the Cousteau closer to the massive columns, its bright light revealing strands of organic material woven into huge cords. "It appears there is electrical energy as well as light in these columns, probably like electric eels back on Earth."

Graham brought the Nansen up towards the ice as well and followed the columns as they spread out like tree branches. Anna pointed at the larger screen, "There are small bioluminescent creatures feeding on the fronds. Do you think they are cleaning the fronds like cleaner wrasse do on Earth?"

Graham shook his head, "I have no idea, I've never seen anything like it, this is amazing!"

Marceau brought the Cousteau again against one of the surface fronds and before anyone could say anything, he used the remote arm to clip a piece as a sample.

Alexey reacted quickly, "Marceau, no samples! We don't know..."

He was cut off as a massive series of electrical pulses starting racing up and down the column originating at the sample site. The whole area started flashing as the adjacent columns lit up as well. Ominously, the small feeders suddenly disappeared into the darkness.

Alexey shouted, "Everyone, bring the submersibles back to the borehole, NOW!"

Alexey turned to Fadek but before he could say anything, Anna yelled out, "Commander there are large objects coming at us fast!".

They had only enough time to see what looked like giant jaws and teeth as the submersibles both recorded impacts and all the communications went dead.

Graham jumped out of his seat and ran over to the borehole. "Fadek, can we seal this?"

Fadek frowned and signalled to the symbiotes to close the opening but it was too late. Something dark and large and wet came rushing out of the hole like the tentacle on a giant octopus.

Chaos broke out as the substance flowed out in giant pseudopods and flailed out around the wellhead. Giant globs broke off and formed shapes which coalesced into terrifying creatures which started smashing equipment and attacking people.

Everyone ran for cover while Graham grabbed Anna and pulled her behind an equipment cabinet for protection. A giant tiger-like beast caught Marceau, decapitating him while Alexey was pinned to the wall by something that looked like a large bear. The lighting suddenly went out as the electronics cabinets were smashed sending the dome into almost total darkness.

The creatures seemed to sense where the crew were in the darkness and were now systematically destroying everything they could find. A giant fanged predator grabbed the symbiote, Ansil, then after taking a piece out of his neck, suddenly paused as if it was thinking.

Then as suddenly as they had appeared, all the creatures

stopped where they were and dissolved back into the dark ooze, recombining into one mass and slithering back towards the borehole. As the pseudopod retreated to the wellhead, it reached out with a dark tentacle and grabbed Anna by her leg and pulled her along with it as it disappeared down the borehole.

Graham reached out, taking her arms, unwilling to let her be taken but it was too late. Anna was pulled down into the hole and Graham dragged with her. He sensed he was falling endlessly surrounded by a dark ooze and then... nothing.

- A beach somewhere -

As he regained consciousness, the first thing Graham was aware of was the sound of waves against the shoreline. He slowly opened his eyes to the blue sky above him with the sun shining.

He pulled himself up on his elbows and looked around, his mind spinning. He was lying on a sandy beach with dark rocks leading up a bluff that was filled with tall pines and evergreens. He suddenly realised he recognized this place.

"Graham, is that you?" He turned to look down the beach and saw a woman walking towards him who he couldn't fail to recognise.

"Anna, are you ok?" She seemed to be walking normally but instead of her pressure suit, she was wearing a floral sundress and carrying sandals.

"Graham, where are we?" Anna had finally reached him and sat down on the beach next to him.

"The last thing I remember is being dragged down the borehole by that thing." She looked at Graham again. "Where is your pressure suit, why are you dressed like that?"

Graham looked down and realised that he was wearing a Hawaiian shirt and cargo shorts with sandals, pretty much his attire of choice when he was visiting his Aunt back on Denman Island on holiday.

The problem was that Denman Island was located off of Vancouver Island in British Columbia and millions of kilometres from where he remembered them being.

"I don't know, Anna; this seems to be an island in Canada where my Aunt lives, but that can't be possible. I don't know what's going on as I remember following you down the borehole as well."

Anna stood back up and surveyed the island as far as she could see. "Look, Graham, there is someone down by the point there and it looks like there is a campfire too. Let's go see who it is and maybe they can give us some answers."

Anna helped Graham up and stood in front of him smiling at him. He suddenly stopped, leaned over and kissed her, much to her surprise. She responded by throwing her arms around his neck and returning the kiss.

Graham pulled back and blurted out, a bit embarrassed, "I don't know where we are or what's going on, but I was afraid I lost you! You are amazing and I ..." Anna put her finger to his lips stopping him from continuing. "You know Graham, I am rather smitten with you as well but now is not the time. So let's go find out where we are and how to get home."

Graham responded, "Then maybe I can take you out to dinner on a proper date." She laughed and smiled in agreement as he took her hand and they headed down the beach.

As THEY APPROACHED the fire, they saw a woman with long dark hair sitting on a driftwood log eating what looked like oysters off a skewer. In her other hand, she had a glass of white wine and was looking over the sea at the sun going down over the main island.

Graham started, "Excuse me, but we are hoping you can help us." The woman looked at them and smiled. She was wearing a flannel shirt over a white t-shirt with faded jeans and bare feet.

"Ah hello, Dr Burd, and I see you found Dr Shirshov. I hope you have been enjoying the lovely weather we are having. I collected a bucket of fresh oysters and I found that if you wrap bacon around them and put them on a skewer and cook them over the fire, they are absolutely delicious! You should try them."

Anna and Graham just stared. "How do you know who we are and where exactly are we? As much as I love the shoreline on Denman Island, I doubt that's where we are. What exactly is going on?" Graham was starting to lose his temper.

"I am sorry Dr Burd, let me explain. You may call me Anahita, and I am the entity that you attacked."

"Attacked? We were just exploring under the ice on Europa; at most we just took a sample of a strand of some organic growth there." Anna looked confused.

"You see, Dr Shirshov, those stands, as you call them, are the synaptic connections of my brain. You drilled into my head and started rummaging around my synapses which triggered my autonomic defences which react to remove infections."

Graham interrupted, "The globs that came out of the borehole after us! Why did they turn into creatures? They killed Marceau and I don't know who else! What were they?"

"Dr Burd, I am sorry about your crew-mates; it was an immediate reaction from my immune system. They read your minds to find images which would strike fear and confusion and took their forms with an intent to destroy the 'infection'. When one of them attacked a symbiote, it recognised the same basic organic matter we are made of, so it stopped the attack. It pulled you and Anna here to my core to find out what you were. Of course, once I had realised I was dealing with beings from off-planet, I tried to repair the damage to your crew. As I had never met one of your species close up, I wanted to speak with you directly."

Graham interrupted, "I'm sorry, did you say your head? Does that mean Europa is a single sentient being?"

Anahita giggled and pulled an oyster off her skewer, savouring it as she took it into her mouth. "These oysters really are delightful, thank you for giving me this experience."

Anna stepped in, "So, Anahita, are we dead? What happened to our crew-mates? Where are we?"

Anahita finished her oyster then looked at Anna. "No you are not dead, you are safe in my care in my interior at the moment as it makes this discussion easier. As you surmised, this is a projection based on memories from Dr Burd. Once I realised what happened, I arranged to have your people taken care of, though I'm sorry, Dr Frappier was beyond help, even for me. You need to understand, we have more important issues to discuss."

Graham looked at Anna then back at Anahita. "What more important issues?"

"I have existed here for a millennium. I have developed the mental ability to monitor life in this Solar System and influence the thoughts of its life forms, just like I created this world here for you."

The sun was setting and the stars were coming out. Graham sat on the log next to Anahita with Anna curled up against him. Anahita had materialised warm wool blankets to protect them against the cool evening air.

"While our Solar System is old, it is not nearly as old as the Galaxy around us. There are some very malevolent entities in the Universe and I felt it was my duty to protect all the emerging life on the planets in our Solar System from discovery. So I hid all the life forms from each other and the Universe as long as I could."

Graham suddenly put it all together, "Do mean that all of our scientific studies about the planets were influenced by you so we wouldn't find life?"

"Yes, Dr Burd. As you found out when you met the Lúthians, there are many many things that you thought were true that you have gotten wrong. I am sorry for deceiving you and your people. It was necessary to keep you safe but now that you have left your planet and are making contact, there is no point in my deception any longer. Your sensors should now see what's really there."

"That's amazing." Anna looked back at Graham, "That means a whole new era, starting over with our study of life in our Solar System."

"There is a problem though," interrupted Anahita: "while you are now visible to the rest of the residents of the Solar System and they to you, you are all now visible to those predators who hunt the galaxy as well. You are in danger in a way you have never experienced. You will have to learn to work together. At some point, there will be visitors and they may not be friendly."

Graham started with more questions, "What are we supposed to do? What are the other races? How long do we have?"

Anahita stood up, "That is for you and your Lúthian friends to work out. As far as how long you have. I don't know, I felt something probing when your vessel visited Lúth, so you will have to be ready. Good luck and we will speak again."

With that Anahita turned and walked down the beach and disappeared.

The world shimmered, they blacked out and suddenly they found themselves in their beds in the crew quarters. Alexey yelled to the others, "They are back!".

- Office of Co-Director of the Centre
for Earth Lúthian Exploration -

DR GRAHAM BURD sat in the steel and leather office chair in the Office of Director of Space Research watching the Director reading his mission report. So much had happened since that first meeting that it was still hard to take in all the new revelations.

Director Richotte leant forward in his desk, "So not only are the Keltans not on the best terms with the Myker and his people, Europa is actually a sentient being who has been using mind control on us and everyone else in the Solar System for hundreds of years? On top of that, there are hostile alien species from outside the Solar System that we may be in danger from?"

Graham shrugged, "That pretty much summarises it. I would say it probably can't get any weirder than that but I think that would be pushing my luck."

The Director just shrugged, "No, at this point, I am getting used to all sorts of weirdness. We will take it under advisement when I brief the EEU commissioners later today. By the way, Alexey has given you high recommendations for your work and Dr Shirshov has asked to continue to work directly with you."

The Director lost his serious face and grinned at him. "It seems you managed to squeeze in a little romance as well?"

Graham flushed, "I think highly of Dr Shirshov as a scientist but I promised her a proper dinner date, so I am taking her to Restaurant Chasse Galerie tonight if you must know."

Richotte smiled, "It's a good choice. Once you two take a few days to relax and get to know each other, I have a new assignment for you both. As you know, we have to redo all our extra-planetary studies now and learn about any other intelligent species on the other planets. We feel you are critical to this effort with all of your experience. Myker has agreed to lend us Elisabeth and Marika and the Crazy Loon to continue exploring the outer planets. We will have teams assigned to the inner planets but I think this is more your area of expertise."

Graham raised his eyebrows, "Lizbeth and her crew are certainly unique. Who would make up the rest of this team?"

"That's up to you and Dr Shirshov, though I understand a certain Keltan mining expert has volunteered along with his symbiote assistant. The final selection can wait until next week so off you go and enjoy your evening!"

Graham stood up and shook the Director's hand then left the room. As he entered the lobby, Anna was waiting for him. He pulled her into his arms and gave her a kiss.

"Anna, it seems we have a lot of work to talk about, but first I owe you a date with some good British Columbia wine and fine Quebec food."

They walked out into the bustle of the city and found a taxi to take them to dinner.

KS "Kaz" Augustin writes genre fiction, but her favourite is space opera. *She cut her teeth on Weinbaum, Kuttner, Russell, Harrison and Smith and loves recreating such atmosphere whenever she can. You can visit her website at* https://www.KSAugustin.com *and sign up to her newsletter at Challis Tower Books at* http://bit.ly/CT-subs

Space opera! What would the Old Solar System be like without plain robust tales of extraterrestrial adventure in the teeth of appalling dangers and long odds? Fortunately we don't have to worry about that dire prospect, as KS Augustin's The Resurrection of Merrick Hardcastle *takes us not back but forward to those thrilling days of yesterday's tomorrows...*

The Resurrection of Merrick Hardcastle

by K S Augustin

MERRICK KNEW HE was only able to keep a hard stare in answer to Judge Ingott's malevolent gaze because he'd been dead for the last fifteen months.

Whatever reputation the judge had, and it was a tough one if one took notice of the televid news, was dwarfed by what Merrick had learnt during his time in the cells. Stories of sentence extensions if a suspect merely looked at Ingott wrongly, whispers of beatings for the more recalcitrant convicts, the encouragement of charge upon additional charge, laid on a man's shoulders till he buckled and broke under the strain.

But Merrick didn't care. Beyond the dome of the Opal Detention Centre, trapped in the centre of a raging inhospitable jungle ringed by swamp, nothing awaited him. Not anymore.

"You stand charged of a serious crime, Mr. Hardcastle," Ingott said, and Merrick was damned if one corner of the judge's mouth didn't twitch with amusement.

He clenched his fists and remained silent.

"Beyond circumstantial, there's enough recorded evidence for me to pronounce the death sentence six times over."

Yes, that would be for the six so-called "Peace Officers" who had trapped his wife in an isolated section of Marine Two. If it were possible, Merrick would have killed each of them again—no, several times over—for what they did. What they had taken. Her life. His dreams.

Ingott's pale eyes were bright and predatory. "Sometimes, I regret the fact that Venus has become civilised, that we've declared a temporary moratorium on the death penalty. Part of me even wonders if that wasn't a motivation for the timing of your crime in the first place."

At this point, any other man would have lunged over the slick, plasteel desk, vaulted onto the judicial platform, grabbed the judge's pudgy throat between two hands, and squeezed. But Merrick knew that was exactly what Ingott and his heavily armed security squad were waiting for. He could tell by the way the uniforms' fingers twitched next to the triggers of their stunguns, how their hips subtly shifted, making sure the shocksticks were ready for instant deployment. In his time at Opal, he had heard a lot of anecdotes about such "amusements".

He didn't move. The judge looked disappointed.

"However, while a death sentence is off the books, it still leaves me in a quandary, Mr. Hardcastle. You see, incarcerating a prisoner for six lifetimes is a very expensive undertaking." He blinked a few times, as if expecting sympathy from the accused. "We're doing well here on Venus, maybe not to the level of Tellus or Europa, but we've made fair strides. At least we're not Mars." A small titter of laughter rippled through the main sentencing room.

Merrick, lips pressed in a straight line, swung his gaze across the enforcers and toadies that let bullies like Ingott and the six Peace Officers trade justice for impunity.

I got six of them for you, Emily.

Then, a second later:

Only six.

"I don't know that I'd call it fair for a man caught so flagrantly killing our planet's finest to get a lifetime of accommodation, free meals and rehabilitation opportunities for the rest of his life." He stretched out a hand. "And I doubt the average Venusian citizen would be happy either, knowing what's being done with their tax money."

Ingott paused theatrically.

"Luckily, there's a solution to our insurmountable problem."

Merrick's head whipped around from regarding the guards and clerks and eyed the judge. He had been prepared to pay for his crime, to be a dead man walking for the rest of his life, but the smirk on Ingott's face told him that there was a worse fate in store. If that were possible.

Ingott leaned forward. "I'm setting you free, Mr. Hardcastle." He saw Merrick's frown of incomprehension and nodded emphatically. "Oh yes, free as a sparrow. Except, unfortunately," he held up a finger, "not on Venus."

He sat back, took up his gavel and banged it once on the specially manufactured strikeplate. The gong reverberated through the room, making the bones in Merrick's head vibrate.

"Merrick Martin Hardcastle, you are herewith revoked of your Venusian citizenship and all associated entitlements and privileges and will be transferred to the ownership—"

Ownership?

"—of the Inner Sun Transworld Mining Corporation for a period of no less than thirty years' hard labour. May God Almighty have mercy on your soul."

It was as if they were killing him all over again. He could only stare in incomprehension at Ingott. Was the man serious? Was he being *sold* to a company? Was he now…a *slave*?

The judge's eyes danced with glee as the guards led Merrick's unresisting form out of the courtroom.

"ALL THE CONDITIONS have been read out to you," said the bored intake clerk. "Your new name becomes valid when you accept the agreement. Do you understand the terms? If so, please repeat that name and the word 'affirmative' at a loud volume and recognisable in the language of your choice."

The trip from the Opal had been swift: bare minutes to collect his meagre possessions before being unceremoniously shoved into a three-person fast transport already waiting for him on the detention centre's landing pad. The glimpse of the transport's exterior hadn't been promising and the interior was no better. The seat upholstery was cracked and stained, the harnesses frayed. There were no portholes, nothing to provide a final glimpse of the planet he had called home for the past thirty-eight standard years of his life.

He was the only passenger.

No guards accompanied him aboard, but he'd been told that the pilot, safely ensconced in a separate compartment in the bullet-shaped nose of the craft, could easily kill him if he proved to be a restless passenger, either by turning off the oxygen supply, stopping the ventilation system or shutting down the cramped cabin's climate controls.

Merrick said nothing but buckled himself in.

The transport rumbled upwards and Merrick's grip on the thin armrests tightened. Maybe they'd evacuate his section once they were clear of Venus and dump him in space? He'd heard of people dying from explosive decompression and a part of him even wished for such a death but, as time dragged on, it became obvious that Ingott had been correct. The Venus Justice Authority had sold him to Mercury and, as the metal plating beneath his prison-issue slippers began heating up, he knew they were at last approaching his new home.

He was met at the docking ring by the intake clerk, his voice as equally dead as his eyes, his expression not changing by so much as a flicker. His words, however, were horrifying. Martin Jones (his new name) was sentenced to corporate servitude for a minimum of thirty years, after which he *may* be eligible for parole. His new identity would be the one he wore for the rest of his life, Merrick Hardcastle's demise only one computer operation away. Merrick couldn't stop staring at the clerk's index finger, unwaveringly poised over a green button on a small console full of buttons and lights. Was that the movement that would end his life? Was that button the one that would declare him dead throughout the System? The clerk didn't notice Merrick's fixation, but droned on.

Should he be approved for parole, he was never to set foot on Venus, Tellus or the Jovian moons—the most prosperous regions of the solar system—for as long as he lived. Seventy-five per cent of his earnings would be garnished by the Venusian authorities as "compensation" for his crimes and basic food, accommodation and medical care would be provided, in return for mining duties. Small bonuses may be paid for the mandatory testing of new industrial prototypes.

"What happens if I don't agree?" Merrick asked. "Don't give you an 'affirmative'?"

The clerk stared at him and his index finger curled towards his palm. "Think you're the first to come up with that line? Your transport has already undocked and is halfway back to Venus, but feel free to take a step back through the ring if you'd prefer."

Suicide.

"And what if I don't want to be one of your guinea pigs?"

"Not want to bravely test and report back on the very latest in space technology?" The clerk shrugged. "Then there's no medical or bed for you, party boy." His voice hardened. "See, I read about your case. You may have had your fun murderin' those six Peacers, but here on Mercury, we do things differently. Disagree with the conditions and we toss you into a dungeon and throw away the magkey. Know what I'm sayin'?"

Merrick should have said no, should have told them where they could stuff those "conditions" of theirs, but he was too weak. He had loved Emily like life itself, but couldn't bring himself to deliberately end his own.

Squeezing his eyes in shame, he let his head droop.

"Affirmative," he muttered.

"What was that? Couldn't hear ya."

Merrick took a deep breath, lifted his head and opened his eyes. "Martin Jones. Affirmative," he repeated, more loudly.

"Thought you might say that, Mr. Jones. Contract accepted. Welcome to Mercury."

IT WAS A hellhole, in its most literal sense. Seen via one of the many schematics that dotted the complex, the Inner Sun Transworld Mining Corporation resembled a giant ant farm. The company made its money carving precious metals and minerals out of the solid core of the small planet, then saved additional expense by repurposing the ensuing caverns. After fifty years of operation, a maze of chambers had built up, connected to each other via straight or lazily spiralling corridors, each corridor just wide enough to take the lumbering mining equipment on which the planet's economy depended.

Merrick learnt all about it during his month-long orientation course. How the forerunners of the corporation had braved fiery deaths while landing on Birchfeld Plateau on the dark side of Mercury. How their very first action was to drill into the protective shell of the fiery planet, making it their refuge from the plasma storms that wreaked havoc on the surface. How they discovered that most rare of metals, palladium, often intertwined with that most coveted: gold. If the pioneers of Inner Sun Transworld had fantasised about a certain path to success, they couldn't have come up with a better way to make money.

But man paid for such riches. Hardly anybody ventured out onto the surface, not even to that delicate ribbon of terrain that marked the boundary line between indescribable heat and bitter cold. Most stayed safe, miles underground, while the Sun's corona waged war with Mercury's eerily smooth surface, solar flares of immense power melting and reshaping the small planet's sunside terrain in the space of minutes. Instead, their thoughts and dreams turned outwards, to talk of retirement on one of the outer planets. The blue cool of Tellus. The majestic windswept splendour of Mars. The self-sufficiency of Europa. The dripping rainforests of Venus.

That last one was what captured the miners' imaginations the most, and every mention of his previous home sent a shaft of longing and sorrow through Merrick's body.

Venus. Rain. Water. Falling from the ever-cloudy sky. No fees. No shortages.

"Just stretch out your hand," was the usual talk in the canteens, "and it'll fall into your palm. You don't even need to do nothin'. Water all around for the taking."

And Merrick knew it was true. Mercury, with only its mineral wealth, had to ship in everything it needed: food, equipment, clothes. But the one thing that cost it the most was water from Venus. There were chambers where vegetables were grown under giant lamps, where even some livestock were kept, but they all depended on one thing. Water. It was the most precious and rare of resources and so became an object of longing for the few thousand who called the mining planet home.

Water was guarded even more preciously than oxygen, needing to come via specially fortified heavy spacefreighters from Venus. That jacked up the price, making the liquid too precious to waste on the mere task of cleaning. Merrick had to get used to the custom of strigilling, using a thin curved piece of metal to scrape the sweat and dirt off his skin. He thought it a disgusting habit but, over time, got used to it, as he got used to most things.

The next most valuable element was oxygen. It was the breath of life and couldn't be monitored as strictly, but there were obvious privileges associated with it. As a result, the job of atmosphere scrubbing was hotly contested. Unlike the miners or small team of suiters, the scrubbers worked deep in the shielded processing plants, the safest areas in the planet, and their jobs gave them opportunity to siphon off pure oh-two and sell intoxicating sniffs of it on the informal market. The conditions of his indenture had made it clear that Merrick couldn't ever expect to get such a job. He was to be part of the mining teams, unless a special assignment sent him to the surface to test equipment that was to be used under extreme conditions throughout the system, a job called being a "suiter". The judge had made the priority explicit—Merrick was a suiter first and a miner second, meaning his remaining life could be measured in months, if not hours. Merrick would have thanked Ingott for such consideration but didn't think it would have been appreciated.

The third most valuable resource on Mercury was women. There weren't many in the tunnels, beyond the medical and some administrative staff. The senior managers had wives who lived with them down in the tunnels, but nobody else on the planet did. If a woman had a brain, she took an employment contract on Mercury, worked her two years for a fat reward then left the moment the last salary (with obscene bonus) hit her account. Only the crazy ones stayed—the ones who didn't have lives to go back to, or the ones who wanted the money, or the ones who thought they were doing what they did for a "higher purpose". They weren't the most stable of women and Mercury was full of unstable men, so maybe they suited each other. But every time he caught a glance at the sway of hips or heard the feminine lilt in an animated voice, all Merrick could think of was Emily, and the thought of his murdered wife was enough to extinguish any interest he may have had towards a member of the fairer sex.

In such a way, by surviving rather than living, Merrick grimaced and toiled through his first two years on Mercury. He came to be known as a good worker, strong, smart and dependable, although often on a short fuse. He found the fight scene and, off duty, worked out his pent-up aggression by pounding other men into the dust for rewards of water, oxygen or extra food rations. He was frequently sent to the surface to test the suits that would then be either refined or mass produced and sold throughout the system. "Designed on Europa—Tested on Mercury" became a standard tag-line that blurred into the scorching background of his new life. Merrick didn't mind being a suiter because it meant extra pay and welcome solitude from the tightly-packed warrens of sweating humanity working beneath the planet's crust. He thought he would end his life on Mercury, paying off his debt till either a fight down below or a sudden solar flare on the surface got him, and he was grimly resigned to such an end.

What he hadn't bargained on was a special prototype suit, the stubborn insistence of Comet Wear and a fateful walk down a narrow ribbon of rock between death and death.

"I DON'T SEE why I need to." Merrick's voice was toughened steel.

His group supervisor, Viktor Hall, tilted his head and grimaced. The man was shorter than Merrick but iron all the way through. Even his voice—rough and rumbling—reminded Merrick of abrasive ore.

"You want a reason why? Because Comet Wear is payin' for it, that's why."

Merrick shook his head. "Twenty minutes out is standard procedure, and *everyone* pays for that. You're asking for an hour. Nobody's done that before."

Hall threw his hands up. "That's because nobody tagged on extra credits for an extension before." He stared intently at his subordinate then sighed. "Look, Jones, I know it's against the rules, but we do a lotta things here against the rules. According to 'the rules', you shoulda been pitched out an airlock for the illegal fights you been indulging yourself in these past years. Not to mention the purchase of those informal water rations."

Merrick remained silent, unwilling to admit his weakness. He was—slash that, *had been*—a Venusian, used to the regular silken touch of water over his body. As red and scraped as he felt after a strigilling, it wasn't the same as a rinsing with cleansing jets of clear, sparkling, astringent liquid. He remembered drinking the water as it tumbled from faucets and showerheads, something he couldn't do with the sticky oil he had to rub onto his dirty skin before scraping the softened muck off.

"Look," Hall said, interrupting his musings, "you do this and we give you a bonus. That's only fair, ain't it?"

Merrick focused on him. That was the kind of language they both understood. "What kind of bonus?"

"One week doubled water rations. All legit. No under-the-panel stuff."

"I may not survive the extra forty minutes outside. One *month's* doubled rations."

"Are you nuts? You wanna start a stampede? You remember what happened the last time some lunatic dropped word of his bonus. Inner Sun had to terminate two dozen asses and the rest of us had to work overtime to maintain production levels. Nobody wants somethin' like *that* happening again." Hall hesitated, obviously calculating something in his head. "Maybe I can give you two weeks and double off your monthly loan payment," that's what they called the debt every indentured was saddled with. A 'loan', "but all that's on the quiet, you understand? You let on to anybody else what our deal is and we terminate *you* like we terminated those others. That's my final offer, Jones."

Two weeks of feeling like a human being again? The next twenty-eight years loomed, hard and lonely, in front of Merrick. He had barely made a dent in the debt he owed to the Venus Justice Authority, so the month of double loan repayments didn't mean that much. Then an imp of mischief inserted itself into his thinking. So what if he died wearing Comet Wear's stupid new suit? What could anyone do? Sue him in Hell for outstanding sums? But if he survived, he'd have two weeks of pretending he wasn't cowering inside the shell of a planet so close to the Sun that, even outside, he hardly ever saw the stars. Two weeks of pretending he had a real life, and that Emily was just outside the door, waiting for him. Two weeks of fantasy.

"All right," Merrick finally said. "I'll do it."

Hall frowned. "You sure? One hour outside? Minimum?"

Merrick nodded firmly. "I'm sure."

But Hall still wasn't taking any chances. The moment he got Merrick's confirmation, he hustled him into the upper levels, snapping commands through his wrist-com as the lift tubes sped them closer to the surface. Already, Merrick felt a fine sheen of sweat beginning to cover his skin.

They stopped at Level Three. It was a bare place, with smooth hard floors and a long corridor lined with anonymous grey panels. Some were wall; others, Merrick knew from experience, were doors that led into small briefing rooms. Hall motioned him into the closest room and, on the table, Merrick saw the cause of his potential demise: the Comet Wear Extreme Endurance Suit.

It looked like a high-quality piece of merchandise. After completing more than a dozen previous assignments, Merrick could tell that a lot of thought had gone into its design. He walked over to it and lifted part of it.

Heavy. That meant lots of insulation.

He peered down the sleeves. Internal tubing, covered by a smooth fabric overlay. No snagging.

It was quite a job to turn the suit over. By the door, Hall merely stood and watched, not saying a word.

Merrick identified the oxygen inlet and carbon dioxide outlet. Clearly marked. Not much room for error there. There was another outlet on the lower back. He bent down and read the small label. "Waste disposal."

"What's the endurance figure on this suit?" he asked, straightening again.

"This one's meant for the 'roid miners out in the Belt. Comet will be advertising ten hours max."

Merrick nodded. That explained why they wanted an extended workout on the surface.

The helmet was another revelation. Merrick was used to a solid alloy case with a fair-sized multi-visored front window. Comet had given them a completely transparent bowl.

"The miners need to know what's coming," Hall said without prompting. "Peripheral vision, the need to turn their heads and see if a rogue is bearing down on 'em."

That could mean either rogue rock or rogue miner. Merrick nodded again, turning the high-tech goldfish bowl over and over in his hands. "How safe is it?"

"They say it's stronger than the standard materials used. It'll bend but won't break." There was a note of doubt in Hall's voice that he couldn't disguise. "Filters are built into the glass and activated by the control panel on your left forearm. The usual. But it uses some special tech to change the glass. Electromagnetic induction it's called or something fancy like that."

Merrick set down the helmet, only half listening. "Okay," he said, turning to face his supervisor. "I'll get suited, then I'll be ready to go."

"You sure?" Hall was watching him closely. "Right now?"

Merrick shrugged. Having already agreed, he wasn't going to back down. "Why not?"

His supervisor finally nodded. "Alright. You know the drill. Strip off, get into the suit. We'll plug you in and seal you up on the way to the surface. I'll go rustle up a tech. Meet us at Elevator One."

Merrick didn't watch as Hall left the room. He pulled out a chair, sat down and took off his creased, grimy boots, followed by his trousers. He left his short-sleeved, close-fitting shirt on and reached for the suit, unzipping the back and folding himself into it. His feet slid into the integrated shoes, the plasgel moving and moulding itself to his contours. In a few minutes, the heat from his feet would activate the gel and it would harden. He stood and walked around to make sure that he still had enough room to shift within the footwear. He then spent a few minutes attaching the plumbing fixtures to his body. He'd never had to use such equipment before but was happy to note that the connections were obvious, if a bit alarming to look at. After he was hooked up, he took a few more experimental steps and grimaced. It felt as if he was carrying a coarse-skinned basketball between his legs. He only hoped the sensation would lessen over time. The gloves were last. They were bulky, but they locked into place with a satisfying click. He looked down at the small rectangular panel on his forearm and pressed a few of the raised buttons. They gave good feedback, even through the thick material encasing each digit. The rest, the helmet and the backpack every suiter wore, he would need help with.

Rotating his shoulders, Merrick felt the weight of the suit as it moved against his body. It was comfortable and didn't constrict movement. As long as he didn't think about the tubes snaking out around his groin area, he couldn't remember wearing better. He shuddered to think what Comet Wear was going to sell the market-ready suit for. Probably the price of a small shuttle. Then again, for the 'roiders, it was probably worth it.

After a quick scan of the room, Merrick picked up the helmet and headed for Elevator One, his thoughts focused on his upcoming reward.

Two weeks of double water rations.

And all for just sixty minutes bouncing around on Mercury's surface. He couldn't wait to collect.

Hall and a suit tech were already waiting for him when he entered Elevator One's anteroom, the shielded backpack resting between them. Without saying a word, the tech turned him around and completed the suiting up.

"Lot of 'roiders are solitary," Merrick said, as much to try out the helmet's comms system as to satisfy his curiosity. "They're not going to have someone around to help them into their suits."

Hall moved to a console propped up against a wall and pressed the two-way comms button. "Prototype," he said, before launching into instructions. His voice came through the helmet loud and clear. "They want ten minutes in the hot zone, forty on the dark side, the remainder in between. Comms will be on throughout. Hop around a bit. Jump. Bend over. Kneel. Get up. The tech is fitting a toolbelt on each thigh now." Merrick felt tugs against his legs. "Take out each tool, use it a bit, put it back. Report on ease of use and quality of tools. Gloves too."

Merrick's lips twitched. "Is that all? No flaming hoops of fire to jump through?"

He felt two taps on his upper arm as the tech indicated that he was done. Everything was ready to go.

Hall ignored his attempt at levity and jerked a thumb at a wide metal door. "We'll be timing you."

Merrick glanced at the hatch leading to the Evacuation Room. He turned his head and was pleasantly surprised to see that his line of vision wasn't suddenly cut off. Maybe Comet Wear was onto something. Hall looked expectant.

Merrick grinned. "What are we waiting for?"

BRAVADO WAS EASY with a hundred feet of rock between the threshold of safety and the interior of a furnace, but Merrick's cocky self-confidence evaporated as the elevator lifted him upwards. Two thousand people toiled within Mercury for the Inner Sun Transworld Mining Corporation, but fewer than a hundred had ever walked its surface.

The elevator shuddered to a halt and the large doors haltingly slid open. Merrick felt the change in surface beneath his boots as he exited the metal floor and stepped onto gravel. He was in a deep rectangular well, protection for the frail electronics and mechanisms of the elevator. Before him was a heavily fortified stairway hewn into rock. He took a breath before ascending the roughly crafted steps…and stepped out into a wondrous vista.

The top of the stairs was facing the Sun. Without needing to do a thing, his helmet darkened and he felt vibrations from his backpack ripple against his spine as the refrigeration function kicked in. Still, nothing could distract him from the awe-inspiring sight of being so close to the centre of humanity's solar system. The Sun dominated the heavens, its bulk and brightness crowding out sight of any other stellar object. This close, and with various protective filters activated, it appeared as a living thing, pulsing before him in tones of yellow, orange and brown. Licks of red-tinged gold played across the star's immense surface, like sprites chasing each other in a game. It was as if Merrick was gazing straight into another world comprised of beings who were both more powerful and more playful than he.

He looked down from his vantage point between the planet's hot and cold zones, and watched as pools of molten rock facing the Sun solidified, melted and flowed into each other. Small plates would darken to stone as they hardened, then fissure open again as the stresses of heat broke them apart. Like ice floes, regions of cooling rock knocked against each other, collided to form higher, angled structures, or disappeared under a glowing river of molten minerals. It was a slow, rippling dance as old as the solar system itself.

Merrick took a few moments to lose himself in the spectacle before he reported in.

"Jones here. I'm on the surface."

There was a pause before Hall answered him and, when he did, his voice was crackling with static. This close to the Sun, a lot of the technologies the rest of the system took for granted were next to useless.

"...have started the clock...you walk...DMZ? I'll let... when time's up."

That's what the workers on Mercury called the thin strip of rock that circled the planet between the infernal tempest in front of him and a landscape of near absolute zero behind him. The DMZ. The Demilitarised Zone. The only region of relative safety on the planet's surface.

He knew what he had to do—he really didn't need Hall babysitting him—but his supervisor was also a psychological link. It had been before his time, but Merrick had heard of suiters losing their minds on the surface, unable to withstand the illusion of a giant ball of gas about to fall on them. The problem was, nobody knew whether a particular man would crack or not until he was on the surface and, in that case, the first test was also his last. But what some men couldn't cope with enthralled Merrick. Reluctantly, he tore his gaze away and turned, dutifully trudging forward along the DMZ and careful to keep one side of his suit facing the Sun at all times. To be alone with his thoughts was already a delight. Inner Sun packed them in like sardines below the surface and nobody could cough without at least a dozen others hearing. But on the surface, he was surrounded by blessed silence and in the presence of the most magnificent object in the system. If his suit malfunctioned, if he slipped and fell into the turbid sea of lava, if a solar flare flicked out towards him at the wrong moment, he would be dead within seconds. It was a terrifying prospect. But also exhilarating.

"...around now," Hall said.

Merrick did as he was told, turning and walking back the way he had come, interspersing his walk with small jumps, bends and kneels. He knew the suit would be recording each of his actions on a data unit that the techs would extract once he finished the trial and descended to the safety of Mercury's interior.

He did the requisite time at the very edge of the DMZ, as close to the eternally bubbling pools of lava as he could get while still remaining safe, making sure all sides of his suit were exposed to the heat and hard radiation of the Sun. Near the end, however, he noted that the internal temperature of his suit was rising, something the atmosphere-control unit in his backpack, with its deeper vibrations, was trying gamely to combat. Frowning, he looked down to the suit's control panel on his left forearm, but the status indicator still glowed green. Still, he moved further into the DMZ with a sense of relief, and carried on with the exercises that Comet Wear had paid for.

"...going now?" Hall's voice interrupted.

"I'm in the DMZ now," Merrick replied, "just running through some sequences."

"Remember....most time...dark...tools..."

Merrick nodded, even though he knew Hall couldn't see him. Although the hot and DMZ sections were important to the suit manufacturer, it was really performance in the cold zone that interested them. After all, 'roid miners didn't usually ply their trade while surfing the Sun's corona.

"Heading there now," he said.

The dark side of Mercury was a complete contrast to the light. The light side was dynamic, in constant movement, smooth and blindingly bright. The dark side was static, sharp-edged, and plunged into eternal abyssal darkness.

Merrick turned his back on the Sun and trudged across

the DMZ, watching as his shadow slowly melted into the approaching gloom. Here, if he looked straight ahead, he'd finally see some stars, the white pinpoints of the brightest ones steady against the relative blackness of space. He did this as he reached the fuzzy border between light and dark, idly wondering what constellation he was currently peering at, when the ground beneath his boots suddenly gave way. Flailing, Merrick reached out, attempting to grab something, but there was nothing to grab onto. He tried to gain purchase by kicking back with a leg, but it didn't help. In a sequence of movements that seemed to stretch out to eternity, Merrick felt himself fall and tumble head over feet, down a steep slope he should have taken notice of. Mistakes like that could get a suiter killed, he thought to himself, trying to capture an outcrop, a large boulder, an angle of rock, *something!*, but failing. He felt an impact to his fishbowl helmet that caused his head to jerk, saw a quick flash of multicoloured light in his left field of vision, then it was darkness and vertigo as he continued to plunge downwards.

Somersaulting in zero point four *g* shouldn't have hurt, but it did. When Merrick finally came to a sliding stop, he felt as though he'd been put through a commercial vortex sorter. His breath came in loud gasps and his ribs hurt.

"Hall," he called, "I've taken a fall, but I, I seem to be alright." He steadied his breathing and listened for a moment. "Suit seems to be holding, but I don't know where I am. Get a team with a salvage winch ready, just in case."

To his consternation, he didn't even hear static but a dead silence.

Raising his voice, Merrick tried again. "Hall? Hall, can you hear me?"

There was no response.

Groaning, Merrick lifted his head and looked around, but all he could see was blackness.

Of course! He needed to reset the filters in his helmet.

The fall must have messed with the automatic controls. With effort, he lifted his left arm but couldn't see a thing. With his right hand, he felt for the rim of the panel, oriented his fingers and punched at where he thought the right buttons should be located. Nothing happened till the second press, when his surroundings were suddenly bathed in the faintest green, except for a spear of black to his left and...what he was lying on. Frowning, Merrick looked right towards a far crater wall then back down at the ground, wondering why contours of rock appeared so fuzzy and far beneath him. That should only happen if...if...he was somehow suspended in mid-air!

With an energy he didn't know he still had, Merrick gasped and scrambled backwards across the strangely smooth surface, panic overriding the pain radiating throughout his body. His gloves could feel solidity, so why was his helmet telling him nothing was there? He stumbled against a rising slope of rock and threw himself against it, getting as far away from the mysterious surface as he could, air escaping his lungs in panicked spurts.

He lay there for many minutes, willing his body to relax, for his ribs to stop hurting, for his comms unit to start working again. From the corner of his eye, he noticed the panel on his forearm blinking amber and red. Something was wrong, but he didn't know what. There was writing beneath the warning lights but it was too dark to make out the letters. Something else to inform Comet Wear about. He took a deep experimental breath and held it for a moment before exhaling, but his suit still felt okay. No obvious signs of a puncture. The heater was working. Maybe the refrigeration unit had taken a hit?

Merrick angled himself up on one elbow. There was no feeling of dislocation, no betraying hiss. His backpack still appeared to be firmly attached. His head was turned, staring across the slope's transverse, drawn to the far end of the crater and the smooth nothingness in between. The crater bottom was a hazy blur a dozen feet beneath him, but it was still visible, when it shouldn't have been.

"Think," he said to himself. "Why didn't you fall down there? What exactly were you on?"

When he thought he got control of himself, when the tremors in his hands subsided, he let himself sink back against the slope and stared upwards. The Sun's nimbus was visible directly overhead, dimming the starscape.

"What *was* that I fell on?" he asked aloud.

Hall would be going crazy right now. Or maybe he was expecting some communications glitch to occur. They weren't unheard of. How long would it take before a rescue team was despatched? Would they find him with all the electromagnetic disturbances around?

With growing impatience, Merrick finally levered himself into a sitting position and stared out over the mysterious surface he had landed on. Blinking hard in an effort to clear his eyesight, he ignored the blinking warnings and punched another filter button. This time he saw a play of yellow light overlay the green. That didn't look right. He deactivated that and tried a third filter that turned everything black, except for glints of silver deep below the surface. One at a time, sometimes with several together, he cycled through the filters. He could take a guess at what each did, but didn't know for sure as it was too dark to read the text on the small control panel.

He went through the overlays several times, trying to make sense of what he could see, and his eyes widened when he finally realised what it was he was looking at. The coloured lines were sharp at the crater wall but grew fuzzier as they descended because…they were following the contours of rock plunging deep beneath the surface Merrick had collided with. *Beneath* the surface. Lines that he shouldn't be seeing if the surface was also rock. Which meant that the surface of the crater he was in *wasn't* rock. With rising excitement, Merrick cursed the clumsiness of his gloves as he looked from crater floor to rim and back again, shocked into silence when he got the answer he was hoping for. Somehow, he had stumbled across a lake of frozen water!

Ice! On Mercury!

How? When? Why? He knew he couldn't answer those questions, but it didn't matter. All that mattered was that he had found a lake of ice seventeen feet deep in one of Mercury's craters. And where there was one, he thought to himself, there must be others.

"Hall!" he shouted, with a tongue suddenly thick. "Can you hear me?"

Silence.

With effort, Merrick turned over onto his stomach and began the arduous task of climbing back up the steep slope, stopping whenever his body protested. But at least he could still breathe. At least there was air in his suit.

When he reached the summit, he fumbled for a pick from one of the tool belts and stuck it into the ground. It would do as a temporary marker. Having done that, he tried getting to his feet, but couldn't.

"Hall," he rasped.

His head spun as he half-crawled in the direction of the elevator. Or, at least, where he thought the elevator should be.

"I can't...."

Why was his body still hurting? Why did his limbs feel so heavy? Why was he feeling so dizzy? Why didn't Hall answer?

Blearily, he thought he recognised a landmark. If he was right, the Sun should be to his east.

Why was it getting so hard to think? East! East was... right.

Merrick, blinking hard, used to the limited-vision helmets, shifted his shoulders to bring the helmet around. He gazed at the huge pulsing orb for a moment, before its heat seared through the damaged left-hand section of his helmet.

Too late, he remembered the flashing warnings. And now he knew what they meant.

Fifteen feet from safety, Martin Jones screamed his pain. But nobody heard him.

TRAVIS INGOTT STOPPED and stared at the old damaged suit on display outside the Controller's office within Inner Sun Transworld Corporation's brand-new (and plush) tunnel complex. The words "Comet Wear" were still faintly visible running across the suit's torso and down one leg. The antique helmet, with cracks crisscrossing it, was a mess.

"That's the suit that changed history for us," the aide beside him said, her voice full of pride.

Travis tried hiding his distaste. Yes, he knew all about the suit. Ever since *that suit*, things hadn't gone well for Venus. The discovery of ice on Mercury two decades ago had cut water shipments from his planet to almost zero. Now Tellus had moved into first place on Mercury's trade table, sending foodstuffs to a hungry and prospering population on the system's innermost planet. Europa was sending engineers, experienced in low-delta exotic technologies, and the Outer Consortium was buying up palladium as fast as Inner Sun could plough it out of the rock.

Travis hated everything about Mercury: its disconcerting lack of gravity, the upside-down settlements beneath the surface, the smugness of its workers. But, most of all, Travis hated the fact that he'd been sent by the Venusian authorities to try and negotiate larger shipments of precious minerals from what had previously been the solar system's penal colony.

"And see if you can't sell them more goddamned water," the Trade Minister had growled, irritation lacing his voice. "Lie about it if you have to but we need a two hundred per cent increase at the very least."

It was all very well for the minister to give him orders,

but he didn't know the gruelling conditions Travis had so far endured: transport on a ship barely above scrap; only one assistant, to be left at their assigned quarters during the negotiations themselves; accommodation that looked like it dated back to the foundation of Inner Sun; not to mention the appalling food. Travis had tolerated all this for the past two standard weeks because he had to. Now, finally, he was poised to meet the power on Mercury's throne and this simpering fool was delaying him.

"Let's get moving," he said. "I didn't come here to sightsee." He knew he was being rude, but he didn't care. The young aide was a nobody, one of a wave of poor anonymous young women who'd been drawn to the system's newest money frontier. He, on the other hand, had descended from one of the most renowned families on Venus. The difference could not have been more stark.

The aide seemingly took no offence, bobbing her head and gesturing Travis further down the corridor to a set of double doors. The door panels were made of a black ore. They were ornate, garish, Travis thought. They depicted an underground industrial scene, each figure and accent line meticulously outlined in gleaming gold and palladium. Tasteless. The aide pressed a decorative pin on the lapel of her jacket and the panels slid apart.

The office itself was large but sparse. Modern. High-quality. Subtly lit and furnished. None of the words that could be applied to his so-called "hotel room".

Travis had been briefed on the way to Mercury, knew what to expect, but as he faltered to a stop, he realised that he was still unprepared for the reality of what confronted him. Behind him, the doors shut and he knew the woman had not accompanied him inside.

The Controller of Inner Sun Transworld Mining Corporation politely stood up. He was a tall man, broad-shouldered and still trim, despite his obvious years. But that wasn't what made Travis draw a quick breath. It was as if the Controller's face was divided in two: the right side normal, handsome even; the left, burnt black, wrinkled and immobile. Two eyes, one natural, one bionic, tracked him as he edged closer.

Swallowing his distaste, Travis stuck out a hand. "Thank you for making the time to see me, Controller, er, Jones. I'm Travis Ingott. I represent the Trade Authority of Venus."

The Controller's right eyebrow twitched. "Ingott? I think I know that name. Any relation to Judge Ingott of the Venus Justice Authority?"

That was more like it! Travis straightened and couldn't conceal the triumph that curled his lips. "That's, I mean, that *was* my father," he said. "In his time, he was one of the most respected magistrates of the inner system."

Controller Martin Jones indicated the empty chair next to Travis.

"In that case," he said, "please take a seat. I'm looking forward to our negotiations."

Dylan T. Jeninga is an enthusiast of the fantastic yet (perhaps marginally) credible, and it was this interest that drew him to science fiction when he was a young boy, and more recently to the classic tales of our Solar System as it ought to have been. Born near the Wisconsin / Illinois border on the last day of 1993, he now lives in Chicago with his wife (who, the reader may be sure, has a hand in shaping everything he creates). He works as an improvisational actor / hopefully temporary shop clerk, and he writes everything from realistic adventures among the planets to sojourns to the distant stars.

Tales of monstrous creatures on distant worlds are of course staples of the Old Solar System, as they are in every other genre of imaginative literature from the Epic of Gilgamesh on. In Pirates of Titan, *Dylan T. Jeninga adds a lively contribution to that classic theme. As in many of the best such stories, the monster in question is not quite what it seems...*

The Colorless Colossus of the Cold

Dylan T. Jeninga

S HERIFF GILMA LIKED a good show as much as the next guy.

For sure, you didn't get many of 'em in Conamara. Or probably on Europa at all, for that matter.

And it wasn't like she didn't like seeing ponies and Marsrats and Venusian Mantidonts and frankly any animal that wasn't a weird Europan fish - ice fishing was the only real way to make a living on that snowball moon, and Gilma was one of the few people in town who didn't get up every morning, pack up a sledge, auger and nets, and then snowmobile out into the white. In fact, about the only time she ever left her cabin was when Jesus or somebody else was drilling through the ice too close to town.

Yep, a dazzling display of otherworldly wonderment was exactly what she and the townsfolk could use to get them through the winter, especially when summer was years away and wouldn't get much warmer anyways. Which was why, when the Mikkel Mobile Menagerie and One-Ring Circus slid into town with the monthly caravan, Gilma had gone out with the mayor to personally welcome the performers. And, in Gilma's case, to catch a peek at the critters.

Only that was three weeks ago. Overnight a glowing tent city had popped up, sheltered behind the same hard-packed windwall that protected Conamara from the intense glacial gale from the north, and it seemed the performers only ever came into town to drink and get into trouble with the local desirable youths. It wasn't the kind of show Gilma had hoped for. It was the kind that bred paperwork.

Finally, after rescuing a drunk, idiotic roustabout from freezing his face off outside Lecia's Cantina one evening, Gilma'd had enough. She marched into the circus camp and burst into the biggest tent, which turned out to be home to a pair of elephants. With wide-eyed apologies to the disturbed beasts she quickly stepped out, asked a passerby for directions, and tapped gently on the taut entrance to the Ringmaster's tent.

"Come in," came the irritated reply. The Sheriff quickly entered and zipped the door shut behind her, cutting off a flurry of flakes. "What is it?"

The Ringmaster, Majorie Mikkel, looked smaller out of her snowsuit. She was diminutive, almost, with bright eyes, a nose that was clearly familiar with frostbite, and a booming voice that outmatched her size. Gilma unclasped the hood of her own snowsuit so the circus director and proprietor would recognize her.

"Oh, Sheriff! I'm sorry, I thought you were someone else. Take a seat!"

Gilma obliged, plopping her heavy form into a folding chair near the thermal unit in the corner. It was nice for a tent, she thought, decorated with photos and a dresser and a real mattress and even one of those desks with a mirror on it performers were supposed to own. Mikkel was seated in front of it, assembling something Gilma recognized.

"That a K&M blaster?" She asked, eyebrow cocked.

"Oh, this? Yes, good eye! This one, though, is modified only to stun. A necessity when dealing with large creatures, you understand."

Almost imperceptibly, the tent began to shake, as if it were shivering. Ice quake. Common enough, what with big, fat Jupiter in the sky, tugging on Europa's innards. Neither Gilma nor Mikkel acknowledged it: if a quake got bad, there wouldn't be much they could do anyways.

The tiny Ringmaster got up and trundled over to a table with an electric burner, coffee machine and microwave. "Coffee?"

"Sure, thanks.

"Cream? Sugar?"

"Black, thanks."

Gilma watched Mikkel fill one mug to the brim, then reach for a second mug which she filled only halfway, making up the rest with cream and a heaping helping of sugar. Gilma winced, that stuff was pricey.

"I have an old friend who owns a number of plantations on Ganymede," Mikkel said, apparently reading Gilma's expression, "he sends me some necessities every few months, just as a token of brotherly love. If you ever make it out there, I will introduce you!"

Gilma returned the ringmaster's shining smile. "I appreciate it, but I'm pretty much a homebody."

"Ah, too bad. The Solar System is a wondrous place, I have seen much of it."

"I bet." The coffee was good. Gilma tried not to drink it too quickly.

"Not to worry, we are preparing a spectacle that will bring the stars down here to your charming little village."

"Actually, Ms. Mikkel, that's what I wanted to talk about."

"My friends call me Majorie, and I always like to think the local law officials are my friends."

"Right, sorry. Majorie. I wanted to have a chat about when you're going to be putting on this show of yours. It's been three weeks, and your people are starting to cause trouble."

She might not have had much police work to do in Conamara most of the time, but nevertheless Gilma prided herself on her perceptiveness and ability to read people. The Ringmaster was starting to sweat, and she wasn't even the one sitting next to the thermal unit.

"Oh? Trouble? Of what kind?"

"Drunken disorderlies, homewrecking, getting in fights. It's making my life a real hell, I'll be honest."

"I'm deeply sorry, Sheriff. If you give me names of the offenders, I will see to it that they are duly disciplined."

"Appreciate it, Mikkel. But what I really want to do is find out when your show will be on. I think your folks need something to keep them busy."

Mikkel swayed, tapping her finger on her mirror-desk (vainery? vanery?), seemingly lost in thought. Finally, she looked at the gun by her hand.

"Sheriff, I have not been entirely honest with you."

There's a surprise, Gilma thought. She sipped her coffee.

"Mikkel's Mobile Menagerie and Circus did not come to Conamara solely to delight and astonish." Her eyes were hard, frozen. "I am hunting the Colorless Colossus of the Cold."

Gilma stared. She set her coffee down. She laughed.

"I am serious, Sheriff!"

"Right, right, I believe you," Gilma waved. "A big monster would interest an animal person like you - only, you're not from here, are you? Europa, I mean?"

The Ringmaster eyed her quizzically. "I hail from New Memphis, on Ganymede."

The sheriff nodded. "I thought so. Look, Mikkel, sounds like someone's got your rocket. The Colossus isn't real."

"Not real?"

"I'm afraid not. The only things aside from people on Europa are fish. Now, I'll admit, some of those fish get pretty colossal, and I know a few people who could be called 'colorless'. But a great, ten-foot-tall, fish-stealing, snow-white beast with fangs and claws and glowing eyes - it's an icefisher's tale. Admittedly, it's a new one, I hadn't even heard it 'til a month ago, so you can't really be blamed for falling for it."

"But it's not a myth, ma'am. I've seen it."

Gilma stopped short of accusing the ringmaster of trying to pull one over on her. She seemed to believe her claim. Instead, she said, "So, you're after the Colossus. Alright. But that still doesn't explain why the show hasn't gone on."

Mikkel fidgeted, and it was obvious there was something else she had yet to come clean about. Gilma waited patiently.

"My master of beasts, Andre, and I have been following stories of the Colossus from town to town. Interviewing witnesses, examining tracks. We arrive somewhere, he spends a week or so out on the ice, looking for clues, and then returns and the show, indeed, goes on. But this time he hasn't come back."

Gilma's expression hardened. "There's a man missing? In my jurisdiction? And you didn't tell me?"

The ringmaster regarded her with alarm. "Oh, no! I didn't mean to keep it from you! I was sure he would come back, I said to myself, 'he has stayed out for a long while before.' Except now so much time has passed, I fear…"

"That he's dead. You should have told me."

"Again, I am sorry. I fear my little group has caused nothing but endless trouble for you. As soon as the next caravan arrives, I promise, we will be gone."

Gilma emptied mug and left it on the floor by her chair.

"I'm going to get a sledge together. We're going looking for this Andre. You and me."

Without waiting for an answer, she got up and closed her hood. Angry as she was, she still made sure to seal the door on the tent on her way out.

SHE SWUNG BY the general store to let her only deputy, Miguel, know where she was going and why. Since Miguel also happened to own the shop, she picked up filtered water, thermal unit batteries, emergency fish paste and a pair of flashlights at a discount. Then she went back to her cabin, put another layer on under her snowsuit, strapped goggles to her face, threw on her snowshoes, and went outside to hook a sledge up to her snowmobile. Almost as an afterthought, she threw her stunner in with the supplies and first aid kit. She'd never had need of a gun, but the stunner was sometimes handy for driving off some of Europa's more amphibious and aggressive beasties.

Then she checked to make sure her snowmobile had a full charge, and, satisfied, drove to Mikkel's tent.

The short woman was again as they'd first met, bundled in enough layers to appear downright stocky. The dark fabric of her snowsuit was stitched with floral patterns, apparently by hand. She waddled around behind the tent, emerging on a colorful snowmobile of her own. "MMMC" was painted on the side in bright colors, above the K&M blaster hanging in a holster.

"Andre set off to the south," came Mikkel's muffled voice, and she pointed out of town. Gilma nodded and sped down the furrowed path, Mikkel following her into the white.

GILMA MAY HAVE considered herself a competent detective, if the need ever arose, but she was not a tracker. Fine white grains snaked over the sheer ice, driven by the northern wind which sometimes meandered, sometimes blasted, but always blew. Snow banks were pushed along with it, migrating south like dry icebergs, filling the chasms in the ice left big icequakes. On top of all that, it was starting to lightly snow. The wind, the weather, the quakes, all of these things would have made it hard to find someone who'd gone missing a day ago, much less at least two weeks ago. Finding this Andre alive was a long shot. She didn't even hold out much hope for a body.

They drove for hours and hours, late into the night, but nevertheless, Gilma felt like they were barely covering ground, forced as they were to stop and shine a light in every crack, around every snowbank, and into every shadow that might conceal their lost man. Adding to her frustration was the fact that her numb fingers were stiffening with cold and her snowmobile's charge was more than halfway drained. Once, she unclasped her hood to tell Mikkel to investigate a crevice, and the wind burned her face. Her bladder was angry, but after that she wasn't about to open her snowsuit to relieve it.

"Ho!" Mikkel called suddenly, swerving to the right. Gilma brought her vehicle around to follow the Ringmaster.

Mikkel came to a stop a few yards later, the lights of her snowmobile illuminating something on the ground before her, half-buried in the thickening snowfall. Something bloody and shredded. Gilma's heart sank.

Then it rose again. The bloody, shredded thing was a redbeak, a fish.

"He must have been here!" Gilma exclaimed. "We're on the right track!"

Mikkel slid from her snowmobile, stomping over to the dead, frozen creature and picking it up.

Gilma looked away from the frankly unpleasant scene. She didn't know why the ringmaster had to touch it like that. "Gotta say though, this lion-tamer of yours is a messy eater."

"Perhaps."

"Hey!" Came a sudden yell from behind.

Gilma spun, shining her flashlight on a strange sight - something was sprouting from a nearby snowbank. As the snow fell away and a head emerged, her jaw dropped.

"Andre!" Mikkel dropped the redbeak and rushed to pull

her lost Beastmaster from the snow. The man looked ragged and frostbitten. His scraggly beard was flaked with ice, and frost caked his snowsuit. He was clutching something in a gloved hand. "Andre, I can't believe you're alive!"

Gilma shared that feeling. The "snowbank" was actually a quinzhee, a warm-ish shelter made of refrozen snow. "God, I have to say, this is unexpected. Are you alright?"

The tall man clasped his hood against the outside cold and nodded. "Hungry. Cold," he said, then he held the thing in his hand out to Mikkel. Gilma leaned in for a closer look.

It was dung.

"Uh…" she had no idea what to make of the bizarre display. Mikkel, for her part, regarded the frozen poop excitedly. "My god, my god! Droppings! Where did you find it?"

Andre shook his head. "Not sure. Miles away. Back by wherever my snowmobile ran out of power. But he's close, closer than he's ever been, that's why I didn't come back. Wait—" He looked over his employer at the ruined fish. "My bait!"

Gilma was truly confused. "Your bait? The redbeak?"

The beastmaster rushed past them both. "The last of my food. I was trying to lure him out with it, but I must have dozed off. Damn it!"

"But, my friend, he is still close. If he did not take his prize with him, that can only mean he was here when the Sheriff and I approached, and we frightened him!"

"Who was close?" Gilma asked, unheeded.

Andre appeared to steel himself. "You're right. He might have lift prints." With that, he took off into the dark.

"Wait—what in the— ?" As far as Gilma could tell, their missing man just bolted without explanation. "Come back!"

"This way, Sheriff!" Mikkel called, grabbing her gun and running after Andre. "The Colossus is within our grasp!"

Of course. "No, you idiots! Come back! You'll get lost!"

But they were already gone. Swearing, and conscious that she still needed to piss, Gilma grabbed a flashlight and set off after them.

If the surface of Europa was tough to a driver, it was brutal on foot. The falling snow was swelling into a blizzard, and a blizzard was the absolute last thing living people wanted to deal with out in the white, cuz it would turn them into dead people. Plus, the deep rumble in her chest felt an awful lot like the beginnings of a big ice quake.

She trudged after the rapidly vanishing footprints of the others, cursing all the way. The beam of her light was crowded with heavy snowflakes.

"Mikkel!" She shouted hoarsely, "Andre, damn you!"

There was something else, something she hadn't noticed before. Some of the footprints were big. And not human. And in sets of four.

She finally caught sight of a silhouette: Mikkel, he assumed, and Andre, oddly huddled together. The rumbling that signalled an ice quake grew louder and more immediate, and now that she thought about it, it didn't really sound much like an ice quake, it sounded more like the animals at the circus—

She saw the thing clearly. It rose to its hind legs, huge, white, and vicious looking.

Gilma's bladder no longer concerned her.

"MIKKEL!" She screamed, and turned to run.

Fleeing in the deepening snow was next to impossible, but Gilma managed, and berated herself. The Colossus was real, of course it was, you idiot, you don't know everything, and you should have seen the signs, the chewed fish, the tracks, the roaring—idiot, idiot, idiot. Crunching, thumping footfalls behind her cleared her mind of any further reprimands.

Somehow, she made it back to the snowmobiles. Breathing raggedly, she threw herself at the sledge and fished around inside for the stunner, finally grasping it and priming it to fire. Nothing surrounded her but emptiness, the great erasure of the world that came with a snowstorm. The white.

There was a claw.

It dug into the thick cushion of her snowsuit and lifted her into the air. She screamed and pulled the trigger, firing wild sonic pulses that whined even above the wind and the growls of the monster. Then she was flying through the air and plowing head first into solidified snow of Andre's quinzhee. Bright spots blinked in her vision. Blind, dazed, she fired the stunner wildly.

And apparently got close enough. The hot breath of the monster retreated.

Gilma blinked, her sight clearing. She couldn't see the Colossus, but she could hear it grumbling in the direction of the snowmobiles, cutting off her escape. Her little stunner had frightened it, maybe, but she didn't think it would be scared for long. She needed somewhere to hide, like -

She was lying beside a quinzhee.

Painfully, she crawled on her hands and knees around the small shelter, pushing herself through the entrance feet first. It was tight, and harder that way, but she didn't want to turn her back on the stalking Colossus and give it a chance to take her by surprise again. Kicking at Andre's bags made a little more room inside the cramped space, allowing her to squirm in further. Finally, she was lying on her stomach inside, stunner trained on the opening.

For a while, the only sound was the whistling of the blizzard over the mouth of the quinzhee. The insulation of her snowsuit was falling out where it was torn, she stuffed it back in. Unclasping her hood, she gingerly felt the spot where her head had met the ice. Her gloved fingers came away red and sticky. Well, there was a first aid kit in the sledge. She thought they'd need it for Andre, funny how that turned out-

There was a growl outside. She saw the steam of the monster's breath, and hoped it couldn't smell blood. She didn't even know if it could smell. A claw the size of her

head reached into the hole and pawed around. She fired. The claw jerked back with an ear-splitting roar and Gilma prayed to no one in particular. As if in answer, the quinzhee groaned under a sudden impact. The monster was trying to crush its way in. Spiderweb fractures streaked across the low ceiling. She hoped, when it reached her, she could hit it with a good, solid stun and make a dash for the snow mobiles. Even as she pictured it, she couldn't see herself being that adroit. God, was she really about to die?

The high, hard whine of a stunner sounded again, followed by an indignant bellow from the Colossus. Gilma looked with surprise at the weapon in her hand. She hadn't fired it. Again, the unmistakable noise of a stunner resounded through the crisp air outside. The monster shrieked, but the whining continued, and finally, with a crunch, she saw a giant white mass collapse before the opening of the quinzhee.

Slowly, careful not to bump her head, she crawled out. Her heart still pounded.

Mikkel appeared atop the damaged shelter, K&M rifle in hand. "The Colorless Colossus of the Cold," she said, a smile on her voice. Andre was beside her.

"Good shot," he said, and strode over to the unconscious beast. The snow was already beginning to bank against the broad hulk of the thing, which rose and fell slowly with its breath. "Are you hurt, bud?"

"I'm okay," Gilma said, "might need stitches though." She realized Andre was talking to the monster. "Are you gonna kill it?" Her mind was still muddled.

"No. His name is Yutu," Andre said, brushing the thing's white fur with his fingers.

"It has a name?"

Mikkel came to stand at her side. "Um, yes. He is one of ours. He escaped, unfortunately, during an accident on the caravan... I hope deeply that he didn't hurt anyone seriously in the months since."

"He hurt somebody."

"I'm sorry he attacked you, Sheriff, I swear it. Polar bears are mighty predators, but I fear Europa isn't as brimming with seals as Yutu might typically have liked. He's been subsisting on the catches of terrified icefishers. Which is good, in a way, as it left us a trail of witnesses to follow." The ringmaster looked apologetic. "Allow me to thank you for finally finding him. Now, we can carry on with the show!"

It was a polar bear. Of course, look at it. Gilma must be the least perceptive woman on Europa. "The show?"

"Yes, and with Yutu back, what a show it will be! Andre, help us load him onto the sledge. It's a good thing Europa is a world with easy gravity, eh? On his home planet, he weighs almost 1500 pounds!"

"Wait, why didn't you tell me there was a 1500 pound polar bear on the loose?"

"Well, you see…"

Andre looked up from his unconcious charge. "We didn't want you to try to kill him."

"Andre is right, I'm afraid. These animals, they're expensive. Additionally, I thought that if we told you, you might think it our fault he was 'on the loose', and maybe not take too kindly to us, being a lawman. I really can't apologize enough."

"There was a bear. Polar bear. Running amuck."

"Well, yes, but, well, accidents happen and all that. Ahem. Perhaps we can make it up to you? The show must go on, as we say. And it will be a good one, I guarantee it."

THE SHOW DID go on, and it was everything Mikkel promised. The old Ringmaster was fiery and energetic, a real showman, and Andre handled the creatures deftly. Gilma even enjoyed it, although she stepped away when Yutu came out. Nothing personal against the animal, he'd been lost and hungry, but…

She allowed Mikkel and her people to perform, despite having kept the town in the dark about the possible hungry bear nearby, on the condition that they permit all of the residents to see the show for free. When the next caravan came, they were to leave with it, and never return. It wasn't a bad deal for either side. The kids, especially, were gleeful as they watched the menagerie unfold. That felt good, at least.

For now, though, Gilma was taking it easy. The last thing she wanted was any excitement. A nice, long, boring winter would do just fine.

She was in her cabin, resting her bandaged head on a pillow, when there was a knock at the door. Sore, she yelled for whoever it was to let themselves in. Miguel rushed inside and unclasped his hood.

"Sheriff!" He said, "we need you at the circus."

"What?!" Gilma shot up, so fast she felt dizzy. "Polar bear?"

The man sounded surprised. "Uh, no. Just, uh, a couple of roustabouts got drunk, and there was a fight."

"Oh," Gilma sat on her bed. "Oh, thank God. A fight. That's excellent news."

Miguel was puzzled as she happily pulled on her snowsuit.

James W. Murphy spent his childhood near the tide pools and harbors of Los Angeles, his adolescence in the forests and plains of Oregon, and most of his adulthood in the cozy alleys of Taipei and dusty boulevards of Beijing. He's made a living flipping hamburgers in polyester, stocking groceries in a red bow tie, and painting houses in canvas pants, all while lifting heavy objects with proper form. He's also been a teacher, a translator, a technology industry analyst, and a publisher of research books and journals, spending over a dozen years terrorized by millions of emails and presentation slides. He currently lives in the misty hills of southern Taipei with his wife Monica, enjoying the regenerative power of their three dozen houseplants and doing whatever he wants, like writing science fiction stories.

Tales of adventure on the high seas doubtless started being told about fifteen minutes after the first dugout canoe came back after venturing out of sight of land. The same classic genre also has a place in the Old Solar System, where there are many more than seven seas—and James W. Murphy's Cutter Pristine sets sail on one of these adventures in a tale set on the oceans of Neptune.

Cutter Pristine

by James W. Murphy

J ENSON COULD SEE the hydrofoil bobbing next to the shore. The running lights were off, but its silhouette was unmistakable thanks to the light cast by Neptune's numerous moons reflecting off the black water. The island's major port town was now far behind him, the ambient light from the town now so faint as to make the rest of the way to the shore pitch black. It would be tough to get to the boat in the darkness.

He opened his duffle bag and felt around for his flashlight. He continued ahead, aiming the beam at the ground and avoiding the rocks and dead-looking plants jutting out from the chalky dirt. After a few moments Jenson looked up and saw he was closer to the boat, relieved to see he was making good progress. He would have no problem getting there before the appointed time.

Heavy steps approached rapidly behind him. Before he could turn around a pair of hands slapped on his back and pushed him face-first into the ground. A tremendous weight bore down on his back, pinning him.

"Moron!" said a deep Terran voice in a hoarse whisper. "The

hell you doing running around here with a damn flashlight?!"

Jenson rocked side to side, trying to get the weight off of him. A hand grabbed a fistful of his hair, then jerked his head back with such force that he wondered which would give first: the hair out of his scalp or the bones of his neck. He could see part of the man's profile. Clearly Earthman. Likely part of the boat crew.

"How the hell else am I supposed to get to the boat? Can't see anything out here." Jenson seethed.

"You do it without running around with damn flashlight. If anyone from the town sees us, we're done."

The man let go of his hair and dismounted, slapping the back of his head. "Get your ass up and get to the boat."

Jenson scrambled to his feet and took in his attacker. The man was huge, standing a foot taller than Jenson, his body thick with age, clearly at one time heavily muscled but now yielding to fat. He pointed to the boat. "Get your ass on deck. The crew is prepping. Help them out so that we can get underway."

Jenson picked up his duffle bag, and made his way to the boat. The man stayed where they had been, eyes fixed on the lights for the town, searching for movement.

As Jenson approached, he realized he could have found the vessel by smell alone. The stench was overpowering, like walking toward a mountain of rotting squid covered in a gravy of raw sewage. He wondered if he should just run. Use the darkness as cover and just forget the whole thing. But he was out of options.

Despite the darkness he could see the decks, railings, and walls of the wheelhouse were covered in oily grime. On any of the other boats he worked on, the entire crew would have been keelhauled before the captain let it get to that state. The man who hooked him up with the job said the craft was named Cutter Pristine, proving the rule that ship names somehow jinxed the vessel to a fate opposite of what the namer intended.

Jenson could hear talking in low tones. He headed toward the voices, and saw two figures sitting next to a tower of traps and working the lines. Two Earthmen. One about his age, and one elderly. Both rail-thin and malnourished. The elderly one tied knots with incredible speed and precision despite his swollen, arthritic hands. The younger one—roughly mid twenties—was noticeably slower, punctuating his numerous failures to tie knots with bursts of foul language.

He heard the approaching slap of wet naked feet on the deck, and the deckhands turned to look at a Neptunian stepping out from behind the traps. He was shorter than the usual Neptunian, about one and a half Earthman-lengths tall compared to the usual two. He held a coil of line in his two hands, while the flippers situated below his arms extended out to balance out the movements of the vessel. His giant, froglike eyes fixed on Jenson. The other deckhands followed the Neptunian's gaze, discovering Jenson standing there. The silent Neptunian continued on, heading astern.

"You our new greenhorn?" asked the younger one. "You better get to work before the Captain sees you just standing there." He pointed up to the wheelhouse. Jenson looked up, and could see a shadow of a head in the window. He dropped his duffle, took a stool next to the younger man, grabbed some line, and started working quickly through some knots. He wasn't able to match the speed of the old man, but he worked faster than the other youthful deckhand.

"Where'd you crew before?" asked the young one.

"I was on Mars before this," said Jenson. "Crewed on the airships there. Work was easy but the pay sure as hell doesn't match this. I knew this would be tough but I wasn't expecting to get attacked just walking to the damn boat."

The two crewmen smiled. "Finbar's like that," said the old man. "He's the First Mate. Worst crewmate I ever worked with. And I worked with a lot of crazy mean bastards. Ain't even sure why he's on the boat. Don't do much, other than loaf around and bitch."

The three continued to work in silence, hearing nothing but the sounds of the water lapping at the boat.

"I'm Efan," said the young one. He motioned to the old man. "This is Hendrik." The old man nodded at Jenson.

"The Neptunian you saw lurching around is Ogorris," said Hendrik. "And don't ask me why in the hell we have a Neptunian on board. Would think he would rather die than catch any of their sacred sea bugs with a bunch of criminal Earthmen. He musta done something real bad to be skulking around the oceans with us. Good worker though. Need him on these trips. This is gonna be pretty different than anything you've done on Mars."

"Before Mars I crewed on Earth. On the ocean. Up north. About this cold but the seas are a lot calmer in this part of Neptune I hear."

Hendrik chuckled.

"Did I hear wrong?"

"No, you didn't hear wrong," said Hendrik. Efan and Hendrik shared looks. "Difficult to describe. But you'll see soon enough. Hope you're a sound sleeper!" Hendrik smiled and knocked his fist on the deck three times, then reached into his pocket, and pulled out a rotting fish. He held it under his nose, sniffing deeply as if it were a fine cigar.

"Put that damn thing away," said Efan. "Can't you bring a good luck charm that doesn't stink up the whole boat? As if it didn't smell bad enough."

Hendrik put the fish back in his coat, smiling a toothless grin.

Jensen could hear Ogorris returning. They all went quiet as the Neptunian made its way to starboard behind the stack of traps.

A scream of sirens pierced the silence. The deckhands' heads shot up, looking in the direction of the town. Jenson could hear the sound of Finbar's pounding steps coming from the shore.

"Time to head out!" the First Mate yelled from the shore, followed by a thump as his feet hit the deck. Finbar rounded the wheel house, leapt through the cabin door, and slammed the door behind him.

The boat shuddered as the engines roared to life, and the hydrofoil began moving away from the shore. The boat began to pick up speed, slowly lifting higher in the water as the jets powered up. Jenson caught a flash from the corner of his eye in the direction of the port, followed by a succession of loud booms. He looked over to see three missiles arcing above, headed toward their position. He looked to the two deckhands, who were focused on tying themselves to railings.

The loudspeaker crackled and buzzed to life. "Get yourselves secured. We're about to launch," said a staticky voice in a bored monotone.

"Damn Captain never gives us enough time," said Efan, the young deckhand now tying knots with a higher degree of proficiency than before.

Alarmed, Jenson searched around for some spare rope, not finding any.

"There's some line right there," said Efan, pointing to a pile of filthy rope coiled next to the outer railing. He scrambled over and started working it around his body, looking up to see the missiles getting closer. Once the line was tied off at his waist, he began securing it to the railing. The ship started to cant into a steep angle, the stern submerging, the bow now aiming up into the air. His feet slipped on the deck, and he looped his arm around the railing, catching himself just in time. He could hear the whistle of the missiles as they drew nearer, his hands shaking as he frantically tried to complete the knot.

The hydrofoil launched into the air, the thrust of the ship throwing Jenson back against a pile of traps. He could feel the bars of the traps pressing into the flesh of his back and the bone of his skull as the gravitational force continued to build. The two deckhands were pressed against the railing: Efan prone, belly down. Hendrik was grinning manically into the air, his rotting back teeth clearly visible. Jenson heard a distant splash and explosions as the bombs hit the water. The boat began rapidly to decelerate. The pressure on his back eased, and he started to float. As the other deckhands float-ed away from the railing, Hendrik began making swimming motions, positioning himself upside down and scissoring his legs open and closed as if he were performing water ballet. Efan swam himself over to Jenson's failed knot, tightening it up into a constrictor knot, and then giving Jenson a thumbs up.

The boat was angling downward, and starting to accel-erate again. The two deckhands floated back to the railing, grabbing hold. Jenson reached back and held the bars of the traps as the gravitational forces started pushing him back again. He could barely hear the wind over his pounding chest as the hydrofoil hurtled downward. They were approaching the dark ocean at a terrifying pace. He could feel his stomach crawling up into his chest. The darkness of his ocean filled his vision, until everything went black.

JENSON WAS SHOCKED to consciousness by the torrent of warm water splashing down on his body. Unable to breathe in, his body convulsed, then coughed out a what felt like half a lung of the metallic-tasting water. He lay on the deck, gasping for air. The engines shuddered off, leaving only the sounds of water running off the deck into the ocean and Hendrik's hys-terical laughing. Jenson reached down and pulled the line off his waist, and rubbed his bruised, rope-burned skin.

The loudspeaker crackled, "All clear. Lay the traps." Efan made his way over to Jenson, and handed him his duffle bag, the sides bloated from a mass of water trapped inside and slowly pouring out at the ends of the zippers.

"Surprised your bag survived the jump," said Efan.

Jenson opened the bag and let the remainder of the water out. "I don't suppose I'll get a chance to go down below and dry off?"

"Nope," said Efan." We're going to have a mountain of bugs coming our way with all that sound. Gotta get to work. You can hang up some of your gear to dry on the bow. There's no way Finbar is going to let you in the cabin before the traps are set. So hang your stuff up quickly and then join us on the stern."

Jenson went up to the bow and spread his clothes on the railing, and spaced out his gear on the deck. There wasn't much wind, and although the warm seas had taken the bite out of the cold, his gear wasn't going to dry out anytime soon. Satisfied he had done what he could, he made his way to the stern.

"You're working with Ogorris," said Hendrik as Jenson approached the team. "You can load and he'll shoot."

The Neptunian had already secured line on five of the traps. Ogorris walked over to the trap cannon, and grabbed both handles with his hands. He looked over to Jenson and used his fin to point at the traps, then to the loading barrel. Jenson watched Efan load his cannon, then did the same, kneeling down and placing one of the traps into the loading barrel, making sure the rope aligned correctly to avoid tangling with the mechanism. The design was much better than anything he had used on the fishing vessels Earth, which seemed optimized to cause injury. Once Jenson finished loading the traps, Ogorris did a slight bow of approval, and looked over to Hendrik.

"Fire!" yelled Hendrik.

Both guns popped, and the traps shot out over the ocean on both sides of the boat, one a mirror image of the other, a squiggle of line trailing behind them followed by a spinning buoy. The traps splashed, then sank until there was nothing but a half-submerged buoy bobbing on the sea's dark surface. Jenson saw Efan loading up the mechanism for the next trap, and did the same. Ogorris and Hendrik aimed in and lower, letting the traps to fall closer to the boat. Then wider on the next one, repeating this pattern on subsequent shots. They kept on, a zigzag of buoys growing behind them.

For Jenson, it was easy work compared to the fishing trawlers on Earth. Too easy, for the money he was getting, which made him nervous.

The crew settled into a smooth rhythm. Load. Pop. Load. Pop. When all two hundred traps were in the water, Ogorris and Hendrik pulled the trap guns off their mountings, and placed them on the deck.

"Time to head in," said Hendrik, motioning the crew toward the cabin. It seemed a bit early too wrap up. Jenson was used to going for days without sleep. But he chose not to voice any objections.

While the others filed into the cabin door, Jenson went on to gather his things on the bow. As he approached, he saw all the clothes he had hung up to dry were gone. Confused, he looked around. There was no wind to blow them off. The boat barely rocked in the eerily calm ocean. He looked around the bow, to see if they had been blown around. The clothes were all gone. His heart sank, as he thought about trying to get through the rest of the journey with whatever he had on. He grabbed his bag, picked up the remainder of his gear, and headed toward the cabin.

As he opened the door, a gust of hot, acrid air gusted out. Like the smell of ten-thousand souls with morning breath exhaling in unison. With shallow breaths, he descended the stairs.

As he entered the galley, Jenson saw Finbar sitting with his legs propped up on the galley table. He looked away from a book he was reading, directly at Jenson. "You're on food detail tonight, kid. Get your skinny ass in there and get to it." "You sure about that? I can't really cook," said Jenson. Finbar took his legs off the table and threw his book at Jenson's head. Jenson dodged it just in time, hearing the book smack across the wall behind him. Finbar stood up, his eyes blazing and fixed on Jenson, his complexion reddening. As he started to work his way out of the galley booth, Efan blocked his way. "Here's your book sir."

Finbar, distracted, looked at Efan and took the book, seeming to relax. "Well at least somebody knows the chain of command and how to show proper respect." Jenson was surprised at the First Mate's abrupt change in attitude. It was clear Efan knew how to handle him.

Efan walked over to Jenson and grabbed him by the arm and shoved him into the galley. Jenson could see Finbar squinting with a thin, approving smile on his face just as Jenson stumbled in. Hendrik emitted a wheezing laugh.

"Why'd you push me like that?" asked Jenson.

"Got to put on a bit of a show for Finbar," said Efan. "He's old school. As the greenhorn he expects you to suffer some. Better me making a show of it than having Finbar do it. He once chucked a greenhorn over the side. At least that's the story. But I'd believe it."

"Other than him and the bombs this boat's a cakewalk compared to others I've worked on. Is a first mate even needed?" asked Jenson.

Efan pointed to a row of matching boxes on an upper shelf. "See that box? There's a bunch of freeze-dried meals in there. Take one of the packages out, throw it into the bowl over there, then boil some water and add it. Mix it up, then bring it out to the table. Then bring out the bowls and silverware: two sets for Finbar, one each for the rest of us. "

"What kind of food is it?"

"Stew."

"What kind of stew?"

"No idea. It's just some kind of stew. Meat and carrots and crap. The package just says 'stew.' We have it every meal and it's all we eat on these trips. Finbar says the Captain loves the stuff. Must be 'cause it's cheap. Sure as hell isn't for the flavor."

With that Efan walked out, and Jenson went to work reconstituting the crew's dinner.

THE MEN IN the galley were silent save for the sound of spoons scraping against bowls. The First Mate had two bowls in front of him, one left untouched as he used his fingers to get every last dripping from the bowl into his mouth. He then got up, grabbed the second bowl, and took the stairs up into the wheelhouse.

As Finbar's footsteps faded up the stairs, Jenson turned to Efan. "So the Captain and Ogorris don't eat with us?"

"No, the Captain pretty much just stays up there." said Efan. "There's a toilet and bed in the wheelhouse. Finbar relieves him at night, but he doesn't come down. Never even seen him. The guy just lives up there. Not the chatty type. I have no idea what Ogorris eats."

"I tried to offer Ogorris some stew once," said Hendrik. "I swear the bastard smiled before he walked away. Like he was laughin at me. Sure I was seein things 'cause I don't think Neptunians have the facial muscles for that."

"How long you been crewing here?" asked Jenson.

"'Bout a dozen trips or so," said Hendrik. "Probably be about a dozen more before I have enough to live on without workin'. Don't want to end up like those old sad sacks you see, lyin' around out in the elements like a forgotten turd with no family and no money and no friends. Just lyin there waitin' to die." Hendrik brought the bowl up to his mouth, and licked the remainder of the stew like a dog.

"How 'bout you, Efan?" asked Jenson.

"This is my sixth trip. Tough at first, but you get used to it. Got a lot easier when Ogorris joined the crew a couple trips ago."

"You keep taking about how tough it is, but other than other than Finbar acting like a—"

Jenson went silent as he heard footsteps coming down the stairs. Finbar emerged from the doorway, and made his way to the dining area with an empty stew bowl. He sat down, and let out a long sigh.

"Better hit the bunks," he said, taking out a bag of pharma tablets from his pocket. He took one out, pressed it against his skin. As it melted in his head rolled back and his body seemed to crumple for a second.

"Want one?" he said, to no one in particular.

"No thanks, sir," said Efan. "I don't need one yet. But maybe later on the trip."

Finbar put them back in his pocket. "You all better get to sleep quick," he said, getting up and lumbering clumsily toward his bunk.

"You're bunking with Hendrik," said Efan. "Through that door and the first door to the right. Head's the first door to the left if you need to use it."

Jenson got up and walked toward the bunk. Opening the door, the same rank smell that hit him when first entering the cabin wafted out, only stronger. He put his duffel on the top bunk, took off the tattered and gloriously stained bed spread, and shook it. A cloud of crumbs and debris rained onto the floor. Jenson took off his still-wet clothes, hung them up to dry, and crawled up onto the bunk naked. He was too tired to care about the disgusting state of the bunk, and ignored the thought of what his skin would be rubbing against.

He heard Hendrik shuffle into the room, crawling immediately into bed without changing. The old man coughed and wheezed, and he could hear the rustling sound of his stiff and dirty sheets as he settled in. Hendrik started snoring within seconds.

JENSON KEPT WAKING up from the precipice of sleep, his mind buzzing with the odd events of the day. The surly First Mate. The silent Neptunian who shouldn't have been with a crew of Earthmen illegally fishing in his planet's sacred waters. The pitiable Hendrik, a body racked with age and nothing much left in life but toil. Efan, the only one on the boat that seemed to be looking out for him.

He thought about the boat. The dirty deck. His foul bunk. The head across the way, which he was in no hurry to visit having relieved himself on deck. He could smell it from where he slept. His mind wandered into the galley. Bags and bags of desiccated stew. His mind wandered further, up the cabin stairs, then to the door leading to the deck.

Everything suddenly felt off; he no longer felt like he was imaging the door, but actually standing in front of it. Everything he saw seemed to be a negative image of what he remembered. The white door was black, as were the stairs and the walls. The black grip-tape was now white. He looked down at his naked body. Green, like the color of tarnished copper. He reached out to the door handle. It felt real. He could feel the cold metal in his palm. He opened the door and stepped out on the deck, his head suddenly filled with a maelstrom of horrible roars and screams.

Like the cabin, the world on deck was lit in reverse image. The black ocean appeared white, punctuated with black-caps. What he remembered as calm seas were now roiling with giant waves. Some crashing into each other. Some cresting over the railing and washing the deck with black foam. On the side of the boat, white, smooth, tentacle-like appendages were coming out the water, lightly touching the railing, as if feeling an optimal point of purchase. Some were already wrapped around. Some just seemed to tremble in an erect state, flapping back and forth like fleshy windsocks. Jenson saw Efan pounce over with a club, slamming down one of the appendages. The tentacle let go of the railing, trembled as if shaking out the pain, and then retracted back into the water. Efan hit the remaining tentacles that were wrapped or probing around the railing, and the group of tentacles nearest Efan began to slither back into to the ocean.

The young deckhand turned to Jenson. "What the hell are you doing out here naked?" he shouted, trying to be heard over the din of crashing waves and bestial screams. Jenson just stood there, confused. "Just stay close to the cabin, and watch. You can see what we do and pick up on the next shift," screamed Efan. He then ran down the railing, hitting more tentacles.

Jenson looked out at the roiling sea. It was teaming with life. He could see schools of fish jump from wave to wave. He saw the humps of something large and serpentine climbing up another swell. Just as its head broke the surface, the serpent screeched as a giant whale-like creature with a mouth full of sharp teeth broke the surface, biting it in half. Thousands of small fish descended on the two halves, consuming it in a frenzy in a matter of seconds.

The whale creature re-submerged. Jenson could see its tremendous black bulk underneath the water. It looked to be about as big as the boat. It suddenly launched itself out of the water next to the boat, raising itself higher than the wheelhouse, roaring. It stayed in place, tail-walking above the surface of the sea like an enormous dolphin.

Jenson heard feedback and a snap from the intercom system. "Ogorris. Toothwhale to port." announced the Captain, again sounding inappropriately matter-of-fact.

"Hurry up! It's looking right into the wheelhouse! And it's pissed off!" screamed Hendrik's voice from somewhere.

The toothwhale reared back to attack. Jenson heard the slap of wet feet. Turning, he saw Ogorris launch himself high in the air with a spear. Mid-air, the spear shot like a piston from Ogorris's hand and into the toothwhale's mouth and out the other side. Ogorris landed on the railing, on top of two tentacles. He stamped his feet, and tentacles winced back into the water. The toothwale made a groaning sound, and toppled into the sea, causing a tremendous wave threatening to engulf the boat. Jenson saw Ogorris do a back-flip just as the wave was hitting.

"Wake up!"

"Wake up Jenson!"

Where the hell is that sound coming from? thought Jenson.

"Dammit ! Wake up!"

Jenson opened his eyes to see Efan looking at him. A normal Efan, not the greenish reverse-image version.

"Get your clothes on and get on deck. Finbar will have us keelhauled if we don't get those traps in."

THE FOUR DECKHANDS stood on the stern as the boat neared the first buoys.

"What'd you think?" asked Efan.

"About what?" said Jenson. He figured he knew what Efan was asking about but he still couldn't believe what he experienced.

"Last night's shift. Do you think you can help us out a bit more on the next one?"

"So that wasn't a dream, was it? What the hell was that?"

"It's how we spend our sleeping hours on these tours. The price we pay for placid seas and a big catch of the bugs when we're awake. It only happens on certain parts of the ocean. Where the bugs are. When you go to sleep you're forced into a nightmare. And we have to keep whatever's out there from taking over the boat. Or killing you."

"What happens if they take it over. It's just a dream, right?"

"If the boat goes down in the dream, or if we get picked off one-by-one by the sea monsters, you don't wake up. Just go vegetative."

Hendrik cut in, "Happened to the guy you're replacing. Was a real treat sharing a bunk below him when he blinked out. Think the cabin smells bad now? Sometimes I wish we could just capsize the vessel and clean the whole damn thing out."

Jenson recalled the stains in his bunk, and regretted not bringing his own sheets.

"It's happened before with other crews," said Efan. "Neptunian patrol came across a hydrofoil filled with rotting bugs in traps, and the mummified remains of the crew in their bunks. Just a ghost ship, bobbing in the ocean for who knows how long." Efan shuddered.

"That ain't gonna happen with Ogorris on board," said Hendrik. Ogorris stood nearby, studying one of the winches. He appeared to ignore the comment.

"Ogorris seemed a bit more limber than he normally is," said Jenson.

"Yeah, it's not the same rules," explained Efan. "If you focus, sometimes you can do things you normally can't. Once lifted a stack of traps with one hand. I saw Hendrik here climb up to the wheelhouse like some sort of spider to slap off an anemone that was trying to eat through the window. We can't do it consistent like Ogorris. Just sometimes."

"What's going on now? In the dream world now that were are awake?" asked Jenson.

"It only exists when one or more of us sleeps," said

Efan. "That's why we sleep at the same time, so that there's enough of us to handle the beasts. If we were to take shifts, it wouldn't be enough."

"Why not just have the crew stay awake the whole trip? Or do pharma uppers? Then you wouldn't have to deal with all that," said Jenson.

"Our trips are just too damn long," said Hendrik. "Been tried. Drugs help. But by the end, crews start hallucinatin'. Acting weird. Crew starts doing dangerous stuff. Starts to screw with your head permanently. It's why Finbar's a little off."

Efan leaned down to pick up a hook with line attached to it. The young deckhand and Ogorris threw the hooks out at the buoys, and pulled them into the automatic winches. Hitting the buttons, the winches whirred to life, tightening as the line as the gears sped up. Black seawater dripped down the mechanism as the winches wrung the water out of the line.

Jenson could see the trap drawing near. The cage was teaming with what they called "bugs." They looked like badly deformed crabs about the size of a king crab of earth. They had the same reddish color, but instead of an oval body, they were spiral shaped, with one giant claw at the outward-end of the spiral, and a small, round carapace at the center. The bugs were still feeding on the bait in the trap, using their claws to tear off chunks and meat and passing them into their mouths at the center of the spiral.

Hendrik opened the up a trap door, and pulled out a slide, connecting it to the trap. He opened the trap door, and bugs slid down into a holding tank deep in the hull. A few stragglers held onto the side of the slide with their tremendous claws. Efan took a crowbar to the remainder, grunting and cursing as he worked to pry them off. When he was done, he presented Jenson with the twisted crowbar. "See how bent that is? Don't want to any of your body parts near those claws."

"Well it's a good thing I'm fully clothed today," said Jenson. The two Earthmen chuckled. Ogorris turned and looked Jenson up and down, and then went back to readying the winch for the next trap.

AFTER A HUNDRED or more traps, the holding tank began to fill up. The crew began stacking the full traps on the deck, each one packed with live bugs.

"How long can they survive like that?" asked Jenson.

"A few weeks," said Efan. "They're hearty."

The intercom crackled. "Time to head in."

Jenson noticed the crew did not display the sense of relief that normally comes at the end of a shift. If anything they became tenser. A feeling he couldn't help but share after his experience the night before.

As they entered the galley, Jenson headed toward the storage area to make some stew.

"Get to it you little crumsnatcher," said Finbar, chuckling.

Jenson looked over and noticed Finbar wearing one of his shirts. One of the shirts he thought went overboard. It was a poor fit. He paused, staring at the shirt, then looked at Finbar in disbelief.

"What of it?" said Finbar, grinning. The other crew members focused their attention elsewhere.

Jenson felt his temper blaze. The same temper that got him kicked off other boats. "What the hell's wrong with you? Take another man's clothes? They barely even fit you, you lazy, fat piece of crap."

Finbar's grin evaporated, his face twisting with rage. He scrambled over to Jenson, and before Jenson had a chance to move away, pinned him against the bulkhead. Jenson worked to struggle free, but the man's bulk and strength prevented any movement. Finbar reared back to deliver a punch, and then paused, a confused expression taking over his face. "Get your ass in the kitchen and make us our stew." He pushed Jenson toward the food prep area, and Jenson stumbled in.

Jenson couldn't wait to get this trip over with. The traps would probably be full during the next haul, and then they would go to offload. He'd be done, and with enough cash to get off the damn planet and try something else. Anything else.

He went about fixing the stew, then brought it out to the crew. Finbar took two bowls and went up into the wheel-house. The deckhands ate in silence, and then went off to bed.

THE TENTACLE RECOILED back as Jenson slammed his club down on it. It felt like a game of whack-a-mole. Hit a tenta-cle, move down the railing, hit another. And another. Again and again toward the bow, then back toward the stern.

There were more creatures than the previous night, and every so often some new horror would emerge from the depths to threaten the ship. The Captain would call for Ogor-ris, and Ogorris would come and dispatch the creature.

He had seen something that looked like a hairless goril-la, hissing just before Ogoriss's spear went through its eye. There was a creature that looked like a giant turtle without a shell, but with claws that came close to breaking the railing before Jenson batted its head. He was surprised at his own strength—how fragile the animal's hard-looking skull felt as it caved in under his bat. He also found he could jump higher than usual, as he discovered when he intercepted a lizard-like thing flying at a speed which would have put a hole in the wheelhouse window. Were it not for the constant feeling of being in peril, and the ear-piercing shrieks and screams, it would have almost been fun.

Jenson continued whacking tentacles, when an alarm

sounded from the intercom system. He looked over to where the rest of the crew was fighting off a horde of angry sea life on the bow. Off to starboard a giant beast was emerging from the surface. It looked like a fat worm, with a long proboscis pointing up into the air, which slowly lowered down to point at the traps teeming with bugs. They began to grow agitated, their giant claws clanging against the sides of the traps.

Jenson stumbled as the ship veered hard to starboard, angling the traps away from the creature, and pointing the bow toward it, exposing Hendrik and Ogorris, who were wrestling with a giant snake covered with black hair. Efan looked up to the wheelhouse with disbelief. "You're going to get them wiped out," Efan screamed. "Turn to port! Get those traps between that thing and the crew!"

The boat continued to angle starboard, the engines gunning louder as if in defiance of Efan's demands, putting the two deckhands dead center in the path of the monster's proboscis. A blue fluid shot out, covering Hendrik, Ogorris, and their serpentine opponent just as Efan jumped away. Hendrik let out a piercing scream as his skin started dissolving, the scream eventually subsiding as his body melted together with Ogoriss's, turning into a pile of combined soupy flesh on the deck. The creature bowed down, its proboscis entering the heap of flesh, and began sucking up the runny, gelatinized mass.

Jenson grabbed one of the spears fastened to the wheelhouse, and threw it directly at the creature. The spear hit just above its proboscis, travelling with so much force that it went out the other side of the creature's head. The monster went slack, and slid back into the ocean.

Jenson looked at Efan. "The Captain did that on purpose?"

Efan just looked at the pieces of the deckhands that remained. Feet and hands that didn't get dissolved by the creature's fluid. "Greedy bastard put them in danger just to save a bunch of bugs."

"But they're still alive right. Just out for the rest of the trip?"

"Not sure. Never seen it happen like this."

The intercom crackled. "Crewman, proceed with your work."

"Screw this," said Jenson. He slammed open the cabin door and slid down the steps, making his way to the wheelhouse stairs. Finbar was standing in the entryway, a smirk on his face. Jenson tightened his grip on his baton, and charged over to the First Mate. Finbar vanished just as his baton swung out to his head.

Jenson stood there confused. *Time to take this up with the captain*, he thought. He stormed up the wheelhouse stairs, and entered the wheelhouse itself. He could hear Efan coming up the stairs behind him.

As he looked in, he froze, not quite understanding what he saw. The figure in front of the controls was not a man, but what appeared to be a low-tech robot. The parts looked to be an assemblage of different department store mannequins from Earth, and its arms jerked as it adjusted the wheel to keep the boat on course. The deck below was swarming with sea creatures. "Captain?" said Jenson. There was no response.

Efan walked into the wheelhouse, and stood there, confused.

"The Captain's a damn robot. And cheap one at that," said Jenson.

"But a robot this basic wouldn't have the memory cores fit for piloting a boat," said Efan.

Jenson saw a cable connected to a transceiver. "Looks like it was operated remotely. He looked at Efan. "What is the point of that?"

"I saw Finbar carry a control set with him. Assumed it was for system diagnostics." Efan shook his head. "No idea why he'd need or want to control it remotely."

Jenson was suddenly rocked with a horrible pain. He fell to the floor, as he heard Efan say "Ah hell." His eyes fluttered, and his vision was suddenly filled with Finbar's sneering face, framed by the water-stained ceiling of his bunk room above. He tried to get up, but was unable to move anything but his head. He looked down, and saw he was bound: his hands tied to his sides, his legs tied together.

Finbar pulled his fist back, and smashed it into Jenson's face. Jenson's vision went white with pain along with the sickening sound of his nose breaking. Finbar moved down to his chest, hammering his fist repeatedly in a rage. Jenson tried to squirm away. He hoped for a moment that his ribs weren't broken, and realized there was too much pain to tell how bad the damage was. Finbar stopped momentarily, laying his forearm across Jenson's chest and holding him down. His other fist paused to take aim, and smashed down on Jenson's solar plexus. Jenson made a croaking sound, struggling to take in breath. Finbar laughed, and Jenson could see the man's mad smile as he lifted his fist again, aiming again for his face. His view of Finbar began to fill with a dark cross-hatch as the lack of oxygen started to affect his vision, covering Finbar's smiling face until everything went black.

"GET UP! GET the hell up, Jenson!"

Jenson could feel light slaps on his cheeks. He opened his eyes, wincing, and saw Efan standing where Finbar was. He moved his arms, then groaned as his chest exploded with a sharp pain.

"Jenson, we've got to get out of here," said Efan, helping him up.

As he sat on the edge of the bed Jenson saw Finbar lying on the floor. "How did you manage that?" he said, his voice hoarse.

"Used his pharma tablets on him. A lot of them. Fortunately they act fast. Then put him in a sleeper hold. Damn that man's strong, but I managed to do it long enough to get him to fall. With the sedatives he'll be out for a bit. I've got one of the dinghies ready."

Jenson looked down at Finbar's limp body. "We won't get far enough before Finbar wakes up. He'll find us and run us down."

"No, I mean we can put him in it," said Efan.

"And then we take the boat. Do you know where to land so we don't get caught by the coast patrols?"

"No idea. Finbar knows. But even if we tie him up we won't be able to get it out of him. If anything he'd head us right to the worst possible place just to spite us."

The room was quiet save for the hum of the engines as they sat there thinking of options.

"Here's what we do." said Jenson. "The boat has an autopilot. We leave Finbar on board, and set the pilot for port. We take the dingy. We're not that far from the coast. It takes some time to get there, but with the hydrofoil running into port it will take some of the heat off of us since the coast patrols will have their prize. We should be able to get to shore without running into one."

Efan sat there, considering. The shrugged. "That's what it will have to be."

"I'll take care of the autopilot. Can you get Hendrik and Ogorris into the dingy?"

Efan looked down at Hendrik in the bunk below. He could see the man's skinny chest taking in shallow breaths. His pants were wet with urine. "Hendrik's light as a feather. I can take care of him but you need to help me with Ogorris."

"I'll do what I can," said Jenson, carefully running his hand over his ribs.

EFAN WORKED THE controls of the dingy as Jenson watched the

hydrofoil in the distance, making its way toward port. Lights in the harbor flashed, followed by the wail of sirens barely audible over the roar of the dinghy's engine. He looked back at Efan. "How much longer?"

"We're getting pretty close. This crappy little boat is louder than the damn hydrofoil. But with all that action going on in port I can punch it a bit harder." Efan pulled back the thrust lever, and the engine let out a deafening roar, without any perceptible increase in acceleration. Efan growled in frustration.

Yet the shoreline was getting closer. Jenson looked down at Hendrik and Ogorris. They'd need to drop them off at a medical care unit somewhere. Would be best to not have to answer any questions, and it would be tough to get them there without being seen.

The shore was just a couple boat-lengths away when the engine sputtered out, dying from the sudden strain and years of neglect. "We'll have to swim it from here," said Efan.

They jumped into the water and pulled the bodies in, Efan with Ogorris and Jenson with Hendrik, working to keep their heads above water as they made their way to shore. Reaching the shallows, they strained and cursed to get the bodies onto the rock, then paused to catch their breath.

"What now? What do we do with 'em?" said Efan, pointing at the bodies. He was starting to shiver in the cold.

They heard a sudden yelp, and Hendrik shot up, head swiveling around in panic. He felt the ground with his hands, and then looked up to the two confused deckhands. They heard a shuffling sound, and the three men turned in unison to see Ogorris working to get to his feet.

Hendrik began laughing. Meeting the other deckhands' confused faces. "The coma only lasts on the ocean. You get to shore and away from the bugs, you wake up. Takes a while for our dreamselves to regenerate, but they'll come back."

A far-off siren burst grabbed their attention. They all

turned toward the ocean and watched as the flashing lights of the harbor police surrounded the boat.

"S'pose this ends our fishing careers on Neptune," said Efan. "Sure word will get around we mutinied now that Finbar got caught."

"Somebody'll take us in," said Hendrik. "Most captains'll understand, Finbar being what he was. I know other skippers. Might need deckhands. You all still interested?"

Jenson wished he could say no. He and Efan both nodded, and Ogorris made his customary bow of acceptance. The Neptunian's face was unreadable as usual, but Jenson caught a hint of sadness in his posture.

As they got up and headed back to the town, Jenson walked behind the three deckhands, their defeated forms slouching as they made their way in the darkness. Shivering as the water dripped from his clothes, Jenson silently cursed himself for coming to Neptune, wondering how much longer he would have to endure the endless horrors and disappointment of fishing the ocean planet.

David England is a ponderer, generalist, and student-of-every-thing who, in the words of his daughter, "does math for a living." *Following a nomadic childhood typical among military families, and supplemented by wanderings of his own, he now resides in the well-rooted community of Two Rivers, Wisconsin (birthplace of the ice cream sundae) with his wife Anne, her incredible artwork, and the half-dozen or so unwritten novels which have taken up residence inside his head over the years.*

In one sense, it's unfortunate that the authors of science fiction's golden age didn't know in advance about the steampunk genre—that dizzy blend of Victorian esthetic and advanced technology that's carved out its own landscape in the contemporary imagination. In another sense, this is good news for today's intrepid explorers of the Old Solar System. As David England's Lady Penelope and the Drug Lords of Venus *demonstrates, steampunk and the Old Solar System is a match made in the heavens...*

Lady Penelope and
the Drug Lords of Venus

by David England

THERE ARE THOSE, my lady," her host said carefully, "who would assert that your inquiry is no business for a woman."

Lady Penelope Hillcrest, Fifteenth Baroness Botelier, sipped her tea as she considered the man seated in the armchair across from her. Lord Reginald Darsey, Earl Ashbury and His Majesty's Viceroy of the British Venusian Concession, examined her casually with calm grey eyes.

"I understand, my lord," Penelope replied as she lowered her cup. The liquid shimmered a fluorescent blue, smelled of cinnamon, and had a sharp, peppery bite which she very much enjoyed. She would be looking into acquiring some for her stores during her stay here, she'd already decided, as well as the possibility of obtaining native stock from which she might develop a hybrid crop suitable for her Martian estate. "Nonetheless, I have a commission to fulfill and I would not care to disappoint Lord Salisbury." She set her teacup on the saucer resting on the side-table to her right. "How official might this attitude to which you refer be, if I may ask?"

Ashbury smiled tightly. "Rest assured that you will receive the full cooperation of this office in your efforts. I only wished to apprise you of attitudes at large with which you may have to contend, both within the society of this Concession and more generally with respect to the Territorial government of the Franco-Spanish Empire." He looked at her pointedly. "The prime minister believes—and not without cause, as I understand—that you bring certain elements into play which may prove more fruitful in the destruction of this interplanetary scourge than the efforts to date." Pausing to sip his tea, he continued. "I will certainly not be one to gainsay Lord Salisbury's opinion."

"I see, my lord," Penelope responded as she crossed her legs beneath her skirts. The cultural blend of the Franco-Spanish was indeed heterogeneous and contradictory. On the one hand, it had embraced the French republican proclamation of the Natural Rights of Man and Woman on the legal front, yet on the other hand displayed a somewhat narrower view of gender roles societally. Penelope did appreciate that Venusian women's fashion had adopted the pantalons, suitably loose so as to disguise the female form, though frankly she preferred the riding breeches of her outback fieldwear. For a woman, these were a scandal to all proper British society, whether one was speaking of London or Barsoom, but extremely practical in the Martian highlands. As a newly-commissioned agent of His Majesty's government, however, she was finding it necessary to be more diplomatic and therefore she had selected rather conservative attire for this particular meeting. Her modestly-tailored dress layered muted blues with dusky greys. Raven-black hair, quite short for current fashion, was cut to a page-boy style. Emerald eyes met her host's gaze evenly.

"However," Ashbury cautioned, "the management of an empire is a delicate balancing act. When her late majesty the

Queen passed on two years ago, there was great concern that the stability that her reign had come to represent would similarly pass from these worlds. It has been the focus of His Majesty's government to reassure on that score." Ashbury set his own cup aside.

Penelope nodded. The death of Queen Victoria had come on Christmas Day, 1897, following a sudden illness and her eldest son had consequently assumed the throne as Edward VII. While her reign had been long—some sixty years—and her death not unexpected, the swiftness of that end had left many of her former subjects unsettled.

"What is a traditionalist to do, my lady?" her host inquired. "On the one hand, we crave stability, certainty, and a steady hand at the tiller of the Empire. On the other hand, the turning of the century will be upon us in a matter of weeks. No one is so naive as to think that the changes of this coming twentieth century will not eclipse those we have witnessed already within our own lifetimes." He gestured vaguely with one hand. "The youth, if you will pardon me, do chomp at the bit and shake off the efforts of calmer hands to restrain them."

Penelope kept her expression bland. At twenty-six, she was undoubtedly a member of that group to which Ashbury had referred so casually, and the notoriety of her upbringing was still the subject of whispered gossip in certain circles. Her mother had died at her birth and her father had chosen not only not to remarry but also to raise his only child in a manner he saw fit for his heir. That her education and childhood had been unusual for one of her sex was a gross understatement. It had been little more than a year ago, shortly having reached her majority, that she had inherited her title and the family's Martian estate in the wake of her father's assassination by an American agent just outside a London cafe. And it had been her subsequent quest to unravel the mystery of her father's secretive final project and to bring his killer to justice that had brought her to Salisbury's attention. That first task had been accomplished, as she had uncovered her father's research into alternatives to the vulcanite crystals which propelled the vessels of the various powers through the aetheric currents of space. Her second task, however, remained undone.

"Yet change is upon us," Ashbury continued. "My own daughter Francine, for example, has taken a most unwomanly interest in marksmanship and hardly a week goes by without one member of the family or another commenting on how troubled my late wife must be in her rest. However, I can only register my public disapproval—to uphold social standards, of course—as she is of age and free to enter the exhibition tournaments along with any inhabitant of Venus." He eyed Penelope deliberately. "The fact that she can out-shoot half the men of the best drill regiment of La Grande Armée de Vénus has absolutely no bearing on the matter."

Penelope only just managed to suppress an amused smile. "I do believe that I understand your lordship's meaning," she replied with equal nonchalance.

"Excellent," Ashbury responded and leaned back into his chair. "With that business out of the way, I rather suppose we should discuss this mission of yours."

"Agreed." Penelope settled her hands on her lap. "I understand that you were provided a précis of my assignment. While I have an outline of the situation here on Venus, I would appreciate any relevant information that you might be able to provide."

"I can provide you with something far better than information, Lady Botelier," Ashbury replied. "This noxious trade is a scourge upon the worlds and it is the duty of every right-minded government to work toward its eradication."

Penelope could only nod in agreement with her host's vehemence. There were any number of vices which proliferated across human civilization: prostitution, gambling, and liquor, to name only a few. Generally, these were activities acceptable within moderation, but ruinous when taken to excess. The drug trade, however, had no positive aspect to it. Opium had long been a source of trouble and additional addictive and debilitating substances had been discovered among the native flora of the new worlds as the space age had extended the horizons of human settlement.

In these last several years, though, even more potent varieties of known drugs had been appearing on the underground markets across the worlds. While these new versions produced a set of common symptoms, there seemed to be no linkage in cause and rumors surrounded the phenomenon like an impenetrable fog, leaving authorities stumbling blindly as recognition of the shifted terrain slowly dawned on them. It had been after some years of futile efforts by various organs of His Majesty's government that Salisbury had asked her to pursue an independent investigation. That had been over seven months ago.

She had begun her inquiries on her native Mars, which she knew best among the worlds, but it quickly became apparent to her that the web of which she was encountering a few strands actually spanned the entire system. Carefully making her way along the seemingly isolated threads, she had worked her way slowly, determinedly, toward the heart. That trail had now brought her to Venus.

"I would be most appreciative of any aid which your office could offer," Penelope replied. "What might your lordship have in mind?"

"There is a young man on my staff," Ashbury responded, "who is most passionate in the pursuit of this evil. My intention is to release him from his current duties so that he might assist you in your inquiry for the duration of your stay on this planet."

Penelope's eyebrows rose. "That is exceedingly generous, my lord. I would gladly accept such assistance."

Ashbury rose from his seat and walked over to the edge of his desk, pressing a button on a small box that sat at one corner. A moment later, the office door opened and his secretary stepped into the room.

"My lord?"

"Please have Phaesphoros come in, Michaels," Ashbury directed the man.

"Yes, my lord."

"He is a most energetic, somewhat excitable, young man," Ashbury continued after Michaels had shut the door behind him. "Likely due to his heritage. His mother is of Greek extraction, as I understand it, but he is a most precise and effective clerk with a bright future ahead of him in this administration. Those qualities, along with this personal interest he has apparently taken in this matter, ought to serve you well in your efforts."

Penelope stood as the door opened once more and she was mildly surprised to see a sensibly-dressed man in his twenties with light blond hair and sky-blue eyes enter.

Ashbury turned to the young man. "This is Lady Botelier." To Penelope, he said, "My lady, Thaumiel Phaesphoros."

Phaesphoros bowed gracefully. "My lady."

Penelope inclined her head. "Mr. Phaesphoros."

Ashbury looked at the clerk. "You have been briefed on Lady Botelier's inquiry, I understand." Observing the silent nod in response, Ashbury continued, "For the duration of her stay on Venus, you are to assist her in any manner she requires. All of your present duties will be suspended for the interim."

"I understand, my lord," the young man affirmed.

"Very good," Ashbury replied. "If the two of you would now excuse me, I have other matters of state to which I must attend. I leave you to your commission, Lady Botelier. Perhaps Phaesphoros might better acquaint you with the fair city

of Aphrodite as you begin your investigations here?"
Penelope nodded in agreement. "Thank you, my lord.
That is an excellent suggestion and would be most welcome."
Phaesphoros smiled and politely gestured toward the
door. "After you, my lady."

"I UNDERSTAND THIS is your ladyship's first visit to Venus?"
Phaesphoros inquired as the pair stepped through the doors
and beneath the covered porch which held off the day's driz-
zle.
"It is," she replied. "But, if I may be so bold as to offend propriety, please call me Penelope. If we are going to be
working together this closely, it might be helpful to dispense
with the 'my ladys' and 'your ladyships'." She looked at him.
"Thaumiel."
Her companion grinned as he flagged down a passing cab
drawn by a large four-legged, ostrich-like creature with blue-
green feathers and a prominent black beak. "I am hardly offended. However, in that case you must call me 'Tom.' It's
just easier."
Penelope smiled back. "Tom, it is."
"And if I, in turn, may be so bold, Penelope, where is it
you are staying?" The cab came to a halt in front of them.
"The Queen Elizabeth."
Tom nodded. "The restaurant there is quite good; however, might I suggest another location for dinner where we
might 'talk shop,' as they say?"
"I place myself in your hands, good sir."
Tom held the cab door for her. "I will endeavor not to
disappoint you." He looked up at the driver. "Chez Martin,
please."
The two of them settled in their seats facing one another
as the cab pulled away from the walk and entered the flow of
traffic along the covered streetway.

"You are undoubtedly wondering about my appearance and my family name," Tom said after a moment.

"I was, in fact," Penelope admitted. "But I did not wish to be rude. Lord Ashbury mentioned your mother's ancestry, which quite frankly, does not seem much in evidence. And yes, 'Thaumiel' is a rather unusual name."

"My maternal grandfather was something of a student of the old lore and my naming was an inspiration of his. As to my appearance, the explanation is a bit more prosaic. My mother was herself of mixed ancestry and my father is English. My features are one of the few things I received from him."

Penelope sensed where this discussion was leading. "A prominent family?"

Tom nodded. "One with whom you might be familiar, given your family estate on Mars. My father is the Earl Redgrove."

Penelope looked at her companion levelly. "The Earl Redgrove is a fourteen year-old boy."

Tom blinked. "Oh, my. Yes, that did happen, didn't it? I meant the previous Earl Redgrove, of course. I fear that I am not in contact with the family, being born on the wrong side of the sheets and all that."

"You don't seem terribly bitter at your situation," Penelope commented.

Tom shrugged. "I've had all of my life to become accustomed to my lot. It would seem that I am the eldest of a whole brood of bastard-children, yet I have managed to make my own way without any assistance from a family who refuses to acknowledge my existence in any event. Phaesphoros is my mother's family. I feel that my name suits me quite well."

"I see," was all that Penelope could think of to say.

Tom shook his head. "Do not trouble yourself, please. It is the way of these worlds." The cab began to slow and then came to a gentle halt. "But here we are. Please allow me to introduce you to some of Aphrodite's finest cuisine."

Penelope had to admit to being rather impressed as they were greeted and shown to a tastefully-appointed table for two off to one side of the main dining space. The wide window next to them provided an expansive view of the bay below and the churning waters of the Sea of Eros beyond. She allowed herself to be guided through the menu, as she was unfamiliar with most native Venusian dishes and accepted Tom's suggestions gratefully, including a mixed appetizer that she might sample an even wider variety of native fare.

"I would expect," Tom began as their food was served, "that the most effective course of action would be for us to pool our information and share what each has uncovered in our respective investigations." He inclined his head slightly as he gestured casually. "Would you like to go first?"

Penelope nodded. "I agree, and thank you." She gathered her thoughts for a moment before continuing. "After my meeting with the prime minister over half a year ago, I initiated my inquiries on Mars, as its territory and society were the most familiar to me. The size and scope of the drug trade has grown significantly in these last years, exploding from an unfortunate but ubiquitous societal illness to something more akin to a plague." She felt Tom's assessing gaze as she spoke. "I have known too many people--of all ranks of society--who have fallen into this web of darkness, never to emerge again." She looked at Tom with a certain deliberateness. "Including your late father."

"I see," Tom commented. "I actually had heard vague news of his passing, I now recall, but nothing of the cause."

"What I had found most perplexing," Penelope continued, "was the commonality of effects across such a broad spectrum of drugs, the majority of which were already known but had never demonstrated this kind of potency. Even within the Martian trade, this phenomenon has been observed."

Tom nodded. "From what I have seen here on Venus and read in the reports from the other worlds, your experience is not an isolated case."

"I have come to the tentative conclusion," Penelope said carefully, "that the common element is yet another substance. A drug within the drugs, one might say. A singular substance of incredible potency which requires a carrier or vehicle for some reason."

"Like a substrate."

Penelope examined her dinner companion. "Something tells me that I am not alone in my reasoning."

"You are not," Tom replied. "Your thoughts in that regard closely parallel my own, actually. My investigations have begun to center on that very notion and I have, in fact, stumbled across a whispered name for your mysterious substance."

Penelope's eyebrows rose. "And what might that name be?"

"Le voleur d'âme. The thief of souls."

Penelope took that information in as they ate. She observed her inner reactions to this outing with some interest: the discussion was engaging, the food delightful, and the company equally so. This last was of a kind with which she had little practical experience.

"You haven't mentioned," Tom commented as they began to sample the crisp sorbets which had just been delivered to their table, "how your trail came to Venus."

"Mr. Jefferson Broadstone."

"Pardon me?"

"I have been tracing these threads, attempting to gain sight of the bigger picture," Penelope responded. "Stands of a web, you might say, and I have gradually worked my way toward its heart. My investigations have identified Mr. Jefferson Broadstone as a significant player, possibly the most significant player, in the Martian drug trade and I have followed him to Venus."

"Where is he now?"

"Registered at the Queen Elizabeth."

Tom inclined his head with a small smile. "My dear Penelope, you are a most impressive investigator."

"Thank you."

"I am actually quite encouraged that you have managed to identify this man," Tom commented. "Your puzzle piece completes a picture I've been attempting to put together for some time."

"What do you mean?" Penelope inquired.

"I do suppose it is my turn," Tom acknowledged, placing his spoon on a small saucer. "In the course of my investigations, I have uncovered suggestions that this mysterious substance was controlled by an equally mysterious cabal of individuals who call themselves Les Trois Obscènes. The Three Obscene Ones. I have managed to determine probable identities for two, but the third has yet eluded me. I wonder if your Mr. Broadstone might not be the man I've been seeking."

"That is fascinating," Penelope replied. "I, too, have stumbled across a whispered name for the central figure of this web: Ombre."

Tom gave a small chuckle. "I hadn't heard of that, but I must admit that it is clever."

"How so?"

"This is the territory of the Franco-Spanish Empire," Tom gestured vaguely about them. "Ombre in French means "shadow," as I'm sure you are well aware. A similar-sounding word in Spanish, hombre, means "man." So in one word we have an ambiguous term meaning 'shadow-man.' Rather ingenious, I'd say."

"Do you suspect that such an individual exists?" Penelope inquired. "A single mastermind behind this entire network?"

Tom shook his head. "I doubt it. The complexity of this affair, the management of such a widespread operation...it would be difficult to imagine a single individual able to do such a thing. Far more likely the cabal I spoke of has encouraged such an image in order to confuse and befuddle. At most, it might be the name for the organization as a whole." He shrugged. "You have to admit, however, that the notion of a sinister, shadowy mastermind has a certain appeal to the imagination."

"I am less interested in the imagination," Penelope replied, "and much more interested in in putting an end to this evil."

"I quite agree."

"What are your thoughts as to our next steps?"

Tom considered the question for a long moment. "As I mentioned, I've identified those whom I believe to be the remainder of our supposed trio: namely, a Herr Rudolph Fleischer of Mercury and a Gospodin Daniil Lebedev of Ceres. I have information that these men have recently arrived on Venus, but their present whereabouts are unknown. If our suppositions are correct, your Mr. Broadstone is our best link."

"That makes a good amount of sense," Penelope agreed. "If there is a gathering of these men in the offing, we would do well to find out about it." She paused in thought. "I would like to speak with relevant authorities of the Territorial government as well. Is this something you would be able to arrange?"

"Yes," Tom nodded. "I have worked with the chief inspector for a number of years now. I ought to be able to arrange a meeting with him for tomorrow afternoon." He looked at her, curious. "I've hesitated to ask this, but I sense you are as deeply-dug into this quest as I am."

When he paused, Penelope prodded. "Yes?"

"Have you noticed," he said slowly, "any peculiar aspects of this network as you've followed the threads toward the web's center? Anything that struck you as unusual for a simple drug cartel?"

Penelope nodded. "I was wondering if you had observed something similar. Yes, in fact. A secretive dynamic, almost cultish in nature. It has certainly served them well for cloaking activities and deflecting the curious."

"I am glad I'm not the only one who has seen that," Tom replied, a look of relief washing across his features. "It is one of the things that have made it difficult to convince others in authority of the existence of this central network in the first place." He reached over to his wineglass and lifted it in a toast. "To our endeavors and the downfall of this sinister cabal."

Penelope mirrored his gesture and their glasses clinked. "To the destruction of Ombre."

"HAVE YOU HAD much interaction with the Franco-Spanish?" Tom inquired politely the following day. The two of them had just finished a very pleasant lunch at the Queen Elizabeth's in-house restaurant, the Sir Francis Drake, and were now en route to the appointment with the Territorial chief inspector that Tom had arranged.

"Not to any significant degree," Penelope admitted. "I know their history, of course."

The age of space exploration had exploded in the collective consciousness with Joseph Henry's pioneering flight in 1821, fundamentally altering the dynamic among the contending world powers. The paths taken by the two great empires which had coalesced in that turbulent third decade of the nineteenth century could not have contrasted more. The Austro-German Empire, comprising all the Germanic states but ultimately a union of the Austrian and Prussian camps, had been a result of practical assessment and considered negotiations. A miracle of German engineering, some historians had quipped. The formation of the Franco-Spanish Empire, on the other hand, involved all of the drama, tragedy, and spectacle one would associate with the Gallic and Latin temperaments.

Penelope recalled how, at the age of twelve and during her second-ever trip to Earth, her father had taken her to the Louvre and she had stood before that famous painting by a young, daring Eugene Delacroix titled simply "Le Duel." With rapt attention she had listened to her father describe the meeting of Ferdinand VII of Spain and Louis XIX of France on the field of honor between the Mediterranean port cities of Cebère and Portbau on that fateful first of August, 1825. Only months prior, the two kings had been in attendance at the wedding of Prince Alberto of Sicily, cousin of each of their queens, and during the festivities following the ceremony a card game had been played. Accounts differ, one suggesting that Louis made a jocular comment regarding Ferdinand's unusual streak of luck, another indicating he directly accused the Spanish king of cheating. The outcome of the encounter, however, was not in dispute. Flared tempers, an overturned card table, and a glove across the face.

Both courts strove to prevent the meeting, but each king refused to stand down: Ferdinand considered his personal integrity impugned and Louis felt that the honor of France was at stake. Even Pope Leo XII called for the men to reconcile, appealing to Catholic charity and Christian brotherhood, but stopped short of forbidding the contest outright.

It turned out that both monarchs were excellent marksmen and in the space of a handful of breaths, two kingdoms passed from one reign to another. The throne of Spain fell to Ferdinand's twenty-one year old son. The crown of France, on the other hand, went to Louis' twenty-four year old daughter, as the French monarch had assented to a number of reforms in a nod to republican sentiment when he'd assumed the throne in the wake of his unpopular father's abdication years prior, including a nominal constitution and the abolition of Salic Law.

"I think you are going to find," Tom replied, shaking his

head, "that the knowing of a thing and experience with that thing are very different propositions." He gave her a half-smile. "Particularly when it comes to the Franco-Spanish."

Penelope pondered his words as their cab came to a halt before one of many administrative buildings in the heart of Aphrodite and her thoughts turned to the second half of the tale her father had told those many years ago. If the confrontation between Ferdinand and Louis was a tragedy fit for bardic lore, then the story of Alphonse and Louise was worthy of the songs of troubadours.

The people of Paris had been stunned when, one grey morning less than a week after their fallen king had been laid to rest, a carriage stopped before the Cathedral of Saint Denis, where Louis had been interred, and the still-uncrowned king of Spain had exited, a black armband clearly visible. Flanked by a mere pair of guardsmen, he had then knelt on the stone steps of the great church and begun praying the rosary for the soul of his father's killer. As the hours went by and it became clear that this was to be a vigil of some length, a crowd had gathered, murmuring and muttering. The shock could not have been greater when an entire company of French soldiers had marched out, on the young queen's orders, and taken up a perimeter about the kneeling monarch as he continued to pray through the night and into the next morning.

Word of that deed spread across Europe like wildfire and so the people of Spain were only somewhat surprised some weeks later when a carriage stopped outside the gate of El Escorial, the palace-monastery outside of Madrid where Ferdinand had been buried, and Louise emerged to kneel at the entranceway to pray. What had shocked observers was the company of palace guard that had marched out to stand watch over the queen during her vigil, led by Alphonse himself in full military dress.

Penelope had always prided herself on her practicality, but the recollection of that childhood episode with her father brought up in her a long-forgotten wistfulness for such a romantic pairing. She frowned to herself as she followed Tom into the headquarters of the Bureau des Gendarmes. This was no time to be day-dreaming.

"Just a mild warning," Tom whispered as they were led to their meeting by a young junior clerk. "François can be... challenging...to deal with sometimes. He has rather fixed opinions about things, you see." Penelope nodded discreetly, guessing this might be one of those moments to which Lord Ashbury had been referring.

François Sebastián Alphonse Louis Durand, chef inspecteur des Gendarmes Territoriales de Vénus, was the epitome of the Franco-Spanish union. Named for each of his grandfathers as well as the improbable couple whose marriage had created the empire three quarters of a century ago, he was a stoutly-built man in his middle forties with a Latin complexion, jet black hair, sharp blue eyes, and a prominent aquiline nose.

"Thaumiel!" he greeted them enthusiastically as they stepped into his spacious office. "You did not tell me this this was to be a social call."

"François," Tom nodded in response. "It is not. As I had indicated, the prime minister has asked--"

"Yes, yes," the chief inspector waved his hand, brushing Tom's comments aside. "And while we wait for your Baron Botelier to arrive, please introduce me to this charming young woman you have brought with you."

Tom's eyes flickered over to Penelope for just a heartbeat. "Lady Botelier, this is Monsieur François Durand, chief inspector for the Venusian Territory of the Franco-Spanish Empire. François, this is Baroness Botelier, the investigator sent by His Majesty's government of whom I had spoken."

A look of surprise flashed across Durand's features, though he recovered a moment later and gestured grandly to the vacant chairs before his desk. "Welcome to Venus, Lady

Botelier! Please have a seat, both of you, and tell me how I might be of assistance to the British government."

"Monsieur," Penelope began carefully as she and Tom sat in the proffered chairs. "I have been tasked with looking into this dark and destructive drug trade plaguing the several worlds." She looked over to Tom briefly. "Mr. Phaespheros has told me that you have been his point of contact with regard to related enforcement activities here on Venus."

"That is quite so, my lady," Durand replied with a full smile. "Although my friend here is rather caught up in his twisted labyrinth of shadowy cabals. We focus on more practical measures here. Gritty street-work, one might say."

"I take it then," Penelope inquired politely, "that you do not put much stock in the idea of a more centralized operation behind the scenes?"

The chief inspector laughed heartily. "For an Englishman, Thaumiel has quite the romantic imagination." He shook his head. "No, Lady Botelier. What we are dealing with here on Venus, just as on the other worlds, are loosely-affiliated street-gangs, mere scum operating in the cracks and crevices of society. Nothing more."

"Nothing more? No coordinating force? Ombre, for example."

Durand gestured dismissively. "Even more outlandish than my friend's secretive cabal. No, my lady, while these notions may seem terribly romantic and mysterious, I'm afraid that the truth is much more mundane and the solution to our problem here is straightforward police-work."

"I see," Penelope said flatly.

The nuance of her reply was lost on Durand as he continued. "You would do better to focus your attention on those practical aspects of our efforts." He smiled at her again. "But I cannot see why a beautiful woman such as yourself would be involved in such sordid and seedy matters. I would be more than happy to provide you a tour of our marvelous city and introduce you the delights of Aphrodite during your stay."

"Thank you, chief inspector," Penelope responded as she stood. Tom and Durand mirrored her actions a moment later. "I will certainly give your offer the consideration it is due."

"Of course, of course," Durand replied. "Thaumiel will know how best to contact me. Bon soir, my friends."

Penelope's mouth was set in a firm line as they left the office. Tom said nothing for the moment, apparently choosing discretion as the better part of valor. As they stepped from the building, however, he spoke up, laying a hand gently on her arm.

"At the risk of being terribly obvious in my diversion, there is a lovely horticultural garden nearby showcasing examples of carnivorous Venusian flora. Perhaps we might take a casual stroll and entertain one another with tales of our various adventures." He smiled disarmingly. "Although I fear you have the better of me in that regard."

Penelope's shoulders relaxed and she allowed herself a chuckle. "I suppose that would be a useful distraction for the moment. Lead on, my good sir."

PENELOPE ROSE EARLY the next day as was her habit and proceeded to shift the furnishings of her sitting room in order to clear space for her morning exercises. She's packed the traditional, loose-fitting cotton garments worn during training, but opted to go without this morning and relished the air moving against her bare skin as she began to move through the particular pattern of blocks, punches, and kicks she had selected. If her punches were a bit more forceful and her kicks a tad more energetic because of a lingering reaction to her encounter with Monsieur Durand the day before, she did not dwell on that fact.

A rinsing off followed, as she had managed to work up a good sweat, and she took advantage of the newer device installed in the hotel bath, called a "shower." The sensation of falling water cascading over her body was unquestionably invigorating and she decided that having such a device installed at her estate house on Mars was something she was going to have to investigate further.

She had just gotten dressed, choosing to don a comfortable pair of billowy sea-green patalons and a complementing blouse of ivory when a frantic knocking sounded at her door. The portal opened to a troubled-looking Tom.

"My apologies, Penelope," he greeted her. "I realize the hour is early yet, but I'm afraid that I bring unhelpful news."

"I was already up," she assured him. "What news?"

"Our Mr. Broadstone checked out of the hotel in the small hours of the morning and left for the train station. I fear that we may have lost our link."

Penelope muttered something quite unwomanly under her breath and Tom's eyebrows rose slightly, a small smile forming on an otherwise forlorn countenance. "Do we have any options at this point?" she asked. "Any contacts he might have made during his brief stay?"

Tom shook his head. "None that I've uncovered in my questioning of the desk staff just now. He seems to have kept to himself these past few days." He raised a finger indicatively. "We might have one path forward, although I admit it to be long odds."

"And that option is?"

"I may have overstepped myself, but I leaned on my authority in aiding your investigation at the behest of Lord Ashbury to have Broadstone's suite remain untouched until we have had a chance to search it." Tom shrugged. "It is possible that we may find a clue as to where he has gone."

"Well-played," Penelope replied approvingly. "Let's be about it then."

Securing her own door, she followed Tom down the hall to the central staircase where they proceeded to descend to the floor just below. Turning down the leftward hall, they came to a door with a man in the hotel livery standing outside.

"This is Lady Botelier," Tom stated as they approached. "She is conducting a vital investigation on behalf of His Majesty's government." He looked at the man sternly. "Are you certain that no one has entered these rooms since Mr. Broadstone departed?"

"Yes, sir," the man answered. "The rooms were secured just as you ordered."

"Thank you," Tom replied. "Please remain here until we have completed our examination." He turned to Penelope. "After you, my lady."

The suite was noticeably smaller than hers, though the fundamental layout was similar: a sitting room with a writing desk and armchair, a separate bedroom, and a small bathing room with a tub, sink, and watercloset. An initial review of the space revealed a rumpled, unmade bed and a prodigious amount of ash in the ashtray at one corner of the writing desk. The lingering scent of heavy cigar smoke hung in the air. Otherwise, nothing of significance was apparent.

Tom stared at the ashtray for several minutes. "I cannot say that I'm hopeful, Penelope," he said finally. "But let's look again. Perhaps we missed something." Nodding, she moved to the far side of the sitting room to begin a more thorough search, but paused to look back at her companion. He stood with his back to the writing desk, deep in thought. Brow furrowed slightly in concentration, his clear blue eyes focused on some spot on the floor several feet away. His right hand rested at the small of his back while the left cradled his chin. Penelope found herself appreciating his lean form and aristocratic features, a frozen fire ruthlessly harnessed but capable of being unleashed at any moment. Unbidden, the idea of a sculpture capturing that beauty flitted through her mind.

Then the moment passed and Tom stepped away from

the desk, breaking the spell. Penelope began to turn back to her task when something caught her eye which cast all other thoughts aside.

"Tom!" she said, pointing. "The waste bin."

He looked up at her, startled, and then turned back to the desk. Partially obscured and unnoticed by both of them initially, a small waste bin was tucked away just to one side of the writing desk, almost directly behind where Tom had been standing.

Tom knelt beside the bin and reached inside as Penelope rushed over to him, a cry of triumph on his lips as he lifted a crumpled piece of paper in his hand.

"But does it tell us anything?" Penelope inquired as Tom stood. He turned and laid the paper on the desk, smoothing it with impatient motions. The note proved to be a scrap of paper torn from a larger sheet, evidenced by the ragged edges along two sides. Three lines were scrawled diagonally in loose script:

Kyth via Adon
Los Disp
SW

Penelope examined the note, puzzled. "Can you make something of this?" she asked, looking over to Tom.

His eyes gleamed. "I can indeed." A fierce grin spread across his face. "You may wish to gather your gear for the hunt, Penelope. I believe I know where the cabal is meeting!"

A SHORT TIME later, after Penelope had returned to her suite to retrieve a few belongings and don a light jacket, the two of them had settled into their cab seats and were en route to the aeroport. Penelope had cast a questioning glance at her companion when he'd called out that destination to the driver, but he offered no further explanation as the cab pulled away from the hotel.

"Is the drama of suspense truly necessary?" she asked finally. "Or would you care to disclose your conclusion?"

"Please forgive me, Penelope," Tom replied somewhat sheepishly. "I became caught up in my own thoughts. This has been a work of mine for some years now."

Penelope nodded sympathetically. "I can certainly understand that feeling," she said, thinking of her own ongoing quest to bring her father's killer to justice. "So why the aeroport?"

"Mr. Broadstone is travelling initially by train and lastly, I suspect, by mount. The first line of the note," he explained, "indicates his first destination is Adonopolis and then on to Kythira. Passenger rail runs from Aphrodite along this route. Kythira is situated in the foothills of a series of mountains in the British Concession officially known as the Prince Albert Range." He looked at her knowingly. "However, those mountains have another name: Los Disputados."

"The second line of the note," Penelope observed.

"Exactly," Tom affirmed. "Prior to the 1832 Treaty of Geneva, which established the boundaries of the primary territories and national concessions across the worlds, that range was part of a region in dispute among the old kingdoms of Spain, Britain, and Prussia based on their initial explorations in the early 1820s. As the kingdoms consolidated into today's empires and those boundaries became defined by treaty, that range ultimately ended up entirely within the British Concession."

"Interesting," Penelope commented. "Where does that take us?"

"To the final line of the note," Tom responded. "During that earlier period, the Prussians actually constructed a small fortress in those mountains along the northwest coastline of the Sea of Eros. I forget its original name, but in the aftermath of Geneva when it became apparent that the fortification would be of little value, it acquired the moniker Fort Worthless."

Penelope's eyes widened slightly in understanding. "Schloss Wertlose," she said quietly. "SW."

"Yes," Tom replied as the cab slowed and came to a halt. The driver dismounted and opened their door.

Penelope stepped out of the cab and turned to her companion. "So what is your plan? Are we flying to Kythira?"

"Not exactly," Tom responded with a small smile. "Aphrodite sits on the southeastern shore of the Sea of Eros, while the mountains and the fort are along its northwest shoreline. Mr. Broadstone's journey takes him west from Aphrodite into the British Concession at Adonopolis and then northward to Kythira." He led the way as they followed the covered walking path toward the airfields. "I am proposing that we take a short-cut across the water directly to the fort." He stopped and gestured toward a smaller zeppelin tethered off to one side of the larger field. "I give you my humble vessel, The Queen of Night."

"You're an aether pilot?" Penelope asked, rather surprised.

"No." Tom shook his head as they approached the airship and he opened the cabin door. "She is only an atmospheric craft, but an indulgence I have allowed myself over the years. Soaring within and above the clouds of Venus, it is much easier to dismiss the cares of one's life, I find."

Penelope nodded at that and climbed aboard. Tom began to make preparations for casting off. Penelope followed her companion's directions, helping as best she could as the ballast was trimmed and the engines churned to life. With a final signal to the ground crew, Tom brought the engines up to speed as the tethers were released and the vessel rose into the clouded sky.

"What are you expecting we will find when we reach the fortress?" Penelope inquired as the aeroport fell away and the waves of the inland sea rolled beneath them.

"I'm not altogether sure," Tom admitted, his gaze fixed

ahead. "It may be only the three we suspect to be the leadership of this cabal. On the other hand, it is possible that the fortress is in fact a more substantial headquarters." He glanced over at her. "Given the odd cultish behavior we've both observed, I'd lean toward the former. Groups like that tend to favor secrecy and small, elite gatherings over more prominent presences."

That reasoning seemed fair, Penelope thought to herself. "What do we know about the fortress itself?"

"Schloss Wertlose is officially catalogued as Eros Defense Structure 11-B," Tom replied. "It is under the Viceroy's administration, but has been admittedly neglected for many years now due to its low importance strategically. The Empire has more modern and effective positions placed appropriately for what is deemed necessary defense of this portion of the Concession." He shrugged. "There are greater needs and more attention placed elsewhere. Unfortunately this may have provided an opportunity for unscrupulous individuals to utilize the fortress as an operational base of some kind. I cannot tell you offhand the last time the Inspector General's Office reviewed that facility."

"Do you anticipate a fight?"

Tom nodded. "Quite likely. These people are not going to surrender easily." He looked over at her again. "Are you prepared for that eventuality?"

"Certainly." Penelope opened her jacket and held one side away from her hip, revealing a holstered pistol.

Tom smiled. "I am most impressed."

"My father's views on my education were rather comprehensive."

"I think I would have liked to have met your father."

Penelope felt a sadness rise within her chest, the ache that was slowly becoming familiar now accompanied by a vague sense of something else. "I would have liked for you to have met him as well," she said quietly.

Tom did not respond, but held his gaze forward. Silence settled in the cabin. Only the steady vibration of the propellers accompanied them.

After a time, Penelope asked, "When we arrive, how do you plan to secure this vessel?"

"Your question earlier," he replied, "was, ironically, not too far from the truth. While I am no aether pilot, the Queen was once an aethership, which I purchased as salvage and retrofitted as an airship. While I scrapped what remained of her aether engine and the Henry-Germain lens—the vulcanite crystals having been sold off long before, of course—she retains some of the equipment from her former life." He grinned mischievously. "Such as her grappling claws, for example."

Penelope's eyebrows rose slightly. "Oh?"

"As I recall," he continued, "the upper level of the fortress provides sufficient space to land a vessel of this size and there ought to be outcroppings or other structures that we will be able to grapple."

"You are proposing we adopt a strategy of speed over stealth," Penelope observed. "We could easily be seen if we are landing on their roof."

"If they are manned to any substantial degree, then you are quite correct," Tom agreed. "My suggestion is premised on the belief that they are not. I fully admit it to be a gamble."

Penelope nodded. "But one worth taking, in my opinion. Let's do it."

THE MOUNTAINS GREW from an uncertain line on the horizon to uneven rows of broken, jagged teeth protruding above the green-grey of the Venusian sea. Tom steered toward a collection of peaks further northward and then toward one peak in particular which stood above its immediate neighbors, a truncated summit overlooking the churning water below. As they continued nearer, Penelope was able to distinguish the walls of the fortress rising from the rock.

Schloss Wertlose.

It did not seem a large fortification, but well-positioned for its original purpose. From Tom's description, however, the lowermost levels were actually dug into the mountain itself, a significant effort rendered useless by the political turn of events.

They could see the fortress long before they reached it. Tom brought the Queen high and at an oblique angle off the sea, commenting to Penelope that in the event someone would spot them, it might be presumed that they were en route to some other aeroport. He maneuvered the vessel expertly, dropping her down toward the fortress at the last possible moment and bringing her to the edge of the curtain wall that ran along the upper battlements. Penelope felt a shudder beneath her feet as the grappling gear unfolded itself from the sternward belly of the undercarriage and wondered at the precision with which Tom brought the targeted wall within its grip.

The airship perched on the edge of the battlements, bobbing slightly in the wind. "We need to tether the nose, but should be well-anchored once that is done," Tom said as he turned from the controls.

Penelope exited first, stepping into the wet air and moving swiftly to the nose-line. Gathering the tether in her hands, she turned to the first anchor-point which caught her eye, a gun-emplacement only a short distance away, and quickly secured the vessel. Examining the knot briefly and giving a nod of satisfaction, she stepped back.

She was still staring at the gun-mount when Tom came up alongside her a few moments later. "What's the matter?" he asked.

"This," she replied, pointing at the fifteen-foot barrel, "is a QF 4.7 Mark II." She looked at Tom's astonished expression and explained. "My great-grandfather was the artillery commander at the Third Siege of Barsoom. The history of field pieces is something of a hobby of mine. Besides, ballistics makes for excellent mathematical exercises."

Tom shook his head, a half-smile on his lips. "I ought not find myself surprised by you, and yet still do. What is it about this gun that bothers you?"

"It is in remarkably good condition, for one thing," Penelope replied. "And for another, that it is here at all."

"I believe these guns are typical for small coastal defense works," Tom suggested. "That would make their presence here somewhat understandable."

"Yes," Penelope agreed, "but as I said, these have been maintained exceptionally well for being at an abandoned fortress." She pointed to a large metal locker set to one side of the emplacement. "The padlock on that ammunition locker looks terribly new."

"Perhaps the Inspector General's Office has been more active than I had presumed," Tom commented. "Although I am beginning to suspect that some other force is at work here."

Penelope looked at her companion levelly. "We should not keep the gentlemen below waiting." Tom nodded in agreement and gestured toward an enclosed stairway spiraling down into the fortress. As the two of them began to descend, Penelope cast one last questioning glance back at the gun-mount before following Tom into the shadow.

The staircase was wide enough for two abreast, but she lagged just behind Tom's left shoulder as they wound clockwise. Coming to the final turn, Tom stopped suddenly, his hand coming up in a sharp gesture. He turned his head to look back at her and mouthed a word: "Listen."

Penelope complied. At first there was nothing. Then, at the edge of her hearing, she caught a low, guttural rhythm, slowly rising and falling away again. Like a chanting of some kind, she thought to herself.

The stairwell opened into a long, unadorned corridor of hewn stone that ran in both directions. The sounds seemed to be coming from the left. At a questioning glance from Tom, Penelope nodded and the two of them began to move along the hallway. The corridor bent to the right, obscuring its far end. As they proceeded along its length, however, the sounds began to resolve themselves into syllables, harsh and aspirant. Penelope did not recognize the language. The chanting continued to rise and fall in its slow, monotonous rhythm.

They slowed as they came to the end of the corridor where an open archway marked the entrance to a windowless chamber with a low ceiling. An eerie luminescence filled the space. Three large copper braziers sat at the points of a black triangle outlined on the stone floor, each bearing a large, phosphorescent crystal which emitted the strange light. At the center of that triangle stood a block of dark stone, distinct from the surrounding rock of the mountain, perhaps two feet square and roughly waist high. The archway at which she and Tom crouched was in the center of one of the four walls of the square chamber. Archways were set in the centers of two other walls, to their left and directly across the chamber. The wall to their right was blank stone.

Three men stood at the midpoints of the sides of the triangle in loose, black robes. They faced inward, their cowled heads bowed slightly as their guttural chant continued. That stone altar—Penelope could not describe it as anything else—appeared to be the focus of their attention.

She felt Tom's body shift next to her and glanced downward to see a pistol in his hand. Bringing hers out as well, the two of them positioned themselves carefully in the entranceway. Tom looked over to her, the unspoken question in his eyes. Penelope nodded in silent reply.

"Hold there!" Tom's command sounded forcefully in the close space. A startled silence replaced the chanting as the three cowled heads jerked towards the archway. Something glinted in the right hands of each of the figures. Weapons. Tom's pistol cracked, Penelope's a split-second later. Another pair of sharp reports echoed from the stone walls and moments after it had begun, the fight was over.

THE BODIES OF the three men lay sprawled upon the hard floor among the blood and debris of the brief battle. Two of them, Fleischer and Lebedev, had taken shots to the head and were very much deceased. Off to one side, Broadstone emitted a wet sputtering noise as Penelope and Tom approached. Blood flowed freely from a pair of chest wounds and the man's head flopped loosely in their direction as they stopped, standing over him. Dark eyes blinked slowly, widened and then glazed over as the last seconds of life slid away.

"Ombre," he gurgled in a final bloody whisper before lying very, very still.

Penelope looked over to her companion, who gazed down at this last of their quarry. "It would seem," he said as he lifted his eyes to hers, "that this whispered word you discovered was the organization's name after all."

"Perhaps," she replied and turned from the scene. She walked back to the center of the room, its archaic design on the floor, that block of stone set at the heart of the black triangle.

"What are you doing?" she heard him inquire to her back.

She did not look at him but examined the strange design. "Something doesn't feel right." She stepped within the triangle to look more closely at the waist-high block of stone. "As though we're missing something." She walked around the block to the far side, standing before it with the apex of the triangle behind her, and placed her hands along the edges of the hard, cold surface. Running her fingers along the back and sides and finally the edge in front of her, she prayed fervently that she was wrong.

She wasn't.

A small piece of the stone yielded to her touch and slid fractionally inward. A hollow click echoed beneath her feet and she turned as a low, grinding noise sounded behind her. A section of the blank stone wall had pivoted on unseen hinges, revealing a hidden chamber beyond. Wordlessly, Penelope moved through that opening. Tom followed a few moments later.

The square chamber had a high, vaulted ceiling. The doorway by which they entered was situated in one corner. Diagonally across the space, banks of shelves laden with glassware, earthen vessels, mortars, balances and other laboratory equipment flanked a worktable. A massive furnace dominated the facing corner, cold but the soot about its firedoor showing that it was not unused. To their right, a low bookshelf was set against the adjacent wall next to a large wooden desk. A row of high windows along the wall behind the desk illuminated the room with a dusty light.

Penelope stopped in the center of the chamber, looking about her as Tom made his way over to the desk, its surface littered with several sheets of thick vellum dense with script and diagrams in heavy black ink. She watched as he bent over the desk, rotating one of the sheets slightly that he might read over its contents. "My grandfather spoke to me of this lore," he said quietly. "This is very dark alchemy."

"The thief of souls."

"Yes," he agreed, setting one sheet aside to examine another. "Your shadow-man seems to exist after all. Unfortunately, he appears to have already made his departure. We should consider—" His suggestion cut off abruptly as he looked over to her.

"It would be more accurate, I think," Penelope said as she brought her pistol up, "to say that he has only just arrived."

"Penelope..." Tom began.

"Step away from the desk, Tom," she interrupted him.

"And please keep your hands where I can see them." She looked at him pointedly over the barrel of her pistol. "I mentioned that my father's view of a proper education was quite comprehensive. You are not the only one who is familiar with the old lore."

Tom's eyes lidded slightly. "Oh?"

"You were far too clever with your word-games." Penelope shook her head. "The name of your ship, for example. A title given to Lilith, the demoness. The Obscene Ones. The Disputers. The Worthless One. Leading straight up the central pillar of qliphoth." Her eyes narrowed. "To Thaumiel, the Contending Forces, and the apex of the Tree of Shadow."

Tom nodded slowly. "Quite impressive."

"Did you even find that crumpled note in the waste bin?" she asked. "Or did you plant it for my benefit?"

"I'd sent Broadstone a telegram," Tom replied, "but the idiot actually followed protocol for once and burned the damn thing. Fortunately, I was prepared for such an eventuality."

"Why?" Penelope asked. "Why any of this at all? You had so much. A good position, a promising career. You are handsome, attractive, polite, and intelligent. Of good breeding and family—"

"Family!" Tom spat, cutting her off. "Don't talk to me of family. My mother was a serving-girl who lived with my widowed grandfather, a poor scholar whose only solace was his books." His features twisted with a long-suppressed rage. "She fell into the clutches of my rutting man-whore of a father when he was on one of his many jaunts among the Greek isles. After he ruined her, she was left as so much refuse in his wake."

"Did he even know you existed?"

"Don't defend the man," Tom retorted. "Of course he knew. My grandfather wrote to him when it became clear my mother was pregnant with me. The family did not deign respond."

"But you achieved so much," Penelope persisted. "Why would you throw that away?"

"I did achieve much," Tom agreed. "I studied. I worked hard. I applied myself. Attended the University of Athens on scholarship on the strength of my entrance examination. I did everything I could to make myself into someone."

"And?"

"When I graduated, I wrote my own letter to my father. I poured my heart into those words: what I had achieved, my drive to make something of myself." He paused. "My desire to meet him."

Tom's lip curled into a snarl. "I received a reply. From his secretary. His secretary!I was warned, in no uncertain terms, that any claim of paternity would be denied and deemed libelous. That letter cemented my hatred for the man and all he represented."

"So this," Penelope gestured with her free hand. "All of this is out of spite for your father?"

Tom's laugh echoed, hollow and unpleasant. "By no means. It is far more than that. But his death was a pleasing outcome of my initial project, certainly."

"By 'project,' I assume you mean le voleur d'âme?"

"Exactly," Tom replied. "I had studied the shadow lore for many years. When I arrived on Venus, my research identified a number of compounds present in native flora which, if properly combined and treated, would produce a substance of unimaginable potency. And so I used my position within the administration to isolate this unused fort that I might use it as a base. I built my network slowly, establishing connections, infusing its structure with layers of mysticism, always remaining that shadowy figure in the background."

"Ombre," Penelope said.

Tom bowed his head in acknowledgment. "And as my efforts began to bear fruit and its tendrils began to envelope the worlds, I waited. It was only a matter of time." He smiled cruelly. "A little more than a year ago, I received the word I'd been anticipating. I took a leave of absence and travelled to Mars to see first-hand."

"Mars?" she asked. Then the pieces clicked together. "Redgrove."

"Precisely," Tom replied. "I only saw him from a distance, across the crowded floor of a cafe in Barsoom, but it was enough. He wasn't the shrieking, wasted skeleton he would later become, not then. But I could see the shadows already lingering behind his eyes, the haunted look on his face. The hook had been well-set and there was no escape."

"But then why assist the government in the destruction of this network you had expended to much effort in constructing?"

"Its usefulness was over," Tom responded simply. "My plan had always been to employ the government's aid to rid myself of these miserable lackeys when I was done with them. I knew that eventually the bumbling bureaucratic officialdom would find a halfway competent investigator to delve into this matter. I had counted on that, in fact." He looked at her directly. "What I hadn't counted on, I'll admit, was that the investigator would turn out to be as capable or as intelligent...or as beautiful as you."

Penelope ignored the complement. "You had something more planned?"

Tom's smile showed a harsh edge. "Oh, yes. I have much, much more planned."

Too late, Penelope spotted the small sachet that had dropped from Tom's coat sleeve into his right palm. Before she could react, he hurled it onto the floor between them, an opaque cloud of white exploding in the chamber.

Penelope fired two shots as the swirling fog engulfed her, knowing that her adversary was already gone. Coughing, she plunged forward, seeking the doorway and open air. As she broke from the cloud into the ceremonial chamber, she looked about only to see that Tom was nowhere in sight. Muttering a curse, she sprinted down the passageway along which they had come only a short time before.

Racing up the spiral staircase, she took the steps two at a time. Penelope emerged onto the upper battlements and felt her heart sink as she saw the Queen already receding, a portion of cleanly-severed tether line still fastened to the gun-mount. She hesitated only a moment before running to that gun emplacement and swinging the barrel around with a desperate heave. Looking down at the ammunition locker, she brought her pistol up and fired at the padlock: once, twice. She kicked hard with the heel of her boot, breaking the shattered lock away. Shoving the pistol into its holster, she pulled the breech of the gun-barrel open, then turned back to the locker. With a grunt, she hefted a shell in both hands, managing to load it and locking the breech. She aimed by eye, adjusting the elevation slightly, and turned her head as she yanked on the firing-cord.

The gun roared and Penelope's eyes quickly sought out the projectile as it arced towards its target, sailing over the airship by a fair margin and splashing uselessly into the water beyond. Uttering another oath, she repeated the process, lowering the elevation to correct her aim, and fired once more. The gun spat thunder a second time, but now the shell's path was true, slicing neatly through the rigid structure of the gasbag. Standing silently as the echoes of the gun faded away, Penelope watched as The Queen of Night broke into pieces and tumbled into the restless sea below.

"There was no body found, my lady," Ashbury informed her. "The wreckage was well-scattered by the time the sailing vessels could reach the site, however."

It had been just over a week since that last confrontation at the abandoned fortress in the mountains along that remote coastline of the Sea of Eros. She had found the slain men's mounts tethered in the courtyard of the fort. The hexapedal, lizard-like creatures possessed a mulish obstinacy, but behaved reasonably once she had asserted command. They were nothing like the native jornju of Mars, but she had managed well enough, proceeding down the mountain atop one with the remaining two trailing behind on a long lead.

It had taken some hours to reach the town of Kythira. If the townsfolk were surprised to see a British noblewoman descending the mountainside, soaked to the bone and bearing a grim, determined expression that brooked no dispute, they said nothing of it. A priority telegram to the Viceroy's office summoned the authorities, though it would take some time for them to arrive. Following a change of clothes and a hot meal, Penelope had led a contingent of the local constabulary back up the mountain to secure the scene.

The authorities had recovered what they could from the operation, but aside from the cryptic notes left on the desk in the hidden chamber, little of value had been found. Not even a cache of the mysterious voleur d'âme was found, which might have been analyzed. Tom had apparently already begun the process of abandoning his lair and had removed any material of importance. The cryptic notes were collected, though Penelope was unsure if anything of use could be gleaned from them, suspecting that they were more in the nature of stage props than vital information.

"I see," Penelope replied. "It saddens me that such potential was wasted, such beauty twisted by hatred."

Ashbury coughed politely. "I am not one to speak ill of the dead, Lady Botelier, but I find that I must make an exception in this case. Redgrove was a cad and a disgrace. A disgrace to his family name and to the nobility of the Empire." He raised one hand indicatively. "That said, Phaesphoros' choices were his own and his fate was a result of those choices he freely made. I regret the path he chose, but I cannot mourn him."

Penelope looked past her host for long moments before her eyes met his calm grey gaze again. "I understand what you mean, though I find myself mourning the loss nonetheless. The lack of a body troubles me, however, on a number of levels."

Ashbury shook his head. "I would not be so concerned. Given the depths and the creatures which inhabit them, I very much doubt any body will ever be found. The Sea of Eros will be his final resting place."

"Perhaps, my lord," Penelope replied, her features pensive. "Perhaps."

Augustus Keden is currently writing a series of inter-related stories based on the oral narratives of real people of various ages spanning the years 1880 to the present. The narrations are his-story, her-story, not history. The narrators are: Irish, English, Scottish, Canadian, French Canadian, German, American, Polish, Mexican, Peruvian, Guyanese, Punjabi, Trinidadian, Jamaican, Barbadian, Nicaraguan, Costa Rican, Ghanian and Nigerian.

Lenore Keden is an African American woman from Philadelphia. She received television Emmy recognition while working for NBC. Her ancestors were kidnapped from Africa and brought to the USA to become slaves. Her mother born in America was not even issued a birth certificate. Augustus and Lenore live in a small apartment on the side of a cliff, on the slopes of a volcano, overlooking the ocean, just off the coast of Africa.

The Old Solar System is not necessarily a pleasant place. The most brutal features of terrestrial history can also be found out there along the spaceways—and so can the courage and the desperate necessities that drive individuals to pit themselves against those horrors. Augustus Keden and Lenore Keden's Ghosts of Saturn *is a lively and kaleidoscopic tale of one such confrontation...*

Ghosts of Saturn

By Augustus Keden and Lenore Keden

F OR A MOMENT Ryun was on Saturn looking out through Cy's eyes staring out at blue, red, orange trees and yellow, red, turquoise black vegetation, purple earth, oblique rings gold, red, blue, purple, brown tilted towards him. There were strange orange, red bird creatures flying through the sky, and yellow and blue striped animals that resembled cows. And then he was back in his prison, blind.

Ryun had been the Blaster for Zydon mining, in Africa. Zydon being the new rocket fuel for interplanetary travel – believed to have come to Earth from Saturn via a meteorite crashed in the Congo long, long ago.

According to international agreement the crater mine, originally hidden by tall dense jungle, was part of and belonged to the Congo Nation Republic, which had an internationally recognized government, and unofficially pocketed large sums of money to allow the Congolia Corporation to mine what government officials called "a lawless, backwater, human cesspool."

Therefore, from the perspective of law, Congolia was legally permitted to mine, but the locals perceived Congolia as predators, oppressors, takers, and exploiters. And in Ryun's opinion, "that's basically what they were, but what difference can I make?"

The Congolia Mining company was a World First Corporation, that had named itself Congolia in order to make it internationally appear to be of local origin. According to their contract with the government, all mining was to be monitored, and the quantities of Zydon mined were to be measured, and accurately quantified and taxed, before export. But in practice most of the ore was transported from the mine in unmonitored armed jeep caravans, with what was tantamount to a small army—to a private air base in the Congolia Mining compound, and smuggled out of the country to be flown to Asia.

Having been paid a great deal of money to allow the mining, and to turn a blind eye to the details, Government officials strongly proclaimed their support for Congolia, and justified the overseas export, stating:

"The Zydon fuel is being mined and exported by an International corporation because it has no intrinsic value to our nation."

Though, it nevertheless required armed guards to protect it.

On account of officials' questionable actions, Congolia's destruction of natural habitat, and various other irregularities, there were native and overseas protestors, who argued, "Congolia is desecrating, contaminating, despoiling and mutilating the native home land of our people, poisoning our land, our water and our food and dispossessing us of our native homes, homeland and birthright."

But that was not Ryun's concern. And he told himself he could not have stopped it or significantly interfered with the process even if he desired. "Mining exploitation has been happening since at least Roman times, certainly long before me. Most likely from the day mining first began. Mines invariably destroy the landscape above. I can't change that. I'm only a Blaster."

"Blaster" was an archaic term still used and a family tradition! His great grandfather had been a Blaster near Sheffield, England, many, many years ago, followed by his grandfather and father after that.

"Some families have doctors..."

Cy, a Black man, currently enslaved on Saturn, had on Earth been "executed" for farming. His parents, before him, had their North American farm taken away from them by force, and were physically terminated for protesting their dispossession.

Years later, beginning in his late twenties, Cy initiated, instigated and participated in many non-violent protests of his own.

Because he wanted to be independent of his own history, Cy's main "revolutionary" activities did not concern farming. He published audios—as most people could no longer read—criticizing the Establishment. He preferred audio to video, because society was prejudiced towards blacks and he did not want his face seen when he was questioning and criticizing the legitimacy of the Government.

Most of his audios actually focused on Belief. "Unconscious belief", he said, "Controls everything." He was not talking about belief in God, though that could have been equally as pertinent. He was talking about "Belief" in and of itself—any belief.

"Modern society, without realizing it," he stated, "depends on Belief more than any before it. Without beliefs, invisible though they pretend to be, modern society would fail as completely as the collapse of the Incas.

"Primitive humans, who had many beliefs, could survive without them. As long as they practiced the skills they had learned as children: farming, or hunting and gathering, they could live, regardless of whether their belief continued.

"Modern man does not have that luxury."

In his audios Cy stated:

"Everything in our modern society depends upon Mass Belief.

"Without belief the authorities would no longer have power.

"Therefore, the authorities do everything in their power to coerce and maintain Belief.

"This includes mass propaganda, persuasion, coercion and force to maintain belief in what is the current hierarchy.

"If our entire society, including the members of the military and police forces, were to no longer Believe, the power structure would instantly cease.

"The maintenance of every discriminatory difference in our society depends upon Mass Belief."

"Change Your Beliefs!

"Entitlement depends upon Belief. (without belief why would we allow some to be much more entitled than others?)

"Wealth depends upon Belief. (without belief why would we allow some to have a million, billion times as much as others? Do we really think they contribute that much more?)

"Change Your Beliefs!

"Belief in modern times relies on—memory—that has been corrupted.

"Memory is the recollection of what no longer is!

"Today is not yesterday!

"Yesterday has passed!

"Change Your Beliefs, Today!"

Such were Cy's audios. They were annoying to the authorities but since almost no one listened and Believed, they were mostly disregarded.

It was for the High Crime of Farming that Cy was executed.

The Prosecutor stated: "This Reprobate has been an ongoing blight upon our society and state for many years. He has never made any contribution to our society, and has always displayed disrespect to Authorities."

In the court room, Cy lived up to his reputation.

Instead of sitting respectfully before the court, as required, he stood up when his name was called and said, "I am a Sovereign Person. I refuse to accept or acknowledge the jurisdictional authority of this court, this judge, or give the judicial officials of any country the right to pass judgment on Me."

Police came to remove him from the court at that point, but he physically resisted them, and began to speak quickly.

"I refuse to submit or be told what I can and cannot do or say. I refuse to be numbered, monitored, regulated, and reduced to a subject receiving Allocations decided by Authorities!

"I am and continue to be a Free and Sovereign individual."

More guards arrived, and as Cy refused to walk or stand and support himself, they lifted him off the ground, and carried him out of the courtroom.

In spite of his many transgressions it was only for the crime of "Farming" that Cy was sentenced to Death.

After he was removed from the courtroom, the judge passed judgment in absentia:

"The accused has committed the Abominable and Unspeakable Crime of traveling to the NoGo Zone and Farming on what he declared was his parent's farm-land, before it was legally declared part of the International Park Ecosphere.

"The accused repeatedly and regularly violated the Code

of NoUtility—which in summary states no individual shall have the right to self-sufficiency, but shall always be dependent on the state. Therefore all business, land and occupations are owned by the state or their corporations. Individuals must be employees to maintain proper safe social management.

"This is further justified by the Governmental Proclamation of 24666 which declared: 'People without authorization from Corpco are not to perform any function contributing to livelihood for fear of Contamination. All land not utilized by Farmation will be designated Ecosphere. All business. all labor, all process not belonging to Corpco shall not be.' "

As a result, in Cy's era private business had disappeared. There were no longer any private farms, private hair salons, private anything. There were only giant corporations, Government Management, and employees or subjects.

Cy's parents had argued that not allowing individuals to farm and grow their own food, or start their own business, reduced them to dependency. In so arguing, Cy's parents had refused to leave the farm that had been in their family for generations. And were killed while defending it.

More than 30 years later, Cy was found guilty and sentenced on four counts.

"For violating the Prohibition Against Free Public Speech...One Hundred and Twenty years.

"For violating the prohibition against self-publication and criticizing Authorities in said publications... One Hundred and Forty years.

"For the Grotesque and Extremely dangerous and Unsanitary transgression of Farming...Death by Firing Squad."

But instead of being killed as he expected, and as the world would have its citizens Believe, Cy was slave-traded to mine on Mars, with a new name and identity, his own having been deleted and erased.

Mars was Central Slave Management for the entire Solar

System's Slave Work Force. Deportation to Mars meant immediate forced-labor mining on Mars, which was often followed by deportation for mining purposes to one of the other seven Slave Planets. The Solar System had become Earth's Slave Mining System. And the slaves referred to themselves as "The Living Dead".

On the planet Mars, all slave miners, guards and management lived and worked underground. Cy never once saw the planet, or the horizon, the sun, or the Martian sky, or even earth in the distance. He was instead immersed in near blackness, with only the dimmest of lighting to work in. And like all the miners he was daily abused, bullied, coerced, and compelled to labor, to mine in dangerous, toxic, radioactive conditions, for the privilege of being allowed to continue to live.

RYUN WAS BLIND and imprisoned in an underground Copper Mine Cell, or so he was told.

This had been his state since the Revolution. A Revolution of which he was the victim.

Living in his private despair in endless black blindness, one day Ryun awoke to "see" Ghosts peering in at him, trying with their fingers to pry open his pupils.

This was horrifying. To Ryun it seemed like the Ghosts were trying to escape into the real world through the holes in his eyeballs. But when he opened his eyes, the Ghosts— crowding round his pupils, prying with their fingers, trying to rip them open as if they were doorways into another world —stepped away.

He was not sure if the ghosts were trying to look inside, or out—trying to escape into another world, another universe— or what. But as soon as he opened his eyes wide, they retreated and resumed living their normal life, the life of an earlier, or perhaps current, African era, as if nothing untoward had happened, and he did not exist.

To be exact the fingers prying were those of black men, women and children, otherwise living in a village, cooking, eating, talking, laughing, going about their business, as they always had done.

But as soon as he closed his eyes the native people, in that closed-eye moment, rushed back again, to pry, as if by so prying, at the edge of his eye craters, they would have sight into— he did not know what—his soul—the current era—or something else—it was absolutely horrifying.

And so, sitting up, he kept his eyes open, and was safe as long as he kept them open. They withdrew and returned to their lives, and their daily local village business, until he closed them.

He therefore told himself, "Keep your Eyes Wide Open, and Limit Blinks."

But that was impossible!

Ryun found the situation more than frightening, and he remained in that state of terror until the point at which he passed out from exhaustion.

But strangely, aside from the terror, he found the situation somewhat interesting, if only because he could see – and puzzling because he could not figure what the people were really about.

The next time Ryun fell asleep (he could not stay awake forever) he was startled upon opening his eyes to see a giant luminescent, incandescent fish swimming by. Red, gold, striped, translucent, there were schools and schools of them. Some looked like whales, some looked like marlin, some looked like squid. But he knew they could not be fish, as they were swimming through the air, and through the walls of his cell, as though the walls, the mine, the cave itself, did not exist.

"What the hell are these fishes?" he asked himself.

"You can see us?" he heard a voice answer, which in reality was not quite a voice and he was not sure he had heard it.

"If you are fish, then I did," he timidly thought, not sure he was not making a fool of himself.

"We are not Fishes. We're from Saturn. And we don't talk in words; we use telepathy."

"Then why do I hear you?"

"Apparently, your mind is translating into a form your brain can understand."

"What are you doing here?"

"We're cleaning your air."

"Why?"

"So the people of Earth will stay on earth and stop invading, infesting, contaminating and polluting other planets."

"You think that'll keep people on Earth? Just because you clean our air?"

"It is our hope."

"You don't know much about humans."

"But that is our intention, to learn. That is why we came here in the first place and why we allowed the first settlements on Saturn. How is it you can see us?"

"I've no idea. I'm blind. I'm in prison. My eyes were damaged in an explosion."

"Ah, that explains it. Your eyes, your perceptual orientation must have been phase-shifted. We've been trying to communicate with humans telepathically for years and years, ever since we first came in contact. Until now we have been unsuccessful. No human has ever before seen us."

"Telepathically? You're talking to me in words."

"Not words. We don't know words. We're putting thoughts in your mind and you're translating."

"I am? I don't think so. What are you called?"

"We don't have a name. We don't have names, we only think in images and emotions."

And so he decided, because—although he was being friendly towards them—he didn't really like them, because he did not believe they existed, that therefore he would call them whatever he wanted to. In this case, derogatory names. They were not entitled to real names, because they were not real. And so as the mood struck him, for comic effect he called them: Saturnaliens, SaturNeons, Rayons, Spike, Rainbow, Seethrough, Whale, Horseface, Dog, Bluebeard, Sabre, Orange Squid, CandyStripe, Tooth-Fairy, and most often just plain Fish.

AFTER A YEAR of being enslaved in the mines on Mars, Cy was assigned the position of Blaster. This "promotion" occurred because: "The previous Blaster blew himself to pieces," the guard laughed.

And as Mars did not have a replacement Blaster, and as the guards had generally taken a racist dislike to Cy's skin color, and since Cy was the only one who could read, and the previous Blaster had left a Blasting Instruction Manual from 1910—which was not exactly reassuring considering its antiquity—and since they did not care if Cy died or lived, they declared, "You are our new Blaster."

And tossed him the 1910 manual, and said, "If I were you I'd read it."

Cy managed to survive and this eventually garnered him grudging respect and made him a sort of leader.

As such, 5 years later, he played a large part in organizing the Mars Rebellion. The revolt was successful, insofar as rebellion went.

But eventually they needed re-supplies, which only came from Earth. And although they thought, believed or hoped, that they were negotiating in good faith, the rebellion was overwhelmed and quashed by Earth troops hidden on the re-supply ship.

Cy was again tried in a court, he again refused to recognize, and was again convicted, found guilty, and executed. This time he was sent to Saturn.

CY HAD ORIGINALLY come from an African, Amish, Mennonite family on Earth that had incorporated the principle of self-ownership. They called themselves Sovereign Men and Women, and claimed they belonged only to themselves. For centuries they had lived independent of modernity. They farmed and owned their own land, grew their own food, raised their own livestock, made their own clothing, and traded with nearby like-minded families. Only in this way did his parents believe they could remain independent.

In the 120th year of our modern era, independence was declared illegal.

"In order to maintain and enforce standards of disease, infection, contagion and hygiene control, as well as biological purity, sanitation and the necessary disease pandemic control of our citizenry, the Government has decided it is necessary that all citizens desist from dangerous independent activities. No citizen however skilled will be allowed to perform any "self-employed" activity since that could lead to quality control issues. Therefore, such activities as Farming, Fishing in the ocean, and raising livestock, or owning a business, shall henceforward be illegal for individuals, and individual pursuit of these activities will be strictly forbidden. Only corporations, under strict quality control supervision, will be allowed to engage and perform in these activities."

"Citizens are to live in cities, and city suburbs, constructed for them in the midst of our modernity. Citizens are to work in employment, without regard to the perceived utility of such employment. In return all citizens so engaged will receive the Pay Allocations, necessary for them to purchase what they need to live."

For the Sovereign People this was sacrilege. "A free sovereign individual needs to be able to support himself and his family from his and his family's own efforts."

"And if you don't own your own land, if you're not growing your own food, building your own shelter, making your own clothes, then you are completely dependent on others for handouts," his mother had said.

"And when it comes to allocations, working for the Man or an Employer or whatever they want to call it nowadays, they can give you whatever they want, and change that when they want, or fire you and give you nothing, whenever it suits them," his father said. "You don't think they divide the pie fairly, do you? It's entirely up to someone's whim, and of course, over time, they like to keep more and more for themselves."

His parents were adherents to what was considered a bizarre mixture of North American, African, Amish Mennonite beliefs and practices, living in what was still called North America, and through remoteness and indifference been overlooked and ignored, and thereby managed to remain self-sufficient farmers long after the proclamations banishing such activities had been decreed.

Although farming and living on the land had been declared unnecessary, unsanitary, unhealthy and dangerous. And all food was to be grown by Farmation. And all land not needed by Farmation was declared Ecosphere...

His parents and surrounding locals resisted, and supported various anti-current government initiatives, for back-to-the-land movements.

"The Sovereigns do not want to be 'paid' for 'doing something' in order 'to buy what we need to live."

"The Sovereigns believe in maintaining their own independence and supporting themselves."

And even though Individual Farming and Back to the Land movements had been outlawed and declared illegal generations earlier, because of the remoteness of their community, the color of their skin, and their lack of contact with other humans, Cy's folk had remained unmolested for many, many years.

Eventually, there came a government that announced,

"This wanton flagrant disregard and violation of our Law cannot be tolerated any longer."

Cy's parents were executed while refusing to give up their land, which they had been "Farming Illegally."

Cy was placed in a nuns' orphanage in the city.

Except for being raised in an orphanage Cy's young life was not considered exceptional, or insufficient by the authorities, or significantly different from that of any other child.

And aside from his color, Cy's only deviations from everyday normalcy were that he liked to keep himself to himself, which if truth be told the authorities preferred, and he retreated into fantasy and read books. This was unusual but it kept him out of sight.

Most modern adults and children could no longer read and only listened to words read to them. Books, to the extent they still existed, were an anachronism and only "read", if that could be called reading, by allowing a computer to narrate, in the same way people listen to music. Words where they existed were CAPITALS. In the beginning this had mockingly been called Cap-Speak.

Cy's parents had begun teaching him to read when he was very young and he continued the practice even after he was rescued and returned to "city civilization."

His favorite stories were sci-fi. As a child, he only had access to the books in the orphanage's antiquated library. These were books that had not yet been thrown out, in a room that had not yet been emptied. In that archaic anachronistic atmosphere Cy found and read the sci fi books from a much earlier era.

He did not, for the most part, take note of the authors' names and therefore as he grew older references to the books he had read were for the most part lost to him.

He did, however, remember reading Burroughs' Mars adventures of John Carter, beginning with A Princess of Mars. These books still existed in the orphanage where he was raised, primarily because no one had bothered to remove them. They were his hidden treasure, overlooked because the library had not bought new books in decades.

Cy's predilection for books and fantasy might have given warning of anti-social tendencies, or cautioned the guardians of his social well-being with regard to some sort of maladjustment, except that most of the nuns themselves read, and considered reading relatively harmless.

And, since the nuns were female, they did not perceive how archaic fantasy could harm a young boy. In fact they were proud of his ability to read. Most children could not, and had no desire to learn, since reading had gone out of fashion, and there was no need of it.

Modern people preferred videos and talking books.

Therefore, the nuns reasoned, reading, though an archaic skill, would have marketable value for employment in the future.

As he came into adulthood, Cy began, without at first realizing it, to follow in directions that led him back into his parent's footsteps. And this later, inevitably lead to his clashes with Authority and the Government.

AFTER BEING "EXECUTED" on earth, Cy's still live body was exported, as all the still live bodies of executed humans were, to Mars for slave labor. The Authorities called it "Constructive Labor", but the prisoners called it Slavery.

On Mars, Cy was at first assigned to forced manual pick-and-shovel labor, as were all new slaves.

Eventually, as mentioned earlier, he was assigned the position of Blaster, after the previous Blaster had exploded himself.

There had always been a shortage of Blasters on all the planets, because blasting was still a very lucrative and highly desired profession on Earth. Few Blasters needed to do anything illegal. Therefore few prisoners had any Blasting knowledge.

Cy only had the 1910 Blaster's manual, but he managed to teach himself enough to survive.

And although he remained relatively un-versed in the more modern techniques of blasting he had at least learned enough to continue to live.

Many of the guards had hated Cy because of his skin color. They had given him the job in the hope that he would die. But Blasters have a certain status, and Cy, in surviving, quickly gained respect amongst many guards and most of the slaves. Their lives could depend on him.

RYUN, HIS WIFE and his children, lived as proscribed, in a city on the northeast coast of North America. But Ryun's job as a Blaster, 3 months on 1 month off, was in Africa. He was Congolia's African Demolition Man.

Although Ryun had never directly participated in killing anyone, if he thought about it logically, people had died, and people's lives had been irrevocably changed for the worse, because of his actions.

But he did not like thinking about that. He kept telling himself, "Nothing I can do will really make a difference. Mining will continue with or without me. Even if I stop, they will just go on. Mining will continue, as it always has.

"Therefore all I can really do is earn an income to support my wife and children, and make the best of our family tradition."

USUALLY RYUN LEFT his family at home. But in being away so often he missed his family and they missed him.

The company had been promoting their mining base for years, as "Bigger and Better than the Best Resorts."

And for the same number of years, Ryun had been insisting to his wife, "It's better, and safer, for you and the kids to stay home."

But nothing hostile or dangerous had ever happened at any of the mining Home Bases he had been in and he was always alone.

He had allowed himself to be persuaded by Sonya, his wife, and by Congolia's promotional advertisements, and his co-workers, who had been safely bringing their families for what they called "Great Vacations", that it would be perfectly safe to bring his own family. And so he had.

It should here be noted that Ryun's family was particularly unsuited for tropical African weather. Ryun, though tall, was very blond and pale. His wife Sonya was even blonder and paler. And their children had white hair and skin so pale you could see their veins through it, and some people even thought they were albinos. But they did not have pink eyes, so it was generally believed they remained so white because they never went outdoors.

On first getting out of the Sonic, on the tarmac, while still on the runway landing, Erin, his 10 year old daughter, complained, "It's too hot! I don't think I can take it."

"It's Africa, for god's sakes."

"We'll be indoors soon enough," Sonya added.

And his son Jesse said, "I don't like it. I want to go home."

"We just got here. Give it a chance."

And it was Hot!

But in the compound the children and Sonya found it delightfully, air-conditioned cold.

Styled after the most expensive, exclusive luxury resorts on Earth, the compound had super air conditioning, and numerous stores, restaurants, bars, movie theaters and three large shopping malls, stocked with goods imported from all over the world. There was even an indoor air-conditioned, 18-hole golf course.

And outdoors on the surrounding grounds there were palm trees, lining the long, ocean-breeze-cooled, sandy beaches, paralleled by palm-tree-lined golf cart roads, which carts even the kids were allowed to drive, plus jogging paths and walkways. The company claimed their location was the Biggest Baddest Resort anywhere.

"I can eat whatever I want all day long," Erin said, "This is Heaven."

"You better watch what you eat, young lady, or you'll get fat," her mother said.

Their company-compound residence was a palatial beach house far larger than their much more modest real home.

They were living an extremely luxurious and pampered life, though all the time invisibly and distantly surrounded by armed guards. This was not much different from many other world resorts, except that their compound was the largest, most luxurious resort on Earth. And their outer guards were so remote, they were almost non-existent.

To top it all off, instead of taking a car into town, they took a skypod into the local African cities, or a Sonic to old cities-become-museums in Europe, or alternately they flew to the most advanced cities of Asia.

This was the very first time Ryun had brought his family along. And he was very glad he had.

It was very good.

THEN ONE EVENING the power suddenly went off, there was silence and extreme stillness for moments, and then they heard gunshots and explosions. The rebels were attacking in the dark and all that could be heard were the bombs and the bullets and the blasts, repeated over and over again, terrible escalating and descending booms and echos in blackness, and all that could be seen were momentary bright flashes, followed by more explosions.

When the power was restored, and the rebels found the Congolia personnel gathered together and still alive, the leader said, "Kill everyone but the Blaster and his family."

Ryun, his wife and his children watched in horror as the rebels individually put a bullet through the forehead of everyone still alive around them.

The leader said, "We need the Blaster. And his wife and children make good hostages."

The leader had been educated at Oxford, and said in English, "We accuse you of: the High Crimes of Desecration, Contamination, Despoliation, Pollution, Destruction of Lives, Destruction of Habitat, Destruction of Livelihood, and Culture, in short, of not caring, of being indifferent to the consequences of your actions."

Sonya began to argue, to indignantly, belligerently, scream, "You can't do this to us. We have rights... We have..."

The leader shot her in the head.

"Too much talking," he said.

Ryun was in a state of rigid shock. Wanting to protect his children, protect them from what they had just seen, from what could happen, he froze, and was helpless. And there was nothing he could think to say or do about any of it.

"We don't need her," the leader said as Erin shrieked, and Jesse cried, and they dragged his dead wife away. "We can do whatever we want to you, or your children. We own you. That's what ownership means. We control your bodies, the bodies of you and your family. You are our white slaves."

Ryun went as if to speak but nothing came out.

"So long as you do what we want," the Leader said, "we will raise your children. You will not know where they are but you will know they are alive."

"But..."

"We are holding their lives to ensure your cooperation. We don't have to do this, but we are willing to do so out of consideration."

"What do you want?"

"We need you to blow up the mine. This mine is occupying, destroying, contaminating and desecrating our land. If you do that your children will live."

"I'll do whatever you want. Just don't hurt my kids."

"We know you will."

They took him away from his children, and then a few days later he was taken to the Zydon mine and given directions. He set up explosives to close up the mine, blow up the dam and flood everything underwater.

He then detonated the charges, as instructed.

But the explosions that resulted were far larger and far more powerful than the charges he set. He instantly realized, "They planted additional explosives."

Explosion after explosion shook the earth, and rock filled the sky as he stood under shelter, shocked and stunned, hearing, watching explosion after explosion, as if they were fireworks, until suddenly there was a blast right above and rock rained and crashed down upon him.

Days later he awoke in the Rebel's makeshift camp hospital, and found he was blind.

Weeks later, after Ryun had healed enough to stand and walk, the Congo Liberation made a great show trial presentation of him, which trial he could not see but only heard.

Before the sound of a large crowd of people, he was charged, they translated to him, with the aforementioned crimes of "Destruction, Desecration, Sacrilege, Disrespect and Violation of Ancient Tradition." The leader summed this up as, "The general crime of Indifference to the Consequences of Your Actions."

He was expecting, "Death," but the sentence declared: "Instead of death: for your blasting our land, you are to be imprisoned in a cell in the bottom of a mine shaft for the remainder of your life.

"We will raise your children, as our own. As our White Slaves they will learn to hate the white man for what he has caused to be done to them. And they will not even know who their father was. But they will hate you and all white exploiters for if it were not for you and what you have done to us, they would be free. And we will remind them of this every day.

"And they will therefore know some of how African people feel."

Ryun blindly lunged towards the speaker. He absurdly felt like he should do something, which even in lunging he knew was pointless. He was held down, taken away, then drugged, sedated and transported.

HE AWOKE IN a cell in the dark, in what the leader said was formerly a copper mine.

It seemed to him, he had been unconscious for a very long time, and now that he was awake there was nothing but blackness, and the smell of toxic gases.

And then he remained like that in the darkness, off and on, waking and sleeping, awakening and falling back to sleep, for what seemed weeks, and perhaps months, in and out of physical, emotional and spiritual deliriums in darkness, for he did not know how long. But there was no real reason or desire to be awake—awareness brought memory and pain. He knew he was blind, he knew he had lost his entire family, and he knew he was unable to see or do anything about it.

Every day he woke up. And waking was the most painful thing he could do.

He lay and lay or sat, in the extreme blackness, and over time he discovered it was not completely black. There were sparks, flashes of light, in his periphery. He was becoming confused, disorientated. In his blindness he was not sure what had happened, or was really happening. He had no idea where he really was, or what was really going on.

He kept re-seeing in his mind, the explosions, far bigger and more prolific than they should have been, his wife shot, his children being taken away. He also saw himself in front of a firing squad. This was untrue and preposterous, insulting even.

The bullet missed and exploded beside his face. The world went black—except this never happened. He was blind in both situations, then, some light began to return in the one. But not in his cell, not in the mine, but in the other world, then everything became black again in both. But not exactly. There was fire and bright light at the edges and other things.

Cy AWOKE HIS very first day/night on Mars to discover he was not dead.

But he was told: "You have been given a new name and number. And you are Dead! You might not feel like you are dead, but you are! You are Deleted! You are deleted from memory, from existence; you no longer are.

"Once Deleted you are not even part of Yesterday.

"We do not have to consider what you were or what you will be, or what is fair or unfair, or right or not right, we only consider what you can do for us Today in the Now.

"You have been erased from living Memory."

Cy thought it ironic a "dead person" who was actually still "alive" could be deleted, erased and exist no longer, but entrenched authority and power that was only Belief, "like a virus lived on."

Even though Cy was not actually dead, he had been executed.

He had become, in the style of one of Burroughs' titles, "A Slave Miner of Mars".

RYUN AWOKE. HE had no wish to awake. He often tried not to awaken, but eventually he always did.

Black, black, black. Hot, sweating still, even in prison.

He remembered everything. And memory was a horror beyond description.

And in spite of his blindness and having provided the rebels assistance he was still imprisoned in a deep black hole in the ground.

Was this prison cell really in a copper mine? He had doubts. It was a great deal of trouble to feed a prisoner underground. And it was still very hot.

Nevertheless, wherever he was, he was left, almost abandoned there, except daily, someone brought food and water and took his pail, or he believed it was daily, for that is how he kept track of time.

He could not see anything he believed to be real. His only functioning senses seemed to be heat, discomfort, and aches and pains from sitting and lying on concrete. No sound, except delivery.

Yet, as he had already discovered, the Blackness was not entirely black.

He was repeatedly drifting, no longer sure any more of what was real and what were imaginings, blind in blackness, nevertheless seeing things, daydreams, nightmares, three-dimensional visions, with light and color and sound, of a sort which he had never experienced in the light of day.

The Ghosts prying at his pupils always returned. Perhaps they were ancient peoples, or worse, ghosts of people he was responsible for killing. And then came the Fishes.

But neither the Ghosts nor the Fishes were always present.

In the times between visitations when he felt like he could think clearly, he kept questioning, asking himself, what is real, and what is not, picking at the scabs of his beliefs and perceptions.

"Am I really blind?" he kept asking. "Is it black because I can't see, or is it black because I am in a black prison? Or is there actually a light on in the corner?"

Every day, every night, in his recurring sleep, he kept re-living, re-experiencing the rebel attack, the great endless explosions, the rain of rocks. And then he remembered, sometimes in his sleep and sometimes when he awoke, that he was Blind.

But in blackness there was no way to verify his blindness. Without the presence of someone he trusted who could see light, how could he be certain? But he had been told by insurgents, whom he did not trust, that he was blind, and would be blind forever, and he believed it. Why?

Where were his children? What had happened to them?

And also, and this made no sense, in his dreams he kept seeing himself in front of a firing squad.

Kept seeing a bullet miss him and explode beside his face, blinding. But that never happened.

But the world was black.

SOMETIMES, INSTEAD OF Fishes or Ghost people, he saw abstract patterns and images and flashes, bright lights at the periphery, and other indescribable things which he almost but could not quite make out.

Then always it became black again, and he was asleep or awake.

And then sooner or later there came and went the Ghosts of an earlier era, and the Ghosts that were Fishes, who talked, through telepathy. And – except for prisons and blindness —it was all quite ridiculous and preposterous.

HE DECIDED HE was not going to believe in Ghosts or Fishes. And he convinced himself for a time.

But the Ghosts and the Fishes returned and they would not go away.

Then he decided, instead of fighting what he could not control, he would watch them, as you might watch a movie or outdoor action from the periphery.

EXCEPT, THE GHOSTS and the Fishes both insisted on engaging. The Ghosts kept trying to rip his eyes out. The Fish never stopped talking.

The Ghosts' clawing at his eyes terrified him far more than the Fishes ever did. There was no getting used to someone clawing at your eyes. When he awoke and saw them grasping, trying to rip his pupils open, it was all too much.

He kept pushing them away with his arms and hands, but that was as ineffective as their eyeball clawing. He could not push them, just as they could not claw out his eyes.

Though perhaps they were pushing their essence through his pupils nonetheless? He was never sure about that. But it made him queasy.

Even when he opened his eyes just a crack, they always noticed, and withdrew, but hovered, right up on him, as if thinking he might fall back to sleep.

And whenever he opened his eyes wide, they moved away. Instead of them watching him, he watched them as they carried on their daily lives, except that some of them kept looking back.

And every day he told himself over and over, that these daily visitors, these Ghosts and Fishes, were created by sensory deprivation. But that did not really make him feel any better, or more at ease. They still kept visiting and interacting.

Fortunately or unfortunately the Ghost People did not speak to him, or at least they did not seem to. And when they spoke to each other, and they were constantly moving their lips as if speaking, he could not hear them.

The Giant iridescent, floating Fishes in contrast never shut up.

But since the Fish lips never moved he was never sure which Fish was talking.

Was it Red or Blue, Squid or Whale? Sometimes he thought he knew but they never declared themselves and he was never certain.

But Fishes that float in the air don't exist.

And they don't speak telepathically, and they don't come from Saturn either. And logically, these were not Fishes or Saturnaliens, floating in the air or speaking telepathically, in a cave, in a cell in a mine, where he was blind and there was only blackness.

It was all perfectly unbelievable. Iridescent floating Fish as large as dirigibles, that he could see through, were speaking to him. As if.

And although he had nothing else to do, and therefore had time to carry on very long-winded conversations with the Fish, when he was bored, he could not take them seriously or really believe a word they said.

One thing was true, real or not real, these Fish did not move their lips.

He had a flashback once again, of the explosions, the bullets, his wife, his children, oscillations in and out between one memory and another, and then the relief after memory, of the Ghosts and Fishes. There was nothing else in the prison in the blackness.

AND SO HE slept. And he awoke.

The Fish were looking at him.

He said, "What are you doing?"

"We have come to talk to you."

"Why?"

"We need your help."

"For what?"

"We need you to help us stop Earth from Zydon mining."

And now he was irritated. It was bad enough that he was talking to Fish and they were speaking back to him, but now they wanted things.

"What's with all the words? I thought you couldn't speak. I thought you only communicated telepathically."

"We try to keep things simple for you."

However, as a response, as if they felt he'd challenged them, they showed him a kaleidoscope-whirl of images and beings he had never seen, in places he had never been, and he did not understand what they were getting at. He found all this very confusing.

THEN THEY SAID, "The Council of Planets. What you call Mercury, Venus, Mars, Jupiter, Uranus, Neptune and Pluto. They are trying to decide if Earth shall continue to be inhabited by Humans."

This sounded an awful lot like the Congolese natives talking about Congolia.

THE SATURNALIENS SAID, "We are showing and connecting many different things for you. Things you do not understand but they will have an influence and meaning eventually."

He was moving in and out of different minds and consciousnesses of aliens and humans on other planets.

He began to feel and be overwhelmed by the discontinuities, the insertions and disconnections, the apparent wakening, in so many different beings, so many places, so many different awarenesses, living multiple separate lives.

The only real difference between their life and his own was that he kept returning to his dark cave.

They said to him, "Your spirit lives" (or did they mean

"your spirit can live") "in many different lives simultaneously."

"If I can live many lives simultaneously why does any one of them matter?"

"That is the point," a Fish answered.

"What is?"

"Why lives are kept separate."

"Each and every life must be valued as if it is the only one," another voice chimed in.

"Whatever are you talking about?"

It was the smaller "Fish" that seemed to be communicating most of the time, but Ryun couldn't be sure, perhaps the smaller Fish just were closer and looked into his eyes. Certainly all of the Fish he could see chimed in when they wanted to, like an orchestra of discordant conflicting voices.

He asked again, "What is all this?"

"As we told you before, we primarily communicate through images."

—As if that was an answer.

"But you need to see this:" – and then one or another or all together they showed him images of the polluted air on Earth and how they were cleaning it, through their gill filters.

"What has this got to do with needing me?"

FOR THE NEXT few days, or was it weeks, he awoke over and over again in different bodies, in different places. As soon as he began to orientate himself they moved him. Oftimes he was waking in blackness in other prisons.

BUT THROUGH ALL this multitude of lives one other was taking priority: the life of Cy the Blaster on Saturn.

One life, Ryun's, was entirely in blackness, imprisoned on earth, Cy, the other life, was an African, a Black Slave on

Saturn, a large muscular black man, a Blaster, underground mining in semi darkness without much light, but on Saturn.

"Not really that different," a Fish said.

"He's nothing like me."

"I see a similarity."

Who said that? Was it the green and blue Fish right in front of him?

"You think!"

"He is of the exact same essence and profession as you."

"He's nothing like me. I'm a professional. I have a wife, a family and kids. He's an African criminal."

"From North America. Not so different."

"What've I got to do with him?"

"We need you both. Him especially."

"If that's the case, why don't you just let me be?"

"You can see us, he can't"

"So?"

"We told you before...

"We're on what humans might call, a different, normally unseeable frequency, we're often in the same space, but not exactly. And as you must know, every atom is composed mostly of empty spaces. We're in the spaces between your spaces."

"What do you want of me?"

"As we've already told you, many times, we're trying to save the Earth, and Saturn."

"So?"

"You can see us and he can't"

"I already know that."

"You will be our transmitter. Through you we can talk to him. Telepathically."

AFTER DAYS AND days of back and forth in and out of consciousness drifting, half between sleep and awake, it became hard to tell what state he was in, if he was truly awake. Yet suddenly he felt clear headed and wide awake. He had woken up. And he could clearly see there was nothing visible in his cell, and he now believed he was not just imagining he was blind.

He was in absolute blackness sitting on a concrete slab, with a bucket to his right for a toilet, a water bottle on the floor beside him, and one blanket to lay on the concrete slab. The room was barely four feet wide, and every day he felt his way to the door when he heard the food and water delivered, and left his plate and empty water containers at the door after he was done.

But now he was sitting lucidly hyper aware in the blackness, figuring for the first time in days, with a clear mind, before he was disturbed by Ghosts and Fishes. He had few moments like this. "I am awake, I am here," he thought, "there are no Ghosts or Fishes, or any one else. It is just me thinking, perceiving. And that is a relief."

But after a very short time the accusatory Ghosts reappeared, and then the Giant translucent phosphorescent Fishes all around him, nudging him with their minds, telepathically, into telepathically conversing.

"WHY THE HELL do you keep coming back?"

"We still need you on Saturn."

"Well, how am I supposed to get there?"

And suddenly he was...

Looking at..... Orange trees, purple clouds, turquoise soil....

And then he was back. And then he was there. And then he was back in his cell again.

"What do you want me to do there?"

"Not you—Cy."

"What? The African?"

"We will put you inside him."

"I don't want to go there."

"You've already been visiting."

"Crazy visions, and dreams."

"Saturn."

"Doesn't make any sense."

"Many of these things we have discussed with you before, many of the images we have shown you many times. But you keep denying or forgetting, or failing to absorb."

"Fleeting images, that's all you ever show me, is fleeting images."

"We've shown you your spirit doubled, tripled, multiplied. We've shown you reincarnation. Not reincarnation exactly, but incarnations simultaneously."

"Everyone has them."

"Working things out."

"Working out what?"

"Multiple consciousnesses."

"Working things out simultaneously."

"Existence. You have connections, independent incarnations, all working on the same life problems simultaneously."

"Independent linked incarnations."

"Cy is an incarnation of you on Saturn, who also knows blasting. Saturn is another place you live. You can see us, we can merge you to Cy, you can transmit directions and follow our instructions."

"Lucky me. I am blind and in prison. My wife is dead. I have lost my children. I can only see Dead people and Fish floating in space. And now you're telling me, you need me, just like the Congolese needed me, 'to blow things up'. But this time on Saturn, in someone else's body, that you say is actually me or part of me, I can't figure out which. Whoopee. And all because I'm blind and can see you and am imprisoned in a mine, and therefore can't escape from your nonsense."

"And you're a Blaster, and that's what we need."

"On Saturn. I'm not helping anyone blow up anything for anybody."

"The Earth rockets on Saturn."

"Why would I do that?"

"The Zydon fuel humans need for their rockets only exists on Saturn.

"We and the Council of the Solar System, have met and decided we need to stop Humans from pillaging and desecrating our planets. We therefore need to stop all human space travel, until humans are more ready."

"NEWS FLASH! HUMANS have already been to all the planets. There's no life on any of them."

"Different phase shift. We already told you this."

"Alternate Physics."

"There are entire civilizations on all the planets that humans just cannot see. Rivers of energy flow across Martian riverbeds and humans never even noticed them."

"The Ridiculous Human assumption that humans are the only intelligent life in the Solar System, is justified by humans—just because they can't see what is there. You can't see bacteria either, or electricity or molecules, or energy."

"The assumption that advanced beings must have digits is fallacious!"

"Digits are a temporary advantage in developing tools, but too many tools distracts from higher development and learning."

"Earthlings are not welcome on any of the planets. They are an infestation of polluters, exploiters, desecrators, and beings that create slaves. Humans are, for the Solar System, what you call cockroaches."

"Humans can't see the inhabitants of the other planets because humans can't see the primary phases that exist elsewhere. Human senses, human sensory organs are so limited, compared to us, and many of the other species, it is worse than if you were blind or color blind."

"I am blind!"

"But now you see and communicate with us. That is so much more important than your human seeing!"

"You are proof humans can or could perceive us. There has been much contentious argument over this. Many of the inhabitants of other planets had decided humans would never perceive other beings."

"Every planet resonates on a different frequency, but humans are out of sync."

THEY LEFT. THEY came back. It is as if they had never left.

The Saturnaliens resumed their argument, "We and the aliens from other planets are very upset and disturbed with Earth, not only for what Earth is doing to Earth, which is a disgrace, but because Earth is busy mining and turning into prisons every other planet in the solar system without consideration or concern for the consequences to the native inhabitants."

"We and the Council of the Solar System don't want Earthlings traveling through space. We have all agreed we want this stopped immediately."

"We are tired of human despoliation."

"If we're in a different phase what difference does it make?"

"There remain intersections. What you do in one phase can still poison or pollute another."

"Earth occupies a Space; if we were to destroy that space, in any phase, that would destroy Earth in all phases."

"THE MARTIANS AND the Venusians, want to destroy your

planet permanently, especially after Earth's savage pollution of Mars, and the fact that Earth has turned Mars into an Interplanetary Slave Trade Center."

"But destroying Earth would destroy the Balance and Harmony of the entire system."

"Each planet is necessary to balance the others, yet is required to develop independently."

"We have what we call an official agreement, or policy of interplanetary non-interference."

"Each planet is supposed to develop independently. The phase shifts not only create and allow different worlds but are the protection that allows each planet's separate development."

"Humans are violating the non-interference agreement on every single planet."

"We don't even know you exist."

"That doesn't change the disgusting things Earth beings are doing: slavery, mining pollution, contamination. If humans had any respect, any reverence, even for their own planet, they would not do this."

"So?"

"Since your fuel comes from Saturn, it has been agreed we will manage the problem."

"So."

"You are the conduit. We need your help to stop your fellow humans."

"How do you expect me to do that?"

"As we said, your alternate self on Saturn can do it. But he needs your professional expertise and guidance. We just need you to transmit your knowledge to him. We can merge you. You will be linked. In talking to you we will be talking to him."

"Like a forwarded telephone call? I don't think so. Why

would I ever help you?"

They showed him an image.

"YOUR CHILDREN," THEY said.

"What's this got to do with my kids?"

"Maybe we can help?

"Help, how? Why?"

"You help us. We help you."

"I'm blind and I'm in prison, how you gonna help me?"

They didn't answer and he didn't think they would, or could, since he doubted they were anything more than his own wish fulfillment fantasy.

"That happens in prison, from sensory deprivation, in the dark," he told himself.

THEY WERE GONE.

But after a time they always returned!

"You will be able to see through his eyes."

"Yeah, we already did that."

"At first you will only be able to influence. But eventually, you'll be able to control."

"Control Cy? I don't want to."

"Then let him access your knowledge. He'll do it. We need you, to communicate with him. We influenced the Congolese rebels in dreams and visions, and you saw how that turned out. Not good."

"You were responsible for that bloodbath?"

"Not exactly. As we said our influence was very imprecise."

"Imprecise! They murdered the Congolia employees right in front of me. They shot and killed my wife. They kidnapped my children. I'm blind and in prison. And they tortured me. Why in hell would I help you after that?"

"Because your children are still alive and still need you."

"My children again!"

He wasn't at all sure he believed in the Fish or that they could help. He wasn't sure they or anyone needed him or that everyone wasn't better off without him, but on the other hand he couldn't imagine anyone else caring for his son and his daughter as much as he did.

He still remembered Erin and Jesse being dragged away screaming. And how helpless and useless he had been to do anything about it.

And now here he was enraged, talking, conversing with the very beings who were responsible for that, and they wanted him to help them?

But either the Saturnaliens were real or they were not. And as he was helpless, blind and in prison, what difference did it make?

HE THOUGHT ALL this as he watched a dirigible sized Fish float by, and he remembered for the first time really, they can read my mind.

And he also thought, aside from the Fish, I have no one to talk to.

But the Fish, when they were present, monopolized the conversation.

He couldn't get them out of his head.

Sometimes he thought, "If I were to play along... like Alice, in Wonderland... I'm blind, I'm in jail, what the hell else is there to do?"

He said to the Fish, "All right, whatever you want."

"For your planet. For Saturn. For your children. For the solar system! For the Universe!!!"

"Yeah, right."

EVERY DAY THE Fish kept returning and adding details, "Except for the meteorite being mined on earth, which you exploded, there is no other source of Zydon on any other planet."

"Without our ore…"

"Humans will be stranded on Earth. But we must act soon!"

"WHY?"

"The 'geniuses' of your Earth planet decided after you destroyed the Congo mine that with all the difficulties of reaching Saturn, it is easier just to explode our planet—which to the Human way of thinking, was only created for humans —and harvest the debris.

"Easier than to keep mining Saturn."

"They have accumulated a large supply of explosives on Saturn and are now sending a very experienced professional Blaster to explode our entire planet. We need you there first."

"They don't seem to realize exploding Saturn will block out the sun."

"Wouldn't it be easier to manipulate human minds?"

"It would if they could hear us. We can't physically interfere, or interrupt. We would pass right through your matter."

"Like Ghosts?"

"Like Ghosts. Our matter will not interact with your matter. And if humans blow up Saturn they will destroy earth and the entire solar system. We need humans to give up space travel until they are more evolved; that is why we need you."

"You know what, you're not real! So why am I even listening to you? I can say and imagine whatever I want. It's not going to make any difference. Fish, go away! Find someone who cares, who's not in jail!"

"We need you."

"I heard you the first time."

My life is a crappy story, Ryun thought, "OK, not ok, off on, binary components, with – millions of tortuous sounds, colors, emotions, and feelings in analogue."

"Actually," the Saturnalians said, "Life, existence, has nothing to do with a story. But for you it makes it easier to understand. We resuscitated Cy after his suicide attempt. We need him. We need you!"

"As Saul/Paul must have wondered, 'Why me?'"

"Because you can talk to Cy. And after your accident you can see us."

"Why don't you just use Cy?"

"He's not evolutionarily developed enough."

"But I am?"

"You're broken. Breaking you, the explosion altered your perception."

"I still don't see what you want from me?"

"Telepathic connection."

He awoke again and again.

This is the condition of human existence. Awaking: there really is no choice—unless I'm dead. And who knows even then? I've seen Ghosts.

And of course it was blackness. He lay half asleep.

Saturnaliens… it was all so absurd! Ryun churned the terms, Saturnaliens, Saturnalians, as his own disrespectful joke.

The aliens do not call themselves anything. In fact they do not have any words. Therefore I call them, Squids, Flat-Fish, Whales, Marlin, Minnows.

And since he was in blackness and darkness, seeing only the imaginary and nothing real, and should not be able to see Fish at all, real or unreal, he could imagine them doing anything he wanted. Therefore, he imagined the Fish madly copulating.

"After all why shouldn't they?"

Whether or not they saw his joke in his mind, which is half what he intended, they did not say anything, which seemed to defeat his purpose. He meant to offend them. But perhaps imaginary beings can't be offended?

THEY ANSWERED HIM.

"Our earth manifestation is not our real being. We have created it from earth elements in order that we can manifest ourselves on your planet, while still existing at home."

"But you can't be in both places at the same time!"

"We can."

"WE NEVER INTENDED to be involved. We first came to earth centuries before space travel. We were trying to make contact with humans, as we had already made contact with all the other planets. But for various reasons, earth intelligence has been developmentally delayed."

"Is that another word for retarded?"

"As we observed, we took note of earth's strange propensity for self-destruction, and we could do nothing about that. Then we noticed earth's self-pollution, and we began to help clean the air to help protect humans from themselves. We were hoping humans would have grown out of polluting by now.

"Instead, humans have accomplished space travel and seem intent on polluting and contaminating the entire solar system. This is the reason the Council of Planets delegated us to end human space travel. Because the ore that makes Zydon comes from Saturn.

"But now Earthlings have the grandiose plan to explode our planet."

"IF YOU'RE REAL, if you're so all powerful, I still don't see why you can't rescue the planets yourself."

"We've been through this over and over."

"Excuse me! I keep forgetting!"

"We're not allowed to intercede directly."

"And this isn't interceding?"

"We've been through this. You communicated with us."

"I saw you."

"You were in our minds and we were in yours. That is as far as we can go. We can't force you. You must want."

"I don't."

They showed him his children in enemy captors' hands.

"Stop. I don't want to remember this! I want to go back to sleep."

"You may. But you can't stay asleep forever. Soon we're going to need you."

"To save Saturn."

"To save your own planet."

"To save your children."

"I already told you. I don't care."

"Your planet will survive."

"Our planet will survive."

"Your children will continue to live."

"Do I look like it matters?"

And then they showed him an image of all the exploded pieces of Saturn in the sky blocking out the sun. And another image of his children in agony, dying.

"But perhaps even more important, than that, will be the destruction of the Tonal Harmony."

"Tonal harmony?"

"Saturn emits harmonic tones."

"Terrific. The music will stop!"

These conversations occurred in his head. Since there were no words ever actually spoken, they were in essence imaginary; they were not the Fish's words, regardless of whether the Fish were real or not. So why believe in their existence?

Yet at the same time he was thinking of his children. But what chance had he, blind and imprisoned? These Fish are my mind's method of distracting me.... Or are they the means of torment?

SUDDENLY WITHOUT PROVOCATION they said, "Your wife is dead."

"Why the hell did you have to say that?"

And now there was a great pain.

He deliberately, repeatedly forgot his wife's death. As far as a person can forget a thing like that. He was now in great agony.

He had until this moment attributed his ongoing emotional agony and physical pains to blast injuries, the blackness, the hard concrete bed and imprisonment. He hadn't allowed his mind to go beyond that.

He doubted he would ever see his children again. And he certainly was never going to see his wife or leave this prison.

"YOU STILL DON'T believe we can help you!"

"I never said that."

"You know we can read your mind?"

"Three wishes. Can you do that?"

"Possibly. What exactly do you want?"

"I thought you can read my mind!"

"We can but there is so much confusion, pain, hostility, rage, anger, belief and disbelief, hope and despair. It is not a pleasure to go very deep."

"My children. Give me back my children. Help me rescue my children. Get my children back to me safe and sound!"

"Whatever we are capable of doing."

"What the hell does that mean?"

"What we can."

"Damn you. If you can't help get out of my head."

They didn't answer.

IN BLACKNESS THERE should have never ever been anything to see. But the Fishes. glimmering, slithering, kept coming into his vision. And the dead people. Every time he awoke. It was either Fishes or the Dead. Or he was dreaming he was in an alien body on another planet. And then he was back in his cell again.

But wherever he went, whether he was on earth or Saturn, or some other planet, he saw these Fishes floating and they had an agenda.

HE SUDDENLY BEGAN to feel ill, physically—a sort of telepathic interplanetary motion sickness from alternation, fluctuation between bodies and places, awakening with different eyes in different human and inhuman bodies, being pulled in all directions, before being thrust back into his own body again. He began to doubt or forget or wonder which body he really belonged to. Any body was better than being torn between them. He wondered if he could enter another being and forever forget his current existence.

Considering his own life (blind, helpless, imprisoned in darkness), that could be preferable.

BUT MOSTLY, HE alternated between his body on earth and Cy's body enslaved on Saturn. And this itself was very disconcerting—but what was even more disturbing, "Every single human body I inhabit is a Slave in prison."

The Saturnaliens said, "Except for the guards, and their

minds are especially unreceptive, the only humans living on other planets are Slaves."

"How far we have come through the ages, killing, oppressing, mining and enslaving."

"That is the problem."

And then he was asleep again, and then awake back on Earth, and then suddenly a giant translucent Squid was on his face. He tried to push it away but he could not move it.

"Stop it," he screamed.

But the Fish kept telepathically speaking. "You are progressing too slowly. We need you faster."

"Stop it! Get off!" And afterwards he thought, No wonder species of different planets are kept separate.

AFTER BEING IN the dark for so long, and in so many different persons on eight different planets, and trying to hurry as the squid had demanded, Ryun was finally beginning to believe, or come to terms with their existence.

"EARTHLINGS SHOULD HAVE suspected from the very start, that Saturn's atmosphere was artificially created and not a natural environment," he overheard images.

"But we concealed and disguised that," another responded, "so that they wouldn't know!"

"But any intelligent being should have figured it out."

"They don't even believe there's life on other planets."

THE APPARENT NATURAL habitat of the Vortex was easily accepted and welcomed by the Earth First missions. And in Earth's arrogance only two possibilities had been considered. Either this anomaly had been created for humans by God, or the solar system itself had organized itself for human benefit.

Even when alternate perspectives were proposed they were ridiculed and rejected. The Governments declared "Alternative Theories of Solar System Origin" subversive.

In spite of the governments' official proclamations, numerous speculative underground rumors to the contrary proliferated.

THE "OFFICIAL VIEWPOINT" never mattered to Cy. He hated officials and authorities.

He lived underground in a windowless barracks without external natural light, and only saw sunlight through a window while being transported to and from the mine in twilight hours.

Cy's job as a Blaster was to blast shafts and tunnel underground openings to mine the local ore from which they made Zydon.

In the beginning of his Saturnian incarceration, Cy worked hard as a Blaster, while he took stock of his situation.

They mined 10.5 hour days a day, half dark half light, underground, where they could not see the difference between day and night. They left in the morning for the mine and returned in the morning to the barracks at 10.5 hour intervals, the entire day and night of Saturn being only 10.5 hours long.

After being returned to the barracks Cy was locked up. With eight official hours for sleep, he and the other Slaves had two whole hours to do anything else. Mostly they sat or lay on their bunks. But they also bullshitted and played cards. They even had a chessboard, chess pieces and checkers. Except for the ride back and forth they spent their entire Slave lives without ever having access to natural light. CY found he needed natural sunlight.

Therefore in the early morning drives, when they were driven in the armored vehicles to the mine, he had fought for the seat under the armored bulletproof window. He then stood on this seat to look out at the light. He was stunned by the nature of the surrounding countryside.

In the beginning, he found it necessary to fight every day in order to obtain this seat. Eventually the other prisoners just gave it to him, perhaps realizing it could be dangerous to fight with the Blaster.

As the days passed, in the drives, back and forth, Cy was also given a certain respect on account of being, comparatively speaking, a good and cautious Blaster.

The men said, "All Blasters are crazy."

"It wouldn't do to have the Blaster angry with you."

"Not if you don't want to get buried or blown up."

Bizarre as it was, under the strange light and the distant view of Saturn's rings, Cy was shocked to see miniature people, farming in the distance – there were even houses, and towns and villages.

But although the men tolerated and acquiesced to Cy's idiosyncrasies they still mocked and harassed him.

"There's no point seeing."

"It'll only make you crazy."

"We're never getting out of here."

"You're driving us nuts."

"Africans are crazy."

Cy BEGAN TO imagine escaping, living a simple life: farming, growing his own food, building his own house, and maybe, if he was lucky, finding a good woman and having kids.

This imagining, though it seemed utterly impossible, kept him going.

There was nothing else to hope for. He needed a reason to live.

He certainly did not want to return to earth. He had found life on Earth smug, limiting, meaningless, entitled and unbearable.

He began to plan. Escape from the barracks seemed difficult, but not impossible, especially with explosives. He believed he could accomplish escape, but then what? Where to? How? Alone, or with the other prisoners? And what would he or they do when Earth sent troops?

He had been through this before, on Mars, but unlike on Mars he could breathe the air on Saturn and if he could escape and be left alone, he was sure he could survive farming. He could escape into the interior, but he was very uncertain what would happen after that.

He needed to make his escape permanent. He was determined to fight to the death rather than go back to being owned. He was not going to be imprisoned any longer.

There remained difficulties; he continued to puzzle on the planning and strategy.

His big worry was Earth. He could not think of any means of preventing Earth troops returning to search for and recapture him.

THE HABITABLE AREA of Saturn was relatively small. There was nowhere remote enough in which to hide completely. He knew Earth would send troops and search, and search, if it could. Whoever was in control would not tolerate insurrection. And there was no means of escaping off the planet, and nowhere to go even if he did. That is why they called these worlds prison planets.

And although it was clear from his window that there were humans who had farms and settlements, which would have been completely illegal on Earth, he was not sure what kind of people they were, or if he could trust them. How would they respond to a stranger? Would they think of him as a dangerous criminal?

How hostile would they be? He could not count on friendliness, especially towards an escaped Slave.

He had no idea why these settlers left Earth. Were they political, religious, ideological or some other sort of refugee? Were they sympathetic to others who were persecuted?

The guards did not explain or elaborate Saturn info, and likely did not know. They tended to know little, and didn't want to know more, and their employers and the Authorities in general preferred both guards and prisoners ill-informed and uneducated.

The Officials didn't want either the guards or the prisoners having ideas about escaping, or leaving the compound premises.

In general the guards only spoke to give commands and brusque monosyllabic orders.

There was never any news, or input from the outside world. And no one, not even the guards, had any real idea of what was happening off-planet. The government and their employers maintained the only things the guards needed to be concerned about was the ore, the mining, the arrival of new slaves, and the next shipment.

"What happens off world does not impact you."

Cy, however continued to fantasize, to imagine his escape and becoming a farmer with lasting freedom. Though he did not know how he was going to accomplish his desire, he imagined and believed he would. His determination to make it so, helped keep him from going crazy.

His great fear, in all his plans, was: he would escape, he would find a place to live, he would farm, he would find a wife and have kids, he would accomplish all this, and just when he was sure he was safe he would be recaptured and they would send him to an even more inhospitable planet. And torture him just for the fun of torturing. There were certain guards who seemed to love torture more than anything.

He felt he would never really be free, never be sure his escape was permanent as long as there remained any connection to Earth.

And so he began to think of ways of disconnecting.

But no matter how he pondered on it, and tried to structure and organize a plan that would work—even if he could organize, as they organized on Mars—even if they revolted, as they had on Mars—and even if they destroyed the Earth bases, as they were destroyed on Mars—and even if they destroyed the prisons—as they destroyed prisons on Mars—and even if after all that they managed to flee into the countryside and were accepted by the local people, Earth would not let it go. Earth would send ships with troops to recapture them eventually. There would never be any certainty of permanent escape as long as Earth needed Zydon.

IN HIS CAVE/CELL Ryun was asleep again. In sleep he could sometimes see and be free, alive with his wife and family. While awake he was stuck with the pain and depression of reality. Was his current situation really true?

He re-membered. And wondered at that. Is memory real? Did life really happen in sequence? Or was that merely the way he recollected?

He sometimes re-lived incidents of his former life out of sequence, and they sometimes seemed more real than anything that was "now", and he wanted to believe that the almost-real really was "now", or really had happened, but sometimes he wondered if all memory was deception and therefore might never have been. Life sometimes seemed like a deck of cards, and he could rearrange the sequence. Did such-and-such really happen? And in what order? Had he once lived a life above ground with a family and children, and lost it? Could he live life backwards as Merlin did? Time normally seemed one way, but not in darkness.

Of course he already knew about the invasions, the rebels, his wife dying and the kidnapping of his children in a memory sense. But even memory rearranges. There were parts of him that still had not received the messages, and were absolutely shocked when they realized. Not all parts of his being were synchronized. The terrible happenings, the terrible incidents were still in the future for the parts of him that had not been informed, which made it all the more painful upon their sudden discovery, while for other parts what had happened had already been forgotten.

Which is what made waking so difficult. Waking was the moment of putting everything back together again. But which order? That is what he was afraid of. Reassembled self, remembered, forgot, erased, omitted, was not notified and was yet to know. But did everything have to be? Or were there alternate realities?

Surely there was more to life than this. Surely there was something beyond, that he could not see, either in the past or the future, or something that he should have done differently, that could have prevented all this, some thing he had done wrong, that perhaps he could still change, even in the future, or perhaps something in his past that made him guilty and responsible for everything forever, and therefore he deserved it!

But what of his children? How were they responsible? Except, perhaps they had been too pampered?

He had to rescue his kids, only half innocent as they were. The Saturnaliens said they would help him. If he believed in Fishes, if he trusted them. He definitely was not sure about that. And he was blind. How was a blind man, Blasted Blind, ever going to rescue anyone?

But: if the Saturnalians really needed him? If the Saturnaliens really could or would help him, then he had something to hope for. If there really were Saturnalians? How much wood would a wood chuck chuck, if a wood chuck would chuck wood? Were there really Saturnaliens and did they really need him?

And would they really help?

The Fish who were telepathically listening said, "We do.

And we will."

"I wasn't talking to you."

"But we are communicating to you."

THE SATURNALIENS HAD imaged for Ryun many out-of-sequence series of events.

As the Saturnaliens did not believe in stories, they imaged incidents or situations in any order, and left it to the receiver's mind to organize and put together.

And there were always many different Fish imaging him at the same time, and the images of different Fish disagreed and he did not know which image came from which Fish.

But the general story, he had organized into words, so that he could understand the conflicts:

One voice: "When the humans first visited Saturn we created the Vortex, a safe zone, as a place where humans could live. We wanted humans to visit and live on Saturn in order to study them."

Another voice, "We didn't realize most of the humans were only visiting to take."

Another: "Earth beings are currently engaging in slavery, and utilizing their slaves to despoil and desecrate Saturn, mining Zydon."

Another, "Although we do not approve of slavery, or Zydon mining, our belief system has always compelled us to tolerate other species' differences."

"But not all of the humans are mining?

"True. Some did come to farm and live."

"And that is what we wanted."

"We strongly disapprove of mining and slavery – but until this time those were mostly human issues. What we cannot tolerate is what humans are planning next."

"After you, Ryun, exploded their mine, Earth decided mining is too slow and laborious."

"It is easier, Earth Authorities decided, to explode the entire planet of Saturn, to harvest the debris."

"These human fleas haven't really thought this through. The consequences of exploding Saturn will not only destroy Saturn, but will destabilize and end life in the entire solar system."

"The explosive debris will black out the sun. Destroy life on every planet."

"There are humans who suspect the dangers. They are trying to warn others of the possible consequences."

"But they are not being listened to."

"Other humans oppose destroying our planet on principle. They do not believe in desecration, destruction and despoliation of any planet."

"But all the humans with rational thought lack the power to make a difference and are outnumbered, ridiculed, dismissed and sidelined by louder, more powerful, greedy vocal interests, who call them 'Fear Mongers', and 'Chicken Littles'."

"The human Authorities in charge still intend to proceed with Saturn's destruction. To them it is the most logical and practical plan. And they insist they have the right to follow through unless it can be proven otherwise."

"But by then it will be too late."

THE FISH HAD never actually created an exact image of what they wanted Ryun to do.

But Ryun and Cy were both Blasters, and therefore the only logical explanation was that they wanted Ryun and Cy to blow things up.

But when Ryun asked, "Do you want us to explode the rockets?" —the Saturnaliens suddenly became non-committal.

"We can't tell you what to do."

Which as far as Ryun was concerned was either a lie, or self-deception.

Furthermore, the Fish refused to admit what they were doing. It seemed more than a little clear they wanted blasting. They had encouraged the Congolese to blow up the Congo mine and dam.

The Fish would not even admit that events made a difference to them. "What will be will be," though it was more than obvious they would prefer their own planet's continuance.

He became impatient with the Saturnaliens' ambiguity. Real or figments of his imagination, they were annoying him.

They claimed they did not possess meanings for the words "hint", "insinuate" or "manipulate". But as far as Ryun was concerned, that was all they had been doing since their first arrival.

And, images seemed to be a convenient method by which to retain deniability and remain imprecise.

THE ENTIRE TIME the Settlers were farming Saturn, and the miners were mining, neither settlers nor miners were aware there were living beings already inhabiting the planet.

The Saturnians had invited the humans – by creating an environment humans could live in, in order to learn more about the inhabitants of the third planet.

BUT HUMANS BROUGHT mining, slave prisons, human pollution and contamination to Saturn. And the human plan to explode the planet did not fit in with the Saturnians' continued existence.

But the plans of "the slave" Cy did.

The Saturnians had discovered Cy long before they discovered Ryun.

And they had correctly calculated they could use Cy's intentions to their advantage. But they were frustrated they could not directly communicate with him.

They had been trying to figure how to coax his plans into synchronizing with their own. They had tried dreams, but dreams did not seem to have much influence on modern humans.

And the situation on Saturn was considerably more complex than the Congo, and needed more precise handling. The Saturniens did not so much care what happened on Earth, but they were trying to avoid being exploded.

Yet in spite of all the efforts they made to communicate with Cy, for him the Saturniens did not exist.

It was for this reason that the Saturn-aliens, were so pleased to discover Ryun in his underground prison on Earth.

RYUN, SITTING IN his black hole, incommunicado with everything in the entire universe, was the perfect transmitter. He overheard:

"He really has no choice. Imprisoned, blind, having lost his children, what does he have to lose?"

"Though he's blind in human terms, he can see and communicate with us.

"Even though he keeps refusing, and denying our existence."

"Insisting we are no more than Ghosts or phantasms,"

"We are working on his disbelief."

"We can use him"

SINCE BEING A child, Ryun had thought: if I find myself in an Alice Through the Looking Glass world, why not go along with it?

So why do I keep resisting?

Since there was nothing else for him to do, he continued to daily communicate with the Fishes when they spoke to him. Ryun could not help but hear them because they were inside his head. The Saturnaliens digressed and discussed many wide ranging subjects whether or not he wanted to know or was listening. But of one thing he became more and more certain: they always had their own agendas. And he did not think they were being quite forthright.

RYUN WAS SEEING through Cy's eyes! The Fish did not give advance warning. Where only a moment before Ryun's cell was black, and he had been blind and swallowed by blackness, suddenly Ryun/Cy was standing on a seat, staring out the window, at the most bizarre Saturnien landscape.

Then the truck entered a fenced barrier, and went underground. The miners disembarked into their prison barracks —communal sleeping room, with bunks, food served from a counter, on trays. Shortly after arrival they prepared to go to sleep.

Ryun could see the bunk above him, the room, the dim lights, which remained on, became dimmer after lights out.

And then, in the darkness Ryun could also see the Saturnaliens, who seemed to be the exact same individual Fish he had seen on earth. Red stripe, Blue stripe, Whale etc..

"We told you we could be in two places at once."

Strangely, it felt almost a relief to see them. The Fish had become almost familiars and in these strange circumstances familiars were welcome.

Once Cy was in bed, closed his eyes and was asleep, Ryun and the Saturnaliens began to upload Ryun's Blasting knowledge. Cy tossed and turned, and for a moment woke up, but there was nothing to see; he went back to sleep.

Ryun continued to communicate with him telepathically while he slept.

WHEN HE WOKE, Cy thought he had had the strangest dream, "The dream where I finally solve all my escape problems – with a guide."

But like any knowledge, in dreams or otherwise learned, he did not really know or realize what he knew until he began to utilize it.

Throughout the next day at unexpected moments Cy found he seemed to have the solutions he was looking for.

He had finally figured exactly how to best set the detonations: the sequence to use, the optimal placements and amounts to destroy the mine, the base, the communications headquarters and the rockets. And the means to prevent Earth forces returning.

And although his plan had risks, Cy wasn't worried about danger. For the first time he had a chance to escape. To live free he would gladly risk everything.

If he could not live as he wanted, he did not wish to live at all.

As RYUN HAD subliminally communicated, Cy would set charges to destroy all the Earth rockets on Saturn, as well as any coming or going. Earth would no longer have access to the Zydon fuel, and would no longer be able to engage in interplanetary travel.

There were currently two rockets on the planet. One had just landed, one was about to take off, and another was due to land. If Cy timed it just right, for a few moments, all three would be on Saturn, or in the process of landing, and could be destroyed together at the same time.

If they were destroyed simultaneously, then Earth would be stuck, with no rockets and no fuel. And even if Earth built or sent a new rocket it would have to use an alternative fuel.

"THIS WILL CREATE a new equilibrium," a Fish said.

"The 'equilibrium', the interruption, will not last forever but it will give us time to save Saturn, Earth and the entire solar system, for the moment."

Ryun had the feeling the Fish weren't telling him everything, but he couldn't figure what they were leaving out.

Sensing his thoughts they said, "You're just a small part. Important, but small. You don't need to know everything."

"Why would I?"

And so it became.

ALTHOUGH RYUN HAD been inside Cy, looking out through Cy's eyes on Saturn many times, he was not 100% sure that the Saturn he was seeing was not another clever hallucination.

A very detailed hallucination. And certainly better than blackness.

As an experiment, looking through Cy's eyes, he went to a mirror to see how he appeared. He saw before him, looking back, a muscular African man with dark curly hair and a thin short beard.

He then discovered he could access Cy's life in memories.

And the aliens said, "Cy was always your life, your alternate life, simultaneously," or something like that.

"THEN WHY DIDN'T I know it?"

"For the same reason you can't remember reincarnation. Humans find this confusing. They weren't designed for awareness of more than one life at a time."

"So why can I do it now?"

"You have a reason. Besides, in the blackness you are not even living a half life. This has made the consciousness of other lives more manageable. Which is fortunate for us, because we need you in more than one place."

"To play your silly games?"

"You don't need to believe. Just do what we need."

"What about my children? How does this help?

They did not answer.

"If I help you, Will you help my children?"

"We've had this conversation before."

"And?"

"We'll do all we can."

"That's not a promise."

"As we've told you repeatedly: we'll see what we can do."

And still Ryun continued to help them.

It was always more than a little strange for Ryun to be on Saturn. It was new and not new. He had been half remembering, half dreaming it. And yet the actual real experience was unnerving. Cy, whose emotions he shared, was accustomed to the setting.

Saturn, even in its strange remarkableness, had for Cy become familiar. Everyday he looked forward to viewing the rings, the moons, the multi-colored vegetation, all of which for Ryun was still amazing, disorientating and confusing.

Ryun was trying to look at, perceive and see things as Cy did, so that when the plan became active he would not become distracted by his surroundings. But sights were so breath taking, it was difficult not to get lost in what he was seeing.

Ryun probed Cy's memories, in order to know whom he was dealing with. Even though they were Cy's private memories, Ryun cycled through them, perceiving from his own perspective.

IT BECAME CLEAR to Ryun, although it did not appear to be clear to Cy, that Cy had long rebelled against the establishment. And it was obvious, even though Cy hesitated to make the connection, that he had begun to rebel because the Authorities had killed his parents and seized their farm. As a child, as a citizen, Cy had been conditioned to parrot the idea that the state had acted for his own benefit, and to believe that their seizure of his parent's land was just and right. And therefore, when he first began to protest, he was unaware why he was behaving as he was. He thought his actions were completely based on logic.

Cy had been sentenced to death for emulating his parents. Ryun witnessed the execution through Cy's eyes, and saw through Cy's eyes his awakening and discovery that he was now a Mars Mining Slave.

Was Ryun looking out through Cy's eyes similar to the Ghosts trying to pry Ryun's pupils open and look out through Ryun's eyes?

Searching Cy's memories Ryun saw Cy studying, learning how to blast, experimenting with simple detonations, to become good enough that he managed to survive. And Ryun saw how this earned him respect amongst the guards and Slaves.

So it continued for six years. Ryun saw in Cy's memories that the mining on Mars had been arduous, exhausting, toxic and extremely dangerous. But strangely what had bothered Cy most was the complete lack of sunlight. The same thing that was bothering Ryun, in blackness. And it had been that lack of sunlight, that led Cy to organize a Mars revolt.

RYUN SAW CY captured, and ritualistically "killed" once more. He saw, on Saturn, Cy's name changed once again, and his re-enslavement to Blast in Saturn's mines.

AND RYUN SURMISED that Cy's skill as a Blaster was the reason why, after the Mars revolt, Cy was sent to Saturn instead of Uranus or Neptune.

Ryun was surprised Cy was even still alive. The 1910 manual he had learned from had many errors.

RYUN BEGAN TO live Cy's life in preference to his own. It was a good way to influence Cy, as he worked.

The Fish said Cy's life always did belong to him. "Your lives belong to each other."

Ryun wasn't sure about that.

The Saturnaliens said he could even control Cy if he wished. Ryun didn't want to be a puppet master. But nevertheless, in a hallucination or a dream, the Fish showed him how to seize control, should it become necessary.

But Ryun decided that the first necessary move was to get Cy out of prison.

AFTER CY HAD completed calculations and planning, there remained one thing he was uneasy about. He had heard rumors that the Zydon mine and the Zydon fuel on Earth had been completely destroyed. But he was unsure whether that was really true.

And without certainty about Earth's Zydon fuel, and the Zydon mine's status, Cy was still worried that Earth would send another rescue fleet, as they had on Mars, to recapture the outpost.

There was only one remedy Ryun could think of. He took Cy into his mind on Earth.

Ryun had been preparing Cy for this by placing hints in his subconscious. And then without even the briefest of explanations, Ryun took Cy into his mind in his cell on Earth.

CY WAS TERRIFIED at being possessed, transported. At first, there was only terror; blackness and heat; and gigantic, annoying iridescent Fish floating by. But then Cy noticed a deeper undercurrent of memories and pain, which he could see his possessor was still having trouble dealing with. Cy heard the bullets and the explosions, saw Ryun's wife being shot, his children abducted. Cy saw Ryun blowing up the Congo Zydon mine, with the resultant massive super-explosion that blinded Ryun.

Cy saw the hospitalization, the blindness, the trial, the fake shooting—he had been through similar himself. Cy saw the imprisonment in absolute blackness, which Cy found an absolutely horrendous fate, the subsequent disorientation of Ryun, the Ghosts and the Fishes from Saturn visiting, and Ryun no longer sure what was real and what was not.

Cy said to himself, "I've never seen any Fish or aliens on Saturn."

"You will now," a multitude of Saturnien voices answered. And they showed him images of themselves swimming everywhere on Saturn.

That was enough. Cy believed! And was distressed by it.

Yet he wanted to escape slavery. He needed to take advantage of the situation.

Having decided that, Cy ejected himself from that terrifying space that was Ryun's mind, without any desire ever to return.

CY HAD FOUND being in Ryun's White mind completely unnerving. And to be permanently cut off from light, in complete darkness, in that mind, was more than he could bear.

Even his own Blaster life was preferable.

Having ejected, he confirmed to himself that yes, he was still a Slave in prison, in his own bed, on Saturn. He was still Cy and not Ryun, or a dream.

He was disconnected. And he hoped to remain discon-nected permanently!

He fell asleep.

AND WHEN CY awoke, he was relieved, to be still himself.

But as he readied for work he remembered the plans and the knowledge he had gained, and he was confident he could blow up the mine, destroy the rockets, the outpost and com-munications.

He put aside worries or concerns that Ryun was still in his mind guiding him, with the Saturniens guiding Ryun. He needed all the help he could get. All he wanted to do was es-cape. And then they could be damned. He began to anticipate, see, taste and smell his freedom.

To hope.

The thought of Freedom, escape, he knew, is a very dan-gerous thing for a prisoner or a slave—it can cause impatience, recklessness.

And for a slave and a Blaster it was especially dangerous when, in order to succeed, he most needed to be careful.

Cy tried hard to put all such thoughts of escape out of his conscious mind.

He was successful for moments at a time, but his uncon-scious mind kept working on it. He kept repeating to himself, one day, one day, one day at a time, to override his thoughts.

He attempted to remain unexcited, negative, half pessimis-tic. Not easy, but safer than enthusiasm. There would be plen-ty of time for hope and excitement if he actually managed to escape.

NEVERTHELESS, FLICKERS OF hope kept flashing through his mind. And when he tried to go to sleep, Ryun and the Sat-urniens disturbed his calm.

No matter how many times he pushed them away, his visions, and Ryun and the Saturnians kept returning. Hope and excitement were draining energy and were very dangerous. He kept repeating, "I am not hoping, I am not expecting." Yet he was already visualizing the where and the when, the explosions, seeing himself running, hiding in the night. There were only 5 hours of dark in which to set the charges, detonate and escape.

And he even found himself fast-forwarding to his hoped-for future: his own land, his own farm, his own family, under a pink Saturnien sky.

ESCAPE SHOULD HAVE been difficult but with the Saturniens's guidance it was easy.

There occurred a preemptive, unanticipated, riot.

The Saturniens, though invisible, were inside the prison.

When the riot occurred, the Saturniens told Ryun/Cy what to do, where to go and when, in order to escape.

In this manner Cy, with his fellow Slaves following in his wake, escaped the slave prison compound.

Most of the slaves were focused on creating chaos, confusion, insurrection, destruction culminating in the explosion of the mine. They then intended to commandeer a rocket and return to earth. Except for creating terror, Cy could not see any benefit to these plans, and he feared the explosion of the mine.

The mine was located on the edge of the farmland. If they destroyed the mine they might contaminate the habitable land, and leave nowhere to live.

Cy's plans involved permanently disconnecting from Earth.

CY DID NOT inform his fellow insurrectionists where his intentions differed from theirs.

He set explosives within the prison base. With Ryun and

the Saturnien guidance, Cy and the revolting prisoners entered, took control and set explosives in the communications base. Alone, without help, Cy set explosives in the rockets, and on the landing fields.

A GLORIOUS SEQUENCE of orange explosions brightened the Saturn night sky. The prisoners commandeered and crowded onto one last soon-to-be-departing rocket.

Cy watched it go, then exploded all the buildings that remained and ran for a prison vehicle to drive into the countryside.

CY HAD NOT planned to allow the Slaves to depart Saturn, but then thought better of it. He did not trust many of them; it was better they returned to Earth.

And the Slaves had no desire to remain on Saturn or farm. Why not let them depart, he had suddenly thought, ridding the planet of numerous undesirables, and exposing the fakery of the executions with their return, and reappearance on Earth.

After destroying the remaining rockets, Cy re-mined the landing fields with more explosives to ensure he could destroy any rockets daring to touch down. He still had a great fear of Earth returning with forces to re-enslave him, as they previously had on Mars.

His actions were guided by Ryun and the Saturniens.

Cy then fled in the dark in an armored prison vehicle towards the most distant side of The Vortex.

The Saturniens said to both Cy and Ryun, "Humans will eventually return to Saturn and space, but we hope by then they will be more evolved."

Cy said, "Maybe not. In any event, I mined the landing area to destroy any ship that lands."

EVEN THOUGH RYUN told Cy, "The Saturnaliens don't need you anymore; you're free now," Cy made it his life's mission to protect Saturn from earth. He monitored the one remaining communications radio, which he had taken for himself, to anticipate and prevent future landings.

Cy had accomplished all of his primary objectives. Everything that could bring Earth, the rockets, the communications, had been destroyed.

Ryun was gone, out of Cy's head. Cy was free on Saturn, looking for work, a farm, a wife, a family, a homestead. This had all become possible. He found this success the most intense, exhilarating and exciting moment of his life.

And then at the dispensation of the Saturniens, new frontier land suddenly became available. The Vortex mysteriously expanded.

And Cy free at last, felt happier than he had even been.

THE ROCKETS THAT came from Neptune and Uranus exploded upon landing,

THE SATURNIENS HAD created the Vortex for human settlement.

Within the limits of what was possible on Saturn, with a 10.5 hour day, the Saturnians had created the perfect environment. The atmosphere, the oxygen, the gravity, had all been adjusted to provide optimal human living conditions. Plants and vegetables were provided or modified to flower and fruit in the shorter daylight environment.

And although the plants that could be grown on Saturn and most details of the growing conditions were different from Earth's, it was all adaptable to human requirements, with effort and experience.

The Saturniens surreptitiously helped the humans in their cultivation endeavors. They were the invisible hand that assured a successful planting and harvest. They wanted to ensure that the isolated humans on Saturn thrived. They believed isolation would allow these humans to evolve more quickly and perceive the Saturniens, while at the same time retaining their ability to communicate with Earth humans, when Earth eventually reconnected.

AFTER DISCONNECTING FROM Cy on Saturn, Ryun found himself right back on Earth in his cell, blind. "The Saturnaliens did nothing for me." And he felt betrayed.

As he sat on the concrete in his cell, still blind, in the dark in despair, he began to wonder: "What now?"

Suddenly he began to have vivid, horrific visions of rebellions, explosions, people dying dismembered—guards and soldiers burning, on Mars, then Earth, Venus, Jupiter, Mercury, Uranus, Neptune and Pluto. These intense and nightmarish visions arrived sequentially, one after the other, but when he thought about it, they seemed to have occurred more or less at the same time, the sequence being caused by distance-reception delay.

He was highly agitated, disturbed and unclear how could this be happening. How was the same plan, with even more violence, manifesting on all the planets, more or less simultaneously?

And then he realized, "The Saturnalians."

He knew they were listening. "What's going on?"

"We broadcast your connection with Cy."

"Why? What?"

"All your Blasting knowledge."

"To all the Blasters enslaved on all the planets."

"Some of them were very angry."

"They became explosives experts overnight."

"They used your memories, your knowledge and experience."

"With your guidance and connection with Cy we coordinated everything."

"We destroyed earth's prison system and slave network on every planet.

"All the slaves are free."

"You didn't explain this to me! You didn't warn me. They brutally killed people."

"We told you, you had an affinity, a connection to many different lives simultaneously. The Council of Planets is very happy with the resolution. We were afraid you would object."

"I would have."

And now he understood why his conscious possession of inhabiting other beings kept flickering and was always disconnected before he could get his bearings. They had deliberately disorientated him, during the connections, disconnecting and confusing his awareness.

"All Earth rockets, Earth bases and communications have been exploded on Saturn, Jupiter, Mars, Venus, Uranus, Neptune, Mercury and Pluto," they repeated. Only the guards are dead."

"All slaves are free or rocketing home."

Ryun felt betrayed, and used. He hadn't agreed to mass murder, or the destruction of all earth bases.

And this manipulation and exploitation, reminded Ryun once more of the Congolese, who had also murdered carelessly. And who were the instigators of that betrayal?

AND NOW SUDDENLY Ryun knew why Cy kept half singing a tune, he thought he recognized, but with different lyrics, "First we take Saturn then we take Neptune."

THERE WAS STILL no light, he still could not see.

Sometimes he began to wonder, once the initial visual and

auditory shocks had passed and were over with, what had really happened? Anything? No difference with him. What was really going on? Was it all imaginary?

In his black hole nothing seemed to change. He was disconnected from the world. Had he imagined the whole thing, including the deaths and all the explosions?

He was still blind. He was still in prison. The Fish seemed to be gone, and he still couldn't go anywhere, nothing good had changed. He had been blind for months. He was still locked in a cell in a mine or a cave.

Once again, one more time, he went to the door that he had gone to a thousand times before, to shake.

But this time, it was unlocked.

The door was open. Had they opened it? Had it been open for a while? Why hadn't he noticed before?

HE FLED HIS cell immediately, walking as fast as he could in the darkness even though he could not see. As he felt his way down the halls, the Saturnalien's thoughts came into his mind: turn left, turn right, stop, stairs, lift your leg. He did not know where he was going.

As he walked he stumbled, avoided a guard here, missed a guard there. And it was dim but it was not dark.

But he could not see that.

For him it was Black, black black, and hot, hot, hotter as he climbed. Africa.

He walked and stumbled in and through the blackness for a long time. Even blind, he was perspiring heavily, and his sweat burned as it dripped into his blind eyes. All sweaty and sticky, his shirt was sticking to his body. He was soaking wet.

And then suddenly, he turned a corner, and there off in the distance was a light.

A BRIGHT WHITE light, and it seemed to be the end of a tunnel. Was he walking into escape or death?

He walked closer, ever closer, towards the increasingly blinding white light, that hurt. And then he stepped out into daylight. And he had to close his eyes.

Slowly, slowly, he opened his eyes in bursts. And then quickly re-closed, re-opened, then re-closed, opened and quickly closed again and again, until he could keep his eyes wide open.

He could see. He could see colors.

It was the most amazing, exhilarating thing, to see once more, to be outdoors, everything was so bright and intense and green. He felt like he had stepped into the Garden of Eden. It was indescribably delightful to be outside, to feel the air, to see plants, to breathe.

But in the midst of the exhilaration and joy he felt, he began to notice his sight was different. He saw not as he always had, the light had new different shades and substance, his eyes seemed to focus differently.

He closed one eye, then the other. Each eye saw different things. The right eye perceived almost conventionally, but the left eye saw very differently. He had lost conventional perspective using both eyes. The left eye saw new colors, and could still see alien beings, and other things he had not yet deciphered in daylight.

HE BEGAN RUNNING, turning right and left. He did not know where he was going, but he was being guided. He was at another compound, he was in the compound. And there were his children!

And then another door, and there was his wife. Alive!

How could she be? Was it all a dream, a terrible dream, her dying? Was this possible?

And then he had a vision.

The Saturnaliens were present during the rebels' attack.

His wife was shot. He could see her life force leaking, oozing away, he could see her dying.

And then, as he was taken away, he saw the Saturnaliens, stopping her life force midair, and pushing her life back into her, and healing. The Saturnaliens put her back together again. There was not even a scar on her forehead.

But that meant they were already interested in him!

They all walked out of the compound together, into the daylight sun. The Fish swimming around him said, "Keep walking, you will not be seen."

Even though they were in plain sight.

AND IT WAS all like a dream, except he was acutely conscious and aware of every detail, he couldn't quite believe it, and from his very disbelief, he knew it was real. He could never have imagined.

He was fleeing; where to, what to do now?

He urgently wanted to go directly to the airport and fly home. But he was instructed in words, "Do not take a plane, travel overland, use cars, and buses, without onboard communication."

He was terrified yet found it thrilling, and unbelievably exhilarating, as if he was really alive for the first time!

"Flag a ride." A car stopped for them.

"Take a room." They saw a hotel, a room and cash was waiting for them.

"Wait till dark. Hire a car. Drive through the dark, on back roads, around, through check points."

"Abandon the car."

"Drive the car into the river."

They walked till they found a boat with oars. "Get in." They got in and he rowed across the river.

"That was the first border."

In the days that followed they found and slept in rooms

in the day. Found drivers at night: Crossed unmarked borders in various cars, with different drivers—Ryun, his wife and children—in the dark. His children weren't complaining anymore. Day after day, night after night, for 5 days.

As the Fish who were talking to Ryun, kept saying, "Drive in the dark, sleep in the day, drive in the night. Drive and drive, until light comes."

He was directed to a small airport, with a pilot and a small skypod. Another country was left behind. They landed, and took off, in another skypod, more driving. A bigger skypod.

They had escaped the Congo, their imprisonments, but they were not safe yet.

HE WAS DIRECTED to a post office. There was money in a package with new passports and cash.

Another and another skypod. Immigration and border crossings

Eventually they were in a white country, where they no longer stood out.

They had escaped. The whole thing seemed unbelievable.

AND WHILE AT moments it seemed just too good to be true, and he wondered if he was still in the prison hallucinating. At other times, he thought it felt so good to be alive with his family—alive, in the moment.

But there were other times when he remembered what it had cost: his wife's "death"; she seemed very different after her resurrection. Did she really live? Had they really saved her? Was she really the same person?

And sometimes, remembering his life and all the tragedy, it seemed just too, too painful to live.

AND FOR A time, even though they were all safe now, and he had found the terrible adventure thrilling, he became so depressed, he almost wanted to commit suicide, but still, there were his kids, an almost albino girl and boy. And they still wanted life.

He could hardly kill himself and leave them alone.

And he was more than afraid to leave them with his wife.

And his children, in wanting to live, wanted this and that and most everything. They had to be fed and clothed, and looked after. And how could he leave them alone to fend for themselves, if he could not cope himself? He had to look after and protect them. And their endless wants and needs, complaints and desires distracted and kept him alive. They gave him a reason to live.

THEY HAD DISAPPEARED and were living amongst people, white people, who looked almost like them. But that was not enough.

"In order to create a discontinuous trail," the Fish explained, "you must move several more times. You must have different names and different passports with each disappearance."

Eventually they moved into a large house, with new lives, new wealth, and the children were home-schooled by a tutor. Ryun had become independently wealthy.

He was glad and depressed it was finally over. They were finally safe.

But he was still concerned about what could still happen, and about all the ways in which his wife was a different person. Did they put her back together correctly? Was she really the same being? Perhaps an alternate incarnation?

A YEAR OR two passed.

SUDDENLY THE FISH were back, he could see them, they were in his head.

"We need you."

"I can't leave. I have my children."

"Your wife can take care of them.

"She's not the same. What did you do to her?"

"She'll be ok. There's more we need you to do."

"Why?"

"You're our translator Blaster."

Ryun went with them. But he no longer trusted the Saturnaliens, if he ever really did.

And he reflected: even in his childhood, and the stories of Alice and Gulliver, there was no one the hero or heroine could really trust.

There was no reason to believe the Fish would be any more benevolent.

CY ON SATURN had found a place to live, found a home and thought that the revolution, the liberation, the cry for freedom, was over with.

He had discovered that most of the settlers on Saturn were Black of African descent just like him. And that was the secret reason why no one mixed with them. It was also the reason the authorities let them go.

They had left earth to escape the racism, to have their own land, their own place, their own freedom to work for themselves instead of someone else.

Many of these Black settlers came from the same heritage as Cy's family: Mennonite, Amish, Black Sovereign People. Some had even met his parents. They all wanted to farm and remain independent.

Cy was happy to be a farmer, and to be part of a society that valued him.

Several of the families had daughters. He married and in

the new Vortex territories they found and farmed their own land.

And, for the first time in centuries the Black Sovereigns had Freedom: the equivalent of Moses' Promised Land, of milk and honey.

Earth was still full of division and racism, no longer black and white, since most blacks outside of Africa had been eliminated in the Biovirus wars, but light skin, dark skin, Asian, Redskin, whatever.

Anything, to be better than. No one wanted to be equal.

Earth Authorities were glad to be rid of those "really dark ones". "They were always problematic and were never going to fit in."

And these Africans, these really dark ones, they were glad to be rid of Earth. They had no desire to be Better Than. They were happy to be amongst equals.

Cy felt lucky and happy. He had fulfilled his family's desire, ambition and quest.

But the Saturniens returned for Cy too. Ever since his connection with Ryun Cy had been able to see and hear them.

"There's a ship coming. We need you to blow it up."

Cy was excited. He liked his part as "Saturn's Defender!"

He had used all the earth explosives. The Saturniens showed him how to make new explosives from what was native to Saturn.

Cy liked being, "The Defender of My People."

And he liked blowing things up. He was now teaching his children "The Fine Art of Blasting…"

Ron Mucklestone resides in Toronto, Canada, where he works as a consultant and spends his free time engaged in organic gardening, carpentry, mystical pursuits and raising a family. He has recently resumed his childhood passion for writing science fiction and other forms of fiction.

What's not to like about an old-fashioned story of love, peril, and adventure? The Old Solar System lends itself to such tales at least as well as any fictional universe, and better than most. Thus it's fitting that this series of voyages across the Old Solar System finishes with Ron Mucklestone's Love in the Mountains of Venus, *in which a most unlikely pair of adventurers face dangers together and find true love...*

Love in the Mountains of Venus

by Ron Mucklestone

Encounter

HIMANSHU PARTED THE leaves of the copra tree to see what was making the strange noises. They sounded like a mix of bird and animal talk, but it was not like any animal or bird he had ever heard. And the crunching and crashing of vegetation like some boars drunk on fermented cacamusa juice. He saw a flash of red, then yellow, then black. Very odd indeed.

Curious, he leaned further over on the branch than was safe. He knew it. But he couldn't stop himself. Everything in the forest had its place, and he knew all that lived in his forest. But whatever it was that was trespassing through his allotment did not belong here.

The branch broke. Vines escaped Himanshu's grasp as he desperately sought a handhold while airborne. He tumbled down ten feet onto the ground and felt exposed and vulnerable.

Then Himanshu saw the strange beings and gasped while trying to comprehend what his senses were telling him. One of the strange beings started making noises with its mouth.

"Well, what have we here? Oh, it's a Formanian sloth—

named after the Forman Mountains to the west of here," said the tallest being who had a bushy beard and was covered in something loose and tan in colour. "Note the extremely short fur and bright orange streak of long hair along the top of its head—that is the distinct marking of males belonging to this species," the tall being continued.

"Excuse me, Dr. Jenkins," said another being—this one shorter in stature, with long black hair and covered in red on top and black on bottom. Its feet were covered. "I heard that some Venusian sloth species have nearly human capabilities such as the ability to make fire, count into the thousands and even produce beautiful sculptures using a variety of tools. Is any of this true?"

"Ah, Judy, you must be talking about the research of Dr. Vermeer," replied the tallest being. "He ended up getting lost in the Epsilon Mountains and wasn't found for six months, if I recall correctly. A windfall for exobiology and exoanthropology, if there ever was one. He was adopted by a tribe of the Klaxo Sloths, observed them closely and even learned a great deal of their language. All what you heard is true, but there is much more. Vermeer has even hypothesized that the Klaxo Sloths must have had a great civilization in the past and that they are presently living in a Dark Ages of some sort right now because the things that this tribe knows and describes, including knowledge about the Sun and other planets in our solar system would be impossible without the use of sophisticated telescopes. It may sound far-fetched, but Vermeer has gone out on a limb time after time with seemingly fantastic claims about life on Venus and every time he has been vindicated. I see no reason to doubt that he will be proven right about this, too. We have barely scratched the surface of life on this planet and nearly everything we learn is truly astonishing."

All the while Himanshu sat watching these strange beings babble in a peculiar tongue. So far they showed no aggression towards him and at most mild interest in him, and the colours he saw emanating from their bodies—blues, greens and pinks—proved to him that they meant him no harm. Himanshu therefore decided to watch and learn all he could to tell his extended family and the Chief of his tribe once he got home. His only concern was that the story he had to tell them would be so outlandish he would have a hard time convincing them that he hadn't just imagined it all after snacking on hallucinogenic ferns.

Himanshu quickly realized that the tall bearded being liked the sound of his own voice. "Everybody," Dr. Jenkins thus addressed his group, "you'll notice that even though we call these species 'sloths', they also have several primate-like features such as opposable thumbs and their claws are remarkably short—more like nails, really. They are also much faster here than our sloths back at home—but, then again, all life on Venus seems to operate on a 'higher gear' than life on Earth. We are still trying to figure how it is possible for life on each of the inner planets of this solar system so closely to resemble life on Earth in term of morphology and even in the environmental niches that they occupy. All evolutionary theories say that this cannot happen, but here we are looking at the facts straight in the face right now!

"Anyway, we mustn't tarry any longer. We know precious little about the Formanian sloths yet, and now is not the time to find out. It is quite a jaunt to the next cabin and it will be nightfall in just a couple of hours. And I've got to show you a grove of giant blue rubber trees that grow just a mile up ahead. Come along!"

The troupe of a dozen botany students followed Dr. Jenkins like a gaggle of goslings following their mother. Himanshu saw many of them looked at him with an expression of mild interest on their faces as they noisily stomped past him. Except for the last one in the group. She looked different: shorter and rounder than the rest with straight black hair cut quite short. She also walked differently—her steps were smooth and quiet as if she knew how to walk in the forest. But what was most different about her was that when she walked past him she had an expression not of mild interest, but of happiness or even recognition! And even as the troupe walked further away, she kept on looking back at him right until the time they rounded a corner in the trail and disappeared from view.

Himanshu didn't know what to make of this. He was sure that the look on his face must have been total bewilderment. He had never even imagined these odd-looking beings before: walking only on their long hind legs, practically no hair on their short arms, and covering their feet and much of their bodies and heads with objects of various shapes, sizes and colours. How could one of them look at him as if it recognized him? It made no sense to him.

Intrigued and happy that his fall had led to a harmless adventure, he clambered back up the copra tree and headed back towards his tribe.

Peril

THE FOLLOWING DAY Dr. Jenkins and his troupe of young botanists started the morning leg of their journey through the botanical wonders of Venus's Iona Plateau. It would be possible to walk for about three hours until the heat became too unbearable under the gigantic blur of the Sun bearing down through the cloud layer. How the sauropods that dwell in the even hotter lowlands manage to thrive still baffled Earth biologists.

The plan was fairly simple. The students would gather seedings of various palms and ferns along the way and take them to the next botanical station up the path to study their suitability for habituation to Earth conditions. Over the past two decades, nearly all palms and ferns had perished from the increasingly hot conditions in Earth's tropics, and all attempts at genetic engineering of species native to Earth to withstand the raised temperature had been futile. Although Jenkins kept a casual and jovial manner among his students, he and all other senior botanists the world over were panicking over the unravelling of ecosystems across Earth as many plant and insect species succumbed to unbearably fast changes to the climate. And Venus's heat-loving plants were the only possible hope for preventing a repeat of the Permian-level extinction event on Earth.

The troupe were in high spirits as they started their day. The weather was clear and there was a breeze that, though not cool, was at least not searing.

After an hour into the walk, an extraordinarily thick mist rolled in. Visibility was reduced to a few yards and sounds barely travelled a few feet. The ordinarily cacophonous forest became eerily quiet. The troupe walked forward slowly.

Himanshu had got up extra early in the morning and had managed to find the troupe's tracks. He wanted to study them to find out what these curious aliens were doing in his homeland. He caught up with them shortly after the descent of the blanket of mist. He sensed danger as this part of the trail was close to the home range of the seven-horned rhinos and they spook easily when it is misty. A snort of alarm reached his ears. He dreaded what would happen next.

In an attempt to alarm the troupe, Himanshu came out into the open and screeched as loudly as he could. The troupe looked at him, baffled. Now that he had their attention, he screeched again, fell onto the ground and curled up into a ball. Again, he screeched, commandingly.

Dr. Jenkins shouted to his troupe: "Everyone: do what this sloth is showing us. NOW!"

The next moment was a jumble of motion and sound. Students dropped to the ground. A huge quadrupedal form suddenly emerged from the mist, heading towards the troupe.

One young man was slow in getting down, and the giant quadruped collided with him. The youth went flying into the air and came down onto the ground in an awkward position. He was shouting and writhing in agony. The quadruped disappeared into the mist.

The troupe gathered around the young man in shock and confusion. "First Aid," said Jenkins firmly, and one of the students dropped his backpack and took out a box. The student that had been struck had been gored badly in the legs. One leg had three holes gushing blood, and the other leg had one hole, also bleeding quite profusely. The student who had taken out the First Aid box took out a roll of gauze and started to apply it to the leg with the three wounds. "I have only enough gauze for one leg," he said in an alarmed voice; "how can we staunch the bleeding of the other leg?"

Immediately one student stood up and walked away from the troupe and into the forest. Himanshu looked closely through the mist at the person: it was the one who had looked at him yesterday.

"Jacintha," said Jenkins amid the din, "what on Earth are you doing? Come back here immediately! There's a seven-horned rhino on the loose out there!" But she continued walking. She took about twenty steps into the forest and bent down low, her hands touching the tops of the bushy vegetation that clung to the forest floor. Then she stopped and breathed slowly. Swiftly, she moved both hands to the left, clutched a bunch of broad-leaved plants, and pulled off the leaves. Immediately, she turned back to the troupe. Confidently, she placed three broad leaves on the untreated leg of the injured youth. The bleeding stopped almost immediately.

Jenkins was beside himself and he scolded Jacintha. "You can't just go picking plants at random. This species could be poisonous! We haven't even tested it yet!"

"I understand how this looks, Dr. Jenkins," she replied, "but it is alright."

"And how do you know that?" retorted Jenkins.

"Because the plant told me," Jacintha stated in a matter-of-fact way.

"Now just hold on here," began Jenkins.

"Please, just hear me out. I am from Colombia. I belong to the Muisca people of the Amazon. Our medicine people learn everything from what the plants teach us. I know it must sound crazy to you, but it is true. You've got to trust me. Ask Robert how his leg feels."

The injured youth had stopped moaning. "You'd better listen to her, Doc," he said; "my right leg has stopped bleeding and it hardly even hurts. I am sure that I can walk on it. But my left leg is still bleeding and hurts like the Devil."

Himanshu had been watching the scene unfolded with rapt attention. He saw how Jacintha's aura had turned pink as she moved among the plants and chose the right species. He thought: "She is a healer and knows how to talk with the plants—just like me!"

The incident forced the troupe to return to their camp of the previous night, since the mid-day rest stop that they had planned was more than twice the distance. As it was, with Robert hobbling slowly it took nearly three hours in the increasingly hot mist to get back. Dr. Jenkins took some samples of the plant species, which Jacintha had used as an emergency poultice, for analysis and testing.

Reflection

BACK AT CAMP the cabins were abuzz with talk about the close encounter with the seven-horned rhino, Robert's close call and his nearly miraculous recovery. The leg that had received the herbal poultice was healing better and was less painful than the leg that had received the latest generation of antibiotic/anti-inflammatory cream. He received numerous stitches and was ordered to take one week of bed rest. It had been decided that the entire troupe would be staying put until he was well enough to walk with them again. There was also a lot of talk about the warning given by the sloth and everyone wondered why it was so visible, since they are rarely seen out in the open and rarely on the ground.

Jacintha didn't know how or why, but she was convinced that it was the same sloth that they had encountered the previous day. Before she knew it, Jacintha was immersed in thoughts about her early childhood in the Amazon, where she had had a pet brown-throated three-toed sloth. She had named him "Happy," because of the nearly perpetual grin on its face as well as because of the way he made her feel. Happy would come down from the nearby trees at dawn every day and give Jacintha a hug; he would be grumpy until she gave him a hug. They would even play together, in slow motion, and Happy liked to hear Jacintha sing. But to her, Happy was not really a pet. He was her closest friend and confidant. She was unusual in her community in that she was an only child and her father was a vegetalista—a traditional healer – who was highly respected, but also somewhat feared in their increasingly Western-influenced society. Some families who had converted to Christianity forbade their children from playing with her out of fear that her family practiced 'witchcraft'. But as long as she had Happy's friendship, Jacintha was care-free. Unfortunately, when she was nine, tragedy struck her family: with both parents dead, she had to live with her aunt in a nearby town. She never saw Happy again.

Jacintha obviously knew that the sloth she had encountered on Venus was not Happy, but since the first encounter the previous day, she couldn't get Happy out of her mind.

Shortly before sunset the same day, Jacintha was looking out the window of her dorm, when she saw a male Formanian sloth move among the nearby trees. He looked straight at her. And then he descended to the ground and walked straight to her. Finally, he peered back at her through the window.

Though he neither blinked nor averted his gaze for a long time, Jacintha did not feel like she was being stared at; rather, it was an inquisitive but kind gaze as if he wished to befriend her. It was markedly like the way Happy had looked at her more than a decade ago.

Jacintha decided to go out and meet the sloth at close quarters. It was safe to do so due to the triple barrier that had been constructed around the camp which kept out predators and other large animals. And, fortunately, the Iona Plateau did not have any poisonous snakes or other dangerous small fauna to worry about.

Slowly, Jacintha went out and walked around the dormitory to the side where her window was situated. The sloth was still there. She stopped about five yards from the sloth and sat down on the ground, waiting to see what would happen next. She looked at the sloth, expectantly.

Himanshu liked this approach. He waited a minute or so, and then cautiously ambled on his hind legs to Jacintha. He stopped two yards away from her—a safe enough distance should she lunge at him. But he was sure that she would not attack. After another minute, he ambled right to her side and sat down beside Jacintha. After another moment, he reached out and touched her shirt. It felt very strange to his hand; not at all like the baskets and purses that his people weave out of grasses and thin vines. He smelled it and found it vile – it did not smell like life at all, more like something that had been dead for a very long time. But despite the barbaric things that covered her body and head, her aura was calm and peaceful: that is what he trusted, rather than what his senses told him.

Himanshu wanted to attempt to communicate with Jacintha through actions. Placing his palm on the ground beside her to tell her to "stay," he went up into a nearby tree and plucked a brown nut about the size of a baseball and threw it on the ground near Jacintha. He then walked to the nut and showed it to her. It had several slits along the five ridges that ran down from the top to the bottom. Striking it on a stone, the nut split into several pieces. Nested inside each section were about twelve black spheres each about the size of a chickpea. He squeezed one, showing Jacintha that it was somewhat soft. Putting one into her hand, he told her that it had soporific properties by looking her in the eye, putting it to his mouth as if eating it, and then slowly closing his eyes and falling over on his side as if fast asleep. Jacintha immediately recognized what he was trying to tell her and showed him so by imitating the motion. Himanshu was delighted. "Fulbit," he said to her and she repeated it to him.

Now that he had successfully communicated with her, Himanshu wanted to show her where his tribe lived so that she could see how they lived. He gently took her hand and pulled at it and, with the other and he pointed into the forest. Her eyes told him that she understood.

Jacintha put her hand on the ground, telling Himanshu to stay put. She then got up and went back into the dorm. Attached to the dorm was the lab where Dr. Jenkins could be found most of the time. She briefly told him about the latest incident and in particular the sloth teaching her about the medicinal properties of a nut. Jenkins was enthralled, but did his best to keep a cool, professional demeanour. He readily agreed to accompany Jacintha to see for himself.

Returning to the clearing beside the dorm, Jacintha motioned to Jenkins to position himself a safe distance away while still having a good look at her interactions with the sloth.

Himanshu immediately noticed Jacintha's return and waited for her to come back to his side. After a moment with her, he returned to the forest and was gone for a moment. Jenkins gave Jacintha a puzzled look and she said to him, softly, "I'm sure he is finding something else to show me." A minute later, Himanshu returned with some leaves which were about four inches long, almond-shaped, and grouped in threes with one sticking straight out from the stem and one leaf sticking out on each side. Himanshu plucked one leaf, rolled it up and acted as if putting it into his mouth to chew. Then he opened his eyes really wide, took a deep breath and puffed out his chest. "Marma," said Himanshu.

"Extraordinary," exclaimed Jenkins; "it is telling you that this plant is some kind of stimulant or narcotic! See if you can get it to give one to me."

Jacintha looked at Himanshu and pointed to Dr. Jenkins, motioning for him to give Jenkins a sample. Himanshu hesitated and looked into Jacintha's eyes, but then ambled over to Jenkins, handing him two leaves. Jenkins beamed.

Again, Himanshu pulled on Jacintha's hand.

"See, Doctor, I think he wants to take me somewhere. Judging by our interactions so far, I would say that it could be of great value to us, scientifically speaking. Since we are stuck here for a week, could we go on an expedition with this sloth to learn from him?"

After some hemming and hawing, Jenkins agreed under the condition that a small team of three or four people go out the following day, himself included.

Jacintha smiled at Himanshu and pointed at the Sun, and motioned it moving to the western horizon, and beneath their feet, and stopping just above the eastern horizon. Himanshu smiled back at her and promptly returned to the forest, where he disappeared.

Expedition

JACINTHA AND THE expedition crew hand-picked by Dr. Jenkins were up a couple hours before dawn. Early rising was the norm for humans on Venus, anyway, due to the mid-day siestas forced upon them by the intense heat. Outdoor activities were restricted to the hours around dawn and sunset. By sunrise, the crew was equipped and ready for the expedition. Besides Jacintha and Dr. Jenkins, the crew consisted of Carl—a PhD student—and Angus—a survival expert and extraordinary marksman. Both Carl and Angus had been stationed on Venus for more than two years and were very familiar with the territory surrounding the camp.

At dawn the air was thick with dozens of species of birds flying from their rookeries to their feeding grounds. Jacintha's favourite was the Blazing Toucan – a bird covered with bright red and orange plumage so that it almost looked like fire on wings.

Himanshu showed up a few minutes after sunrise. Delight was evident on his face when Jacintha exited the dorm and walked towards him, but his expression soured somewhat when Dr. Jenkins, Carl and Angus joined Jacintha. In particular, he did not like the look of the two strangers: their auras were complex with no colour predominating. He motioned to Jacintha to make the strangers go back, but she motioned to Himanshu that they were all part of a single team. He sat down in despair.

Being a keen observer, Jenkins said to Carl and Angus, "Gentlemen, I want you on your best behaviour out here. We are likely interacting with a species that is highly intelligent and seems willing to teach us botany. A breakthrough like this is almost unprecedented. Mutual trust is absolutely essential. Screw this up and you are on a one-way ticket back to Earth." The two nodded in assent.

Himanshu led the party, followed by Jacintha and the others.

Soon after the team entered the forest, Himanshu stopped, looked back and cupped his tiny ears with his hands. He then demonstrated, in an over-exaggerated manner, how to walk quietly in the forest. They all tried, but, with boots on, success was limited. Himanshu was still irritated by the racket but noticed that the noise was somewhat reduced and so he accepted it as better than nothing.

Locomotion by tree was natural and faster for Himanshu than walking, so when the forest canopy was low, he would move from branch to branch, coming down occasionally with a new botanical lesson to teach. When tree canopies were high, Himanshu would walk with the rest of the party. Dr. Jenkins and Carl busily scribbled in their field note pads, while Jacintha took mental notes. The party moved at a leisurely pace.

Angus found the expedition to be tedious, but he was mindful of the route they were taking through the forest and knew that he would be able to find their way back to camp once the time came for returning. He was also on the lookout for aggressive animals and had two loaded rifles strapped on his back, as well as a concealed pistol and several hunting knives, in case of an attack. Fortunately, much of forest they were moving through (people would call it an "old growth forest" back on Earth) was fairly easy to walk through, as the mature trees that towered 300 to 500 feet in height left little light to reach the forest floor and so smaller trees and plants were relatively few and far between.

After about two hours of walking, the forest undergrowth suddenly became very dense and the amount of sunlight increased considerably. Soon it was an impenetrable mass of vegetation. At this point, Himanshu turned to the right and the team of humans followed him. He became much more animated and virtually each minute he would find a plant and explain through signs its medicinal or other uses. Carl and Dr. Jenkins scribbled even more furiously in their notebooks.

Soon, various hooting sounds became audible on top of the orchestra of other sounds (mostly birds and insects) that permeated the forest. A half-dozen Formanian sloths came within view among the lower branches of the smaller trees nearby. Their eyes were wide with wonder. Himanshu went up to them, hugged each one in turn and began to chatter with them, pointing to each human in turn. Most of them grinned at the humans, but a couple of them had a stern look as though they were not sure that interacting with these strange creatures was a good idea. The smiling sloths descended to the ground and ambled towards the humans, where they reached out and touched their clothes and boots. Himanshu assured Jacintha and her party, through gestures, that all was fine and to not be bothered by his curious clan-sloths. After about fifteen minutes, their curiosity now largely satisfied, the sloths headed back to the trees and followed the team of humans about ten feet off the ground.

Dr. Jenkins noticed that they were very gradually turning left as they followed Himanshu. "Has anybody noticed," he said to the group, "that this impenetrable thicket appears to form a regular curve?"

"I was just noticing the same," spoke Angus, "do you think it is a natural formation?"

"It seems to be too regular," replied Dr. Jenkins; "I would say that this may be a deliberately made fortification pro-duced by these sloths. Look how closely and regularly these thorny trees are spaced; nothing natural about that."

Jenkins could not be more correct. A moment later, Himanshu turned left – apparently right into the thicket – and when the human team followed, they saw two stern-looking sloths standing side by side with about four feet of space be-tween them. Beyond them lay a clearing about ten acres in size, with several tall trees spaced evenly within the space. The two guard-sloths were armed with long spears and each had a bow and quiver of arrows slung across his back.

Himanshu spoke to the two guards and their scowls soft-ened somewhat.

Himanshu motioned to the humans to come, but then clapped his hands loudly, with a very serious look on his face. He pointed to a vegetative "threshold" that was about a foot tall, consisting of a jasmine-looking plant with dark, shiny leaves. Himanshu put his hand close to one plant, pulled back his hand, writhed and jerked on the ground and then lay still. Apparently, this plant was a deadly poison.

"What should we do?" both Carl and Angus asked Dr. Jenkins simultaneously. "We know precious little about these creatures," continued Angus, "so, shouldn't we proceed with extreme caution? It's not as though this is a group of koalas or pandas!"

"I doubt that they are hostile," replied Dr. Jenkins, "or else the sloth who has contacted us could have brought a war party to our cabins and assaulted us there. Still, caution is well advised. Perhaps it is best to have a representative go in first. As the person responsible for this expedition, I should be the one to go."

"No, Dr. Jenkins," replied Jacintha, "I am ultimately the one who has got us into this situation, and this one who calls himself 'Himanshu' so far trusts only me. I should be the one to go."

"I am afraid you are right, Jacintha," said Jenkins; "just make sure that you are always within our sight."

Jacintha alone crossed the poisonous threshold and walked beside Himanshu to the centre of the clearing where the biggest tree stood. A large, plump, and somewhat aged sloth descended the tree and sat at its base. Jenkins commented to the group that it looked like a female, due to the blueish streak in its hair. "Perhaps this is Himanshu's mother, or the matriarch of this clan," surmised Jenkins to the group.

While Himanshu spoke with this elder female sloth, Jacintha observed her closely. Her eyes had a mix of gentleness, sadness, and determination that Jacintha could hardly fathom.

"Oomaa," said Himanshu to Jacintha, nodding (but not pointing) to this elder sloth. Jacintha did not know if that was a name or a title, but she said "Oomaa" in return. This Oomaa motioned to Jacintha to come closer, and when she did, the old sloth put her right hand on Jacintha's head and said words that sounded like, "Alva mahama kadinchi." Judging by the tone of voice used, this sounded like a welcoming or a blessing, and so Jacintha responded by smiling and looking down rather than making eye contact.

Then, from all around the clearing, there came in unison the voices of at least fifty sloths in the trees saying "Haarahaarahaarahaara." And they all fell silent.

A young female sloth ventured forward on the ground with what looked like a clay pot in her hands. She showed it to Jacintha, and Himanshu motioned for her to take it and drink. The pot was filled with what looked and smelled like water. She took a sip and was amazed with the subtle sweetness and vigour that this natural Venusian water had.

A group of at least ten sloths then began pulling branches off trees and tossing them down to the ground in the clearing. Each branch was slender and about ten feet long. Jacintha went close to one branch and recognized it as a kind of neem. Once about one hundred branches piled up, this team of sloths gathered together and in a matter of minutes constructed a dome-shaped hut with an arched entrance, firmly bound with thin vines.

Himanshu motioned to Jacintha to enter the hut. She marvelled at its construction. It felt cool and airy and had a pleasant, clean smell. It was also placed in the shade of one of the big trees. The oppressive heat of late morning was now upon them: apparently, Himanshu's clan had taken the effort of building a shelter for their guests.

At this point, Dr. Jenkins felt that the sloths meant no harm to them and asked everyone to enter the enclosure. The guards stopped Angus, as they noticed the rifles slung across his back. Forcing him to take the rifles down, the guards picked them up and looked at them curiously. One put the barrel to his mouth and tried blowing as if it was a blowgun and had a puzzled look on his face when nothing happened.

The guards handed the rifles back to Angus as if they were useless curiosities and not the deadly weapons that they really were. Dr. Jenkins radioed back to the camp that all were well and had shelter for the mid-day break.

The human team occupied their leafy shelter, where they were given water and a wide array of wild fruits to eat. Jenkins and the team recognized six of the fruits, but there was another dozen types of fruit that were unfamiliar. They spent far more time studying the new fruits and taking notes than eating them. As the heat wore on, the team became lethargic and one by one they fell asleep.

Jacintha woke up first as Carl, who lay near her, had kicked her leg in his sleep. At first, she thought that they had slept right into the evening because it was dark for mid-afternoon. But then, peeking out through a hole in their shelter, she saw that a thick fog had descended upon them.

Dr. Jenkins woke up a few moments later. Jacintha quietly went over to him and informed him about the change in weather. He proceeded to wake up the others.

"This is a predicament," stated Jenkins to the group. "If the fog does not lift within a couple of hours, we will have to spend the night here. Even with a good tracker like Angus, we would easily get lost in either the fog or the darkness. Let us hope it doesn't come to that, but we must be mentally prepared."

Not letting the fog dampen their spirits, the team spent the remaining daylight hours investigating the various plant species that lived within the clearing as well as the vegetative "fortification". They observed and noted numerous uses that the Formanian sloths made of the plants, as explained by Himanshu.

While Jacintha tried her best to pay attention to the vast amount of information that Himanshu was passing onto her team, she was more interested in Himanshu himself. She closely observed every detail of his body; his posture, gait and mannerisms; and even his speech. And she was surprised that even though she did not know his language, she somehow was able to understand what he was saying "beyond" the words. Jacintha could not readily explain it to herself: although she was fluent in several Indigenous languages as well as Spanish, Portuguese and English, learning a language always required quite a lot of conscious effort; but in this case, although she was picking up quite a lot of the Formanian vocabulary from Himanshu, she was more able to understand what he was thinking than what he was saying. It puzzled her until she remembered that the Medicine People of her community sometimes brought news that nobody else knew —and when asked, they would say "I heard the frogs talking about it." She had never known whether to believe it or not. As a small child she implicitly believed it, but as she grew up in the city and learned how to think like an "educated person" she put all this aside in her mind because she could not explain it rationally, yet at the same time she had seen how the Medicine People accurately knew things before anyone else. She had never experienced this "understanding other species" herself on Earth—to her the frogs simply croaked in their undecipherable frog-language.

As night closed in, Jenkins radioed the camp again informing them that all was well and that they would head back as soon as the fog cleared tomorrow.

Himanshu's clan became very active as the light grew dim and the temperature dropped into the 80s. They lit a modest-sized fire using flint and a stone and demonstrated their dexterity in skills such as basket weaving, making pots without a potting wheel, and making arrows. Sloth children were busy alternating between briefly participating in these activities and engaging in play either in the trees or on the ground. All the humans watched in wonder at this seemingly idyllic society where material wants were few and were easily satisfied and there seemed to be no hunger, disease or discord.

After several hours the activities seemed to be winding down and it looked as though Himanshu's clan was getting ready to sleep in the trees, when the tone changed. Several of the adult male sloths started loudly to say "boom, boom, boom, boom," and the two guards became agitated and began shouting at the clan. Suddenly nearly every adult sloth in the community—be they in a tree or on the ground—was armed with either a bow or a blowgun.

The team of humans were at a loss as to what was going on. The alert was definitely not focused on them – it seemed to be an external threat. Himanshu went to Jacintha's side and motioned for her and the others to get into the trees. Jacintha made a sad face to Himanshu and told him that they could not climb trees. She could see fear creep into Himanshu's expression. Jacintha pointed to Angus and motioned the use of a rifle to Himanshu: his expression brightened somewhat. Just the same, he put a copper dagger into her hand.

The enclosure became very quiet as if waiting for something. The minutes ticked by slowly.

Abduction

ABRUPTLY THE SILENCE was rent by the sound of large animals jostling and grunting just outside the enclosure, followed by the simultaneous blaring of many horns. By the dim light of the fire, Jacintha and others could see several massive bipedal creatures with long, thick tails running in through the enclosure's entrance. The first one tripped over the lintel and howled in pain. Reflexively, it reached for its foot with its hands and fell down on the ground. Six of Himashu's clan-sloths were guarding the entrance – three on each side – and were each armed with a spear. They quickly dispatched the giants.

Four more giants poured in. They seemed to have helmets and armour made of leather that gleamed in the firelight. Each had in one hand a club and the other hand a sling. They fanned out and entered into combat with various sloths. One of the invaders received an arrow in the eye, fell on one knee and was skewered by a guard's spear. Another caught a guard by the arm and with a single mighty blow crushed his head. The third giant swung its sling amidst a barrage of arrows and darts and hit a sloth in one tree, rendering it unconscious, and it fell to the ground. Two of the four giants eventually succumbed to their injuries and fell.

There was a pause for a half minute. Then to everyone's amazement—humans and sloths alike—three more giants came in, each riding a seven-horned rhino at full gallop. Due to the size of the giants astride them, the massive rhinos looked almost like the size of ponies. The sloths who were on the ground quickly headed for the trees and ascended. However, the five remaining guards and the humans were still on the ground. Two rhinos headed towards the humans, and the third turned onto the guards. Within a moment one of the guards was gored and then trampled to death. The rhino then set its sights onto another guard.

The two other rhinos had more ground to cover, as the humans were still near the shelter, which was placed opposite the entrance. Himanshu was on the lowest branch of the tree nearest the humans. Seeing a rhino approach, he let out a whooping sound, and a second sloth joined him. Together they rushed to the fire, seized and brandished flaming branches. As the rhinos approached, the two sloths poked the branches into the rhinos' eyes. One rhino spooked and unseated its rider who, while dazed, was attacked with many arrows. The second rhino managed to dodge the fire and continued straight towards the humans.

A 'bang' interrupted the melee. The giant atop the rhino fell. Two more shots rang out and the rhino was the next to fall. Angus lowered his rifle. The giants and sloths alike looked at Angus in shock. The riderless rhino took notice and headed straight towards Angus. After three shots from the other rifle, it, too, lay dead on the ground. But in the confusion, nobody noticed that the third rhino, still with its rider, had swung behind the humans and gored Angus in the back. The giant dismounted and swiftly grabbed both Jacintha and Dr. Jenkins by the hair. The giant roared.

A moment later, more giants filed in on foot, and behind them came one who looked like their leader. He confidently strode in, holding a staff in one hand. Atop the staff was a sloth skull. Adorning his head appeared to be a crown made of skulls and he wore a necklace of skulls. He was a fearsome sight to behold. Not a single sloth fired an arrow or blow-dart at him. "Bagha!" the giant chief roared at the sloths, "Bagha!"

Within a moment, more giants surrounded the three remaining humans, and the remaining four sloth guards had also been surrounded and disarmed. All seven prisoners were swiftly rounded up, arms bound with leather thongs, and led out of the enclosure into the forest beyond.

Marching through the forest at night was particularly difficult for the humans, as there was so little light. The fog was still thick, hiding most of the nocturnal glow diffused by Venus' cloud layer. But the giants had no difficulty navigating through the forest without any artificial form of illumination. They all walked the whole night long without a single break. Their captors were absolutely silent.

Jacintha, Carl and Dr. Jenkins, to keep their fears from running wild, took every opportunity to converse during the forced march.

"I still have my walkie-talkie," said Jenkins, "but I don't know whether we are walking towards our camp or away from it. By my reckoning the village of Formanian sloths is about eight miles from our camp. As long as we stay within 35 miles of the camp, we are within communication range. As soon as I get an opportunity, I will inform the camp of our situation." He didn't want to think how he would be able to find the opportunity to use the walkie-talkie without being noticed.

"I know it is hard to see enough details in the dark, Dr. Jenkins," joined in Carl, "but keeping in mind the morphological similarities between life on Earth and on Venus, what Earthly equivalents do you think could exist for these giants?"

"My best guess at this point, Carl, is Megatherium altiplanicum, a ground sloth that lived during the Pliocene. Here on Venus they seem to have evolved longer legs," replied Jenkins. Both men were comforted by the sound of their voices and talking about biology. It made them think that they were in control even though the events around them made it blatantly obvious that they weren't.

Jacintha listened along, but her mind was dwelling back on the village. How many Formanian sloths had been killed or injured by the giants? Why had the giants attacked the village? What had happened to Himanshu? Was he injured? Dead? She had not seen him since he attacked one rhino with the burning branch and feared that he might have been one of the fatal victims of this attack.

"What do you think they want with us?" openly enquired Carl.

"Could be any number of reasons, I suppose," began Jenkins.

But before Jenkins could start a ten-minute exploration of the relative likelihood of various motives of the giants, Jacintha interrupted. "In the rainforest where I grew up there was a tradition among some tribes to raid other tribes in order to prove their manhood or to settle a score from the past. But these giants are different. They did not slay us on the spot. They have taken us as prisoner. I can only think of one reason for them to do that…" Her voice broke off and she did not want to continue now that her mind had caught up with her words and the full import of her thoughts chilled her to the bone.

"Well, what is it?" enquired Carl impatiently.

"What Jacintha means to say, but doesn't have the heart to say it, is that the giants intend to eat us," stated Jenkins in a flat, matter-of-fact voice.

"No way," replied Carl; "ground sloths were vegetarian… weren't they?"

"That's been the predominant belief for a long time," replied Jenkins, "but there has been some evidence to the contrary. And don't forget that the ground sloths on Venus have evolved in their own way."

"Like Hell I'm going to let them make a meal out of me."

"And how do you intend on preventing that?"

"I don't know, but while we are still walking and not in some little cage or cooking pot or whatever, I'm going to think of something!"

Feast

As DAY BROKE in the forest, Jacintha and her fellow-captives could get a better look at their captors. At best guess they were between twelve and fifteen feet tall, and would weigh close to a ton. They were covered in short tan-coloured fur – somewhat like a Golden Labrador's coat – and were clothed only in a leather loincloth and protective leather armour on their arms, legs and abdomen. Their limbs were massive and their fingers and toes ended in six-inch claws. Their tails, which they kept off the ground, were about six feet long and must weigh as much as a large man. The most noticeable features on their faces were their huge eyes and protruding snout. Their heavy breathing could be heard from about ten feet away. It was hard to say how fast they could run, but it was obvious that a violent confrontation with these giants would be utterly futile.

At sunrise they came to a swift-running river that was about one-hundred feet wide. The Chief motioned to take a rest. Each giant, in turn, walked into the river and drank directly from it. The captives were herded into the river and commanded to do the same. Then they walked through a calm pool in the river. In parts the river was so deep that only the heads of the giants stayed above water. When the time came for the captives to cross, the giant holding the leather thong grabbed his captive and held him/her aloft over his head with both hands.

They walked the entire day, taking only a one-hour break by another river during the most oppressive part of the afternoon. During the break, the giants tore down several fruit trees and completely stripped them of leaves, fruits and small branches, eating them all in the process. They offered leaves and fruits to the captives who, after at least twelve hours of continuous walking, were famished.

During the rest period, one of the captive sloths managed to wriggle his hands free from his bonds and bolted. Seeing the distraction, Carl did the same, running in the opposite direction in the hope that the giants would only notice, and pursue, the sloth. Carl managed to run about twenty steps before a giant began to pursue him, with club in hand. After dodging the giant for some time, Carl slipped on a flat moss-covered stone. The giant was upon him within seconds and with a single blow to the head, Carl was rendered unconscious. The escaped sloth managed to find a tree as large as a mature sequoia and scaled it with remarkable ease hundreds of feet into the air. The giants in pursuit realized that they would not be able to regain their quarry: they shouted at the sloth and threw rocks nearly as high as the sloth had climbed.

While this was going on, Dr. Jenkins discretely sent a message via walkie-talkie to the camp. The message read: "Party captured by giant sloths. Heading south-west. One member killed, one member injured." He was unsure whether the message could be delivered at this distance and did not have time to check for a reply, but if the message was successful, the camp would know the precise latitude and longitude of the message and, hopefully, would be able to send a helicopter rescue team.

The rest of the day was spent walking. One giant had Carl slung over his shoulder; Carl did not regain consciousness. Just before sundown, the party reached what at first looked like a clearing, because a patch of sky became visible. As they proceeded, the other side of the clearing could not be seen—an immense expanse of sky came into view. A few steps more, and they were poised on top of an escarpment that was at least a mile high. The sight took Jacintha's and Dr. Jenkins' breath away. Far below them lay the lowlands and swamps that teemed with sauropods. This area was forbidden to human explorers due to the extreme heat and sheer danger of encountering the monstrous beasts that dwelled there. For a moment, both forgot that they were seeing this as captives whose lives would almost certainly be coming to an end soon.

Their moment of bliss was shattered by the party turning to the left along the precipice. Within a dozen paces they came upon a twenty-foot wide hole in the ground which was a few yards to the left of the precipice. The Chief descended into the hole in a step-like manner. The rest of the team followed.

At the bottom of the forty or so steps, Jacintha and Dr. Jenkins were amazed to see a colossal cave complex, with pillared chambers, arched doorways, and numerous windows open on the cliff-side. Many giants were milling about in the chamber at the bottom of the stairs. Each one greeted the Chief by bowing down, greeted the rest of the party, and looked at shock and disgust at the human captives. Jacintha guessed that there must be about twenty giants in this room: a mix of large males, smaller (ten feet tall) females, and children. There was a lot of chatter going on which, to Jacintha's ears, sounded like a herd of hippos. The Chief disappeared into a separate room.

As the twilight faded, torches were lit and placed in holders along the walls and pillars. Soon the captives were led into a second large room. This room's ceiling and upper walls were stained black with soot. In the centre was a gigantic open fire with a cauldron atop, suspended by numerous boulders at the base. The cauldron must have been twenty feet wide and ten feet high. There were several "vents" in the ceiling which let most of the smoke out, as a breeze from outside gently blew in through a huge window. Other than the party, there were four giants: two appeared to be male and two female.

"So, this is the kitchen," thought Jacintha to herself, "and the end for us." She wondered if there was any possible way of getting out of this dire situation.

One of the female "cooks" put an armful of whole leaves and twigs into the cauldron, from which issued a furious bubbling sound. Another cook held a large snake by the tail and put the writhing creature into the cauldron.

A male cook strode over to the party and pointed to one of the captive sloths. The nearest giant "soldier" clubbed the sloth over the head and handed the limp sloth over to the cook, who gently lowered it into the cauldron. Jacintha and Dr. Jenkins both looked away. The same cook then walked over to the soldier who had Carl slung over his shoulder. Carl was handed over to the cook, who looked with bewilderment at the specimen before him. With a stone knife, the cook cut off Carl's shirt and struggled—but could not figure out—the pants and so put the partially-clothed Carl into the cauldron. Jacintha vomited.

The cooks took no notice of the three remaining captives. After adjusting somewhat to the horror before them, Dr. Jenkins said to the weeping Jacintha, "Looks like they are saving us for tomorrow."

The captives were forced to sit down in the kitchen and to face the bubbling cauldron for two hours. The kitchen was poorly lit and the shadows made weird shapes that moved about as the torches and the cooking fire flickered. At one point, Jacintha thought she saw a small, slim shape descend from outside the window and move towards the cauldron, but she knew that it was just the play of shadows.

The cooking fire died down. The four cooks went to the cauldron and with giant ladles took turns pouring the soup into huge wooden bowls and walking the bowls into the hall, where the sounds of discussion and scuffling could be heard. With nothing else to do, Jacintha counted the number of bowls that were filled. Forty-two. She then felt light-headed and knew no more.

Deliverance

WHEN JACINTHA CAME to, the kitchen was almost pitch-black, with just a few coals glowing under the cauldron. A hand touched her arm. Instinctively, she drew her hand back and opened her eyes. Looking back at her through the gloom was a sloth. It moved its face close to hers: it was Himanshu! She drew a quick breath in surprise. Himanshu moved over to Dr. Jenkins and to the two other sloths and did the same thing. They all sat up and looked around. The kitchen—indeed, the whole cave—was silent. In the dim light, they could see their four captors lying close by, sound asleep.

Jacintha watched in shock as Himanshu touched the neck of one of the captors. It did not stir. He slapped the captor hard. No response. A flood of relief swept through Jacintha and the rest of the captives as it became clear that the giants were not a threat. Himanshu returned to Jacintha and pointed to a flask that he had slung around his neck, and to the cauldron, and fell down to inform her of what he had done. Curious, Jacintha went to the same captor whom Himanshu had slapped, and put her hand to its wrist. She felt around for a pulse: such a large creature would likely have an artery the thickness of a garden hose. But she felt nothing. The giant was not drugged into a deep sleep—it was dead.

Swiftly but quietly, the surviving humans and sloths removed their bonds and retraced their steps through the kitchen, the grand hall (now littered with numerous giant corpses), up the stairs and out under the night sky. They could not believe their good fortune and, momentarily forgetting the horrors they had recently experienced, laughed in sheer relief. But the relief was short-lived.

A sudden rustling came from the bushes close by and out burst an immense male giant who, apparently, had not partaken of the feast. This giant was enraged, his power breathtaking. With one hand he picked up one "guard" sloth, while looking for another sloth to grab. The second "guard" sloth deftly evaded the giant's manoeuvres and climbed up his back. The giant roared as the second sloth sat on its shoulders and proceeded to press the giant's eyes as hard as he could with both hands. The giant's grip on the first sloth loosened in order to grab the second sloth pressing against his eyes, and the moment he fell to the ground, the first sloth found a stout thorny stick. The first sloth ducked under the giant's tail and with all his might rammed the stick as far he could where the sun never shines.

Now in excruciating pain, the giant whirled around and reached down to find his rear assailant. In the tussle, the giant tripped Dr. Jenkins with his huge tail and stepped on Jenkin's left arm, breaking it in several places.

Still blindly feeling around, the giant grabbed Himanshu by the foot and threw him. Himanshu went soaring over the escarpment and plunged out of sight. Next, the giant grabbed Jacintha's foot and she, too, was thrown into the abyss.

Still whirling, the giant caught both his two assailants. For a moment he teetered on the edge of the escarpment, but eventually lost his balance. The giant, along with the two "guard" sloths, plunged over the side.

Silence returned. Jenkins was now all alone on the escarpment. He was in a daze and in terrible pain, but he had the presence of mind to reach into his pocket for the walkie-talkie. This time it was safe to attempt voice communication.

"Station One, this is Jenkins. Come in." Static came in response. He tried again. The seconds ticked past. He tried a third time. Over the static came an extremely faint human voice.

"Jenkins, we read you... [inaudible] determining your location... [inaudible] have a heli [inaudible]... [inaudible] on."

Jenkins fainted.

Twenty minutes later, a helicopter arrived on scene and Jenkins was pulled up in a stretcher, semi-conscious and babbling incoherently. The helicopter returned to Station One.

Home in the Forman Mountains

JACINTHA AWOKE WITH a jolt. Opening her eyes, all she could see was the dimly lit sky of dawn. She suddenly remembered having been thrown over the escarpment by the giant. "Am I still falling?" she wondered. But there was no rushing of wind as if she were plummeting. She was lying on a solid surface. Trying to sit up, she felt a searing pain in her left leg. From her semi-seated position, she saw the leg was twisted in an unnatural position half-way down her shin. She was lying on a small grassy ledge that jutted about thirty feet out from the escarpment and about twelve feet down from the lip of the escarpment. Her life had been saved by sheer luck.

But she was alone. "Dr. Jenkins!" she shouted, "Anyone!" The only response was the echo from her own voice.

After a minute she heard a voice -- but it was not a human voice, it was a sloth voice! And a few seconds later, Himanshu's head poked above the side of the ledge that Jacintha was lying on. He pulled himself up and ambled over to Jacintha with a worried look on his face as he glanced at her left leg.

Other than a few scratches, he was unscathed. He came to her and gave her a long hug.

Himanshu told her verbally, and with gesticulations, that he would make a rope and lift her off the ledge. She nodded in agreement. He deftly scrambled up the face of the escarpment and disappeared for about half an hour. He then came over the edge with a sturdy vine in tow, helped Jacintha to rise on her one good leg and walked her over to the face of the cliff. He then tied the vine around her chest under her arms and disappeared up the cliff again. Soon she felt the jerking motion of Himanshu pulling on the vine. Within a few minutes she was safely off the escarpment.

Jacintha spotted the scene of the previous night's scuffle with the giant sloth. Amidst the maze of footprints and boot-prints lay a pool of dried blood. But there was no sign of Dr. Jenkins. She had no idea what might have happened to him, although she busily imagined numerous scenarios until she told her mind to shut up and turned her attention to the here-and-now.

Working with skill, Himanshu reset Jacintha's broken leg and produced a brace out of sticks and vines. He then helped her to hobble some distance into the forest until they found a large, clear pool of water that was under the thick shade of the forest canopy. Himanshu brought her many fruits to eat and told her that he was going to get help and that during the peak of the heat she should immerse herself in the pool. Although she felt scared to be left alone in this strange world, Jacintha trusted Himanshu and she knew that it was the only option they had.

Himanshu was gone for a full day. During that time, Jacintha heard rotor-blades whirring over her head on two occasions but could not see the helicopter through the forest canopy. She kept as cool as circumstances permitted. She ate and drank occasionally and slept a great deal. No creatures bothered her.

At dawn the next day, Himanshu arrived with a team of

five other sloths. They brought with them a mess of vines which, when unfolded, formed a hammock-like structure strung around two sturdy poles. A team of four sloths (two for each pole) took rotation carrying Jacintha back to their village, taking only a two-hour break in the midday and again at midnight.

Himanshu nursed Jacintha back to full health over the ensuing months. No helicopters came, nor did any search parties. Jacintha had been given up for dead. And so, she moved on with life.

Jacintha learned the language and ways of the village. She found that the Formanian sloths were as caring and generous of heart as the villagers she had grown up with in the Amazon. For the first time since she was a little girl, she felt truly at home.

As Jacintha became more fluent in the Formanian tongue, Himanshu explained to her the customs and history of his tribe, and the dark story about how the giant sloths had made their home on the escarpment many generations ago and would occasionally go "sloth hunting" and attack their village. Himanshu's village declared him to be a hero for exterminating the giants. Nobody had attempted to poison the giants before due to fear of their Chief, whom the sloths believed to be the God of Death incarnate.

Within about half an Earth-year (by Jacintha's reckoning), the village performed a marriage ceremony for Jacintha and Himanshu. Both were delighted, as each knew they had truly found their soul-mate. Jacintha could not have children, so over the years the village gave them six orphan sloths to raise as their own.

Intrigued by the sloths' stories about the "old ones", Jacintha and Himanshu explored the crumbling ruins of the long-abandoned sloth-cities, and found many amazing artifacts of sophisticated mechanisms, writing, and art. And then the epic stories recited by the elder-sloths by firelight about the shining cities, flying machines and interplanetary wars with the Spider-People of Mercury rang true.

Reunion

AFTER DR. JENKINS recovered from the misadventure with the Formanian sloths, he reported the entire incident to the Board of Venus Researchers. It was unanimously agreed that with the discovery of a violent and aggressive carnivorous species of giant sloth in the area, research in the Forman Mountains and Iona Plateau should be abandoned, and within a month the research stations were closed for good. Research moved to other mountain ranges on the planet, where giant sloths were nowhere to be found.

Dr. Jenkins, unable to forgive himself for leading three young adults under his supervision to their untimely deaths, returned to Earth where he built a distinguished career as a researcher adapting Venusian plant species to prosper in Earth conditions. He always believed, however, that the Forman Mountains were the "motherlode" of species diversity on Venus and that many undiscovered species existed there that would be essential for stabilizing Earth's runaway warming.

A full twenty years after the incident, Jenkins returned to the Forman Mountains. Under the protection of a heavily armed guard, he and a team of researchers penetrated once more the teeming jungles of the area. Almost by accident, he found Himanshu's village. As he neared, the sloths who were foraging in the area immediately headed back to the village to tell Himanshu and Jacintha of humans nearby.

Jenkins came to the familiar vernal doorway into the village. The two guards stood resolute and eyed him suspiciously, their spears crossed and forbidding him entry. His eyes fondly scanned the familiar village grounds, noting how nothing seemed to have changed over the two decades since he had last visited.

And then he saw her approaching him. Jenkins could scarcely believe his eyes.

"Welcome, Doctor," said Jacintha somewhat shakily, having neither spoken nor heard English in twenty years. "Yes, your eyes do not deceive you. I am very much alive and am overjoyed to see that you are too."

Jacintha gave the guards permission to let Jenkins and his research party in. She gave Jenkins a hug for a long time. Both were teary-eyed.

After introductions, Jacintha sat down with Dr. Jenkins and the research team and in broken-English told her the story of her rescue and life in the village and—of most interest to them—the thousands of wondrous plants that she has learned about through Himanshu and the other medicine-sloths of the many villages that dot the mountain range, as well as what she had learned directly from the plants themselves.

The following day, Dr. Jenkins returned to the camp and broke the news of Jacintha's miraculous survival and her phenomenal knowledge of plants that would save decades of time in research. Accordingly, the botanical research base was re-opened and exobiology students competed fiercely for the highly coveted research position on the Forman Mountains. Jacintha—who was granted honorary doctorates from six Universities—was invited to relocate to the research base, but she refused. "The students must come to me," was her consistent answer, "for it is only when they are totally in the field, in direct contact with nature, that true knowledge of the plants is gained."

For thirty years Jacintha—along with Himanshu—taught and trained biologists and ecologists in the deeper, non-invasive ways of understanding plants and of nature. Though many people back on Earth fondly (and a few not-so-fondly) referred to her as the "crazy sloth-lady of Venus," Jacintha became famed for her love of students, of nature, of Himanshu, and of life itself.

Acknowledgements

We would like to give a special thanks to the following people for their support as backers through Kickstarter: Steve Tanner, Garrett L. Ward, John Conner - Coop Janitor, Mark Carter, Anaxphone, Robet C Flipse, Jay Skiles, Michael Gonzales, Stephen Ballentine, E.M. Middel, Jason Miller, Jim Kosmicki, Richard Sands, Ryan A. Fleming, BuddyH, Robert Gibson, Eric Richetti, David England, John Robert Mead, Thomas Biros, Clifton Roberts, Serpent Moon, Mog, Hiram G. Wells, Thomas Bull, Olivia Rohan, James Lucas, Thomas M. Colwell, Don C, Justin, Will A Oberton, Daniel G., Catherine Trouth, Jeff Huggins, Mary Gibson, Stephen Rubin, Jim Gotaas, J. Sobieraj, Jerry Koehr, Ruth Ann Orlansky, MJ Silversmith, Luis Manuel Sánchez García, James W. Murphy, Chris Bekofske, Raul Castro, Jill Grow, John J. Senn, Emilia Marjaana Pullianen, Digby, Jeff Hotchkiss, Trip Space-Parasite, Alastair Palmer, Joshua Palmatier, Michael D'Auben, Katy Manck - BooksYALove, Yankton Robins, Eric, Vince Kindfuller, AlmostHuman, Robert Claney, Michael Barbour, Mark Newman, Bobbi Boyd, Gary Phillips, Marko Deablo, Ben Haskett, Richard Dulik, Tim Stroup, Stephen Frede, Edmund Boys, Jen Witsoe, Rob Szarka, Kevin Moreau, Robin E. Douglas, Jean-Pierre Ardoguein, Joseph Guzzo, Cliff

Allred, L.E. Roncayolo, Per Axel Stanley Willis, Sister Crow, Jennifer Barber, Matt Staples, E. Ashby, Sc Fi Cardre, Linda S., Travis Siegel, Jillian Harker, Peter Borah, Andy Dwelly, Daniel C., Keith West: Future Potentate of the Solar System, Silvina & Keren Cohen, Eron Wyngarde, Tanner Nash, Brett Carlson, Michael Ball, Walt Freitag, Justin Patrick Moore, Doug Forand, Orange exiguous piglet - the name bestowed upon me by the Cosmic Oom. Who am I to argue, Harvey L. Lesser, Michael Mudgett, R.J.H., Terrence Miller, Jeff Sigmund, Erik T. Johnson, Joan, Charles Rivers, Ross Richey, Rick Ohnemus, Jeff S., Quin Arbeitman, John Markley, Tim Jordan, Joel Caris, Dagmar Baumann, Niall Gordon, Stacy Shuda, Jonathan Hodge, Ivan Donati, Dan Mollo, Thomas Gaudaire-Thore, Matt Trepal, Howard J. Bampton, Tracy 'Rayhne' Fretwell, P. Robert Thorson, Fred W. Johnson, Dillon Burke, Fenric Cayne, Jeffrey Scarpace, Bill Kohn, Brian Holder, Adrienne, Zack Fissel, Camille Lofters, Michael Carroll, Russell Graves, SwordFirey, Peter Klimas, Ed Matalka, Kelly Mayo, xorx, RvR, Ane-Marte Mortensen, Benjamin, Old Man Sparck, John H. Bookwalter Jr., Robert L. Vaughn, Frank Lewis, and M. Phelps.

Made in the USA
Coppell, TX
04 December 2020

43060402R00204